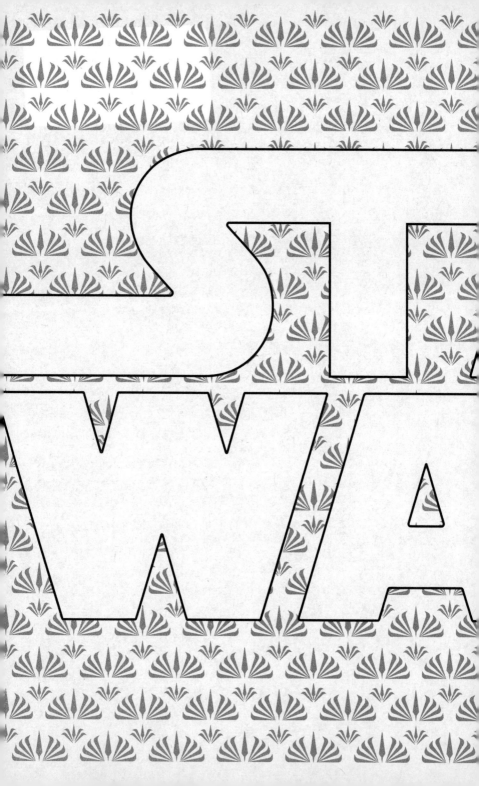

BY LYDIA KANG

CATACLYSM

CATACLYSM

Lydia Kang

RANDOM HOUSE

WORLDS

NEW YORK

2024 Random House Worlds Trade Paperback Edition

Published in the United States by Random House Worlds,
an imprint of Random House, a division of
Penguin Random House LLC, New York.

RANDOM HOUSE is a registered trademark, and
RANDOM HOUSE WORLDS and colophon are trademarks of
Penguin Random House LLC.

Originally published in hardcover in the United States by
Random House Worlds, an imprint of
Random House, a division of
Penguin Random House LLC, in 2023.

ISBN 978-0-593-50037-8
Ebook ISBN 978-0-593-50036-1

Printed in the United States of America on acid-free paper

randomhousebooks.com

2 4 6 8 9 7 5 3 1

To Mom, the original Kyong.
To Dad, who took me to see *Star Wars* in 1977.
And to Bernie, my partner in all the fandoms.

THE *STAR WARS* NOVELS TIMELINE

THE HIGH REPUBLIC

Convergence
The Battle of Jedha
Cataclysm

Light of the Jedi
The Rising Storm
Tempest Runner
The Fallen Star
The Eye of Darkness
Temptation of the Force
Trials of the Jedi

Dooku: Jedi Lost
Master and Apprentice
The Living Force

I THE PHANTOM MENACE

II ATTACK OF THE CLONES

Brotherhood
The Thrawn Ascendancy Trilogy
Dark Disciple: A Clone Wars Novel

III REVENGE OF THE SITH

Inquisitor: Rise of the Red Blade
Catalyst: A Rogue One Novel
Lords of the Sith
Tarkin
Jedi: Battle Scars

SOLO

Thrawn
A New Dawn: A Rebels Novel
Thrawn: Alliances
Thrawn: Treason

ROGUE ONE

IV A NEW HOPE

Battlefront II: Inferno Squad
Heir to the Jedi
Doctor Aphra
Battlefront: Twilight Company

V THE EMPIRE STRIKES BACK

VI RETURN OF THE JEDI

The Princess and the Scoundrel
The Alphabet Squadron Trilogy
The Aftermath Trilogy
Last Shot

Shadow of the Sith
Bloodline
Phasma
Canto Bight

VII THE FORCE AWAKENS

VIII THE LAST JEDI

Resistance Reborn
Galaxy's Edge: Black Spire

IX THE RISE OF SKYWALKER

A long time ago in a galaxy far, far away. . . .

CATACLYSM

There is conflict in the galaxy. Chaos on the Pilgrim Moon of Jedha has resulted in a devastating battle. In the aftermath, the Jedi have learned of the involvement of the seemingly benevolent group, THE PATH OF THE OPEN HAND, in violent interplanetary conspiracies.

With communications down, the leader of the Path, THE MOTHER, races back to the planet Dalna to make her ultimate escape. Little do the Jedi know that the Mother is about to unleash mysterious, nameless creatures with the power to destroy the Order once and for all. . . .

Prologue

Binnot Ullo was pacing inside a meeting chamber on the *Gaze Electric.* To his right, a viewport showed the amorphous light of the hyperlane as the ship sped toward the system that encompassed Eiram and E'ronoh. He had paused once to face the viewport, but the view irritated him. He wanted already to be there, to be doing something.

At the edge of the room, as he paused again to change directions, Binnot was faced with a mirror bordered with inlaid polished glass. This, too, he declined to face. He had been waiting nearly an hour. But for the chance to do more—to be more to the Mother, finally—he would be patient. Suddenly, the door to the meeting chamber opened. The Mother entered alone. He was always surprised at how ordinary she appeared at first glance, yet extraordinary upon further study. She had the wavy brikal-shell-blue lines across her forehead, three of them, though some of the Path had been wearing them vertically of late. Her robes were plain, also marked with blue devotional lines. Since he had last seen her, her dark brown hair had become burnished with more silver strands, and she seemed far older than before. But still, unlike the rest of the members of the Path of the Open Hand, she wore a jeweled necklace around her throat and her robe was crafted of finer, silken material. But more than all of these things, it was the way she held herself, like she saw everything. Knew everything.

From just beyond the open door came a low growl that rumbled at a frequency Binnot felt in his fingertips. The Mother turned to shut the door quickly.

"Has it been fed?" Binnot asked.

"Yes. It's quite complacent at the moment. Much like you, Binnot." She smiled gently, and he felt like he always did when she gave him her full attention. Like he could conquer anything or anyone in the entire galaxy. She sat down at the table in the center of the room, similarly bedecked by cut glass that shone like ice crystals on the table's surface. She did not ask Binnot to sit. He was glad of it. He preferred not to feel too comfortable. There was work to be done.

"My ship is ready to go," Binnot said.

"And Goi Ganok?" Mother raised an eyebrow.

"Also ready."

"He will play the nervous innocent well," Mother said. "But you will have to keep a close eye on him. He doesn't have your talents, Binnot."

Binnot nodded, trying not to smile at the compliment. "The klytobacter is aboard. We'll make sure we are discovered by an E'roni ship as soon as we enter the neutral corridor of space between E'ronoh and Eiram, near their moon." He had helped put the large, liquid-filled storage cylinders into the hidden compartments of the ship. Anyone searching superficially wouldn't find them. Anyone looking for a reason to reignite a war would.

"Excellent." She tented her long slender fingers. A golden bangle slipped down her wrist, disappearing under her sleeve. "You'll blow your engines when you're close to E'ronoh space, and demand to be led to the moon for repairs . . ."

"And the second engine will explode there, once we know an Eirami ship can pick up on the explosion." He had started pacing the room again when he turned. "But what about Jedha?"

"What about it?"

"The peace signing failed. The war will be back on anyway. Are you sure you need me for this mission? I can do more."

"I know you can." The Mother smiled again. She stood and walked toward Binnot. He was far taller than she, almost by a whole head. She turned his broad shoulders around to face the wall. No, not the wall. The mirror.

It was large enough to show them both, but Binnot took up nearly the whole reflection, the Mother standing almost as a shadow behind him. Unlike other Mirialans, he only possessed a scant few markings on his pale-green skin. It had come with joining the Path when he was only ten years old, and not earning more facial markings that would have hallmarked achievements he might have earned if he'd lived his life on Mirial. The Mother's eyes flicked from her own reflection to Binnot's.

"I know what you're thinking. You will bear the honor and greatness of forging your way within the Path, in ways that will reveal themselves not upon your skin, but within yourself. To me, your greatness continues to expand, Binnot."

"Yes, Mother."

"The Battle of Jedha is over," she said, still standing as his shadow. "The Herald has seen to the ruin of the Jedi statue outside Jedha that has marred that landscape since time out of mind. And the permanent peace accords between Eiram and E'ronoh have gone up in cinders." Her hands stiffened against Binnot's shoulders. Something about Jedha bothered her. "The Herald incited a riot against Force users."

"Was that not . . . the plan?" Binnot asked.

The Mother hesitated. She released Binnot's shoulders and began to walk around him slowly as he stood still, frozen before the mirror. "Not exactly. The dissolution of the peace accords was the goal. But the Herald acted without my bidding. It's not how I wish to lead the Path.

It is far easier to act in the moment, as he did, than to manifest the larger vision."

"Your vision, Mother?" Binnot asked.

"That I *am* the Path." She leaned closer to Binnot. "And the Path's hand will soon reach to the ends of the galaxy, far more than the Republic or the Jedi could ever imagine."

It occurred to Binnot that she didn't need to say any of this to him—her hopes, and her disappointment in the Herald. To do so was a sign of trust. He nearly smiled. Her plan was what silently enthralled him, and the Herald's foolish mistake would mean an open place at the Mother's side. He was ready for it, if only she could see his potential.

"If the peace talks are over, then why reignite the war with the klytobacter?" Binnot turned his head. He could not keep his eyes on himself anymore. The Mother must know that it discomfited him. It was a trick he'd learned himself years ago. Throw someone off kilter, and they were more prone to speak the truth.

"A bioweapon against Eiram. Do you not see the irony?" Mother said. "After what the queen herself did with her poison? After she backed out of our deal to create an airborne poison and shut down her research facility before that ridiculous sham of a wedding? It's too good to pass up another opportunity to ensure the war continues. E'ronoh will deny it belongs to them, but its very existence speaks to violence in their favor. And so the war will continue. I need conflict to burn like a fire, Binnot. The Path needs it. We need the chaos. It feeds our ability to do more in this galaxy."

"Chaos," Binnot said. Did she mean Axel? But he was imprisoned. Surely Binnot was more useful than Axel at this point. He turned around and put his hand on his temples. His head was starting to throb a little.

"Are you all right, my child?" she asked, taking her seat again.

"Fine," Binnot said, a little too quickly. He always felt a little unwell in her presence. She didn't seem intimidating, but his body said differently. Or perhaps it was knowing the Leveler was always so close by. The vicious look of it alone was sickening to him.

"Yes," Mother said, her hand pointing to a place beyond the *Gaze Electric*'s viewport. "Chaos. My chaos. I'm speaking of Axel Greylark."

"Axel Greylark," Binnot said blankly, trying to hide his jealousy. "The same Axel Greylark who's in jail right now?"

"Not for long," Mother said. "After your mission to reignite the war succeeds, I need you to retrieve Axel from his imprisonment on Pipyyr."

"He betrayed you. He betrayed all of us," Binnot said.

"He did. And I'll not let him forget it," Mother said. Her lips thinned. "But he does me more good out of jail than inside." She frowned at Binnot. "Why, child. You don't look enthralled at the idea of reuniting with your good friend."

Axel had only ever flitted in and out of the Mother's world when it had been convenient for him these last few years. Binnot had always enjoyed those times when they were younger, and together. But Axel's work on Eiram and E'ronoh had gone horribly. He hadn't killed the Jedi. He hadn't delivered the poisons to the Mother. Now that Axel was gone, Binnot was relieved. The truth was that Axel had always been a shiny object that stole the spotlight away from everyone else when he did show up. He'd been enjoying being of more use to the Mother. Axel would distract her again. So instead, he simply smiled, as if a sun just broke through the clouds.

"So how do we do this?" Binnot said. "Do we have Path members on Pipyyr who can help us?"

"No," Mother said, tapping her chin. "But we have access to the nearby communications buoys. There are ways to intercept and corrupt messages. We just need the right one to go through."

"But . . . he failed," Binnot said. "Why give him another chance?"

The Mother stood and moved toward the door to leave. She sighed, as if speaking with Binnot was starting to tire her. It seemed that Binnot wouldn't be given the chance to know more of her mind. Perhaps she didn't hold him in as high esteem as he thought. As she put her hand on the door, she paused.

"When you know all the moving parts, then you can move them any which way you like, my dear Binnot. Even destroying someone because they failed you can be a useful maneuver, if done with a delicate hand. Axel Greylark is still a piece that can be played." Her eyes flicked upward, as if contemplating the fate of Axel the way someone might ponder which flavor of iced cake to choose for dessert.

"You're going to kill him?" Binnot asked, trying not to appear surprised.

"I might. I might not. But I need him. Make it happen, Binnot." With one last small smile, she left and closed the door behind her.

Seconds later, Goi Ganok, a Roonan male, came rushing into the room, his hands clasped together and his dark, large eyes wide with excitement.

"Goi," Binnot said. "Are you ready? The *Gaze* will be exiting hyperspace soon. It's time to board our transport."

"Let's go. For the Path!" Goi said, his minute teeth glistening as he smiled.

"For the Mother," Binnot replied as Goi excitedly left the room.

Binnot turned back toward the mirror for a moment and forced himself to stare at his own dark-green eyes.

"And for me," Binnot whispered.

Chapter One

THE REPUBLIC EXECUTIVE BUILDING, CORUSCANT

Chancellor Kyong Greylark sat in her spacious chambers. She was facing away from her vast desk, looking out over the skyline. It was near twilight, and the sun's golden light reflected against the spires and domes of shining silver, making them appear gilded.

It was a time of day that usually brought her a sense of peace and calm. But much as she tried to relax, her hands still gripped the edges of her chair as if she were on her ship, the *Aurora Sun,* crashing. A shiver ran down her spine, and the headdress of jadeite—a family heirloom—made a twinkling sound.

A door opened to her chambers.

"Chancellor Greylark," her aide said. "A message is incoming—"

"News about Jedha?" Kyong said.

"No, Chancellor."

Kyong silenced her with an upraised hand. It was the one time today she could have peace. Or at least seek it out, even if it would not come when she beckoned.

"I told you I wanted no interruptions unless it was about the peace accords," Kyong said.

"But . . . it's Chancellor Mollo, on Eiram. It's about your son."

Kyong turned around in her chair, mouth in a fixed line, and nodded. This time, the carved jadeite drops dangling in parallel arches over her head made no noise. She pressed a button on her desk, and a holoimage of Chancellor Mollo appeared.

"Chancellor Greylark," he said in his baritone voice. The Quarren was situated in a room far less grand than hers. His chancellor's robes were dun-colored and edged in silver, and his facial tentacles swayed with expectation. "I trust you are well?"

"I am fine, Chancellor Mollo. Thank you." She allowed a small nod, but that was all. A smile would say that she was inappropriately well considering her only child was incarcerated and the Greylark family was an embarrassment to the whole Republic. A frown would mean that she was not handling the political fallout well. A chancellor with a murderous son? The truth was unfathomable, yet there it was. "How is everything faring on Eiram?"

"Not perfect, but well. There is a slight incident happening on the shared moon, Eirie. I only just heard about it. Something about a downed transport ship that needs repairs. Oh, and the plans for the rebuilding of the Erasmus Capital City are under way. Communications between Queen Adrialla and Monarch A'lbaran are ongoing. Stiff and uncomfortable, but happening, thanks to the newly wedded heirs. Xiri and Phan-tu are keeping the tensions down."

"As always," Kyong said with a slight bow, "I am grateful that you are doing so much outreach in the Outer Rim."

"And I, grateful that you tolerate the hunk of metal that is Coruscant, and the endless political complexities there. Any news about Jedha?" Mollo asked. "Our incoming messages from there suddenly stopped a little while ago. It's concerning."

"We await confirmation of the signing of the peace accords," Kyong said. "Any moment now."

Mollo nodded. "Good. It is a shame that our security wouldn't allow our attendance. Nevertheless, I look forward to celebrating here with both the queen and the Monarch in due time." He paused, tentacles twitching. "There is something else. I wanted to speak to you. About Axel. There's been a proposal passed about by several different members in our advisory committees regarding his incarceration."

Kyong's eyebrows twitched. She had heard of no such discussion regarding Axel. The sentencing had been done swiftly after his capture in Eiram and he had arrived weeks ago at the prison on distant Pipyyr, somewhere near Bakura, but within the Outer Rim. When she imagined him in a cell, she would stop breathing for several seconds, so she had fixed the problem by trying desperately to not think of him at all.

Mollo went on. "You haven't heard of it, because I specifically asked for commentary without your input, so as to gather unbiased opinions." Mollo's holoimage leaned in. "They have proposed lessening Axel's sentence and transferring him to a low-security facility where he can be rehabilitated."

"What?" Kyong was shocked out of her usual stiff and formal self.

"We all recognize the mistakes that Axel made. But he had done some good. He'd saved Phan-tu Zenn from assassins. He helped expose and destroy the vials of poison—"

"By devastating the Eirami capital," Kyong retorted. "He killed that prisoner. Lied to everyone and covered up his actions. He killed an innocent E'roni father. What's worse is he's only part of a bigger picture, and we still don't fully understand the depth of that design. These were no small mistakes of a foolish young person, and we both know it."

Mollo shook his head. "I find it odd that I am the one defending your son, and you are the one reluctant to give him a second chance."

"You are incorrect. I do want him to have a second chance. But wrongs must be paid for, even if he is my only child." Kyong leaned back in her chair. The sun had now set past the skyline, and a lavender-blue darkness began to spread. Kyong turned toward the window for a moment to calm her breathing. The less Mollo could see of her expression, the better. Her distress was becoming difficult to hide.

"The committees came to the conclusion that if, and only if, both of us agreed to his rehabilitation and release to a low-security situation, they would make it happen."

"Both of us?" Kyong repeated.

Mollo's tentacles waved, then were still. His voice softened as he spoke. "I think he should be given a second chance. My answer is yes. What say you, Kyong?"

It wasn't often that Mollo used her first name, and it wasn't lost on her. Kyong tented her fingers. She thought of Axel as a tiny infant. His shining dark eyes and the tuft of dark hair on his head. The purplish birthmark across his low back that would disappear as he grew into toddlerhood. The pure innocence that was in that first smile, so many years ago. She hadn't seen that smile since his father died. They both carried that loss like a never-healing wound.

"My answer is . . ." Her voice hitched in her throat, and she began again. "My answer is no."

Mollo's tentacles waved more vigorously. "How can you—Kyong— I thought . . ."

Chancellor Greylark's aide suddenly burst into her chambers, and both chancellors turned toward the disruption.

"Chancellor Greylark. Chancellor Mollo. I'm so sorry to interrupt!" The Twi'lek aide bowed quickly, her eyes wide and her hands trembling. "Jedha. The peace talks on Jedha have failed! The ambassador from E'ronoh is dead, and the ambassador from Eiram is being accused of treason. There was—"

A holo appeared next to Chancellor Mollo's image, from one of Kyong's high-ranking representatives near Jedha. "Chancellor! I apologize for the intrusion—there's been a riot on Jedha. The permanent cease-fire agreement has not been signed—"

An aide interrupted at Mollo's side, voice flustered and rushed. "Chancellor Mollo! We have urgent news. Both parties from Eiram and E'ronoh have fled Jedha. There are casualties—"

The cacophony of news overtook their conversation as more aides streamed in and urgent calls began piling up. The two chancellors took in what information they could before they quieted their respective rooms and were briefly again alone, both stunned into silence for several moments.

Orlen Mollo closed his eyes tightly, as if he'd swallowed a bitter medicine. His hand covered his forehead. "No. After everything we've done. After the wedding."

Casualties. Treason. A broken cease-fire. It sounded horrible, but Kyong knew from experience that the details to come would be infinitely worse. They always were.

"What will we do? Kyong?" Mollo said, shaking his head.

Kyong Greylark stood, the thought of Axel now pushed aside in her mind. There was work to be done, and this was far more comfortable for her than to think of the transgressions of her family. Sometimes war was infinitely more comfortable than peace.

She spoke to the aide with a sharp voice that made even Chancellor Mollo wince. "Alert the Jedi Council."

THE MOON BETWEEN EIRAM AND E'RONOH
One Hour Prior

The moon hung like a dull pearl between the gravitational tensions of Eiram and E'ronoh. With no bounties of mine-worthy ore deposits, only vast quantities of salts, it was often a forgotten trinket of trifling concern, valued more for the crooning Eiram songs regarding its pull upon its tides. On E'ronoh, the sun boasted a monopoly on the people's lore; the moon was a minor counterpoint in myth, fondly referred to as their Timekeeper.

And so when the explosion had occurred on the moon—a tiny, brief spark on the salt-laden sphere—only Captain Plana Van had noticed.

She had been piloting her transport ship to Eiram, full of algae processing units, when the flash of gold light burst into her field of vision.

"What in the cold moon was that?" she yelped. (Though oft forgotten, the moon came in handy for cursing.) Reflexively, she slowed her transport as two crewmembers ran into the cockpit.

"Did you see that?" said Otto, a young kid learning the business, eyes wide open like a new Sargassum anemone. His skin had brighter-green freckles compared with Plana's, since he'd been on Eiram up until a few months ago. Plana had been living on ships almost nonstop for the last five years, so busy with her work that she'd spent only a scant handful of days on Eiram in any given year. Her time away from the planet showed on her face. Without a regular algae-enriched Eiram diet, her green freckles had become very faint.

"I did."

"I thought the war was over," said Lunnto, her copilot, an older Eirami man. His rounded belly reminded Plana of a golden jellyfish, one of her favorite pets. He tended to speak before he thought, but he had good instincts.

"There is a cease-fire," Plana said. She shrugged, doubting the possibility of true peace, but afraid to jinx it nevertheless. "We aren't receiving any distress signals. And anyway, what on Eirie could possibly explode? The one waystation is hardly ever used."

The skies and space above both planets had been mercifully quiet for the last few weeks. And the quiet had been most disconcerting. Plana, like everyone on Eiram, was used to bursts and explosions near the hyperlane shared by the two planets. If you weren't being shot at by an E'roni military patrol, then you were avoiding the raiding pirates that seemed to be multiplying exponentially in this system. Or trying not to get stuck full of shrapnel from the massive belt of destroyed ships and other debris that hovered near the gravity wells of both planets.

Plana pushed her heavy braids past her shoulders and tied them with a cord, a movement she associated with a coming battle. An incoming alert from Eiram lit up her screen. Of course they must have picked up on the explosion, too.

"Captain Van, this is Erasmus port commander Ailee. Please report your status update."

"Captain Van here." Her voice immediately grew cool and robotic, an old habit from her early years in the Eirami military. Plana was now in the military reserves, since her work as a hauler had been important enough that she hadn't been pulled into active duty throughout the war. "We were on our way home. Cargo is as previously reported. Nothing out of the normal on our mission until . . ." Actually, up until recently, it was expected that something should go wrong. War and all. The entire mission had been too quiet. This felt more normal, to be honest.

"We just witnessed a small disturbance on the moon. A single explosion. No distress signals. Our ship is unaffected."

"Captain Van, be aware, you're in neutral territory. Are you prepared for combat?"

Plana stiffened. "Aren't we in a cease-fire?"

"Nevertheless. Be prepared, as you always should be."

"No one has fired on us. We have no information on what caused that explosion."

As if waiting for her words to leave her mouth, Otto nervously said, "Uh, I'm registering a starfighter from E'ronoh on the moon, by the way. May be the source of the explosion."

"Or the instigator," Plana said.

Lunnto turned to stare at Plana Van. "You know what this looks like. It stinks of piracy. I'll bet that E'roni fighter shot down one of our supply ships. Trying to clean up the mess now."

Plana sighed. This delivery was supposed to be a quick, easy, peacetime job. The communication to Commander Ailee was still open. They heard everything.

"Captain Van," Commander Ailee commed in. "I'm ordering you to land on the moon and check for casualties."

"But there's no evidence—" Plana began.

"Captain Van. You may be a hauler, but as reserve military, you still obey my orders as your port's commanding officer."

"Yes, Commander." Plana rolled her eyes. Oh, for this war to be truly over.

She turned to their tiny crew—Lunnto and Otto. Pell, the navigator, was sleeping in the back somewhere.

"Well. Here we go." Plana sped her ship toward Eirie. Soon, they were descending upon the only active area of the moon. A single way-station, a refueling stop, and a provisions shop. She now had a view of the E'roni ship Otto had picked up on the scanner. It was docked with another transport spewing tendrils of smoke from the engine—the source of the explosion. Not Eirami make, but not E'roni, either. Probably a hauler from another sector making money bringing goods to one of the planets.

Compared with their own transport, the devilfighter from E'ronoh was small, but it was made for speed and power. The injured transport ship was perhaps twice the size, but still quite small itself for anything carrying goods across this sector. The hull seemed intact, but scorch marks blossomed from an irregular hole in the smoking engine.

Plana cleared her throat, hailing the E'roni ship. "This is Captain Plana Van of Eiram. Please state your identification and intentions." Might as well start vague.

There was silence for more than a full minute before a voice commed in.

"This is Lieutenant Gunnaw of E'ronoh, Thylefire Squadron." There was another long pause. Plana imagined him snarling. "Under the terms of the cease-fire, that is all that I am required to say. However. We came across this transport headed toward Shuraden. It was adrift, and we brought it to the moon for repairs."

Plana frowned. "The waystation here isn't capable of handling extensive repairs."

"We are aware of that fact. The ship's crew—there are only two—stated they could repair it themselves if they could dock somewhere safely. They didn't believe the cease-fire was fully legal and requested to come to the moon."

Neutral territory. It made sense, but still.

"What were they transporting?"

"What does it matter? They were looted by pirates. Cargo is gone now. We went inside to do a search and verify the story."

"Can you explain the nature of the explosion while you were moonside?"

"The ship's remaining engine blew. Not our fault."

"And where are you headed?"

"Not your business."

"And the survivors? May we speak to them?"

"They don't want to speak to you."

Plana bristled. This was like arguing with a rock. She commed into Commander Ailee and gave them an update.

"Something isn't right," Commander Ailee said. Plana felt the same, but said nothing. "From a nonmilitary perspective, we have a right to attend to the survivors ourselves and conduct a safety evaluation of that downed ship."

Plana could feel her blood pressure rising with worry. The cease-fire felt so tenuous. Any moment now, the war would be officially over. Then why did it feel like it was an impossibility, even with the union between the two planets?

"I am ordering you to search that ship, Captain Van, and sending four crescent fighters as backup," Commander Ailee said. "Anything that affects the moon affects us, far more than E'ronoh."

"Yes, Commander." The people of Eiram had always felt that way. The moon exerted crucial tidal forces over Eiram. The creatures on their watery planet lived and bred and died by the tides, and by extension, the people of Eiram did as well. If E'ronoh did anything that affected the moon—moved it by a kilometer in some as-yet-impossible but terrifying way—it would destroy Eiram. No one ever considered it, but Plana did at this moment, and it frightened her.

The commander was right. That E'roni ship and the defunct ship were hiding something.

"Oh, and Captain Van?"

"Yes?"

"Make it quick. More E'roni ships will be here in minutes, the second they see ours are on the way. Fire no shots unless absolutely necessary. For all we know, our ambassadors have already signed a permanent peace agreement on Jedha."

Plana Van cracked her knuckles, a habit she had before work got messy. She turned to her crew. "Get on the duo-cannon, and wake up Pell," she said. The navigator's nap was over. "We're boarding that ship."

ORRA LAGOON, EIRAM

The Eirami lagoon was one of many in this region, only five kilometers from the capital city. It was one of the things Phan-tu Zenn most loved about Eiram. In any town or village, no matter how busy or crowded it got, you could go in any direction to find water. And quiet.

Phan-tu was helping with a traditional slek gathering—a water vegetable that was so tender and delectable that he would have traded a boat for a bushel when homesick for a traditional slek stew. It was a favorite of his mother and sister when he was a child, and his longing for it never went away. Now Queen Adrialla and the queen's consort, Odelia, loved it as much as he did, though the fondness existed well before they'd adopted him. Though he was fairly adept at handling the goings-on at the palace, he always sought an excuse to get away back to the water. He'd grown up along the Rayes Canal, and his boyhood would always set him slightly apart from his royal parents.

And yet this lagoon, like so many other areas in Eiram, no longer resembled the memories from his childhood. Lush waters filled with life, greenery growing like tangled jungle around its edges, beaches that glinted yellow and gold like precious metals. Now the sands were often stained with oil and fuel that had leaked from downed ships. The greenery in many places had been burned alive from explosions. And dwellings were in disrepair, with resources being scarce. Incoming ships with supplies were constantly being harassed and raided by pirates taking advantage of the chaos. Finding peace out here was hard with the evidence of war everywhere.

Knee-deep in the cool water of the lagoon, he reached for a tiny, rare tendril near his feet, pulled it gently, and put it into the basket at his waist. Something buzzed at his wrist, and he swatted at it, before he realized it wasn't a biting midge, but his communicator. It was his wife, Xiri.

Wife! The word still seemed so strange.

"Hello, Xee," Phan-tu said, laughing. "I almost mistook your call for a bug bite."

"Well, thanks!" She wasn't laughing. Oof. "Listen, something's happening on the Timekeeper moon."

Phan-tu stood up and grew very still. "The moon? Why would something be happening there?" He reflexively looked up in the sky. The moon was a quarter full just over the horizon. Though not uninhabitable, it wasn't settled by either planet. Eiram loved its plentiful azure waters, and E'ronoh loved its hot temperatures and bronzed landscape—none of which were to be found on the moon. The tiny lagoon waves connected to the Erasmus Sea, and the height of the water lapping against his legs was a result of the moon's pull on Eiram.

"I don't know what's going on, but apparently there are Eirami crescent fighters on their way and I heard we're deploying ships, too." Xiri sounded out of breath. "I was flying when I got the call. I'm on my way to speak to Father and find out more information. You need to come here. Right away."

"Come to E'ronoh? I'm . . ." *Well, I'm up to my knees in water,* Phan-tu wanted to say. Which was the truth, but what he really bristled slightly at was what sounded like orders. "I was on my way to the palace to see the queen and the queen consort. I think we might do more good trying to calm any incendiary feelings on our own planets right now."

"Okay," Xiri said. "The peace treaty will be signed any moment. We're so close, Phan-tu! We just have to keep it together until then."

"Of course. We'll talk soon."

"Phan-tu?"

"Yes?" He waited expectantly.

There was a long pause. "I miss you."

"I miss you, too, Xee. Goodbye."

Sometimes it was still stilted and weird, speaking to Xiri. They were married, yes, and they loved each other. But theirs was still a very young partnership. Half the time they were together, and half the time they were on their respective planets calming tensions during the cease-fire. Phan-tu had yet to feel like he was a prince of E'ronoh, and he knew Xiri felt the same about her relationship to Eiram. Plus, they were always being watched, royalty that they were. Phan-tu had yet to put his arm instinctively around his wife's shoulders. Navigating each other's space was still a new thing. And navigating life as representatives of both planets felt just as raw and new.

Phan-tu strode out of the water. Nearby, children with their bright smattering of green freckles bowed as he walked by. He wasn't born royalty, but was now. Some older teens looked on from afar, slightly mocking grins on their faces. Not everyone was so happy he was married to the princess of E'ronoh. Before their marriage, he had cared less about glances and whispers. There was a war to stop, after all. Now it was often all he noticed.

Phan-tu jumped onto a speeder bike and made his way to the palace. He entered one of the large sitting rooms on the north side, where Queen Adrialla was seated with several of her counselors. Water surrounded the room in a flowing mini river set with floating, iridescent lilies.

"Ah, Phan-tu. We were just going to call for you." The queen waved him forward. She arose from her dais intricately carved of sea wood tree, and reached out a bronzed hand. He touched it to his forehead in respect, and straightened. She smiled at him, eyes crinkling at their edges. Silver hair glinted in the dark braids woven in and out of her crown. Together, they walked into a side room, her shimmersilk robes rustling quietly. The counselors sat on one side of a large teardrop-shaped table. The queen consort rose from her seat to kiss Phan-tu on the cheek, her veil fluttering.

"And not a moment too soon. We need a cool head in this room," Odelia whispered, sitting to Queen Adrialla's right.

He noticed that the counselors were polite, but a subtle coldness had entered their interactions—a new behavior that began the day it was announced he would marry Xiri. He remembered words spoken to him by his guard Vigo, before the wedding. *Half of you belongs to E'ronoh now. How do we know you will love your people as much as you always have?*

It still stung him.

"What news?" the queen asked.

"An incoming transport ship of ours happened to see an explosion on the moon. Our sensors verified it. A small E'roni military vessel is in the area where a trade ship exploded while it was being repaired there."

"On Eirie? Our moon? How odd," one of the counselors said.

Our moon. Phan-tu felt possessive of it in a way he hadn't before. Likely all in the room felt the same way.

One of the counselors leaned in. "Commander Ailee wants the passengers to be questioned."

"The E'roni won't like it," said another counselor—the eldest, sporting a white beard down to his knees.

"No," said the queen. "But in good faith, they ought to allow it, if they have nothing to hide. We cannot do anything that will jeopardize this pending peace accord. We can only wait patiently for news that all has gone well on Jedha."

The counselors shifted in their seats. The planet had been at war for so many years, they appeared awfully uncomfortable with the idea of playing nice with the people that had been shooting down their ships, littering space with metal. And the dead.

Phan-tu looked at the console before him. "We have an incoming transmission. Speak, Commander Ailee." His wrist communicator buzzed as well. Xiri. He put his hands beneath the table and ignored it.

"Our pilot is boarding the ship."

"On whose authority?" the queen asked.

"Mine. There could be Eirami citizens on board. They're in neutral territory."

Phan-tu turned the volume down on his comm and raised it casually to his ear, pretending to scratch his head.

"Tell them not to board that ship!" Xiri said. "Phan-tu? Can you hear me? It's a breach of trust! Tell them—"

The queen gave him a sidelong glance. She couldn't hear what Xiri was saying, but she could tell when Phan-tu was keeping something from her. He put his hand down quickly.

"This is a time to build trust. I think it's unwise to board the ship without explicit permission from E'ronoh," Phan-tu said.

"Of course you do. Or is that your wife that thinks so?" the elder counselor said.

"She does," Phan-tu replied. "But that's beside the point. Both sides carry years of deep war wounds and fear. Working together is the only way to go forward."

Commander Ailee's voice came through the console. "Captain Van has boarded the ship."

Phan-tu's heart sank. It was too late.

THE MOON BETWEEN EIRAM AND E'RONOH

Binnot Ullo straightened up and dusted off his cargo uniform. Goi Ganok stood at his side, hands clasped tightly.

A middle-aged human woman, tall and muscular, entered. She wore a dark blue flight uniform with the water insignia of Eiram on her upper arm. Civilian, but holding herself like she was military. She was armed, as was her companion—an Eirami male who looked far younger, with deep greenish-blue freckles. He seemed about as nervous as Goi was. Just outside the door, the E'ronoh pilot, Lieutenant Gunnaw, frowned and waited.

"I'm Captain Plana Van, of Eiram. State your name, your home territory, and your mission."

"Binnot Ullo." Binnot bowed slightly. He had no interest in using a fake name. Neither he nor Goi was known widely outside of the Path. This would change soon. At least for Binnot. He lightly kicked Goi, who bowed like a squeaky droid that needed oiling.

"Goi Ganok. We're merely shipping folk." He smiled too widely, showing rows of minuscule teeth.

"Originally from Mirial and Roona, obviously," Binnot added. "We were on our way to Shuraden, from our station near Skye."

Captain Van narrowed her eyes. "Strange that you should travel near the Eiram system to do so. Most shippers avoid us because of our junk belt."

"It was faster this way," Binnot said.

"Not by much," Captain Van said. "I understand you were attacked by pirates and came to the moon for repairs. Did your attackers identify themselves?"

Binnot gave her a condescending glare. "They were *pirates*. Of course they didn't identify themselves."

"And your cargo? What were you hauling?"

"Protein concentrates. But the barrels were all taken." Binnot gestured to the empty compartment around him. He watched as the captain and her colleague circled the room. It was about twelve meters long and slightly less wide and tall, taking up the bulk of the small ship's volume. She sniffed the air once, then sniffed again.

The young Eirami man sniffed, too.

Captain Van turned to him. "You smell that, Otto?" She brushed past Binnot, her footsteps making dull thumping sounds as she crossed the storage area. Her steps suddenly sounded sonorous and hollow. She knelt and took a knife from her belt, wedging it against the edge of a flat metal section of flooring underfoot. It lifted, and she pulled it up, hard. She threw the square of metal away and it crashed against the wall.

The hidden floor compartment was full of sealed vats, a window on each showing they were filled to the brim with an inky liquid. They smelled like nothing to Binnot, perhaps faintly briny, but the odor clearly rankled the Eiram captain and her companion. Her nostrils flared and she grimaced, staggering back.

"That's klytobacter." She stared at Binnot. "What are you doing with this?"

Binnot shook his head, as did Goi, a little too energetically. "What's klytobacter?" Goi asked, trying to keep his face benign.

"One dry summer when I was a kid," Captain Van began, "it bloomed on the north shore of my home island on Eiram. Killed the fish, the sea vegetables, birds . . . everything. For years, we couldn't swim or touch the water." Her eyes were full of accusations. "What are you doing with this?"

"We didn't know it was here! We didn't smell anything odd," Binnot said, his hands up in surrender. "We were only paid to bring the protein concentrates to Shuraden."

Captain Van put her hand on her blaster at her side. "You purposely crossed the Eiram system when you could have easily avoided it and now you have a biological weapon that could spell disaster for my planet?"

The Eirami man at her side's fists were clenched as he blurted out, "Are you working for E'ronoh?"

"Choose your words carefully!" Lieutenant Gunnaw had stepped into the room, seeing the tanks and staring hard at Binnot, then Otto.

"Otto!" Captain Van said, silencing him with a glare.

Goi actually looked angry, and blurted out, "No!"

Binnot hit him so hard in the shoulder that Goi lost his footing and shuffled sideways, growling at the cuff.

"This ship is going nowhere." Captain Van touched a communicator on her wrist. "Commander Ailee. They have a biological weapon on board. Klytobacter."

While Captain Van spoke to her commanding officer, Lieutenant Gunnaw was also speaking quickly into his wrist communicator. Goi was dripping with nervousness to the point that half his jacket was darkened with moisture. Binnot held a hand out to him, and Goi met his eyes. Binnot leaned closer and whispered.

"Remember, Goi. This is what we want. Isn't it?"

Goi barely nodded an assent.

When she finished her report, Captain Van and Otto quickly backed out of the storage compartment.

"This ship and you two are never leaving this moon if I have anything to do with it," Captain Van said just before the door to the storage area slid shut. Binnot and Goi heard it lock from the other side. Lieutenant Gunnaw could be heard arguing with Captain Van on the other side.

Oh I'm getting off this moon. Just watch me. But Binnot was satisfied. The Mother would be happy. Binnot will have ensured that this time, the war would rage with plenty of fuel. If there was any wonder if Eiram and E'ronoh should go back to the negotiation table, the klytobacter would destroy that prospect. Just as it would dissolve any goodwill that Xiri A'lbaran and Phan-tu Zenn's marriage ridiculousness ever conjured.

"Hey!" The E'roni pilot commed into the ship's speakers. "Eirami ships are all over the airspace above this waystation. What were you doing with that klytobacter?"

Binnot said, smoothly as possible, "We have nothing to do with that. It's probably not even klytobacter, just leftover sludge from an old protein shipment gone bad. We're just victims here!"

"Hold tight," the pilot said. "We have E'roni backup on the way. In fact . . . they're here."

They heard the low rumble of other craft nearby.

"Oh," Goi said. He put his hands over his earholes. "Here we go."

ERASMUS CITY CENTER, EIRAM

Phan-tu listened in shock as Commander Ailee gave her updated report. A bioweapon? His queen bristled at the word. She, too, had been guilty of gathering a poison to defend her people, only weeks ago. A terrible, desperate misstep. Now she looked at Phan-tu, not with worry, but with a slight self-satisfied expression, as if to say, *See, Phan-tu? Was I not justified for trying to do exactly as the E'roni were to do?*

But they had conceded it was a misstep, and now this was a step toward playing dirty in an already filthy war. Horrifying tactics like using drill ships were old news now. Killing had become sophisticated and brutal. Now klytobacter? Poisons killed warmongers. Klytobacter, however, would kill entire species and delicately balanced ecosystems, if seeded in high enough concentrations. Klytobacter could be a planet killer. This was too much. This was an escalation, plain and simple.

"How do we know it's really klytobacter?" Phan-tu asked.

The elder counselor leaned forward. "We all know what it smells like. Like death."

Phan-tu could feel the room buzzing with rising fury. The queen's consort, Odelia, looked like her fists were on the cusp of breaking the table they grasped. He raised his hand to rub his forehead, whispering.

"Xiri? Klytobacter? Is it true?"

Xiri's voice came buzzing back quickly. "We have nothing to do with that! You have to believe me. I know your people might think it could be a response to Queen Adrialla manufacturing poison to use against E'ronoh. We've got to settle everyone down, and figure this out."

Queen Adrialla raised her hands, bracelets jangling. "This doesn't make sense. We are a breath away from an everlasting peace."

"Xiri is saying they have nothing to do with that klytobacter," Phan-tu said.

"She stood by me when I made my own mistakes trying to protect Eiram. I said I would protect the future of these two worlds. I believe Xiri. We need to discuss this, not act hastily," Queen Adrialla said firmly.

The elder counselor stood. "Princess Xiri means well. But Xiri is not E'ronoh, and E'ronoh is not Xiri. Some parts of E'ronoh will never stop trying to hurt us. Think of Viceroy Ferrol and his son. They tried to kill their own princess because of her ties to Eiram! We have to protect ourselves." He turned to the table of counselors and the royal family. "Since the wedding, we have all agreed to decide action by majority decision after Queen Adrialla's regrettable actions. What say you all to a maneuver that shows strength in responding to this klytobacter threat?"

Of the nine people at the table, six of them placed fists toward the center of the table—a vote of yes. Only the queen, her consort, and Phan-tu left their hands flat on the table indicating disagreement.

Queen Adrialla looked at her son helplessly. "We have no choice."

The eldest held out his hand. "For Eiram."

"For Eiram," they all spoke in unison. Except for Phan-tu, who felt like the ground was collapsing beneath his feet. All he and Xiri had been working toward. It was slipping away.

He could hear Xiri's tiny voice coming from his wrist. Though the sound was extremely faint, it was as good as a scream right in his ear. Answering would do no good.

"Tell them not to fire, please! Phan-tu, can you hear me? *Phan-tu!*"

THE MOON BETWEEN EIRAM AND E'RONOH

Captain Plana Van, back on her ship, hovered above the waystation where the transport ship full of klytobacter was docked. Two crescent ships flanked them, but she'd prefer if they were up front. Since she had last reported to Commander Ailee, two devilfighters from E'ronoh had shown up to join Lieutenant Gunnaw's ship and now faced them at too close a distance to be comfortable. Their transport ship wouldn't take more than a hit or two before it fell to pieces. No, wait. Now there were four devilfighters in sight. Things had heated up quickly.

Commander Ailee commed in. "You have it on my authority to fire on that cargo ship. It's carrying an outlawed bioweapon. E'ronoh has broken the pact of the cease-fire."

"But we can't know for sure that E'ronoh owns those tanks of klyto-bacter. The pilot said—"

Captain Van couldn't get another word out before multiple transmissions came in at once. Five, to be exact. One from an Eirami crescent ship nearby, three from the communications buoy just beyond the moon, and one directly from Eiram's central council.

"What in the cold moon is going on?" She hit them one by one.

"Urgent transmission in. The peace talks on Jedha have failed!"

"Ambassador Tintak from E'ronoh has been killed. It's off. Everything's off—"

"It was a fiasco. Eiram walked into a trap. The city of Jedha is in flames, there are casualty reports—"

Plana Van's hands shook as she stared out the viewport. They needed to fire. They had every right to, now that the cease-fire was dead. But Plana couldn't move. Stepping back into war was the last thing she truly wanted. Was she so sure the klytobacter was E'ronoh's fault? Did she have all the facts? But her gut said to defend her home planet, and the klytobacter terrified her. That was all that mattered. She took an enormous breath.

"On my command," she said. "Fire—"

But before she could even finish, explosions lit up her view. One of the crescent fighters had shot at Lieutenant Gunnaw's devilfighter, hovering above the waystation, while the other crescent fighter targeted the incapacitated transport ship full of lethal cargo still docked far below. Gunnaw's fighter exploded immediately, and the ship with Bin-not and Goi was now smoking. Captain Van saw the two running away from the wreckage, looking for cover, feeling both relief and surprise at their escape. But Lieutenant Gunnaw was dead. Plana squeezed her eyes shut for a terrible moment.

"Get those survivors. We need to know where that bioweapon was made, and how to destroy the source," Commander Ailee ordered.

The ships scattered, with the two Eirami crescent fighters evading the two E'roni devilfighters. Hoping that no one would pursue her very obviously nonmilitary ship, Plana began to descend to the moon's surface to try to capture Binnot and Goi.

Her hope lasted all of five seconds. A devilfighter peeled away from chasing the crescent ships and began to close the distance. Plana made a sharp turn, veering away from the moon.

"We have to head back to Eiram," Plana said to her copilot, Lunnto. "We won't survive a fight with these devilfighters."

Captain Ailee commed in to all the Eirami ships in the area. "E'ronoh is sending out a distress call to their out-of-sector pilots. Both planets sent a large contingent to Jedha, but we're having trouble contacting ours. If those E'roni reinforcements come in—we'll be inundated. We have to stop the message."

"How many ships?" Plana's ship shook—they'd been hit. They stopped accelerating. Lunnto scrambled to bypass a leaking engine drive line. "Fix that! Now!" she hissed.

"What do you think I'm doing?" Lunnto yelled back, scrambling out of the cockpit to head to the engines.

"Captain Van! All pilots! Do you hear me? Destroy those communications buoys or we'll have more E'roni ships flooding in than we can handle!"

Plana growled. She couldn't fight a fleet of E'roni ships, but her little duo-cannon could take out a buoy.

"Leave that to me," she said. "Let's get out of here. The five buoys that serve these planets are C-12, C-13, A-01 through A-03. We have enough fuel and firepower to take them out."

The ship's engines suddenly hummed optimistically. Lunnto had fixed the drive line. As they accelerated toward the first communications buoy, an E'roni devilfighter followed close behind. But it only took one shot for the small buoy to explode in a sunburst of sparks.

Lunnto had returned to the cockpit, his face smudged with grease. "Are you sure we need to blow these up? What if we need them to talk to other sectors?" he asked, hitting buttons so fast his fingers were a blur.

No, I'm not sure, Plana thought, but they needed a leader right now. She spoke, more to herself than to Lunnto. "Why? No one has been helping us," Plana said. "The Republic says it wants to help, but we're not part of the Republic, and the chancellor's own son destroyed Erasmus City. The Jedi were supposed to help with the peace talks, and now the talks have been blown to smithereens. We're on our own, Lunnto." She frowned deeply. "That klytobacter came from somewhere. If E'ronoh is getting help from the outside, it's time to stop that. Let's hit that buoy next." She accelerated, leaving the other fighting ships behind them.

A bright light and a crash sent Plana flying from her captain's chair onto the floor, alarms beeping loudly. Her navigator, Pell, walked almost drunkenly into the cockpit, scratching his bluish beard and blinking slowly.

"Hey, I think someone's shooting at us!" Pell said, voice croaky.

Plana rolled her eyes. That was some nap. She scrambled back into her pilot's chair. She patted the console affectionately.

"Show me your stuff," she muttered, maximizing their acceleration. The devilfighter kept firing on them before an Eirami crescent ship finally cut them off. Plana's transport only had enough shield power for a few more hits.

Another buoy sizzled and died. Plana was a good pilot, but in her youth, she was an excellent shot. Some things, you don't forget. The other buoy was on the far side of Eiram, but they didn't even have to go there.

"Captain Van. The last communications buoy has been destroyed."

"Excellent!" Plana yelled, and her crew cheered. "Which of us got it?"

Commander Ailee sounded exhausted, and they'd only been in battle for minutes. "Hard to tell. E'roni ships fired simultaneously. Looks like they were thinking the same thing."

Plana's skin prickled as she decelerated and turned. From afar, the dark space surrounding Eirie was alight with explosions. Ships from E'ronoh and Eiram alike were being shot down. People were dying again. She thought of all the other planets and people out in the vast galaxy—so many who had come to the enormous wedding celebration only weeks ago. Now they were cut off from help. She thought of all those new communications buoys placed by countless hyperspace prospectors these last several years. They'd connected these two planets to the rest of the galaxy. In a wink, they were gone.

Alone. And once again, at war.

Chapter Two

Gella Nattai sat in a quiet corner of a small sitting room aboard the *Eventide,* cleaning her lightsabers. It felt strange to have her own ship. The sleek curved vessel, a gift from Chancellor Greylark, was now half filled with Jedi. They were all headed to Jedha from Coruscant, where she had successfully petitioned the Jedi Council to become a Wayseeker. The Council had hesitated, wondering if the stress of what happened on Eiram had emotionally swayed her. But Master Creighton Sun had added to the closed-door discussions via hologram, and the request had gone through. Despite everything that had happened on Eiram and E'ronoh, one good thing had come of it. Clarity.

After some time in the Temple there, she thought she was ready to continue her meditative studies in Jedha City, but information from Aida less than a day ago had kept her plans at bay. A bomb at the signing ceremony on Jedha was a shocking show of interference. And now she couldn't stop thinking about Axel, and whether he was linked to the Path of the Open Hand all this time.

Every interaction she'd had with him replayed in her mind daily, like a circuit glitch. Every lie he had told her. Every glance. She'd read Republic reports about Axel's interrogation after he'd been incarcerated, but nothing had been helpful. And nothing resolved the fact that her own intuition had failed her. It didn't help that everywhere she looked she was met with the luxe interior furnishings of the *Eventide* that Axel had hand-selected. The opulence of the marbled floor and brushed-silk surfaces always felt ill fitting. She shook her head and picked up a needlelike scraping tool, digging out bits of dirt from tiny crevices along the hilts of her lightsabers. She followed with a polishing cloth, rubbing so hard she actually grew warm inside the cool ship. The lightsabers were about as clean as they could possibly get by now, but Gella still rubbed the cloth like it was the most important thing in her life. She needed something to do, even if it meant polishing her weapons into a pile of dust.

"Hey."

Jedi Master Orin Darhga stood in the doorway of the room where Gella had been hiding. She braced herself for the joke that usually followed Orin's welcoming *hey.* But he didn't look his normal jovial self. His reddish-brown hair and beard were scraggly as usual, but the blue eyes weren't twinkling. He kicked one of his boots gently against the door.

"What's the matter?"

"Message incoming from Master Creighton Sun and Aida Forte. It's marked urgent. I know you don't have to hear it, but I also know you and Creighton did a lot of work together. It's up to you."

"Of course."

Gella stood up and followed him into the belly of the ship, where a large, polished glass console was set for communications. She had volunteered the ship to help the other Jedi when she could. It seemed odd to keep the *Eventide* all to herself. Truthfully, after she'd spoken to Aida about the bombs, she'd immediately set out to Jedha, just in case. But she'd hoped to hear firsthand that the negotiations were done before she disappeared into the landscape of Jedha's capital city. She wanted to eventually clear her mind of anything having to do with Eiram or E'ronoh—or particularly Axel.

"You okay?" Orin elbowed her.

"Fine, why?"

"That vein in your temple looks like it's going to bust open."

She said nothing.

"Look," he reasoned. "What happened with Greylark on E'ronoh and Eiram wasn't your fault. You did an excellent job. When other people have bad intentions, well, you can't hold yourself responsible for that."

"I should have had better judgment," Gella said.

"But you did. To the very end, you did what was right. That's the hope, isn't it? I hoped not to tell an insulting joke at the consulate reception last week, but I did. How was I to know that toilet humor on Trandosha was considered an invitation to a duel?"

"Oh, Orin."

"Hey, at least I won the duel." He patted his lightsaber. "But lesson learned. Toilet humor is not universally appreciated. Also, I'm clearly not ambassador material. Ah, here we are."

The central chamber of the vessel was large and outfitted with sleek silver chairs. Four other Jedi—two humans, a Twi'lek, and an Iktotchi—waited expectantly. Gella had isolated herself so well that she hadn't even met them yet.

Creighton Sun and Aida Forte's holoimages appeared before them. The transmission was ragged along the edges, no surprise given the sandstorms on Jedha. Creighton's face was marked with a few cuts, and Aida looked exhausted. Both their robes were torn and battle-scarred.

Gella inhaled in surprise. *Oh no. What happened now?* she said to herself as Creighton began to speak.

"The peace talks have failed. The battle has finally ended—"

"Battle? Before you'd said it was an isolated incident with those explosives," Gella said.

"A riot broke out," Aida said. "We can't be sure—but we believe the Path of the Open Hand were responsible."

"Or a smaller faction within it," Creighton said. "We know the Herald—Werth Plouth—was involved in the riot, but whether he incited it or joined in—the story keeps changing. And we don't know if they were purposely trying to obliterate the peace negotiations, or just angry at the Jedi presence. Many of the Jedi are still sick from battle."

"Wait. Sick? Or injured?" the Twi'lek Jedi asked.

"Both. We can't explain it. Some of them had no physical injuries from fighting, but were incapacitated. Not sure if it was a toxin or something else. We've had . . . casualties, and the Jedi weren't the only ones harmed."

"How many?" Orin asked. "How many dead? How many hurt?"

"The total number is unclear, but many Jedha civilians have been injured or displaced, and the damage to the city is significant. The last Jedi statue is in ruins."

There was a gasp.

Aida spoke, her voice more angry than sad. "We don't know the status of the archives beneath it. Buildings are razed. The full extent of the damage is hard to assess right now."

"We're proposing to the Jedi Council and the chancellors that we address the Path directly on Dalna," said Creighton, who continued to relay details from the battle.

But Gella had stopped listening. Her heart ached—she had seen the statue recently on her last pilgrimage to Jedha City. The vision of the breathtaking Aerialwalk being performed by a priestess of the Singing Mountain with the statue on the horizon was still fresh in her mind. She had imagined it would stand firm for millennia and for countless Jedi to see one day. In her mind's eye, she now saw it broken into massive pieces, with dust everywhere, revealing how shockingly fragile it was. For a brief moment, almost like an electric shock, she saw countless Jedi falling, ones she knew, and ones she'd never met.

The image disappeared as quickly as it arrived. She shook her head and reoriented herself to what was happening now.

"Does the Jedi Council know? Do the chancellors?" Gella interrupted.

Creighton shook his head. "We aren't sure. We sent out a message to Coruscant, but our long-range communications buoys were destroyed soon after, possibly by fleeing Path members. We haven't heard back from either of the chancellors."

"The city is a mess," Aida continued. "We need your help with the fallen, and to bring stability. But you must be warned—whatever was making some of the Jedi ill, it could affect you, too. We've searched the city endlessly, but we don't know what caused it, or why it stopped. You must be on your guard."

Gella's head swam from the influx of information, from the voices, from the confusion. Jedha was supposed to mean the closing of this story after Axel ended up in jail. It was supposed to be a new beginning where Eiram and E'ronoh could finally start repairing themselves and building a lasting peace. Everything Gella had fought for in the last weeks—it was all crumbling apart. She thought of Xiri and Phantu, and felt the pain they would feel when the news hit them. Her friends. Their planets deserved better. *They* deserved better.

A kernel of anger grew and knotted inside her. Axel must have known this would happen. He had kept so much from her. He was probably sitting in a cell somewhere, having food handed to him on a pretty tray. She wouldn't be surprised if he was in some sort of luxury resort for lawbreakers in the Republic, being the son of Chancellor Greylark. She deeply regretted that she hadn't followed him and interrogated him in person. The question was, did he care about anything that he'd done? Was he even sorry?

But more important, what else was to come? What if this was only a smaller version of something larger planned? Millions of lives could be at stake.

If he knew, she would make him tell her. Somehow.

Also, she wanted a damn apology. A real one.

"Gella? Did you hear me?"

Orin had touched her sleeve. The other Jedi had left the room, and Gella was standing there, fists clenched.

"I'm sorry. What?"

"The Jedi aboard are preparing to leave for Jedha. Creighton and Aida are flying beyond this sector to make contact with the Jedi Council and the chancellors."

Gella spun out of his grasp to face him. "I can't go to Jedha. I'll bring them to Jedha City, but I need to find Axel Greylark."

"The chancellor's son? Are you mad? He's long gone. I heard he was locked away on a prison on Pipyyr, near Bakura."

"I don't care where he is. I have to speak to him. I know in my bones that he knew this would happen, and he may know if there's more to come." Orin tried to speak to her more, but Gella had already gone to the cockpit to head planetside. She had to focus to pilot the ship, but it was hard to see the smoke rising from Jedha City with her own eyes, the fallen Jedi statue, and crumbling buildings that told of the violence to this city known for its peaceful devotion to the Force. She sensed the pain, the loss, and the anger simmering throughout the city. But her place wasn't here. She could feel the pull toward Pipyyr, where she would find Axel. And answers.

She was closing the doors of the *Eventide* and preparing for takeoff when Orin stepped inside the cockpit, nestling his broad frame into the copilot's seat.

"Hey! What are you doing?" Gella asked.

"I wasn't going to let you crack on without me," Orin said, shrugging. "I'm going."

"No, you're not." She turned to him squarely. "The Council needs you on Jedha. But I know Axel better than anyone. Maybe even better than Chancellor Greylark herself."

"I don't doubt that. But you ought to know that isolating yourself as the sole person responsible for fixing this problem *is* a problem.

You're being swayed by instincts that aren't sound. The fact that you're furious right now tells me that much."

"I'm not furious!" Gella said, a touch more strongly than she expected. She closed her eyes a second.

"At least don't go alone, angry. I can help."

Gella wanted to laugh now. She had known Orin informally for years, and this trip she'd spent more minutes face-to-face with him than ever before. He seemed so optimistic, and that cheerfulness in anyone had a tendency to almost chafe her. She longed for more familiar support in Creighton Sun's guidance. He'd talked her through so many trying times while she was dealing with the two planets.

"How are you going to help?" Gella asked.

"For one thing, I am a Jedi Master. I have been a Jedi far longer than you. And for a second thing, though as a Wayseeker you don't specifically need the approval of the Jedi Council, what you're doing affects their decisions. If I go with you, your decision will seem less hasty. Less like you're following your feelings."

"But I—" Gella closed her mouth and let Orin's words settle for a moment. He was right. And she was angry enough to realize that it might affect her judgment. He looked like he was about to sneeze, which must have been his way of wearing a serious face.

"I sense something large coming, too," he said, looking out at the dust and smoke of Jedha City. The blue sky was somehow defiantly beautiful as a backdrop to what had happened. "I've felt it for some time, and I know now it's not about what happened on Jedha. There's something else." He cinched his seatbelt. "I was put on this ship to put out fires. And here you are, searching for an inferno about to spark. I'm still sticking to the mission. Let's go."

Orin had a way of switching between seriousness and a jovial demeanor that threw her off. It might throw Axel off, too, and that could be helpful.

Gella nodded. "Okay, then. Though I don't think my Wayseeker journey begins right now. The pull I felt from the Force, leading me to be a Wayseeker—I can't quite explain it, but I know it doesn't begin with this unfinished business with Axel. Perhaps later, after I can sort this all out." She began inputting the coordinates for their navigation and Orin took the controls. The *Eventide* rose into the air and soon left Jedha behind. "Thank you, Orin, for coming with me. I'm glad I'm not doing this alone."

"You're welcome, Gella." He looked at her sideways. "Remember that sentiment when you grow weary of my jokes. Speaking of which, have you heard the one about the charhound that tried to work in a Coruscant bakery? He was *fired.*"

Gella rolled her eyes. Lightspeed or no, this trip would be long.

It wouldn't take too long before they made it to Pipyyr, even though it took a zigzag course through the Core and back to the Outer Rim to find established and prospected hyperspace lanes to get there. Thank the stars for hyperspace lanes, because Gella could only take so much cheering up by Orin before she yanked every dark curl out of her head from annoyance. Maybe this was a mistake.

Orin's voice boomed into the rear cabin. "Gella. We're nearly there."

Gella made her way to the cockpit and watched as the blurred light of the hyperspace lane ceased to exist. Soon, they were cruising near a gray-colored planet. Two moons, both crater-pocked, were nearby. A tiny dot in their periphery must be the planet of Bakura.

"I've already told the security checkpoint we're landing shortly."

Gella glanced about as they descended through the clouds. The vapor disappeared to reveal a rocky planet with deep craters filled with water. There wasn't much vegetation, but the edges of the water had a poisonously green hue. There were a few villages perched on the peaks of the rocky mountains and hills. No one lived near the water's edge.

"I see it," Gella said, pointing. On the top of one of the mountains, there was a cube-shaped building that seemed to rise out of the mountainside like a growing crystal. A flat landing pad was etched into the rock next to it, with lights blinking.

"I've seen Axel Greylark on the holonet," Orin said. "Quite the wealthy playboy. Looks like his palace has changed locations."

Gella nodded. She bit her lip. She had to control their first conversation or things might go haywire and she'd get no information.

"What's this boyo like?" Orin asked. "In your opinion?"

"Clever. Conniving. Charming."

"I may have a crush on him already," Orin said.

"He's the walking definition of charisma," Gella said. "But he's got a thing against Jedi because of a bad history involving his dad's death. Don't let him fool you. Under that celebrity sheen, he's painfully insecure."

Orin made a clucking sound. "You like him, don't you?"

Gella cocked her head toward the Jedi Master. "I didn't say that."

"Didn't have to."

Gella steadied her mind and took a breath. "He's slick. But there is a gentle side to him that I sensed. A young kid inside who's still hurting. I looked for the good in him before I had a grasp of who he was." She furrowed her brow. "And I tend to get defensive when I'm reminded of my mistakes in judgment. They had huge consequences, Orin."

He looked down as they drew closer to the landing pad. "I've spent a lot of time in the Outer Rim, fighting sadistic spice traders, rounding up parasitic scavengers that hurt good and honest people. I may have not always been around civilized folk all the time, but I did learn one thing. I'm good at reading people. But it's a skill that has taken decades. You're sharpening those skills even as I speak, but still. Be careful, Gella. Your feelings may alter your judgment."

Gella said nothing, using their imminent landing as an excuse to not speak. She would be on her guard. Not make any snap judgments. And control her emotions. It all seemed so very simple. Then why was she still nervous?

They were welcomed by armed guards, native to Pipyyr. Long-limbed, with fur in shades of black, white, and gray, they stared at Gella and Orin with glossy, rounded black eyes. They were shorter than Wookiees, with fangs that shone only when they spoke.

It was cold and windy. Gella pulled her cloak around her front and nodded when she met the guards.

"We've come to interrogate Axel Greylark, one of your prisoners."

"The Republic has sent you?" one of the guards asked, voice sounding like a low rumble.

"Yes," Orin said.

"No," Gella said, almost simultaneously.

They exchanged glances and the guards shifted their feet.

"I am Jedi Master Orin Darhga, and this is Jedi Knight Gella Nattai. We are working directly in concert with Chancellor Greylark," Orin said. "Our visit will be brief."

The guard looked down at a datapad. "Your ship checks out. The *Eventide* is one of Greylark's fleet." He looked up at Gella. "It looks like the chancellors have left a white list for access without authorization. You are on it, Jedi Nattai. Very well. You will leave your weapons on your ship or locked in our armory."

Neither felt particularly safe to Gella, but they decided to leave them with the guards. Past a three-meter-thick outer blast door and yet another one to the inner building, they were led down narrow corridors of stone. The air here smelled strange, like old seawater. Gella was growing a mild headache, and even Orin looked a little off.

"You'll probably notice the pressure change," said the guard leading them. Her voice was gruff and low. "Our atmosphere is slightly denser than on other inhabited planets. Most get used to it."

Gella rubbed her temples as they seemed to descend lower and lower, and the walls felt like they were pressing closer. The guard led them through yet another set of blast doors, and finally to a row of cells.

The cells were small—containing a cot, washing facilities, and table. Bleak and bare. There was a viewscreen in each room, most displaying a static image of a planet—perhaps the inmate's homeworld. One displayed an old holonet music show that Gella remembered as a child. On another screen was a candid interview with a jovial Chancellor Mollo, his facial tentacles waving.

So this is where they were keeping Axel? It was nothing like what she'd imagined. She'd assumed Axel would be in a cushy prison for the wealthiest convicts in the galaxy. This was harsh for any prisoner.

"Inmate AG-07. Transferred from prison barge CA73Z two weeks ago. Here we are." The guard stepped back so they could speak with relative privacy.

Inside, the disgraced Axel Greylark was curled up on the cot. He wore a white jumpsuit like the other prisoners, his dark, wavy hair longer and mussed, as if he'd just woken up. Gella had imagined speaking to him a thousand times since she'd last seen him on Eiram. Gella curled a fist, but instead of pounding the wall like she'd imagined, she could only bring herself to tap gently on the clear barrier between them. Orin glanced at her, his face showing the tiniest bit of worry.

Axel rolled over. When he saw Gella, he jerked to attention, draping his legs over the side of the cot. He was thinner and paler, with shadowed and hollow eyes. An expression of confusion settled on his features.

"Gella! What are you doing here?" he asked. He had eyes for nothing but her; he didn't even seem to notice Orin standing at her side.

Gella's head throbbed mildly. She told herself to stay clearheaded, but the ache was distracting. She took a moment to reach out with the Force, to steady herself. But it was more difficult than usual.

"We're here to ask questions," Gella said, trying to ignore the pain. "About Jedha."

He shook his head in disbelief. "What—how did you get here? What have you been doing?" Axel looked suspiciously at Orin, finally noticing him. Axel's whole posture changed slightly, like when darkness descends imperceptibly just after a sun sets. He crossed his arms. "So, what about Jedha?" he said.

"Before that, mate. Why are you looking so knackered?" Orin asked.

"What?" Axel said, his face confused.

"You look tired. Or sick. Or both," Orin added.

"If you care, why don't you get me transferred off this fuzz-covered planet?" he said, winking.

One of the Pipyyr guards growled at a distance.

"Insulting the guards?" Orin said. He motioned to Gella. "Maybe he's not as clever as you think."

"You called me clever, Gella?" Axel's eyebrows went up. "I'll take it." But his hand went to his stomach, and he suddenly paled, despite his repartee.

She stepped closer to the partition, studying him. There were several emotions arising from Axel. Relief, distrust, and now . . . discomfort. And he wasn't controlling them well. This was all genuine. "You aren't well," Gella said. "What's going on?"

"It's the atmospheric pressure." He rubbed his head. "Feels like my brain is being squeezed all the time, and I can't keep food down. It's worse when they let us walk outside in the upper courtyard, so I just don't leave my cell."

"Don't they have medicine or something for that?" Gella shouldn't care, but the words left her before she could think about it. Maybe it was her own blossoming headache that made her think less clearly.

"They do. It helps a little, but I'm more sensitive than most to the pressure, I guess. Maybe growing up on some of those high levels on Coruscant with those altitudes. I don't know."

It was disconcerting to see him look so unwell, and Gella knew she was being more sympathetic than she should. They'd passed by several other inmates, and none of them seemed nearly as sick.

"Look, I'm fine. I get boring food, lots of rest, and far too much time to think. Definitely no Chandrilan linen sheets or shimmersilk pajamas here. But you didn't visit Pipyyr's finest high-security prison on the edge of nowhere to ask if I liked the bedding and entrée options. What happened on Jedha?"

Gella studied him, staying silent. She sensed his emotions—the queasiness, the pain, the wondering. He really seemed to not know.

"The peace talks on Jedha failed. There was a battle, with a lot of casualties. Jedha City is a mess. We think the Herald of the Path of the Open Hand started a riot, and things got out of control. Something, or someone, was hurting Force-users. Something powerful." Gella stepped closer to the partition. "You knew this was going to happen, didn't you?"

"No." Axel stood up. He looked down at Gella. "I didn't. I swear."

"What else is going to happen? After everything—you have to tell us."

"I'm not a member of the Path of the Open Hand," Axel said, shrugging.

"But you worked for them. Is the Herald their leader?" Orin asked.

Axel hesitated. He knew something.

"Spill it," Gella said firmly. She was getting irritated. If only this headache would distract her.

"He holds a lot of power, but the Mother leads them," Axel said, his hands hanging limply, as if tired of the questioning already.

Gella and Orin exchanged glances. She could tell by how he said the words that he didn't mean Chancellor Greylark.

"The Mother? Who is that?" Orin asked.

"She's the leader of the Path. She took them from a small religious group on Dalna into something bigger. Much bigger," Axel said.

Gella watched him carefully. Axel had never said who'd instructed him when he wreaked havoc on Eiram. There had been a woman he'd spoken to, but Gella had never learned her identity. And the way Axel was standing now—slightly hunched and not meeting her eye—spoke volumes.

"She was the one, wasn't she?" Gella said. "Who was behind all your moves on Eiram and E'ronoh?"

Axel nodded, still not making eye contact.

Orin frowned. "Does she know what the Herald did on Jedha?"

Axel shrugged again. Gella took a calming breath before saying, "Tell us what you know."

Orin pointed at him. "Aye, or I'll talk for the next seventy-two hours straight until your brain feels pressure of a different sort."

"Trust me, one hour will suffice," Gella said, drily.

Shockingly, Axel smiled a little. "It's so strange, having someone to talk to that's not a wall, or a guard yelling at me." His hands shook a little as he raised them to the partition. "The Path is stationed on Dalna. But that's common knowledge if you ask around. Look, Gella. I need to tell you something. I didn't have a chance before I got taken away—"

"—For murder. Among other things," Gella added.

"I know, I know. And it was wrong. I had a million reasons why it made sense, and why I had to do it. But I didn't have to do anything. It was my fault, and my doing entirely. I'm sorry. But I'm sorrier for losing your trust, Gella."

They stood only a scant meter away from each other. She remembered when she could have reached out to him, clapped him on the back, smiled and laughed over being outsiders on Eiram and E'ronoh. None of this seemed real. And then she shook her head slightly to reset. *Concentrate,* she told herself. *This isn't a time to be reminiscing. He lied. He killed. He fooled you. Don't let him do it again.*

"I'd believe you more if you could tell us what else the Path, and whoever else you've been working with, is up to," she said. "I don't think what happened on Jedha was just the Path stirring up trouble against the Jedi. Tell me what you know."

Axel took a step closer. His palm slapped against the partition hard. Gella and Orin both jerked back in surprise. Axel's head sagged.

"Gella," Axel gasped, and closed his eyes. "I'll tell you everything, but . . ."

"What is it? Axel?" Gella put her hand up as well, and Orin moved to pull her back.

"I'm . . . I'm pretty sure I'm going to black out." Axel's hand squeaked down the plane between them, his eyes closing. He crumpled to the floor as the guard ran over and called for the medic to the lower circle of the prison. The guard ordered Gella and Orin back, opening up the cell to assess Axel. She murmured to herself, checking his vital signs.

"Well!" Orin's eyebrows rose high. "That did not go as I expected."

"I thought he was going to be different," Gella whispered. "Defensive. Manipulative."

"I thought you were going to give him a harder time. I'd no idea the job was already done for us before we got here."

The incoming guards placed Axel on a hover-stretcher and whisked him away. She stared at the empty corridor for longer than she intended, frowning deeply. Axel was doing so poorly. Incarceration was one thing, but this place was physically hurting him. It was cruel, even if it wasn't the intent of the prison itself. The Republic needed to know. Gella wondered if Chancellor Greylark had any idea how awfully her son was faring. She also wondered if the effects of Pipyyr and her distraction from feeling the Force made it easier for him to influence her.

And now her fury toward Axel had morphed into pity, and wanting to help him.

It was a full two days before Gella and Orin were allowed to visit Axel again, who was confined to the infirmary. They themselves had been questioned several times about whether they'd pulled some sort of Jedi trick and sickened the inmate, but the tests were clear that his illness had been progressing since the day he'd arrived. The headaches, the high blood pressure, the inability to keep food down. Gella had been offered medication to ease the atmospheric pressure transition. She felt much better already. But still, her connection to the Force felt off. Orin had noticed it, too.

In the infirmary wing of the prison, they stood at a distance from Axel's bed. He was sleeping, and monitors nearby with numbers and graphs that Gella didn't understand constantly changed colors. One of the Pipyyr medics went to Axel's bedside, her furry hand touching buttons on the monitors here and there. She frowned before moving to exit the unit. Gella stopped her.

"How is he?"

"Stable. Better for now. But his body is resistant to our atmospheric transition medications. The second we unhook him from all this support, he starts vomiting again."

"Why?"

"It happens. Some inmates are more tolerant of our planet, others not so much. It was a poor choice to transfer this inmate to Pipyyr, given his altitude history. And a little unusual given his status. Once in a while, we've had to transfer prisoners for the altitude issues." She left the bedside to work on a wall monitor nearby.

Gella turned to Orin. "If the chancellors don't know how badly he's doing, they need to be alerted. He ought to be transferred."

"I agree. Chancellor Mollo is on Eiram, and I believe Chancellor Greylark is on Coruscant, where she always is. Though they will wonder what prompted this particular visit."

"I'll deal with that later," Gella said. "Anyway, that's why you're here, right? To make sure I don't get into trouble."

Axel was situated near a secured viewport looking out over the gorge. It wasn't much of a view—brown rocks and gray skies, with greenish-colored rainfall. Axel had several tubes attached to his arms where nutrients were being infused. The dark circles under his eyes were less dark, and his face less drawn. He looked almost at peace.

"Should I . . . ?" Gella whispered to Orin, reaching gently toward Axel's shoulder. Before she could touch him, Orin leaned right over Axel's face.

"Oi! We're back!" he hollered.

Axel's eyes flew open and he gasped, hands gripping the bedsheets. "Gah! Why are you so close to my face?"

"Just checking reflexes," Orin replied merrily, leaning back. "Looks like that juice they're pouring into your arm is working. Now, if they could only give that to me after I've had half a barrel of Corellian wine, then I'd be fixed up right smart."

Axel looked at Gella. "Is he really a Jedi? Is he . . . qualified?"

"I assure you, he is," Gella said. "Axel Greylark, this is Orin Darhga, Jedi Master. Sorry I didn't introduce you before."

"Nice to meet you," Axel said, smiling. "My sincerest apologies for the less-than-stellar atmosphere of this place."

"He's polite, this one," Orin said, smiling. Gella didn't smile. *There he goes, Axel with his smooth ways.* "It's not so bad here," Orin said, looking around.

"The water is poisonous. Did you know?" Axel motioned out the viewport to a thin waterfall over the nearby mountain. "It makes prisoners reluctant to try to escape. Pipyyrians have to filter it with carbon to drink it. It's why no one lives near the water's edge, or goes outside when it rains. But they survive. And adapt. I never had to try that hard. Not like you two." He looked back at Gella. "I miss Coruscant. One day, Gella, I'm going to take you back there and show you all my old haunts. The old sable tree with its maze roots, one of the only ones in the galaxy. And the best steamed dumplings on the whole planet."

Gella held back a smile. This was exactly what Axel wanted. To lure her into feeling friendly again. It wouldn't work. And yet her mouth was already watering, just thinking about those dumplings. For a second, she could see herself smiling as he pulled her under a rare, wizened tree for a laugh and a long talk. She forced the image out of her head and blinked hard. *There's a reason he's in prison,* she reminded herself.

"We're not here to go over your childhood memories. We're here to talk about what else the Path has planned," Gella said.

"They didn't tell me that much, but I have some thoughts. It's kind of complicated."

"Well, we don't have that much time," Gella said, trying not to seem anxious. Orin gave her a warning look, probably not to appear desperate.

Axel suddenly put his hand up to his mouth, holding back a retch. The monitors by his bed began to flash in reds and yellows. The Pipyyrian medic came over and growled low, which was apparently a casual way of being disappointed.

"I'm sorry, you'll have to leave. We need to adjust his treatments to get his vitals back to normal."

"Again?" Gella said. "Why does he keep getting sick when we try to talk to him?" She lifted a finger at Orin, who had opened his mouth, probably to make a terrible joke about how repellent Gella was. "Don't you dare, Master Darhga."

Orin closed his mouth.

"If you want to be covered in bodily fluids, then by all means, stay," the medic said drily.

Before they could turn away, Axel grabbed Gella's hand. It was such a familiar gesture that at first she squeezed back, before realizing her mistake.

"Gella. I am sorry. And I want to help. You must believe me."

"We'll talk after you rest more," was all she could manage to say.

Gella pulled her hand away far slower than she should have. She held that hand with her other, as if it had been burned, staring at her palm as she walked out of the infirmary. A few steps down the hallway, she realized that Orin wasn't next to her and turned to see where he'd gone. The door to the infirmary had shut, and Orin was staring through the glass window, watching the medic attend to Axel.

"He seems awfully sorry," Orin said as Gella walked back to stand next to him.

"Don't believe it," Gella said. "I don't."

Orin turned to face her and raised an eyebrow. "But you want to."

Gella didn't shy away from his gaze. "Sure. Who wouldn't want a person to be sorry for killing someone, and lying, and nearly destroying a whole city?"

"There is truth in some of what he says," Orin said, turning to leave.

"Orin. It would be a mistake to believe everything that came out of Axel Greylark's mouth."

He was walking away, but stopped and looked over his shoulder, to where Gella was watching Axel with flinty eyes. "True. But it would be a mistake to condemn him before he had a chance to prove himself, too."

Chapter Three

THE REPUBLIC EXECUTIVE BUILDING, CORUSCANT

Yoda stood in the great conference room on the top floor of the Republic Executive Building, awaiting his meeting with Chancellor Greylark. The view was a little different here compared to the Jedi Temple. Two of Coruscant's moons, Hesperidium and Centax 2, had risen above the skyline in half and quarter phases. With all the light pollution from the buildings, the city was never dark. Something Yoda did not miss when he was on away missions.

Tonight, the watery evening light was beautiful in its own way, but still he could not enjoy it. On Jedha, there was pain and frustration. Tensions between worlds existed at all times, a hum of discord that resonated in the Force like fingers running over a jagged edge of metal. One pair, the aqua-blue planet Eiram and the dry, red planet of E'ronoh, felt particularly dissonant, surging toward even more conflict now that the peace negotiations had failed. There were more disturbances felt in the Outer Rim, but he would keep this to himself. He had always noticed that some in the Republic preferred facts, as opposed to sense, when it came to the status of the galaxy. Speaking of which, he heard footsteps nearby.

"Master Yoda," a terse voice intoned from behind him.

"Chancellor Greylark. You wished to meet with me."

"Thank you for coming. We are awaiting an urgent update from Jedha, any moment now. I thought it best if we both were present."

Yoda nodded in agreement. "Well you are, I hope."

"I'm fine."

The chancellor came to his side, arms crossed. Despite her defensive retort, Yoda noticed her face was drawn with fatigue. Two attendants stood at a distance, and she shooed them away irritably when they offered refreshments. Her billowing robes shone with golden threads and minuscule seed pearls. It was no accident she wore such a grand garment. He'd overheard some local politicians speak of them. The threads were of E'roni make from the cupric ore mined there, and the seed pearls, from Eiram's Erasmus Sea. Her headdress contained three large, intertwined ovals studded with jadeite, the signature stone of the Greylarks. Everything Kyong Greylark did was apparently orchestrated down to the smallest detail.

"Concerned, you seem. Thinking about Jedha, perhaps?"

"Who hasn't? The news is a blow to all who have been trying to broker peace. With Chancellor Mollo staying in the Eiram-E'ronoh system to help keep the diplomatic channels open between the two planets, and me here, we are deluged. It's a good deal of work, even for two chancellors. Not that we cannot bear the honor of the responsibility," she added quickly. Chancellor Greylark was not prone to complaining, but her small slip hadn't been lost on Yoda.

"Chancellor." A third attendant came into their chamber. "The message to Pipyyr isn't going through."

"Try again. Use an Ee-Ex droid if our regular lines aren't working."

"Pipyyr?" Yoda intoned. "Your son Axel is there, correct?"

The chancellor frowned. "Yes. Chancellor Mollo and I have been discussing whether he should be moved to a low-security facility of the Republic where he can be kept out of harm's way—that is, where he can do no harm—" She cleared her throat. "And be rehabilitated. Or if he should remain on Pipyyr to continue his incarceration." She tapped at a datapad, murmuring more to herself than to anyone else, "If I am too harsh, I'm an uncaring parent. If I'm too lenient, then I fail at my chancellor's duties. There's no way to win."

"Perhaps winning is not the answer," Yoda said. "A second chance, everyone deserves." He was about to continue, but the chancellor cut him off.

"Perhaps, but that's not why I requested your presence, Master Yoda." Another assistant came up to her with a datapad, pointing out various appointments and messages. The chancellor dismissed this assistant with a wave of her hand. "I know I'm blamed for what happened on Eiram and E'ronoh, despite the truth about Queen Adrialla and her schemes. People are practically gleeful, learning of the treachery in my own house."

"The greater cause, they will see. Exploration, and connection of the farthest reaches."

"But there is much work still to do." The chancellor crossed her arms. "Many in the Outer Rim see the Jedi as muscle who answer to no one."

"And the Republic, as overreaching," Yoda said.

Yoda and the chancellor stared at each other until a message broke the staring match.

"Master Yoda, there is a communication incoming from Master Creighton Sun."

"Yes." He turned to the table near them, and a blurry holoimage came up.

"Ah," Chancellor Greylark spoke. "Master Sun. We have been awaiting your report." Yoda noticed that Chancellor Greylark's voice was very different now. The irritation was gone, replaced by a firm, confident, and deeper tone. It sounded almost like the thrum of his own emerald lightsaber—ever strong, ever resilient, and dependable. Yoda watched her carefully. Politics were not his forte, but he understood there was a certain amount of acting involved. The small amount of emotion she had displayed just now was enough to show that she was not as calm on the inside as she portrayed. And neither was he—not with that constant sense that the energy in the galaxy was tipping in a direction he couldn't grasp as of yet.

The holoimage of both Jedi Master Creighton Sun and Jedi Knight Aida Forte came into sudden, sharp focus.

Chancellor Greylark gasped audibly, seeing them. Creighton's robes were torn and smudged with soil. He had some cuts on his face that looked fresh. Though only a slight bit of gray shone on his dark hair, his face was haggard and he seemed to have aged years since Yoda last saw them. Aida's green skin was marred with bruises and her clothes were in disarray. The Kadas'sa'Nikto Jedi appeared similarly exhausted.

Chancellor Greylark reached for a nearby chair. Yoda could sense what no one might see—that her hand was imperceptibly shaking.

Creighton spoke. "We have an update on our report. The E'roni ambassador died during the battle. We have reason to believe that the Eirami ambassador arranged to have battle droids at the ready, which turned the Herald's inciting riot into a conflagration."

"Did the Eirami ambassador act under the direction of Queen Adrialla?" Chancellor Greylark asked.

"Not that we know of," Aida said. "And both the queen and the E'roni Monarch may know none of this. The communications buoys around Jedha were torched shortly after the battle. By whom, we don't know. We're only able to speak to you because we've been able to fly far out of the sector. We sent out a message to them but have heard nothing back."

Chancellor Greylark frowned deeply. "I haven't been able to contact Chancellor Mollo, either, since I spoke to him two days ago. I think the communications buoys around Eiram and E'ronoh are down, too. It makes our job difficult, to say the least. And we have much to decide upon."

"Master Yoda. Chancellor Greylark. There's more. We need to speak to you about something. About Dalna," Creighton began.

"Dalna?" Yoda said.

"Yes. Aida and I would like permission from you—from the Jedi Council—to go to Dalna. And we would like the approval of the chancellors as well. We believe the Path of the Open Hand had much to do with the disintegration of the peace talks. Another Path leader who called herself the Mother was there as well, and apparently she has already distanced herself from the Herald. And the involvement with the Grafs made everything complicated."

"Perhaps they were simply expressing their beliefs in the wrong place, at the wrong time?" Aida suggested tentatively.

"Still, it's too much of a coincidence," Chancellor Greylark said.

"Agreed," Creighton said. "And there's something extremely odd about how affected the Jedi and other Force-users were during some of the fighting. I can't explain it. There was another Jedi Master, Silandra Sho, who reported the same effect when she visited the Path headquarters on Jedha. It's too much of a coincidence. We need to know if the Path is responsible, and what their intentions are—and what explains this unusual development."

"You want to confront them?" Chancellor Greylark seemed like she was trying to keep the alarm out of her voice.

"Not so much confront," Aida said. "But gather information. As discreetly as possible."

Creighton held up a hand. "Aida and I both saw what happened. It was messy and seemingly chaotic—but I've seen this before. The signature of what appears to be chaos, but actually is a well-planned event intended to confuse and cause more problems."

"A disturbance beyond Jedha, I have sensed," Yoda said.

"And there's one more thing. Something that Jedi Gella Nattai told me on Eiram. She spoke with Axel about who he had been working with. He'd said, 'They are free—from the Jedi.'" Creighton shook his head. "The resemblance to the Path's creed and way of living is hard to ignore."

"I can't agree to starting a new conflict based on a sense, or a mere resemblance," Chancellor Greylark said.

"We recognize that we do not need the permission of the Republic to investigate," Creighton said. He bowed slightly at the chancellor. "But your approval would mean more, if we were to find important information."

The chancellor rose to her full height. "Absolutely not."

Everyone went silent in surprise. "We could do this with the utmost discretion," Aida said. "Instead of direct talks."

"I understand that you would try. But you are coming right off a conflict. And some of the transmissions that we are receiving are claiming—not definitively, but at least insinuating—that the Jedi are to blame for what happened on Jedha," the chancellor said.

"The Jedi!" Aida took a step forward, her image growing larger in the holoprojector. "We were trying to help! How could anyone interpret that as malevolent?"

"In time, the truth reveals itself. Until then, careful we must be," Yoda said.

"We should go to Dalna," Aida insisted. "We can only find the truth by seeking it out."

The chancellor shook her head. "I can't give the authority to conduct such an investigation without speaking to Chancellor Mollo. And that could take some time."

"We can't wait for that! You said yourself there's no communication with Eiram. We're on our own. If we do nothing, the next time something happens, it could be worse. The Jedi or the Republic can be blamed again, and all the while, we will have sat by and done nothing!" Creighton said, his face suffused with frustration.

"Peace, Master Sun," Yoda said. He rubbed his chin. "There are always those who thrive amidst chaos. Feed off wars, they do."

"It would not be surprising if many wished the conflict between Eiram and E'ronoh to continue," the chancellor noted. She shook her head. "Jedha needs our help. We should put our resources there, in the aftermath of this battle. And renew our work with Eiram and E'ronoh."

"Then go right ahead. Minus two Jedi," Creighton said. "Aren't

Master Char-Ryl-Roy and his Padawan, Enya Keen, nearby? They could easily be dispatched to assist Chancellor Mollo. They participated in the original peace attempts and are already quite familiar with the people of Eiram and E'ronoh."

Chancellor Greylark finally exhaled. "Very well. We'll send a message to have Master Roy and Jedi Keen go back to the Eiram and E'ronoh system. As for going to Dalna—there must be no confrontation, Master Sun. The Mother may have already dealt with this internally by pushing the Herald out of the picture. Tread carefully. Learn what you can, slip in and slip out unnoticed," the chancellor said, planting her hands on the table before her. "One more thing. I insist that some of my security detail accompany you, for safety. More eyes on the facts."

Creighton opened his mouth to protest, but one glance from Master Yoda quelled that. He swallowed down his rebuttal.

Yoda nodded. "Only Jedi Forte and Master Sun, with a limited team from the chancellor's security detail."

"Ten of my people with you," Chancellor Greylark insisted.

"No," Creighton said. "Only four, total. Two of your people. Otherwise, we might as well set off fireworks announcing our arrival."

"Very well," the chancellor conceded.

Yoda nodded. "A fact-finding mission, for clarity, and for information. Nothing more. We will keep this quiet."

"We expect regular updates on your mission," Chancellor Greylark concluded.

Creighton and Aida bowed. Aida glanced at Creighton uneasily before their images disappeared. Chancellor Greylark turned away, staring out the window. The lights across Coruscant were starting to wink out, but not completely. The planet never went fully dark, with its four moons. Small ships passed by, their engine noise muted by the thick, protective transparisteel windows of the building. The chancellor felt small and fragile against the backdrop of the night sky and all the unanswered questions beyond.

"Master Yoda, you're worried about this, too," the chancellor said. "I may not be a Jedi, but I can read people pretty well sometimes."

"Concerned, I am. More information we need," Yoda said.

The communications console before them lit up again. The aide in the corner of the room announced, "Incoming message from Master Yaddle. She's been trying to get through for some time."

The image of Master Yaddle, with her deep auburn hair brushing her shoulders and her neat Jedi robes, came through in bursts of pixels and static.

"Master Yoda. I am on my way as quickly as possible. I am traveling with the youngling Cippa Tarko. I received an urgent message asking for assistance on Jedha."

"Jedha? We did not request your presence there. To Coruscant, you were coming. Yes?" Yoda said.

"But—" Yaddle's image blurred and disappeared. A few seconds later, it reappeared in disorganized static before sharpening in focus. An Arkanian child, slightly taller than Master Yaddle, ambled into the image. She was slight of frame with medium olive skin. Like all Arkanians, she had piercing white eyes and stark white hair, which hung in four braids over her shoulders. She looked at Yaddle expectantly.

"Is he your brother?"

Yaddle waved her hand gently. "Hush, child. He is not. He is Master Yoda, a great teacher."

The child cocked her head thoughtfully. Her image disappeared as she walked out of view.

Yaddle pursed her lips. "My apologies. I have been assigned to this youngling as a special tutor. She is unusually gifted. However, she thinks she knows more than everyone. We have much work to do."

As if on cue, a blue ice apple paused next to Yaddle's head, split into four perfect sections, and sped away. A single section returned, jiggled next to Yaddle's hand, before Yaddle waved it away.

"Not hungry. But thank you, Cippa." Yaddle took a measured

breath. "She is always showing off. As I said, much work to do." She turned to Chancellor Greylark and bowed. "Chancellor. It is good to see you. Though I wish, under better circumstances."

"Thank you," Chancellor Greylark said. "At this time, we have Jedi in the area of Jedha assisting. We do not need—"

Master Yaddle's image suddenly disappeared again.

"Are we having connection issues around Coruscant now? What's happening?" the chancellor said.

An aide began to type furiously into her datapad. She pointed at a readout on the monitor. "It appears that Master Yaddle is near Jedha. That explains the poor connection."

"Repair the communications buoys, we must. Meanwhile, our two Jedi will go to Dalna. It is worth the risk," Yoda said.

A flash of dull green appeared on the console. "Go to Dalna," Yaddle repeated, through bouts of static.

"Master Yaddle. You are to report back to the Jedi Temple here on Coruscant. Later we can update you on the situation on Dalna," Chancellor Greylark said.

"Coruscant . . . later . . ." The static was still terrible. "Situation on Dalna."

The image abruptly disappeared. Chancellor Greylark raised her hands in irritation, and immediately was surrounded by three aides asking for signatures and updating her schedule for tomorrow morning.

Yoda sighed. Though he trusted that Master Yaddle would find her way back to Coruscant safely with the youngling, he also knew she felt the disturbances he did within the galaxy. The pulls to Dalna and to Eiram and E'ronoh where violence was unfolding—they unsettled him.

It was the same unsettling feeling he had whenever a battle crested on the horizon.

THE *LAZULI,* NEAR HYNESTIA

In the end, Creighton and Aida had decided on two guards. That wasn't a lot, but it was enough to get the job done with the minimal amount of backup the chancellor insisted upon. After a brief stay on Coruscant, they had a rendezvous with two of the chancellor's own security detail who had been on a delivery errand on Hynestia.

The guards were grim-faced and heavily armed. One a human male, Lu Sweet, and the other a female Iktotchi, Priv Ittik. The human male was tall and broad-shouldered, with a slightly crooked and wide nose. His pale-brown skin was riddled with small scars, as if he'd survived a pox infection years ago. Both of the guards appeared ready to pounce on anybody, at any moment.

Aboard their small ship, the *Lazuli,* Aida began plotting a course for Dalna on the navicomputer. Creighton exhaled noisily.

"I feel the same way," Aida said.

"Do you?" He squinted at her.

"Yes. Like even though they gave us permission to go, we are somehow doing this alone."

"In some ways, we are. We have no Jedi backup, and two security guards that look spring-loaded for a fight. But we'll get our answers, one way or another."

Aida frowned. "We have to be careful not to cause another ruckus."

"*Another* ruckus? What happened on Jedha wasn't our fault. We were there to promote the peaceful signing of the treaty between Eiram and E'ronoh. Even after the assassination of the mediator Morton San Tekka. Even when the Herald incited that riot after trying to disband the Convocation of the Force. Even after violence erupted. And we did find peace again."

"And yet the blame is being twisted to point at us."

Creighton clenched a fist on his lap. "There will always be finger-pointing after a messy, bloody battle. And I'll do whatever it takes to clear the Jedi from fault. We did much to bring Force believers and good people together to keep that battle from getting even bloodier."

Aida knew Creighton wanted to know that what he did mattered, and worked. That he was keeping good in the galaxy balanced in the way he'd always fought for. But Aida also knew he worried about failure. About all his efforts disintegrating into defeat, again.

Aida finished inputting the coordinates for Dalna. "Ready, Creighton."

Creighton gripped the armrests of his chair. "Punch it."

As they entered the hyperlane and the stars morphed to ever-thinning streaks around them, Aida watched Creighton discreetly. He looked like he was ready for a war.

If they weren't careful, they'd get one.

Chapter Four

"**W**hy doesn't Jedi training include droid repair?"

Enya Keen was sitting on the floor of their Republic ship en route to Eiram, according to Master Yoda's instructions. Her legs were splayed out and tools and broken pieces of an astromech droid were spread out everywhere. It looked like the astromech unit's head had exploded and landed like confetti all around her. Smoke issued from somewhere within the main body. Enya stuck her hand into the depths of the droid and pried out a circuit. The smoke stopped.

"You already know the answer to that, Enya. I'm no maker, and I know less about mechanical moving parts, so you're on your own," Master Char-Ryl-Roy said. He was sitting nearby, reading something on a datapad with minuscule writing. The Cerean's tall forehead was near to the ceiling of the low room. Enya marveled at how he never hit doorways, despite his height. His movements were always so smooth and coordinated.

"Pass me that nine-bolt spanner, please," she said, pushing a lock of dark hair and her Padawan braid behind her ear.

Char-Ryl-Roy lifted a finger, and a metal tool floated into Enya's hand. "Master, that's a bitdriver for a combustion transfer."

He lifted another finger. This time, the astromech's optical lens landed on her knee.

"Not this. But excellent, I was looking for that." She attached the lens and smiled. "Try again."

And again, this time, a scroll of wires.

"Master, are you doing that purposely? Is this a lesson?"

Char-Ryl-Roy closed his eyes, hands folded on his lap. "You can stretch the limits of what's possible, but only after understanding what those limits are."

"Meaning?"

"I already told you that I'm no expert in droid maintenance."

"Okay, okay." She sighed. They'd helped with the recovery efforts on Eiram after the wedding and Erasmus City nearly being destroyed. Then they'd traveled to Eriadu to help protect a delivery shipment of lommite and were now awaiting further orders by the Jedi Council while working on her training. The most recent message from Master Yoda meant they were heading right back to Eiram again.

Enya didn't mind. It was on Eiram that she'd found the droid's almost hopelessly broken body in a pile of debris during the recovery. Something about it bothered her, so when she gathered it up and dragged it behind her onto the ship using an old tarp, her master had said nothing. Enya had a tender heart for broken beings. A whirring sound arose from the droid's head, along with a plaintive set of beeps. It was only attached to the body via a river of wires. The newly re-planted lens glowed pale green, and an attached datapad began scrolling lines of text.

"Well, hello to you, too. He says his name is Forvio-Teegee. Hi there." She tapped the datapad. "Can you tell me what else is wrong?"

The eye glowed, 4VO-TG beeped faintly one more time, and then the light winked out.

"Everything? Well that's not very specific. Then again, your head isn't fully attached." She turned back to Master Roy. "Are we there yet, Master?"

"Nearly. We should be arriving in the Eiram and E'ronoh system in a few minutes."

"What did Master Yoda tell you about our mission?"

"Chancellor Greylark has had great difficulty getting in touch with Chancellor Mollo, on Eiram. She believes the communications buoys have been tampered with, and asks that we look into it. But Master Yoda says we need to give our support to Eiram and E'ronoh in any way possible, now that the peace talks on Jedha have failed."

"Promote the peace. Sounds like a good plan." Enya sat down as the sounds around the ship indicated it was exiting hyperspace. She looked out of the front viewport of the ship and smiled expectantly. "Here we go."

Enya hadn't even blinked when lights burst into her field of vision. Char-Ryl-Roy exclaimed, "What the—"

A loud explosion sounded so close by that it shook the ship. Blinking in shock, they saw a full-on dogfight between E'ronoh and Eiram fighter ships, right between the planets.

"*Promote the peace?*" Enya exclaimed. "We're going to be obliterated! Again! Every time we come here . . ."

"Hold on." Char-Ryl-Roy quickly maneuvered their ship to avoid the conflict, trying to make a wide berth. He opened all his communications frequencies. "This is Jedi Master Char-Ryl-Roy and Jedi Enya Keen. We are traveling alone and are here on a diplomatic mission to both Eiram and E'ronoh. Repeat, we are here on a diplomatic mission."

"Jedi, your timing is absolutely terrible."

It was a familiar female voice. They saw an E'roni devilfighter flying in parallel to them. "This is Captain A'lbaran. I mean, Xiri. Good to hear your voices again, Master Roy and Enya. I can escort you for a short bit, but I cannot enter Eiram airspace in my military craft." She spoke quickly, with that clipped way that told them she was in military mode. So unlike the Xiri during quieter times.

"What's going on here?" Enya asked. She shielded her eyes as an Eirami ship twirled in a shower of sparks before exploding nearby.

"There was an explosion on the moon. An E'roni ship was assisting a neutral transport that had been attacked by pirates. The transport's engine blew during a repair. Turns out, that ship was carrying a bioweapon that could hurt millions on Eiram. People got hotheaded and accused E'ronoh of being responsible. And then in the midst of all of that, the news arrived from Jedha that the peace talks blew up, too."

"Where's the pirated ship?" Enya asked.

"Destroyed. But the two pirating survivors and pilots from both Eiram and E'ronoh are on the moon, at the waystation."

Char-Ryl-Roy shook his head. "What happened to your communications buoys?"

"Burned to a crisp, along with the smaller local beacons. Shot down by both sides. Call it aggressive communications interference."

Char-Ryl-Roy muted the cockpit mic long enough to say, "Well, that's just great. Now we're really alone here." He turned it back on. "Appreciate the escort, Xiri. It is good to speak to you again, though it's unfortunate it's under these circumstances."

They flew toward the aqua sphere that was Eiram, constantly telling nearby ships that they were Jedi, and neutral, but the returning commentary wasn't always friendly. Char-Ryl-Roy and Enya heard a few faint murmurings of "What are they doing here?" and "ruined Jedha."

As soon as Eiram showed large and blue in their viewport, Xiri commed in one last time.

"This is where I leave you. You'll find Phan-tu down there, probably counseling the queen and her aides. Let him know I'm working on getting him an audience with my father, as soon as possible. Tell him—" Her voice seemed to hitch in her throat.

"Xiri?" Char-Ryl-Roy said. He noticed she sounded curt when speaking of her husband. "Is there something else?"

"Captain A'lbaran, out," she said abruptly, and turned away, back into the space shared between the planets, and the ongoing fight.

"This is bad, Enya," Master Roy said. "The peace talks failing is one thing. That bioweapon probably ensures that no future talks will ever happen again. I fear they've descended into a war far worse than the one that preceded the wedding."

"I can't tell if Xiri is mad, or annoyed, or frustrated," Enya said.

"Probably all three," the Cerean said.

Enya raised an eyebrow. "You think it's about the marriage, or the war?"

"Let's hope it's the war," Char-Ryl-Roy replied.

"Ouch. That sounded very pessimistic for a Jedi Master."

"On the contrary. Wars can end in peace, despite unforgivable atrocities. Relationships are harder to repair after even the smallest of slights. Let's hope both are mendable."

Before they could land in Eiram's capital city of Erasmus, they were stopped by a checkpoint ship away from the capital, over waters polluted from warfare. The land in the distance looked oddly parched—not unlike E'ronoh's dunes and mountains—but all the buildings and cottages were abandoned or in piles of rubble. Their ship was thoroughly searched, and guards ran scanners for poisons and chemicals over every compartment. After they were cleared, they finally landed in the capital, with the Erasmus Sea lapping at its edges. The electrostatic dome was once again in working order thanks to generous resources from the Republic, advocated for by Chancellor Greylark herself. Axel Greylark had destroyed it, after all. The interior of the city still showed areas of rubble and water damage. Piles of new stone were awaiting the rebuilding of the highest towers, and several of the smaller structures looked brand-new. Nevertheless, Enya was still awed by the sight of so much water threaded through the land, and the color of the blue sea against blue sky. The capital was awash in tones of azure and gray, but no view could escape the evidence the war was still near. Another landing pad nearby was nothing but ash; a high tower and its sensor dish seemed as if it had been decapitated by a well-aimed explosion.

The landing pad was surrounded by several armed soldiers wearing blue uniforms, along with Phan-tu Zenn. The ring of soldiers visibly relaxed when Char-Ryl-Roy and Enya were the only ones disembarking, and after they shook Phan-tu's hand warmly. The tall Eirami prince was dressed in a tunic of blue and gold linenfiber, but his boots were noticeably muddy. He saw the bulky pack that Enya carried on her shoulder.

"Oh, there's no need to bring a gift."

Enya blushed. "It's not a gift. It's a disembodied droid head. Something I'm working on." From somewhere within the bag, a blurp and a beep issued. "I think it's not happy I'm taking so long."

Phan-tu chuckled. "Very well. Come."

Char-Ryl-Roy tilted his head, his bright-blue eyes catching her gaze for a moment. "Be mindful of the emotions in the room. The droid may be a distraction to understanding the true feelings of those around us." He looked at the bag full of droid parts she carried on her back. "I know it's a distraction for you, too."

"It's useful. This droid may save a life, Master," Enya said.

"It may. However, it's also easier to occupy yourself with busywork when harder study awaits. Also, being that we are working in concert with the Republic, it may be a bad diplomatic look for you to ask the queen to pass you a wrench."

"Point taken, Master."

One of the aides to the queen appeared. "Unfortunately, the queen and her consort will not be joining us."

Phan-tu's disappointment couldn't be hidden.

"And Captain A'lbaran?" Phan-tu asked. "She escorted the Jedi as far as Eiram airspace, but I was hoping she could attend."

"She cannot." The aide bowed. "Now if you'll excuse me."

Phan-tu looked at the Jedi. "This is all news to me. I apologize. Please follow me."

Char-Ryl-Roy and Enya stole glances at each other as they walked forward. Phan-tu spoke as they walked.

"Things have been turbulent since the explosion on the moon. The discovery of klytobacter on that transport ship made the situation especially ugly. I don't believe E'ronoh was responsible but no one is listening to me. I've been in nonstop meetings, and the two royal houses aren't speaking to each other."

"Does that include you and Xiri?" Enya asked.

"No. And yes. Our comms buoys are down." There was something in Phan-tu's voice that implied there were more than just technical problems.

He ushered them toward the palace, an enormous structure that rose into the sky almost like a crown. They passed by several sets of guards, and servants within the palace carting trays and linens. Enya noticed that one of the servants sneered at Phan-tu from afar; a nearby guard blinked slowly after staring at Phan-tu. If blinking could be rude, this was.

"Is everything all right with you here?" Char-Ryl-Roy said quietly as they walked deeper into the palace.

"As well as could be, considering many believe I'm a traitor to my own people," Phan-tu said.

"I remember the whispers at the time of the wedding. I thought things would get better," Enya said.

"They did, and then, when the explosion happened on the moon, it started again. Nothing like having a scapegoat right here on your home planet to be furious about. Apparently I'm a spy, and a traitor, and I've sold my soul to E'ronoh at a high price." He shrugged. "I'm handling it."

"We wish we were here for different reasons," Master Roy said. "After our time on Eiram and E'ronoh and everything that brought you toward peace, it is difficult to see both planets slipping back into war."

Phan-tu nodded, and Enya tried not to sigh.

Another familiar face greeted them from inside. Chancellor Orlen Mollo. The tall Quarren opened his arms in welcome, the tentacles on his face waving gently. His usually refined Republic clothing looked worn, the robes and the edge of his leather sash somewhat shredded.

"Welcome, Jedi Master Char-Ryl-Roy and Jedi Padawan Enya Keen. I am sorry to say that the situation is not that much improved since the last time we met."

"Apparently not. We didn't even realize the war had reignited. We were sent by Master Yoda to keep tensions in check and find out what happened to the communications buoys."

"Nothing more?" Chancellor Mollo asked, his face clouding with worry.

"No. Were you expecting more?"

"I was." The triangular points on either side of his face twitched. "I confess, when the Republic first began our mission to send out the Pathfinder teams, we thought we'd be slowly stitching the galaxy together. More communication, more learning of one another. More tolerance. And yet here we are, having tried to do our best with diplomacy and goodwill, and we still have a war. Our communications buoy is nonfunctional, and there are no courier droids to help out. We are still alone."

They had entered the palace and been led into one of the royal sitting rooms. A central pool and its rivulets fanned out from the room, slipping under walls where they connected with a waterfall cascading outside one of the sheer walls of the palace. Iridescent creatures with tentacles and fins undulated through the water, like decorations that sparkled. The chancellor nodded at them fondly before he and Phan-tu invited the Jedi to sit on chairs and poufs by the water.

"But we're not alone." Enya rested her arms on the mound of 4VO-TG's head, covered in the burlap bag in her lap. "There are things we can do."

"Why are there no other representatives of Eiram to speak with us?" Chancellor Mollo asked.

Phan-tu shook his head. "They are split between rebuilding Erasmus City and renewing their efforts toward military defense. They're stretched pretty thin. As you experienced, we have new testing checkpoints for all non-Eirami ships coming in. And they may be starting quarantines soon, which is going to make our supply problem even worse, and enrich E'ronoh, which has no such guards up."

Chancellor Mollo shook his head. "That's not why they're not meeting with us. They're angry."

Phan-tu sighed. "I won't hide that they are. They're upset about what happened on Jedha. And there are renewed concerns about the Jedi being involved."

"Why?" Enya asked. "Our work here during the last cease-fire was, for the most part, well received. We had a plan and it went forward well, until Jedha."

"It's not that straightforward," Char-Ryl-Roy said. "There are rumors spreading about the Jedi's actions on Jedha. What happened was complicated but what I can tell you with certainty is that the Jedi were not responsible."

"It is good to hear you say that, and I believe you." Phan-tu did look relieved. "We have heard disconcerting news about our own ambassador there, and the death of the E'roni ambassador is more fuel for their fire. But the queen and her consort hear things from many voices."

"Has the queen spoken to Monarch A'lbaran?" Master Roy asked.

"No. They are not on speaking terms," Phan-tu said

"Have you been able to get through to Xiri?" Enya said.

"Intermittently, yes. We're both trying to keep things calm, on both sides. But the news about the klytobacter is making them defensive and everyone on Eiram furious."

Char-Ryl-Roy leaned closer. "The first thing we have to figure out is what happened on your moon."

The chancellor shook his head. "I think that's a waste of time. It's not what the queen and her consort want, and that strains our relationship with them."

"Perhaps. But the fact remains that two people who claim to be innocent were carrying a bioweapon specifically made to destroy Eiram's ecosystems. If it was E'ronoh's intention to go this route, it would have been a heavily protected E'roni ship that wouldn't make the simple mistake of being looted by pirates in a poorly armed, flimsy transport," Char-Ryl-Roy said. "Add to that that it happened almost precisely when the talks on Jedha fell through."

"It's a coincidence that begs for an investigation," Enya said.

Phan-tu glanced at Chancellor Mollo and leaned back in his chair. "What do you propose?"

"I say we speak to the pilots and the two survivors," Char-Ryl-Roy said.

Chancellor Mollo tapped one of his tentacles. "I reviewed the recording of the Eirami pilot, Captain Plana Van, boarding their ship. It's uninformative. I say, we should find another way. A grand wedding to unite two cultures has failed. Peace talks have failed. I propose we concentrate on finding other hyperlanes that connect the two planets to the outer and inner reaches of the galaxy. Fix the communications systems. Stop the looting and piracy. Reinstate the cease-fire, and get both sides to take a breath." He paused a moment, as if to calm himself. "The Republic wants peace more than anything. Our efforts to expand communications and foster alliances in the galaxy cannot move forward without addressing these crises. We've put too much work into this to accept failure. I believe the two planets could still unite if they mutually benefited from something they both believed in. I've been spending time with different villages in and around the capital city. Everyone wants more goods and supplies."

Char-Ryl-Roy exhaled loudly. "I disagree. If the war stopped, the piracy and crime would massively decrease. And there would be plenty of supplies. Eiram and E'ronoh are too busy hating each other to work on exploring and pathfinding new hyperlanes in this sector."

"He's right," Phan-tu said. "It won't stop the war. The two planets can barely handle controlling the one hyperlane now, along with the piracy that increased the second the war reignited. More hyperlanes before the war is over could ask for more catastrophes."

Enya drummed her fingers on the bag with 4VO-TG's head,

thinking. "I say, if something keeps breaking, find out why. Or it'll keep breaking. We ought to find out what really happened on the moon. Like, where did those shippers get the bioweapons from to begin with? Who purchased them? For all we know, there is a third party involved. Which begs for more answers."

"I agree," Char-Ryl-Roy said. "Perhaps the chancellor can get both parties to agree to get another communications buoy up and running, and we can try to do an independent investigation on that pirated ship."

"First you should review the recording of the Eiram pilot boarding the transport ship of the survivors," Phan-tu said. "I don't know what to make of it. I can't tell if they are nervous and frightened, or acting oddly. I would appreciate your expertise."

"Will do," Enya said. "We can head to the moon where the survivors are."

"Sounds good. I'll speak with the queen." Phan-tu stood. Chancellor Mollo didn't seem all too pleased. "I'm sorry, Chancellor. But I think this is the proper direction."

"I'd rather build the buoy myself than have more meetings," the chancellor said with a sigh. "But I understand. We'll work on it."

"I appreciate what you are trying to do." Phan-tu gestured to some attendants. "Prepare the Jedi's departure. We can leave on my ship."

The chancellor nodded, but before he left, he paused to place a hand on Phan-tu's back.

"You're handling this well, Phan-tu. Like you're a born leader."

Phan-tu exhaled, and it became clear to everyone in the room that he'd been holding himself rather tensely until now. "Helping out on Eiram is one thing. Helping on E'ronoh is another thing altogether."

"There is no true accomplishment without challenge," the chancellor said as they all headed toward the door. "It's easy to do what's comfortable. But having two people solve a crisis by dividing the work isn't always the answer."

"Is that why there are two chancellors?" Phan-tu asked.

The chancellor paused, as if remembering something, then smiled. "Perhaps. Good luck, Phan-tu."

As they all departed, Phan-tu touched the comlink at his wrist. It buzzed yellow, a sign that the signal was poor.

"Xee? Is that you? Come in."

There was static, and a voice. "Phan-tu. I'm back on E'ronoh. The fighting has quieted for now. What is going on over there with Master Roy and Jedi Keen?"

"They're headed to the moon. I wanted to give you a heads-up. They're going to interview the pilot and the survivors."

"The E'roni pilot is dead."

"What?" Phan-tu stopped walking.

"I have to go. But . . ." Static filled the transmission again. "Phan-tu, I want you to come here. It would be a great show of support for you to be on E'ronoh, by my side."

"I can't right now. You know that."

"Isn't this part of the reason why we got married? To compromise, and come to each other's side to help both planets?"

Phan-tu let the static speak for him. Their marriage might be a maneuvering business, but hearing it out loud soured his mood. He couldn't help but feel like he was being ordered to go, rather than Xiri actually needing him, in the way that he had felt needed when they were first married.

The question was whether he felt like he needed Xiri. *I should go to E'ronoh,* he thought. *I really should.* But his heart said something different.

Maybe going to the moon would be a compromise.

"I'm going with the Jedi to speak to the survivors. We'll talk again soon, I promise. I have to run."

He could hear her sigh of disappointment. "Okay."

He turned off his communicator.

As he hurried to the queen's war room, Xiri's disappointment hung in the air. When he passed through the door, the guards narrowed their eyes at him but let him through. Inside, there was a vast table with a holoprojector showing both planets and the moon, along with three layered diagrams of figures and vectors detailing their ships, transports, and supplies throughout the planet and beyond.

The queen sat at a table with two counselors earnestly talking to her from each side. It was a familiar scene from almost daily dealings throughout the war from months ago, and everyone had fallen back into that familiar work, as if no time had passed. It hurt Phan-tu's heart to see how easy the backslide was. The queen consort, Odelia, was speaking to other counselors about medical supplies coming in. Queen Adrialla motioned for Phan-tu to approach. One of the counselors, Nolan, saw Phan-tu and straightened up, backing obsequiously away.

"How did the meeting go?" the queen asked, waving away the remaining counselors.

"Well. The Jedi are heading to the moon to pursue the cause of the explosion and the truth behind the two survivors with the biological weapon."

"Without our permission?" She raised an eyebrow.

"It's with my blessing, Mother. I am going as well."

"Very well. We have other things to concentrate on. It will give us reason to show how right we are in this war, when the Jedi and the Republic realize that my need to defend Eiram at any cost was justified. This is what we do, after all. And we are very good at it."

Phan-tu glanced around. "Too good at it. Perhaps too familiar. Sometimes making peace is more difficult."

"There is comfort in what is familiar, my son. Peace has become a fairy tale. Thus far, cease-fires have been unstable, frightful things. Meanwhile, I can fight and defend this planet without rising out of my chair. It's almost easier than breathing." She paused, and Phan-tu could swear for a moment she had held her breath and looked slightly uncertain. It passed, and she exhaled through a strained smile. "And Chancellor Mollo?"

"He will stay here for the time being to work on the communications buoy."

"And after this investigation? Will you stay here by my side, where I need you, Phan-tu?"

Phan-tu looked at his muddied boots. "Xiri would like me to go to E'ronoh."

The queen shook her head. "Phan-tu. We are at war again. I cannot have you go straight from my war room to the enemy's dinner table."

"I did not marry Xiri to give away all our secrets, Mother. You know that. We did marry for love. And because we believe in a future—for both worlds."

A condescending look passed on her face, replaced by pity. "A pure thought, my son. Ah, yours is a young, green kind of love. This is a time when mistakes are made, before your roots have entwined together. Phan-tu—as your parents, Odelia and I know you would never betray us. But we need you here. When things calm down, you and Xiri can be together on neutral territory."

Phan-tu laughed. "Like on the moon, where nothing useful exists? That's a metaphor even too harsh for you, Mother."

"The moon that creates our tides and gives life to Eiram in so many ways. I never thought you the pessimist, Phan-tu."

"I don't think I was until the peace talks failed." He smiled. "There must be another way I can see Xiri without either of our families being worried or upset about it."

"Oh, there's a way." She smiled.

Chapter Five

THE MOON BETWEEN EIRAM AND E'RONOH

Padawan Enya Keen watched the two survivors on a screen. They were inside the small storage area of the waystation that had been repurposed as a holding cell. One guard each from E'ronoh and Eiram stood before the door, trying hard not to make eye contact with each other.

The Roonan male, identified by the guards as Goi Ganok, paced in the locked room, cradling an arm that appeared injured. The other, a Mirialan male known as Binnot Ullo, stared out the window onto the salt flats of the moon, which resembled crumbling sand dunes. The light of the sun cast gray shadows across the plain landscape.

As Master Char-Ryl-Roy and Phan-tu approached to open the door, Enya noticed Binnot's body shift slightly. She knew he couldn't hear anything, as the door was fairly thick, but he seemed to sense they were approaching. Interesting.

Enya quickly joined them from the monitoring room she had been in, just as Phan-tu pressed a button by the door. One by one they entered. Goi jerked to attention, backing himself up to the wall until he accidentally seated himself at a bench by the window. Binnot merely turned and waited, his face calm. He eyed Enya and the lightsaber at her belt, then Master Roy, with the same glance at his lightsaber. At the sight of Phan-tu, he bowed deeply.

"The Honorable Phan-tu Zenn," Binnot said, bowing. "I am Binnot Ullo, and this is Goi Ganok."

Phan-tu couldn't hide the surprise from his face. He only nodded at the greeting.

"I am Jedi Enya Keen, and this is Jedi Master Char-Ryl-Roy," Enya said. "We understand you had a troubling encounter with pirates. We would like to hear what happened."

"There's very little to tell that we have not already shared . . . twice," Binnot said. His voice was smooth. It reminded Enya of how Viceroy Ferrol used to talk. Like it had been rehearsed a thousand times and could be recited in his sleep. "We had a shipment of protein concentrates we were bringing from a station near Skye to Shuraden. E'ronoh and Eiram are halfway between the two, which is when we were stopped by an unidentified ship. This war is making the pirates come out of every crevice of the galaxy to this area."

"They took everything!" Goi said, hands clasped. "I thought they would kill us!"

Binnot gave Goi the tiniest nod. "Indeed, so did I. They incapacitated our engines. We were drifting when the E'roni ship found us. But we wanted nothing to do with the fighting between Eiram and E'ronoh, so we asked to try to repair it on the moon. That is when the second of our two engines exploded." He shrugged. "We are good at piloting transports, but we are not engineers."

"Of course. How understandable. And the klytobacter you had hidden in your ship's base compartments?" Char-Ryl-Roy asked.

"We didn't know it was there. We want no part of the Eiram and E'ronoh conflict. We are only shippers, with families at home to feed."

Enya watched Binnot carefully. His words were sincere, the feeling behind them well matched. But something was missing. She turned to Goi, a sympathetic smile on her face.

"Tell me about your family, Goi."

Goi coughed. He looked at Binnot and then back at Enya. "I . . . I have no family."

"He lost his family as a child. I am his family now," Binnot said smoothly. "I, too, lost my parents. My sister has three young children. We provide for them, and for the people where we come from, on a station near Skye."

"There are no recordings of when the E'roni pilot boarded your ship, or when you were on the moon prior to Captain Van speaking to you," Phan-tu said. "Have you any idea when the ship might have been boarded and the illegal klytobacter stowed away? Do you think it was there since you departed your home near Skye?"

"We do not. All we know for certain is our ship is destroyed, and we will suffer heavily for the loss of our shipments." Binnot shook his head. "We are already in debt. The long-standing war between Eiram and E'ronoh has affected systems beyond this one. Our trade has become more difficult every year that goes by."

Char-Ryl-Roy murmured to Enya, out of earshot. "Their story is consistent so far."

Enya whispered back. "I would like to try one more thing, if I may, Master. But not in here."

Char-Ryl-Roy nodded. The two Jedi and Phan-tu withdrew from the cell. Outside the cell, there was a woman waiting for them, with copper-colored hair in a braid over her shoulder. A traditional E'roni bane blade was sheathed at her belt, along with a military-issue blaster.

"Xiri!" Phan-tu exclaimed, surprised out of his usual calm demeanor.

She crossed her arms and tried to smile. "Why so surprised, Phan-tu? This is our moon, too." She smiled and turned to the Jedi. "Master Roy. Padawan Keen. It is good to see you both again." Enya smiled brightly, but diminished her expression when she saw how awkwardly Phan-tu stood beside them. As Xiri's husband, he had not received nearly as warm a welcome. "I overheard your conversation with the survivors."

"Something is off. I think Binnot is lying," Enya said.

Both Phan-tu and Master Roy nodded in agreement.

"He does seem too polished. How about we give them a tour of the moon? Loosen them up a little?" Xiri suggested.

"A tour that will last all of two minutes?" Phan-tu said, trying not to laugh.

Master Roy gave Enya a glance that said, *We may have to keep the tension between these two calm as well.*

"Let's try. Shall we?" Enya said cheerfully.

Phan-tu was right, Enya thought. There was hardly anything to tour in this area of the moon. Forty meters away on the other side of the way-station, there was the wreckage of Binnot and Goi's ship; Xiri's starfighter; the guards' ships; and Phan-tu's personal ship. The way-station had been maintained by both planets until the war began, which meant that the supplies there were painfully old and out of date, but the dry atmosphere meant nothing rotted or rusted. It was in shockingly good repair. There was a low, domed building with several small wings of rooms holding emergency rations, some dusty sleeping quarters, and storage. The provisions shop was closed, but peering inside, there wasn't much but dusty packages of dried food and trinkets from both planets for sale. Enya assumed it had closed when the war began.

Binnot and Goi had insisted they be allowed to survey their own ship to assess the damage themselves, which seemed fair. They had walked about the ship, touching the burned panels of the engine, patting down the belly of the ship as if afraid it had been tampered with. But soon, they walked ahead of the rest of the party and away from the ships, their feet making imprints in the salt minerals on the surface. With the waystation and shop behind them, there was nothing ahead but more salt dunes and craggy low peaks in the distance. Both planets were in view, with the blue of Eiram cresting over the southern horizon of the moon, and E'ronoh's reddish-and-gray globe on the other. Enya noticed that Binnot had walked slower, within earshot of Xiri and

Phan-tu speaking about their disappointment when the peace talks fell through.

"You know, the moon would be a great place to try to hold more peace talks," Char-Ryl-Roy said. "Perhaps it's more meaningful than having them so far away, as they were on Jedha."

Binnot spoke suddenly, as if he'd been holding the words back and failed. "I would think the Jedi enjoyed war. It gives you something to meddle with." Goi nodded, and held his arm tenderly. Enya noticed for the first time that he had a darkened bruise on his arm.

She approached them. "We don't revel in war. It is the opposite of what we do." She turned to Goi. "Now, that looks painful. Has anyone checked it, to make sure you didn't break a bone?"

Goi reeled back from Enya, his feet kicking up powdery salt. He bared his teeth for a brief moment. "No. It's not that bad."

"Let me see. It's bad enough that you're holding it like that." Enya gently touched the bruised arm, moving the elbow joint. "It looks like you bled beneath the skin from a contusion. Perhaps we could help with the healing?"

Goi pulled his arm back quickly, wincing at the movement. "Don't. I don't want any . . . unnatural treatments."

"Oh. Do you mean using the Force? It can indeed be used to heal, but that is a rare ability. Master Roy and I certainly can't do that. But I was thinking perhaps a salve from the healers on Eiram or E'ronoh. Or something on one of our ships." She motioned to a guard, who nodded and left.

"Ah. A salve. Of course." Goi tried to smile.

"Does the Force make you uncomfortable?" Enya asked.

"I . . ." Goi looked at Binnot, who came to his friend's side.

"Leave him alone," Binnot said, his voice icy. Enya balked for a moment, but Binnot bowed slightly. "We do not wish to burden our benefactors here. Goi is simply shy. We are fine."

Enya smiled politely but she saw Char-Ryl-Roy didn't. He, too, felt it was too quick a turnaround. Binnot began to chat benignly with

Enya about the warmth of the air. Speaking of the weather. How very neutral of him.

They decided to turn and head back to the waystation. It was, after all, a very brief tour. Goi stopped before the provisions shop. This time, he used his elbow to dust off the window and peered inside. He motioned to Binnot.

"Look, Binnot! I think I see a set of pin dice in there. The kind we played on Dalna when we were kids."

Phan-tu frowned. "Dalna? I thought you said you were from near Skye. The only people from Dalna of late who have ventured beyond the planet are members of the Path of the Open Hand."

At those words, Goi's mouth gaped, stricken, like he'd heard a death sentence. He froze in place.

"Ah, no. Goi said it was played on Dalna, as well as near Skye, and Shuraden. It's a common game."

"That is not what Goi said. You said you played it on Dalna. Have you been there?" Xiri pressed.

Goi's eyes shone like dark, wet stones, flicking from person to person as he stood up and backed away, as if he'd been attacked.

"We don't mean to upset you, Goi," Enya said, reaching an arm out. "Just to understand."

"Don't touch me!" Goi hissed.

Enya stopped moving toward Goi.

Binnot held up his hands. "I must apologize for my friend. He is very upset over our recent troubles. Being attacked by pirates makes one distrustful."

But Char-Ryl-Roy ignored Binnot's words, likely knowing they were a deflection. "Goi. You think using the Force is unnatural. We do not own the Force. We do not enslave it. It is the opposite. It flows through us. To deny the Force and how it moves through all beings— including the Jedi—*that* is unnatural."

Enya stepped closer to the Roonan. "Goi. Where did the klytobacter come from?"

Goi hissed at her, his head flicking back and forth between the two Jedi. He was backing himself toward the provisions shop door, with Binnot in front of him, trying to calm everyone down.

"As we told you," Binnot said, now trying to appeal to Xiri and Phan-tu, since the Jedi were entirely focused on Goi, "we had no idea it was there—"

"Goi?" Enya said. "We are trying to help. You and your sister, and her children."

"Yes, my sister," Goi said. He nodded.

"You said it was *your* sister, Binnot, not Goi's. And here you are now, ready to accuse E'ronoh of planting klytobacter on your ship."

The other guards, who until now had remained at a distance, now trained their blasters on the two survivors. Xiri unholstered her blaster, waiting. Goi snarled. "Filthy Force-user," he muttered. "You ruin everything. Everywhere."

"*Filthy Force-user*? Those are words I have only heard spoken by the Path of the Open Hand. Are those your people?" Phan-tu said.

Binnot's face was as benign as before. "I am a freight hauler. Nothing more. What about you, Phan-tu? Are you a traitor to your people?"

Phan-tu recoiled slightly. Xiri clenched her teeth, her fist gripping her blaster.

Enya and her master both stared intently at Binnot. He certainly wasn't acting like a victim anymore. And she'd had an uncertain feeling around Binnot since they'd first met, like she was ever so slightly being pushed away. Enya reached out to the Force around him, not to control or push, but to examine. It surrounded him, centered in his body, flowed inward and outward, even down to the deep bedrock beneath the salt flats. She could sense Master Roy at her side, the brightness of his countenance, how the Force swam like a conduit through him.

"A Jedi with nothing to say?" Binnot said, his voiced drawling. "How odd."

But his casual words were suffused with a modicum of tension.

Binnot's posture grew stiffer. Enya and Char-Ryl-Roy continued to say nothing, simply staring—not with animosity, or sympathy, or anything. It was a blank yet open expression. Binnot fidgeted slightly.

"Stop it," he said.

"What's going on?" Xiri asked. Phan-tu shook his head.

Enya knew what her master was doing, and she pressed on as well. She continued to sense all that was around them. Some Jedi described the flow of the Force as if it had a living quality to it, like grass blades reaching for sunlight. Others would say it was like music whose melody was inscrutable but indescribably lovely. But Enya always felt it almost like it was an invisible, gently blowing wind that connected all things, smooth and gentle sometimes, torrential at others. Always present. But nearer to Binnot, it turned ever so slightly, the way a pebble on a smooth surface would ever so slightly obstruct a wind that flowed over it. No ordinary person would ever notice.

Without lifting a finger, Enya concentrated hard, gathering the Force about herself and pressing it forward toward Binnot. Binnot again fidgeted, now pivoting his feet in the salty ground of the moon.

"I know what you're doing. And I won't be goaded into your tricks," Binnot said, teeth clenched.

The pebble-sized disruption grew to something slightly more substantial as the Force was pushed away from Binnot. Binnot was Force-sensitive, just as Enya had suspected. But he wasn't using the Force so much as pushing it away. A different variation on the same theme.

"Did you sense that, Master?" Enya asked.

"I did." Char-Ryl-Roy spoke in his gentle, knowing way. "You are not who you say you are, Binnot Ullo."

"I'm a hauler. Nothing more," Binnot said.

Xiri lifted her eyebrows. "Too bad. Because you'd make a marvelous politician."

"And you, Goi?" Enya asked. "If I could have healed you with the Force, I would have. What if you were a breath away from death? Would you have let me help you?"

"Dead! I would rather be dead!" Goi turned to Binnot for encouragement. "How can you be so calm, Binnot? Filth, these Jedi are! Using the Force as if they *own* it!"

Suddenly, Goi lunged forward at Enya. He was enraged, his black eyes shining, and almost looked as if he'd bite the Jedi, if he could. She dodged him easily, knocking him back with her elbow so he fell flat onto his belly. Goi scrambled to get up, only to find the guards' blasters all now aimed at him. Goi and Binnot were surrounded by the Jedi and the guards. Xiri now pointed her blaster at them.

"What has the Path made you do?" Enya said, her eyes quickly darting from Goi to Binnot.

"The Path has not made me do anything!" Goi yelled. "The Path is everything—"

"Goi, silence!" Binnot hissed.

Goi cowered at Binnot's words, and he looked at the ground, seething.

"These are not the words and actions of simple freight haulers," Char-Ryl-Roy said. "If you are with the Path, then why meddle in the affairs of two planets that were just on the cusp of securing peace after this Forever War?"

"Two planets that are already back to being at war?" Binnot scoffed. "They would have failed their peace treaty in one way or another. Your theory is weak."

"A clever person carries options with them, like tools. You cannot assume a hammer will fix all broken things," Master Roy said. "If the Path failed at bringing Eiram and E'ronoh back to war at the peace talks, then your plan to make Eiram believe E'ronoh had klytobacter as a weapon was the other option. Wasn't it?"

Goi gurgled, like he'd choked on moon dust. Binnot stared calmly ahead, ignoring his friend. They said nothing further after more questioning, so the guards began walking them back to the makeshift cell on the waystation. Enya and Char-Ryl-Roy spoke as they followed slowly, along with Xiri and Phan-tu.

"Well, this is a turn of events. It reinforces what we believed—that neither planet incited this battle—but now there are more questions," Enya said.

Char-Ryl-Roy turned to Xiri and Phan-tu. "We need to inform the queen and the Monarch, and Chancellor Mollo. And we must confront the leaders of the Path. The Herald, and the Mother. Now. I have a terrible feeling that more is to come if we don't act immediately."

"Our ship is ready to go at any time," Enya said.

"I'm not sure how much of a conversation it will be if we come at them with accusations," Xiri said. "But perhaps bringing Goi and Binnot to Dalna, unhurt, will help show them our intentions. We need diplomacy. For all we know, these are just cries for help, a way to gain prominence and be heard."

"Perhaps they want more visibility in the Republic. We should try to listen, without bowing to violence," Phan-tu added.

Enya nodded in agreement, but Master Roy didn't look nearly so convinced. Ahead, the guards with Binnot and Goi were nearly at the waystation. Beyond it, their ships were docked on a flat of hard, compacted salt. They could see Goi and Binnot, sullen and quiet, held by guards next to the waystation entrance. Suddenly, Goi fell or tripped to the ground, kicking up a cloud of salt dust and obscuring the two survivors. When it cleared, both Goi and Binnot were on the ground and there was shouting. It wasn't clear who was doing the shouting, the guards or the prisoners.

"Stay back, Xiri!" Phan-tu yelled as the two Jedi ran ahead of them, toward the group.

"I'm the one who's trained in combat, you should stay back!" Xiri hollered as they ran, one hand on her blaster and the other holding her bane blade. Phan-tu was running as fast as he could, but Xiri was faster and reached the ship to see Goi and Binnot on the ground, fighting each other.

"What is going on? Break this up!" Xiri yelled. Enya reached down to pull Goi off Binnot when Binnot swung his arm at Enya. She jumped back in time, as Xiri cried out. Something spattering upon Xiri's leg. At first Enya didn't understand. Then she saw it. Something slimy and liquid had immediately eaten through the fabric of Xiri's uniform, making blisters pop up red and angry on the front of her leg.

"What is this?" Xiri gasped, her face contorted with pain.

Binnot had thrown something at the guards, and several of them were screaming, clutching at their faces. Goi rolled away and made a flinging gesture. A clear liquid splashed across a guard's unshielded face. His eyes immediately went opaque and angry blisters sprouted across his face. He fell over in agony. Enya finally realized that Goi and Binnot weren't fighting each other—they had faked the fight in order to take out the guards.

"Get back!" Char-Ryl-Roy warned, his lightsaber drawn and ready. Binnot was holding a canister in his hand, and Goi held one as well. Char-Ryl-Roy held his hand out, ready to push away whatever chemical the prisoners were releasing.

How had they gotten those chemicals? And then a sinking feeling came over Enya. Binnot and Goi had just walked around their damaged vessel and probably had stashed them externally. It hadn't occurred to anybody to search the outside of their ship for hidden weapons, and not just the inside.

Xiri aimed her blaster at Goi, when Binnot swung his arm around. An arc of liquid followed this movement, and Phan-tu pushed her abruptly out of the way, her blaster going off and shooting the air. The liquid saturated the fabric on his left leg, but Phan-tu ran forward and tackled Binnot, his knee making contact with Binnot's ribs. Binnot fell to the ground, the air leaving his chest in a gasp. Phan-tu's elbow came down on Binnot's temple, and Binnot lay still.

Enya reached with the Force to pull the canister out of Goi's hand, who resisted, screaming as he fell on top of it, as if protecting a prized jewel.

"Filthy Force-user!" he screamed again. He balled up with the canister against his belly. "Long live the Mother! The Force will be free!"

He fumbled with the canister, which exploded with a muffled bang. Liquid and heavy gas enveloped Goi, who writhed and screamed in agony. Through the haze, enormous blisters swelled and exploded on his exposed skin, disfiguring Goi's face as he screeched in agony. The torture didn't last long. Goi was dead in seconds.

Binnot lay still, but a canister was in his closed fist. Xiri went to reach over and pull it out of his hand when a glint of metal caught Enya's eye.

"Xiri!" Enya yelled out. Phan-tu had seen the blade, too, dashing forward and forcefully shoving away Xiri, who landed hard on her side. Enya sensed the movement before she saw it. Binnot thrust his hand upward, and Phan-tu staggered back, a knife in his ribs and red blood staining his hands. Binnot scrambled backward, distancing himself from everyone.

Xiri screamed, "Phan-tu!" She scrambled back to her feet and ran to him, pressing her hand over his bleeding chest.

Binnot stood quickly and held up a small device in his hands.

"There are several of these canisters hidden in the market square in E'ronoh's capital city. The canisters will explode if you kill me right now. And they will explode if my escape is in any way impeded, as I have a good friend there with a second detonator who is awaiting my command. If they don't hear from me, they'll all go off."

"He's lying," Master Roy said, his lightsaber aloft.

"He might not be," Enya disagreed, her lightsaber also at the ready. "I think they had this planned out well in advance. You had the acid canisters stowed in an outside compartment on your ship, didn't you?"

Binnot said nothing, only smiled.

Xiri was holding Phan-tu, who was quickly losing consciousness, her eyes wide and furious, darting between the Jedi and Binnot.

"Princess. You'll really bet the lives of your people to call my bluff? The Children of E'ronoh?" Binnot held up the detonator in his hand. "Let me leave, and they will live."

"Monster!" Xiri screamed.

"What if he kills them anyway?" Enya said.

"We don't have a choice," Master Roy said, lowering his lightsaber. "We have to let him go."

Binnot backed away toward Phan-tu's ship, smiling widely, quite possibly the first true emotion he'd shown since he'd arrived on the moon.

"Sorry. I'd love to chat more, but I have other important things to do."

With one more roguish smile, Binnot disappeared into the hatch of Phan-tu's Eirami ship before it disappeared into darkness beyond the moon.

Chapter Six

Aida Forte sat in the main cabin of the *Lazuli*, gently rubbing the green scales over her hands, as if checking they were still there. The planet had dense white clouds over half of the brown-and-greenish masses of land. Dalna's two suns were in the far left of her viewport, golden and mellow. But despite the beauty, she felt unsettled. Like she was being watched.

She felt a tap on her shoulder. She knew it was Master Sun.

"It's me. I sent a message to Master Yoda that we've arrived in the system."

"Good." She turned to him. "Why did you say *It's me*?"

"I had a weird feeling, like you needed to know I was nearby."

"You feel it, too?" Aida said.

"Like we're being watched? Yes."

Aida didn't think it was Lu Sweet, one half of their Republic security detail. He grimaced most of the time while staring forward, as if waiting for the enemy to materialize out of thin air so he could start knocking heads. It must bother him that he appeared more like he'd been sucking on sour, unripe fruit with a name like that. His partner,

Priv Ittik, was just as silent, though the Iktotchi tried to be less than three meters away from Aida at all times. In fact, there she was, standing near the door to the cockpit, like Aida's enormous shadow, her large horns pointing downward and hands folded in front of her.

"Seems I'm never alone, actually," Aida said, eyeballing her so-called bodyguard. "But you're right. It's not them that I'm feeling. It's something different."

"It's probably me," a voice commed in.

Creighton and Aida startled for a second. Aida touched the console. "Who is this?"

"It's Master Yaddle." There was a pause and a tiny grunt that resembled the sound of air squeaking out of a small bag. Or a small person. "And a youngling, Cippa Tarko. I'm orbiting Dalna with you, right now."

"What are you doing here?" Aida asked.

"I heard about what happened on Jedha, and then spoke to Master Yoda and Chancellor Greylark. Our communication was a little glitchy, but my understanding was that I was needed on Dalna to gather information about the Path."

Creighton shook his head. "Glitch or no, Master Yaddle, we welcome having another Jedi with us. I had thought that only Aida Forte and I were authorized to come here." He glanced up, seeing Priv lift a single, heavy eyebrow ridge. "Uh, along with two of the chancellor's guards."

"Well, I'm here now," Master Yaddle said. "I've felt fairly strongly that I need to come to Dalna, not to Jedha, or to Coruscant. This is convenient, however. One of the guards can watch Cippa. Let's meet outside of the Path's compound. It's close to the town of Ferdan. If you have a plan about what you'd like to do, I'll listen, Master Sun."

The communication ended. Creighton spun in his chair. "It looks like there'll be three of us."

"Five of us, you mean," Priv added.

"Four," Aida corrected. "One of you will be watching a Jedi youngling."

Priv snarled, her voice so low and rumbling that Aida could almost feel the reverberations. "I am an elite Republic security guard with fifty years of experience." She balled both thick, muscular hands into fists. "I am no babysitting droid."

"Younglings are not exactly babies. It's necessary for the mission, Priv. You or Lu Sweet. I'll let the two of you decide," Creighton said.

Priv turned around and went into the back of the ship. A low argument could be heard as Aida began to steer the ship down to Dalna. After they penetrated the atmosphere, they descended below the fluffy clouds to find it raining gently. To the northwest were snowy volcanoes, and below them, some flat plains cultivated in geometric grids of farmland. Trees of red and purple dotted the landscape in clusters.

Ferdan could be seen, a concrete and metallic blight on the green land, but small, with one landing pad. There was an occasional small or medium-sized ship coming in and out of Ferdan, which was good. Their own ship wouldn't stand out around here. A few spired buildings were at its center, with square and rectangular ones that spread out to a less populated sprawl around the town. About four kilometers away, connecting with thin, weaving dirt roads, there appeared a small village surrounded by a wooden wall.

There were some plain buildings that appeared to be simple living structures, a barn and other buildings, perhaps for farm animals or meetings. No ships were flying in or out, but a set of raised landing pads of clay and stone could be seen on the western edge of a vast field. They looked newly built, with freshly cut wood walkways connecting them. A set of rolling hills to the south were bare of buildings, and haystacks dotted the area.

"Is that the Path compound?" Aida asked.

"It must be," Creighton said. "Too big for one farmer, and too small to be a town. We'd better not fly in over the compound. We'll land a kilometer away and keep low."

"Sounds good." She peered closer to the viewport. "Odd. Look at the fields. Judging by the season, you'd think they'd be getting close to harvest. But they look kind of messy. Maybe they're fallow?"

"Not so many all at once. Looks like the Path has been too busy to farm. Or too wealthy to need to grow their own food," Creighton surmised.

"Or," Aida said, "maybe they are suffering from a blight and don't have the people to farm. It might be a sign of trouble."

"That they're in trouble, or *are* trouble?" Creighton frowned. "After what happened on Jedha, you know my guess, Aida."

They landed the *Lazuli* far enough away from the compound that it would not draw any attention. They exited with Priv and Lu sulking behind them (the babysitting conversation must not have gone well). About a kilometer ahead, past a grassy expanse strewn with lompop wildflowers and gnostra bushes thick with pink berries, lay the Path compound. The tops of a few brown buildings were visible.

Yaddle's voice came from the handheld comlink that Creighton carried. "We are flying in low and headed your way."

Minutes later, Yaddle could be seen exiting from a grove of trees, wearing the brown Jedi garments for missions. Her hair was braided in tidy plaits over her shoulders. Her pointed green ears bobbed slightly with every footfall, and her large green eyes scanned the scenery. There were shallow lines along her nose and forehead. Her skin was slightly brighter green than Master Yoda's. Aida knew that Master Yaddle was around two hundred years old. Master Yoda was the only other of her species Aida knew existed, and he was older, perhaps by a few hundred years.

A small child walked at her side, slightly taller than Yaddle, but very slight and limber appearing. She wore similar brown pants and a belted shirt with boots, and her stark white hair was in braids like Yaddle's.

Under the light rain and gray skies, Creighton and Aida bowed. The guards, too, nodded quickly in respect.

"Master Yaddle. It is good that you could join us," Aida said. "This is Priv Ittik and Lu Sweet, our Republic support." The two guards were still sulking. But on second thought, Aida realized that these may have simply been their neutral expressions.

Master Yaddle nodded a welcome. "This is Cippa Tarko, the young-ling I am mentoring. We were on our way to the Jedi Temple on Coru-scant." Here, Cippa simply stared at all the new strangers, unblinking. She didn't seem particularly frightened or bothered, as if meeting an enormous Iktotchi soldier or Jedi was utterly normal. "I apologize for the confusion. When I couldn't hear the entire transmission, I took what I heard and then allowed the Force to guide me. I am needed here. Hopefully we shall accomplish more with the three of us."

"We could have saved you from the trouble," Creighton said, gestur-ing to Cippa. "You have a youngling in tow. Surely she needs to be brought to a temple to begin her training."

"My training has been ongoing for many years," Cippa said in her small voice. "And I agree with Master Yaddle. You need her help."

Aida smiled. Cippa was probably right, even if it was forward speak-ing from a youngling. Master Yaddle turned to Cippa.

"Just as your help will be needed, little one. In time, and with train-ing." She turned to the enormous guards nearby. "Priv Ittik and Lu Sweet, thank you for watching over Cippa during our mission."

"Both of us?" Lu almost spat. "Surely only one of us is needed."

"Surely you have never watched over an Arkanian child, much less one so in tune with the Force. I assure you this task demands abilities of *both* your calibers. Keep a close eye on your weapons. Keep all four eyes on her. And do not put down your guard for one moment."

Aida watched Priv look down at Cippa, who stared back with her white eyes. Aida noticed a shadow of fear briefly cross Priv's features. Surely, Aida thought, childcare wasn't *that* terrifying?

"Come, child," Lu said, pointing to the ship, partially hidden be-yond the edge of the forest. He followed Cippa, and Priv came up be-hind. Priv actually turned around a few times to glance back at the Jedi with an expression that looked unabashedly panicked.

"I don't think this is what they signed up for," Creighton said.

"We'd better hurry," Master Yaddle said, leaning into a jog. The wet, green grasses were almost as tall as she was. "We haven't got much time."

"Why the rush?" Aida asked, breaking into a sprint to catch up. Though her legs were short, Master Yaddle was quite fast. She began taking longer leaps to quicken the pace as Aida and Creighton ran.

"Because." Leap. "Cippa will wear them down." Leap. "So before long." Leap. "We shall have a youngling with us." Leap. "For the rest of this mission."

Now Aida was the one a little panicked. "Uh . . . have you taken younglings on missions before, Master Yaddle?"

"Rarely. But I do when the Force has led me to that choice. I am aware of the risk."

It wasn't too long before they were on the outskirts of the Path compound, surrounded by a freshly built wooden wall. They leapt over the wall, hiding behind a building to get a better sense of the layout. There were quite a number of structures here, of all shapes and sizes, many made of pink-tinged stone. There seemed to be only a small number of people around. Some were carrying baskets or blankets. They seemed to be in a hurry. Others were walking toward the hills to the south. Beyond the buildings was a vast field, but the yellow-green plants looked like they were starting to rot.

"Looks like an ordinary farming community," Aida said. "Not many people out, maybe since it's raining. Hard to believe a riot on Jedha arose from people who live in such peace."

"Beware of your judgments. A tree in winter is quiet and unobtrusive, but it has roots that spread far and wide, and can buckle boulders millions of years old," Yaddle reminded them.

"True. We saw firsthand what happened on Jedha. The question is whether the Herald was acting on his own. We need to see if these people are preparing for more conflict," Creighton said.

"There." Creighton pointed to a larger building. There was the sound of metallic clanking, and definitely more activity and people inside. "That's where we'll start."

They hid behind a few vehicles and piles of metal scraps that were being refurbished into other supplies. Three Path members were working in their underrobes of blue or gray, with overrobes of brown with the telltale blue stripes at their edges. Each had the painted wavy blue stripes on their foreheads. They were working with a large set of tanks with enormous tubes running into wagons.

"Could be fuel. Could be a chemical weapon of some sort," Creighton murmured.

"Could be grain," Aida said.

Yaddle said nothing.

"If we're going to find out, we are going to have to pretend we're Path members," Creighton said. "We can abduct a few members to take their clothes, but surely someone will realize they're missing. It'll be a telltale sign of trouble."

"Creighton," Aida said. "I suggest gently influencing them. We won't need to abduct anyone, and we will have the disguises we need."

"And have naked Path members walking around?" Creighton countered.

"Well, they would still have their undergarments." Aida had a flat smile on her face. It was an odd argument to be having, after all.

"Still. People walking around dazed in undergarments. It'll arouse suspicion. I say we abduct a few. We can question them, too, and get more information."

"And when they escape in their undergarments?" Aida asked.

"Wait a moment. Where is Master Yaddle?" Creighton asked, turning his head around.

They looked around from their hiding place. She was nowhere to be seen. Aida listened for a scuffle or fight, but there were no sounds aside from the daily goings-on of the Path members at a distance. Before they could go off and look for her, Master Yaddle walked from around the corner of a shed only six or seven meters away, holding a neat pile of tunics. She quickly came to them and laid the clothing down.

"How did you do it?" Creighton asked, pulling on a plain dark tunic with blue stripes at the hem.

"Laundry building is right over there." She pointed with her three-digit hand. "I also found this inside the building." She took a small clay jar from her robes containing a thick, blue paste made of ground brikal shell. "The steam and sweat must make the markings come off, so they reapply it." One by one they all smeared the wavy blue lines upon their foreheads.

"Oh." Aida looked down. "You brought too many clothes, Master Yaddle."

"No, she didn't." Creighton had ducked back down behind a landspeeder and tipped his head. In the brush far behind them, well beyond a few outbuildings and an orchard of twisted trees, they saw Cippa stealthily walking toward them, rather feline-like, and being followed closely by the hulking forms of Lu and Priv. Lu and Priv saw the Jedi and shook their heads in sorrowful defeat.

"As I said, we only had a short amount of time." Yaddle shook out a child-sized tunic, much like her own.

"Why did you bother having her looked after if you knew it would only be half an hour?" Aida said. "What was the point of that?"

"A Jedi can make a half-hour reprieve feel like a century of peace. One must replenish one's rest when possible." She shrugged. "And I very much needed a rest from Cippa." She turned her head to smile. "Hello, Cippa."

"Master Yaddle." Cippa was already next to Master Yaddle, pulling on her disguise. "Half an hour. That's the shortest minding I've ever had. They didn't last long."

Priv was stooping down next to Master Creighton, still shaking her head.

"What did she do to you?" Creighton asked.

"I don't want to talk about it," Priv said. "Is that disguise for me?" She pulled the clothing over her head, tearing the hole when she squeezed her large horns through. Creighton applied the three blue lines to her forehead.

"What exactly . . ." Aida began, eyes wide with curiosity.

"We agreed we wouldn't talk about it!" Priv hissed.

Master Yaddle smiled. "I think it's time for us to get to work here. Yes?"

"Good," Cippa said as the rain began to fall more steadily. "Because I'm bored."

Chapter Seven

ABOARD THE PIRATE CARGO SHIP
Near the Saaw Moon, Pipyyr System

If Binnot Ullo could have kept the Eiram prince's ship forever, he would have. The Mother, it appeared, seemed to like her trophies. Instead, he had abandoned it—and the trackers it no doubt carried—once he'd left the Eiram-E'ronoh system and transferred himself to the chunky, heavily armed cargo ship full of Path-friendly raiders, courtesy of the Mother.

He had always been in awe of her, but nothing cemented his respect for her calculating mind like when she planned these missions. Despite his worry, he did whatever was asked of him so as to become an asset the Mother could not live without. Even if he didn't quite understand her motivation. Why take Axel back, after his usefulness was spent? After his failure?

She had promised nothing specific to Binnot. A simple, *Do this for me, and you will be rewarded.* The Herald had left an open place at her side. Perhaps it was Binnot who could prove he could stand there.

And so it had all gone, more or less, according to the exact plan that the Mother had laid out. The klytobacter had its effect; E'ronoh and Eiram were at each other's throats again, despite the weak attempts by the useless prince and princess of their planets. True, Goi's death had been unplanned. But casualties must happen. Leaders must accept certain losses.

Now Binnot was in the cockpit of the bulky, well-armed, and well-armored pirate ship.

"We head to Pipyyr, I hear," said one of the Klatooinian raiders in the pilot's chair. He didn't seem to enjoy having Binnot call the shots on his own ship, but again, it was the Mother who was ordering them to. She had been feeding the group of pirates information on where the best raids could happen, in order to keep them in her good graces. They would do at least this favor for her. Possibly more, very soon, she had told Binnot.

"Close. Near the Saaw moon," Binnot said. He was standing in the back of the cockpit, arms crossed and thinking.

"Nothing to steal in that sector these days," the Klatooinian said. Binnot had already forgotten his name; his mind had better things to keep track of, like Axel Greylark.

"We're not going to steal anything," Binnot said.

The ship had already arrived in the Pipyyr system. The gray-and-white planet shone like a tiny marble in the distance, but the almost white moon was now within range.

"Now where's that communications buoy?" Binnot said, peering through the viewport.

The Klatooinian pointed. "There."

It was a tiny piece of cylindrical metal with several antennas poking out of each end. The pirate ship had an extension arm. It easily grabbed the buoy and withdrew it into its cargo hold. Binnot went to it and opened up the belly panel of the buoy. Inside, amid the tangle of multicolored wires, he plugged in a tiny finger-sized drive and had the pirate set it back into space.

"Won't an alarm go off if we tamper with it?" the Klatooinian asked.

"You ask too many questions," Binnot said. "But no. The Mother gave me a code to use. Don't move from this spot. I need to be within a few kilometers of that buoy. Next, we wait."

"For what?"

Binnot only glared at him, then left the cockpit. The other pirates were playing a card game in the belly of the ship, smoking herbs that smelled like pepper and drinking clear spirits. A Nikto, a few other Klatooinians, and some humans were guffawing and hollering at one another. Binnot only went to the nearest viewport, and waited, holding a small handheld device. A line of incoming and outgoing messages scrolled slowly down the screen of his device, and he set it to alert him when the right one went through. He closed his eyes.

It wasn't too long, only a few hours, before the device buzzed and woke him.

MessageType:Holographic/Direction:Afferent/Destination:RepublicCorrection alFacility/Attn:WardenZolehPrin/Pipyyr/Status:Capture successful:StandbyPause

Binnot sat up to attention, smiling.

He put in the order on the device. It was really a clever program, created by someone talented on the Mother's roster of friends. The original message was captured by his program on the buoy. His interference would be erased, and the tainted message sent. He hit EXECUTE and received a confirmation.

MessageType:Audio/Direction:Afferent/Destination:RepublicCorrectionalFa cility/Attn:WardenZolehPrin/Pipyyr/Status:Release successful/StandbyOff

He retrieved the buoy and removed the tiny drive from its belly. No one would ever know they were there. Binnot headed to the cockpit.

"Now what?" the Klatooinian pilot asked. "This had better be worth our time."

"It's worth the Mother's time, so it's worth yours. It's time to head to Pipyyr now. I have a package to pick up."

THE INFIRMARY, REPUBLIC CORRECTIONAL FACILITY, PIPYYR

Gella and Orin had rested for hours. When they returned to the infirmary, it was obvious that Axel had needed more nutrient broth infusions. The Pipyyr medic attached more treatment patches and plasma injections, but Axel continued to vomit anytime he tried to eat.

As they watched him sleep, Gella realized what a very personal thing it was to watch another person in such a vulnerable state. It made her want to protect him.

No, Gella, she thought. *Be mindful. Stay objective.*

"I don't think we'll get more answers from him," Orin said. "We should leave soon."

"We can't leave," Gella said. "He's not well. He ought to be transferred somewhere else."

A Pipyyr guard with gray-and-white fur entered the infirmary.

"There is a message incoming from the chancellors. You ought to hear this."

"What?" The skin prickled on the back of Gella's neck. "I thought they didn't know we were here. Are we in trouble?"

"Most definitely," Orin said cheerfully as they followed the guard out to the hallway and then to the warden's quarters, where a holovid screen was waiting to play the message. The warden, a grizzled, older Pipyyrian, waved them in.

"It's an official Republic transmission. Sound only," the warden said.

Static played at first, followed by the voice of Chancellor Kyong Greylark.

"After much consideration, and given the gravity of his crimes, the Republic High Council has considered altering the punishment assigned to Axel Greylark and a possible transfer."

"Wonderful. This isn't about us. We're not in trouble. At least not yet," Orin said, elbowing Gella.

"A transfer?" she said. "I mean, he needs it, physically, but . . ."

"Awfully good timing, innit?" Orin Darhga rubbed his reddish beard.

Chancellor Greylark's voice went on, the static occasionally obscuring the edges of her words. "However, given the delicate and personal nature of this decision on my part, this cannot be made unilaterally. Our Republic counselors have made clear that a unanimous decision would need to be made by both chancellors. For the record, it is my opinion that Axel Greylark should be released on a low-security rehabilitation program."

"There's no way Chancellor Mollo will agree to this," Orin said.

The transmission continued. "This is Chancellor Orlen Mollo. After much consideration, I, too, agree with the terms offered by Chancellor Greylark. Axel Greylark should be released for rehabilitation, at the Republic Judiciary Central Detention Center near Coruscant, effective immediately."

The transmission ended. The Pipyyr warden, wearing a vest heavy with metal cords detailing his rank, stood. "This is an official Republic transmission. We have to transfer him."

"It couldn't have come at a better time, I guess," Gella said. Much as she wanted him to pay for what he'd done on Eiram, she never wanted to see him suffer. But it was odd, switching her mindset from mining Axel for information about Jedha and the future, to now focusing on keeping him alive and well. He'd said he was sorry, and she wanted to believe him. Perhaps he really could do some good in this new place, instead of rotting away on Pipyyr. A glimmer of hope kindled inside of her.

"I don't think this is a good idea. Transfer to another prison where he won't be sick, sure. But a lesser sentence? You agree with his release?" Orin said, his face suffused with surprise.

"You were the one talking about giving him a chance, weren't you?" Gella said, giving Orin the side-eye. "Anyway, he's not really free," she reasoned. "He has work to do. They didn't say to shorten his term. It may actually be harder for him to actively *work* on being a better person, instead of stewing in a prison where he learns nothing."

"Eh, he might as well head to a hotel on Coruscant or a seaside resort on Naboo." Orin asked the warden, "Can we at least confirm by sending a message out to the chancellors? This seems . . . odd."

"We cannot. As soon as this message was received, our transmissions team noted a burnout of our major communications buoy outside Pipyyr."

"Really? So we can't verify any of this? That seems awfully convenient for Axel," Orin said, eyes wide.

The warden waved a clawed hand. "It's not unusual. It happens when our sun flares are particularly intense," he explained. "Orders are orders. Normally, we would send our guards along with the prison transfer, but it would be even better to have a Jedi escort. And we are short-staffed right now."

Orin started to say, "I don't think we should—" but Gella cut him off quickly.

"Orin," she reasoned, "this way we have more time to speak to him about Jedha, and what else he knows. And if there is anything suspicious going on with this transfer, better we deal with it than a few transfer guards from Pipyyr that they can't even spare."

Orin glanced back and forth between the warden and Gella. "Well—" he began.

"We'll do it," Gella said firmly.

They left Pipyyr within the hour, after all the appropriate forms and legalities were completed. Orin was gesturing to the Pipyyr officials over the last details of the transfer, as if pantomiming his frustration would make things happen any faster. Axel was still attached to an IV bag but walked onto the *Eventide* leaning heavily on Gella.

"My ship!" he said, with more energy than Gella thought he could manage. He smiled widely and his eyes glinted like a kid opening a birthday present.

"It's not your ship anymore," Gella reminded him. "It's mine. Your mother gave it to me."

"She did?" He looked slightly hurt.

"What were you going to do with it while you were in prison?" Gella said. They began walking toward a smaller room where the medical equipment had been stocked by the Pipyyrian medics. She glanced at the polished, curved edges everywhere. "I'm thinking of trading it. It's a bit much for me."

"I'm going to pretend you didn't say that," Axel said, groaning. "Anyway. I cannot wait to get off this sickening planet. I hope I never see another furry guard again."

"Don't be so against fur. I've known a lot of good Wookiees in my life," Orin said.

"And I've known some terrifying ones. Glad the *Eventide* has just us on board. All we need is some champagne and a little less vomiting, and this will almost feel like a vacation."

He was already acting more like the Axel she knew. They'd reached the impromptu medical room in one of the sleeping quarters. Gella set up his IV and prepped a container full of medication for the trip.

"The medic told me what to use, and when, if you feel sick," she said.

"I already feel better. That place was just so oppressive." He paused for a long time, watching Gella set up the tubing. His voice quieted, became serious. "You know, Gella . . . I couldn't do anything there. Try to better myself. To change my life."

"You made a lot of choices in the past when you had a chance," Gella said, organizing packets of nutrients.

"I know. And I blew them all, all because I chased fortune, and then fate chased me right back." He smiled, and the hollows of his cheeks looked somewhat less gaunt than even yesterday. "I have a really good feeling about this trip with you."

She knew he wanted her to say something nice in response. Something chummy. She pointed to the IV.

"Keep that in your arm, or I'll put it in a different orifice."

Axel opened and then shut his mouth.

Orin appeared in the doorway. "We're off. Oh, and I have something for you. I didn't expect to give it to you, but I guess an exception can be made for this trip." He tossed something large and metallic into the air, and it spun and bleeped excitedly.

"Quin!" Axel exclaimed. "I thought he was destroyed!"

"He was," Gella said. "I didn't think he was repairable, but when I returned to Coruscant, there was a technician there who thought differently. He's been working on the *Eventide* ever since."

Quin dodged Axel's attempts to catch and hug the droid. He started making zappy, irritated noises at Axel. It definitely sounded like a scolding.

"Oh. You're mad. I deserve that, I guess. I'm sorry, Quin. Really sorry! I'm so glad you're back. You'll forgive me, won't you?" The droid hovered and looked away. "I guess circuits never forget." He turned to Gella. "So you saved him for me?"

"That wasn't my intention," Gella said. She shrugged. "I just think droids deserve a second chance."

"Like me?" Axel winked at her. "Thank you, Gella. This means a lot."

Quin blooped pointedly at Axel.

"I really do mean it. I'm sorry. I'll make it up to you," Axel said. He reached out, and this time, QN-1 spun around slowly under his palm before keeping a cool distance again. "Missed you, too."

Orin smiled. "That's a faithful droid you have there."

"Well. Quin is more than just a helpful droid. He's been with you through a lot of bad stuff. Perhaps you can take him to the new facility and he can help you work on turning things around," Gella said.

Axel gave Gella a grateful glance, wordless for a change.

"I'd better punch in our first set of coordinates, or else those Pipyyr guards will push us off this mountain soon," Orin said. "We'll be flying for a while until we can enter hyperspace." He left and shut the door behind him.

The ship began to hum and vibrate as it took off from Pipyyr, leaving the atmosphere and gliding far more silently in space. Axel sighed.

He put his hands behind his head. "Remember our first visit to E'ronoh? The color of the sky? I'd never seen anything like that."

"That seems like ages ago," Gella said, leaning against the wall of the cabin, arms crossed. "So much has changed since then."

"You haven't changed," Axel said. "Strong as ever. Beautiful as ever, too."

"Stop," Gella said. She didn't like compliments. Anyway, it was just Axel, buttering her up. "Praise ought to be earned. You can't change how you were born to look."

"You're right. And I can't change that I was born to a mother who wanted me to be something I'm not."

"What do you mean?" Gella asked.

"Perfect. A statesman. Someone who never makes mistakes."

"No one can live up to that."

"Not even a mighty Jedi?" Axel's eyes met hers.

"No. Not even a Jedi," Gella corrected him. But she was taken aback. The question was such a simple one, but it hit her hard and she felt suddenly very exposed, like someone had peeled away her skin. "I . . . yes, it's hard. When you're surrounded by people who are so gifted, and . . . so *good*." Axel stayed silent, and it was an odd thing, feeling the silence around her, letting her fill it with all that she was feeling. All the things she wasn't allowed to feel. "I'm always trying to be better. To work on my emotions, to work on perfecting how I am with the Force, how it works through me."

"Maybe you shouldn't be struggling so much," Axel said, "I mean, maybe if you're fighting so hard, and with respect to the Force, maybe that's a sign."

She thought of a prayer she read during her studies, a sunset prayer by the Guardians of the Whills.

In darkness, cold.
In light, cold.
The old sun brings no heat.
But there is heat in breath and life.
In life, there is the Force.
In the Force, there is life.
And the Force is eternal.

She closed her eyes, answering Axel. "It's not about perfection—"

"It's about other people being disappointed in your imperfection," Axel said, trying to complete her thought.

"Wrong again." Gella opened her eyes. "It's about existing outside of constructs like disappointment and perfection and imperfection. It's about trusting in the Force."

Axel shook his head. "You're right, I don't understand." He pulled his hand through his hair. "I, on the other hand, live amid the very real construct of having an overachieving mother who has no tolerance for my faults. I'm shocked that she's giving me a chance. Chancellor Mollo, too."

"It's because they believe that you can change, and that you truly are sorry."

"I could have done things so much differently. What about you, Gella? Do you believe I'm sorry? Because I am."

Gella wanted to say, *I'm sorry I trusted you. I still don't trust you.* Had he changed? The only way to know was to see him act, but he was a prisoner. There was nothing he could do or say that would convince her now.

Axel reached out to grab Gella's hand, but she was a Jedi, after all. She sensed his intention and pulled her hand away too quickly to be captured. It was time she left him alone. She was always impulsive around Axel, always letting her feelings drive her actions. She needed some clarity and calmness.

"Gella, I—" Axel started, before the door to the room slid open suddenly.

Orin stepped into the room, and Gella stood, perhaps quicker than necessary.

"I . . ." Axel's hand was still extended toward her, frozen in the air. "I think I'm going to be sick."

She managed to grab a basin quickly from the medical supplies. Axel hid his face in the basin and filled it with retching noises and more. Against her better judgment, she sat next to him and patted his back awkwardly.

"Oh! Can't leave quick enough, eh, lad? We're on a set course for a while before we can enter a hyperlane. Huh. You two look like an old married couple after *he's* had too much ale." Orin turned to Gella. "Ship's on autopilot now. After we drop off Axel, I was thinking about our next step. Back to Jedha to help with the damage there."

"Sure. After your help, Orin, I'd like to help you, too. Which reminds me. Axel, during everything that happened on E'ronoh and Eiram, do you remember anyone from the Path being there?"

"Maybe? There were so many people there." Axel yawned suddenly, and loudly.

Orin stared at him for a beat too long, before slapping his legs. "You know what, Axel, you look tired. You should rest." He laid a heavy hand on Gella's shoulder. "Gella, I know you were originally intending on visiting Jedha to attend the Season of Light, and study new forms of meditation. Now would be a good time to meditate. There's a space for you in the other cabins."

"Oh. Sure," Gella said, surprised by his abrupt change of conversation. After she closed the door to Axel's room, Orin nudged her.

"Did you catch that?"

"What?" Gella asked.

"He was lying. About the Path," Orin said. "Almost as badly as me pretending I don't like a hot noodle soup."

"Oh." Gella was chagrined she hadn't noticed. "After he rests, we can press him about that later."

Orin went back to the cockpit, and Gella was left standing outside Axel's door for a while. She really needed to clear her head and concentrate. She craved solace and space, and time away from Axel. So much had happened recently.

Gella stole away for a modicum of peace for a few hours, then returned to check on Axel. He was sleeping, but he'd already detached his IV. The tubing hung uselessly, dripping onto the floor in a pool of liquid. Well, if he woke up feeling awful, he had no one to blame but himself.

An alarm jerked Gella out of her thoughts. Quin set off a piercing complaint of dismay.

Axel sat up quickly, looking around, confused. "What's wrong with the *Eventide*?"

"Stay here," Gella said before the ship lurched simultaneously with the sound of an explosion.

Orin appeared in the corridor, heading for the cockpit. Gella quickly caught her balance and followed him through the belly of the ship, where the luxurious and large central compartment connected the cockpit, the cargo loading area, and corridor to the sleeping quarters.

"Did one of the engines blow?" Gella asked, vaulting over a knocked-over supply container. "Did we hit something? Are you sure you punched in our nav coordinates correctly?"

"Our engines were in perfect order," Orin said, galloping forward. "And I'm a decent navigator! We've been hit."

They entered the cockpit with alarms blaring and lights flashing in all shades of angry red. Speeding slightly ahead of them was a much larger vessel, thick with armor and several cannons at each side. A ship built to attack.

"Blast," Orin muttered as he tried to outmaneuver the ship. "Pirates. That ship is all muscle, and good with short bursts of speed. We can't outrun it before it can shoot again."

"Can we enter hyperspace? Get away?" Gella asked.

"Yes, but we have to maneuver around this ship first," Orin replied. He moved the *Eventide* to change directions, but another blast hit the aft of the ship, lurching them forward. Gella's head nearly hit the viewport. A string of chittering beeps from Quin heralded the entrance of Axel, who was wide-eyed. To Gella's relief, he had the color back in his face and looked better.

"What is going on? Who's shooting at us?"

"Pirates," Gella muttered. "We have nothing to steal."

"What are you talking about? The *Eventide* is worth a bundle," Axel said.

"And you wondered why I plan on trading in this ship," Gella said.

The ship gave an ominous moan and began to slow down. "But we should prepare for a fight. Our second engine just died."

A message alert came through the cockpit right then.

"Are they contacting us?" Orin asked.

Gella looked at the communications panel. "No. It's coming from much farther away." She hit a button on the console.

"Hey! So ah, this is the Pathfinder team Seventy-one-Beenine? Hey, ah, is this, ah . . . Oobin Dark Eye?" There was a rush of beeps coming from the background. "Is this uh, Ooh-man Drunk Eye? What does this say, Pooch? You left your greasy prints on the datapad. Whatever. Drunk Eye! Come in?"

Orin rolled his eyes. "If I had a credit for every time someone said my name wrong, I'd be a very wealthy Coruscant man opening up his own free noodle shop."

"*That's* what you'd do with a ton of money?" Axel said, eyes wide.

Gella shushed him. "Pathfinder team, this is Jedi Gella Nattai and Jedi Master Orin Darhga." She pronounced Orin's name like she was speaking to a toddler. *Ore-innnn DARRHH-gaaa.* "We are under attack by a pirate ship right now. We need assistance, immediately."

After a beat of static, the Pathfinder team commed in again. "No can do, Drunk Eye! We're at least twenty minutes away. Oh! Also, we have Republic news!"

His perky tone was too much for the moment. "They can't help right now," Orin said. "And the last thing we need is an hour-long Republic news update. Turning the comms off." A green light blinked at intervals in the corridor to tell them another communication was waiting for them. There was a loud scraping, grinding noise as the ship lurched. "Wonderful. We're being boarded. Axel, you've got to hide."

"I don't want to hide. I want to help you fight," he said.

"You were throwing up only hours ago. That's a terrible idea," Gella countered.

"But I'm better now," Axel said.

"Awfully quick turnaround," Orin said under his breath as he pulled out his lightsaber. It ignited with a green glow.

Gella pulled out her lightsabers, holding one in each hand. She turned them on, the purple glow reflecting off the walls of the ship.

"I need a weapon," Axel said.

Orin gave Gella a warning look and shook his head. How did he know that she even briefly considered giving Axel one of her lightsabers? But she couldn't, of course. It wasn't a plaything or a blaster you pointed and pulled a trigger. He could instantly kill himself by just turning it on, if he held it the wrong direction.

"Axel," Gella said, "stay behind me. We're going to the cargo area where we can fight with more room to get an upper hand." She exhaled and listened to the familiar hum of the lightsabers. They moved forward, past the central compartment, until they were in an alcove of the general cargo area, which was relatively empty. The ship rocked again, and there was another groaning screech. They were docked, and the cargo door was being forced open. Orin froze in front of Gella, holding up his free hand.

"They're on board," he whispered.

They stood in the shadows of the alcove as footsteps sounded. The first thing that entered Gella's line of sight was a large blaster rifle, followed by the Nikto who held it in his grip. He wore dark clothing with two more blasters at his side. Orin stepped forward quickly, and in one fell swoop sliced the rifle in half.

The Nikto staggered back, pulling out his two blasters as Gella quickly jumped into the main cargo hold. There was a human behind the Nikto pirate, who began shooting at her, the blasts aimed straight at her heart. She deflected them instantly. Out of the corner of her eye, she could see Axel emerging from the alcove.

"Axel!" she yelled. "Stay back! We can handle this!"

Gella took up a wide stance to keep her balance. The shots came quickly and she deflected them over and over, while slowly closing the distance between herself and the pirate. She finally got close enough to slice the human pirate's blaster in half, jumping forward and landing a two-footed kick straight in the middle of his chest, knocking him down and stunning him.

Orin had used the Force to push his Nikto attacker against the wall of the ship, where he pulled away both blasters. He released the Nikto who held his hands up, staring at Orin's glowing green lightsaber.

"Have mercy!" the pirate whined. "We're only here to retrieve the package!"

"What package?" Orin said.

But the pirate didn't answer, because five other pirates filled the entryway to the cargo hold firing blasters. Two more humans and three huge Klatooinians, wearing bandoliers filled with explosives.

Gella and Orin were now deflecting what felt like ten blasts a second, getting pushed back farther toward the cockpit. Orin managed to use the Force to throw empty containers from the cargo hold toward their attackers, but being empty, they only caused a momentary distraction.

Gella glanced back and saw Axel pick up one of the blasters from the fallen pirates and begin shooting over the Jedi's heads. Shooting badly, at that. His blasterfire was only hitting the ship, and not the pirates. But it was enough to make them duck and seek cover.

"Keep it up, Axel!" Gella shouted as she ceased retreating and began to move forward.

"Happily. I'll be your backup any day. Beats having to puke my guts out on Pipyyr!"

The pirates rushed her. One fired on her, and another took out a Zygerrian energy whip and cracked it in the air as he swung it around. It caught Gella's left ankle and yanked her off her feet. She fell hard on her back, the air leaving her chest. She swung one of her lightsabers down and cut the whip off her ankle, swinging her other in a wide arc to keep one of the Klatooinian pirates away from her. She swung her legs around in a twirl, using the momentum to jump back onto her feet.

Orin was fighting the two other Klatooinians, who had abandoned their mutilated blasters and were now fighting hand-to-hand with axes, swinging around Orin and avoiding getting themselves cleaved in two by his lightsaber. As Gella kept fighting the other Klatooinian, the two human pirates scurried around Gella, toward the back of the cargo area where Axel was.

"Axel! Look out!" Gella yelled.

Axel shot at them, but it deflected off the limbs of the pirates. Scorch holes revealed metallic plates sewn into their rugged clothing. One of them tackled Axel while the other stood over him holding a blaster trained on his head.

"Stop moving, pretty boy," the pirate said, sneering. Then he turned toward Orin and Gella. "Both of you, drop your weapons, or your friend here will have a hole in his head."

The pirate who had tackled Axel now had him down on the ground in a choke hold from behind. Axel dropped his blaster and held his hands up, his face expressionless and reddened from the choke hold.

Orin growled, his face sweaty and flushed from the fight.

"Drop your weapon, Gella. They've won this round." Orin turned off his lightsaber and moved to lay it on the ground. Gella also held out her lightsabers, their brilliant purple lights disappearing, and the Klatooinian nearest her reached out to snatch them from her hands.

The ship lurched again, but this time it spun nearly halfway on its axis. Gella went sliding to the right onto her side, as did Orin and all the pirates. The one holding Axel loosened his grip, and Gella yelled.

"Axel!"

She tossed one of her lightsabers to him, and he caught it in his hand. He turned it on and thrust it over his shoulder. In a second, the pirate holding him screamed and released his choke hold as his severed ear fell to the ground. Axel swung the lightsaber downward and bisected the pistol in the hands of the pirate who stood before him. Axel jumped to his feet, taking a fighting stance. Gella and Orin rushed to his side.

"Boss!" Another human pirate jumped into the cargo hold from the pirate ship, waving a blaster. "There's a Republic ship headed our way! It's ready to fire on us, and we don't have our shields up because we're docked!"

"Let's go!" The head Klatooinian who was fighting Orin roared his order. The other pirates began scrambling back into their ship. The human pirate who had lost an ear held his head and ran.

Gella moved to follow them and continue the fight, but Orin held her back. "Let them go. We can't engage them on their ship. There might be a dozen more."

Just as the last Klatooinian, the apparent leader, nearly disappeared from the cargo hold, he paused, grimacing. "I can't have you following us, can I?" He quickly fired toward Axel.

"Axel!" Orin yelled, warning him. But it was too late. The blast didn't hit Axel; it went right past him. Gella knew milliseconds later that she had made a mistake.

The blast clipped her shoulder, and she cried out, clutching the wound.

"No! Gella!" Axel yelled.

The Klatooinian who had shot her was gone. Orin rushed to Gella's side, lightsaber out and ready to ward off any more fire.

"Well, Axel? Are you coming or not?"

Axel, Gella, and Orin looked in shock toward the cargo door. A tall Mirialan man with scant markings on his greenish face stood in the doorway. Unlike the pirates, he wore simple brown garb with a cloak over his shoulders. He leaned against the doorway, lazily. Unarmed.

Axel gasped, "Binnot?"

"In the flesh, Axel," the Mirialan said. He grinned. "You didn't just think we'd let you rot away in a jail, did you?"

Gella realized that Binnot had faint blue streaks on his forehead.

Orin stood from where he'd been hovering over Gella. "You're not pirates. You're the Path."

"And you took my package before I had a chance to retrieve it myself." He made a tsk-ing sound.

Axel's face was awash in disbelief. His expression flitted from guilt, to fear, to resolve. His head swiveled from Binnot, to Gella and Orin, and back to Binnot. Still holding Gella's purple lightsaber, he turned it off and approached the Mirialan.

"Axel!" Gella yelled. "What are you doing?"

Axel turned around at the last moment, his facial expression now inscrutable. "Goodbye, Gella."

The Mirialan grinned at Gella and Orin. "You know, you really should listen to those Republic news feeds. They're quite handy." He turned to Axel, draped an arm over his shoulder.

"Binnot, my friend." Axel smiled at him. "What mischief have you been up to?"

Quin whizzed from somewhere behind them. The droid looked to Gella, and then to Axel, hesitating. Seconds later, he flew off to join his master. The doors shut behind them.

"What just happened?" Gella said, her mind overwhelmed by pain and confusion. "He has one of my lightsabers!"

"I think we've just been had, is what happened," Orin growled.

The lights in the corridor back toward the cockpit were still blinking green. Their shuttle lurched as Binnot's ship detached and sped away. The transmission from the Pathfinder team. Not that it mattered. Gella and Orin headed back to the cockpit, where she sat down and let him dress her wound.

"Pathfinder team, come in. This is Jedi Gella Nattai. The attack on us is over, but our engines are disabled."

"We just saw them fly off. Didn't stop them. Boy, were they in a hurry! You all ready for your Republic news now?"

"Yes, yes. What is it?" Orin groaned.

"Here you go. Direct from Chancellor Greylark."

A holo of Chancellor Greylark wearing a headdress encrusted with beads and silk, spoke.

"Jedi Master Darhga and Gella Nattai. It has come to my attention that you have gone to speak to my son, Axel Greylark. Chancellor Mollo and I held a discussion with regard to releasing Axel to a low-security hold for rehabilitation, the one condition being that we both agreed. Chancellor Mollo favors this lower-level release plan." She took a breath. "I, however, do not."

The blood drained out of Gella's face, and Orin's shocked expression mirrored hers.

"I believe in second chances, and for my son to reenter society after a significant rehabilitation. However, I also believe he must pay his dues and complete his sentence under the original incarceration terms. It is my understanding that another transmission was sent to Pipyyr stating that both chancellors agreed to his release. This message is a fabrication. We are uncertain as to its source. In this case, the final decision between both chancellors was intercepted and altered. The message I am delivering now has been given directly to Pathfinder teams Seventy-one-Beenine and Twenty-one-Seetoo, to be hand-delivered to Pipyyr's penitentiary and to you, Orin Darhga and Gella Nattai. The warden informed us that you were handling the transfer. You are ordered to immediately return Axel Greylark back to Pipyyr."

The holo blinked off.

"Oh, Orin. What have I done?" Gella said.

Chapter Eight

PALACE HOSPITAL, THE ROOK, E'RONOH

Xiri stood outside the door of the E'roni palace hospital. It was a small wing, only intended for royalty and high-ranking personnel. Inside were several patients, all from the recent fight with Binnot and Goi. A few guards had already died from the chemical that Binnot had released. In a lone bed by a window, Phan-tu was still unconscious, surrounded by several attendants. His chest was bound with bandages over his stab wound. She caught a glimpse of them cleansing off the leg that had been sprayed with the chemical. She saw a lot of red, oozing flesh but refused to turn her face away.

It was a shock to see him injured. Until now, they were two married people trying to do the impossible by bringing their planets together. She'd always had a clear vision of what was right for E'ronoh and her people. She'd also felt like being apart from him so soon after their wedding had them drifting back to the people they were before they'd even met. But seeing Phan-tu like this, she suddenly could not fathom doing any of it without him.

"Can I go to him?" Xiri asked when the royal head physician walked by, a woman wearing yellow robes.

"Yes. We've finally neutralized all of the phyteric acid from the attack, so you should be safe around him as well." She paused and looked at Xiri's leg. "How is your own wound, Princess?"

"Healing fine, thank you. The neutralizing compound is working wonderfully."

Xiri went through the door, and the attendants around Phan-tu bowed and departed. Phan-tu was deep asleep. Up close, Xiri for the first time noticed the bruise on his jaw, and how his bare chest was rising and falling faster than she would have liked to see. He was uncomfortable, even while unconscious. Blood seeped through the bandage covering his chest wound, and a flower-shaped bell was hovering near his face, delivering oxygen.

She slipped her hand into his. Her mind went to the fight with Binnot. How Phan-tu had jumped right in, despite the fact that he wasn't nearly the fighter Xiri was. She was so used to being the strong one, the one who had been raised to hold up her fists to anyone since she was a child. Even against her father. Such was the way for the children of E'ronoh. Phan-tu had pushed her to safety and saved her from being stabbed in the heart.

His hand was warm, dry, but didn't squeeze back. Xiri's eyes smarted and she took a deep breath. Crying would do nothing to heal him.

"Daughter."

Xiri turned around to see her aged father in his robes, watching them. The Monarch was accompanied by Chancellor Mollo. Father's face was always set in a stern expression, but this was more from the years that had carved lines and pulled down his jowls. She always knew what he was really thinking by looking into those sea-glass eyes of his—eyes that matched the Erasmus Sea on Eiram, though she had never said this out loud, for fear of angering him.

"My medical team informs me that he will recover well. He's in an induced sleep, to speed the healing," the Monarch said.

Xiri nodded, afraid that if she spoke her voice would break. She refused to let anyone hear that.

"And I have news," Chancellor Mollo said, his tentacles waving optimistically. "Jedi Char-Ryl-Roy and Enya Keen are planning on going directly to Dalna on a diplomatic mission to speak with the Path of the Open Hand. What that survivor, Goi, said before he died—it was clear that they crafted this biological weapon to reignite all-out war. They created or purchased those vats of klytobacter. I've discussed it with Queen Adrialla. In Phan-tu's stead, she is looking to send a representative from Eiram."

The Monarch put his hand on Xiri's shoulder. "Given Eiram's recent poor choice of Ambassador Cerox, I would like you to represent us, Xiri."

"I can't leave Phan-tu, Father."

"Aside from your affection—" He halted, as if admitting the existence of affection pained him somehow. "—you cannot help him."

"And I will remain here," Chancellor Mollo said. The Monarch had turned away to an attendant, and the chancellor spoke low to Xiri. "It's quite bad, Xiri. Both sides are sustaining heavy damage and it's only getting worse. Talk between the royal houses is nonexistent. I must keep shuttling between E'ronoh and Eiram to do what I can." The Monarch returned to the conversation, and Chancellor Mollo shifted to an optimistic expression. "I am negotiating the repair of the mutual communications buoy right now. It will also help improve my conversations with Chancellor Greylark."

"When was the last time you spoke to her directly?" Xiri asked.

"Not since before the war was rekindled. I'm not even sure she fully knows how turbulent it has become. It's very frustrating." He bowed to both of them. "Good luck, Princess. Your Highness."

She nodded. Chancellor Mollo went back to one of the advisory rooms. Xiri walked out with her father, and before they parted ways, she touched his sleeve.

"Father. Many have said that they believe the Jedi were responsible for the failed talks on Jedha. I have been working with Jedi Roy and Keen and I truly believe they are trying to stop this war. What say you?"

He was quiet for some time. "It is difficult for me to believe that the Jedi are purely altruistic and offer themselves to us to forge a peace, with nothing asked in return. If you have lived long enough, you will understand that no such creature exists that is so good-hearted."

"I am not perfect, Father. Nor is Phan-tu, nor are you. But we love our peoples. And we want there to be more good than evil in this galaxy. I believe the Jedi are trying to bring harmony to places of discord. Can you not sense that?"

"I need information, daughter. Bring me information. The Republic wants a piece of us, and I believe the Jedi do, too. If the Path is pulling the levers in our planet's fate, I must know. What I trust, my daughter, is you. Be safe, and remember your training." He paused, as if to embrace her, but walked away instead. Xiri watched him depart down the corridor of bright, reddish marble, walls that had always appeared to her as magnificent and imposing.

Now, as her father's small figure walked away, it appeared he was surrounded by walls of blood.

Xiri quickly went to the hangar where the Jedi were waiting. A shuttle from Eiram was coming in at a distance. She stood behind Char-Ryl-Roy and Enya, who were watching carefully. Enya clutched a tangle of wires in her hand, part of her broken droid.

"Is that the Eirami representative who will be accompanying us?" Enya asked.

"I believe so," Char-Ryl-Roy said. "A new one. The Eirami ambassador wreaked havoc on Jedha."

"I heard. Bringing enforcer droids to a peace talk isn't exactly peaceful," Enya said. "Let's hope this one is skilled in speaking with the Path."

"Until now, I was thinking of the Path as a simple folk with a single-minded devotion to keeping the Force unusable for anyone," Char-Ryl-Roy said.

"*The Force must be free* is what they say, I believe, Master," Enya corrected him.

"Yes. That is what they say. But saying no one should use the Force in any way also refuses its very existence. We cannot help that the Force flows through all of us, alive and inanimate. It is no possession that can be pushed away."

The small Eirami shuttle entered the hangar. The ship was smooth and curved, not unlike some of the water creatures that swam in the Eirami seas. There was some wear at the edges of the seams. The boarding ramp lowered, and a figure in robes of deep blue and azure descended, flanked by half a dozen guards.

Xiri walked forward, but when her guards began to walk at her sides, she raised her hand. "No, I'd like to meet her alone." They paused as she continued forward. She bowed before the Eirami woman.

"Ambassador. I am Captain Xiri A'lbaran, Daughter of Thylefire. I am grateful that you can join our delegation to Dalna."

The figure had a large veil obscuring the face, but Xiri could see a mouth pulled into a scowl.

"I am Toworn Chordata. I regret to inform you that no ambassador from Eiram will be accompanying you."

Xiri was stunned into silence for several seconds. "But I thought—you—there's no ambassador?"

"Well, no. I am only an ambassador in training. In fact, one of my first jobs is to deliver this message to you." She bowed graciously.

"That's not helpful!" Xiri blurted out. "Doesn't Queen Adrialla think this is worth pursuing?"

"She does, but unfortunately we have been unable to procure a suitable replacement under such short notice."

She bowed low again, and turned around to return to the ship.

Xiri clenched her fists. "I can't believe it. We can't do this alone. The whole point is to be a united front!"

Master Roy and Jedi Keen came up to her. "What do we do now?" Enya asked.

"We still have to go," Xiri said. "I don't care if there's no ambassador. E'ronoh needs to defend its name. We need to know about Binnot and Goi. Someone is putting Eiram at risk. I say we continue."

"We're with you, Xiri," Master Roy said.

Enya nodded in agreement. "Let's do this."

They had decided previously that neither party would bring a large security detail—the two Jedi and Xiri were already formidable in their own way. Xiri, after all, was a fairly lethal soldier. So now it was only the three of them. Anyway, a large number of guards wouldn't show that they came in good faith to have a diplomatic discussion.

On board the *Andesine,* a midsized cruiser, Enya had settled the pieces of her broken droid in a corner of the large common area where meals and meetings were to be taken. It took several more hours of preparing the ship before they could leave. It was more spacious than what Enya and Master Roy usually flew with, but for Xiri, it was more than adequate. She only wished it could maneuver like the starfighters she was used to. But she triple-checked their fuel, shields, and ion cannons to be sure they could defend themselves if anything came up.

They took off from E'ronoh without any fanfare, as Xiri liked it. They passed by a tiny, burnt communications buoy—or what was left of it. No actual work was being done on the buoy. Several damaged ships were adrift, being attended to by repair ships. It was a momentary quiet in the barrage of fire, so they took advantage of it as they sped toward the hyperlane. If only the planets could stop arguing for a moment and let Chancellor Mollo help, the communications buoys could be fixed quickly. If only. Communication could end this war, if done right. Xiri thought of Phan-tu lying in his bed, and commed the hospital wing at the palace for a final check-in before messages would likely be cut off during their travels.

"How is Phan-tu?" she asked the head physician.

"He's no longer sedated and is resting. I'm about to examine him again right now. Oh, he's been moved to private quarters. We had some juvan on hand to help with the chest wound. We need more." There was a sigh. "I do hope your trip goes well, Princess. Our people need good news."

"I hope the trip goes well, too. Thank you for caring for Phan-tu."

Enya popped her head into the cockpit. "Hey! We're about to jump to hyperspace, right?"

"Yes," Xiri said, trying to erase the worry from her voice.

"Mind if I plug Teegee into the hyperdrive? I want him to learn by watching. It might refresh some of his basic astromech programming."

"Sure." Enya brought the scuffed and old astromech into the cockpit. The astromech's dome was now attached to his body, with multiple wires hanging from his leg sockets in clumps. The paint had worn off several places, giving 4VO-TG a patchwork look. She plugged one of the dome wires into a port in the cockpit. The green lights on the droid blinked, and Teegee beeped a few times.

"Hi, Teegee. It's very nice to meet you, too," Xiri said, smiling.

The droid whined slightly. "No, Teegee. You don't need to do anything right now," Xiri said. "Pretty eager to prove himself, I see."

Enya smiled. "Well, I did fish him out of a rubble pile. He's got issues."

Xiri turned back to the navigation console. "Okay, coordinates are locked in. Entering hyperspace. We should be in there for about three hours, before exiting and traveling to the next node."

The ship's viewports showed distant stars turning to streaks before they settled into the amorphous light of the hyperlane. Xiri sighed. The Jedi both probably had better ambassadorial skills than Xiri did. She was trained as a pilot, and had learned how to live with the whims and flaring tempers of her father. Though she had received training in diplomacy, it was not her strength. She wished Phan-tu was here. After all, that was the point of the marriage, wasn't it? To work together? It wasn't his fault, but now she was alone.

She hadn't realized it, but a few hours had flown by when Master Char-Ryl-Roy entered the cockpit. Xiri let out a deep breath.

"That's a big sigh for only the beginning of a trip," Master Char-Ryl-Roy said as he sat in the copilot's chair. He stretched and scratched his beard.

Xiri smiled. "I didn't realize I had sighed."

"I practically heard it from the other side of the ship," the Cerean Jedi said.

"I guess I'm worried," Xiri admitted.

"As am I. You go first."

"About Phan-tu," Xiri said. "I wish I could be there while he recovers. And I have the strangest feeling already that this trip is not going to go well. What about you?"

"I have sensed a lot of strife since before you were married," Master Roy said. "With Binnot Ullo showing up, and the peace treaty on Jedha disintegrating into a huge battle—it seems like plans have come to fruition. The question is how far back the roots go to make this all happen."

"Yes," Xiri agreed.

"As well as whether similar things are happening in other systems. Who else could the Path be manipulating, and to what end? You know what they say about space roaches?"

Xiri smirked. "For every one you see, there are a million you don't. So might as well torch your ship."

Char-Ryl-Roy tried not to laugh. "Yes, that saying. Except for the part about burning your ship to the ground."

"Which means the Path may have a lot to conceal when we talk to them. If they let us talk to them."

Char-Ryl-Roy nodded in agreement, and they went into the common area of the ship to relax a little, where Enya had laid out 4VO-TG's legs and body and was working on the joints.

Xiri's wrist comlink buzzed, and Phan-tu's voice said, "It's me."

"Hey! How are you? How are you getting through to us? Did they get the communications buoy fixed?"

"Oh. Must have, yes."

"Are you feeling better?" Xiri asked. "Are you back on Eiram?"

"Definitely feeling better. I'm getting rest. So," Phan-tu said, clearing his throat. "How do you plan on opening a conversation with the Path?"

"I'd been hoping to ask the ambassador for pointers," Xiri said. "I suppose . . . start by not accusing? And shooting at stuff?"

"In the ambassador training I had, I learned a few lessons that stuck with me. It's not unlike encountering the enemy on your starship. There are times you are aggressive, and times you're not. Times to evade, and times to lie low and gather information."

"I never thought about it that way," Xiri said.

"Other times, it's remembering the basics. Find common ground. Come back to it often. Truly try to see their point of view. And compromise." Phan-tu made a funny noise. "Oof. I need to rest. I'll talk to you later."

"Okay. Thanks, Phan-tu."

Xiri looked over at Master Roy, who smiled.

"It's good advice."

"Not to shoot first and ask questions later?" Xiri said, smirking. "This is going to be a disaster."

"That's terribly pessimistic of you. You're the E'roni representative . . . and I guess the Eirami representative, too. Try to see the bright side of things," Enya said brightly, waving a bitdriver.

Xiri plastered a sugary, fake smile on her face. "Well, at least we haven't crashed and burned yet!"

Chapter Nine

Gella couldn't believe what had happened.

Even after she and Orin abandoned the *Eventide* and boarded the Pathfinder team 71-B9's ship, she was still in a daze. She barely registered the pain from the blaster wound to her shoulder as the Pathfinder medic dressed it with a healing salve and bandaged it. Sitting in a supply room adorned with a wall full of random spare communications buoy parts, Gella had recorded a message to Chancellor Greylark already, and now Orin was adding to it before sending it out.

Axel had played her again, and she couldn't forgive herself. She thought she had been careful. On Pipyyr, he had seemed so sick. Even the medics had documented that he was ill. He had been so contrite. And Gella was no youngling—she was well trained in the Force. She had kept him at arm's distance, and still, he had fooled her.

Orin stepped into the supply room, leaning against the wall.

"Message is sent." He crossed his arms. "You okay?"

Gella touched her bandaged shoulder. "It's not that bad. I'll be fine."

"I wasn't talking about your shoulder."

Gella looked up after a long while and met Orin's blue eyes. "I can't believe he lied to me like that. And I completely fell for it."

Orin sat down on a ledge next to her. "Perhaps he wasn't lying."

She shook her head. "You're just trying to make me feel better. We both know he was."

"I don't think it's that obvious," Orin said. "Perhaps he was sorry—truly sorry for hurting you. Some who are skilled in being deceptive all their lives can hide behind true feelings to get their way. I suspect Axel did this." He rubbed his beard for some time, before murmuring, "You know, when Binnot showed up, Axel looked genuinely surprised. Like he had no idea that there was a plan to rescue him."

Gella concentrated on the memory of him, the changing expressions on his face. "By the stars," she whispered. "I think you're right. And yet, when it came to the decision, he chose what was best for Axel, didn't he? Rather quickly, I might add."

There, in that moment. That was where Axel had a chance to do the right thing. And he turned away from whatever goodness she ever saw in him, yet again. Sometimes it seemed like Axel was still a wounded teenager, grasping for things to make him feel settled in a terribly unsettling galaxy.

"Yes," Orin said. "And now he's a fugitive."

They were interrupted by a tall, lanky human wearing work clothing with an absurd amount of pockets. The clothes were too short for his arms and legs, and his hair was a mass of light-brown curls. He had to duck to speak to them in the supply room.

"Heyoo, Jedi DarkEye, and Jedi Natty. We hope you are making yourself comfortable. It is an honor to have you here."

"We appreciate the help. It's Kenny, right?" Orin said.

"Yes. Kenny of the Kenny Night Clan. Communications for Pathfinder team Seventy-one-Beenine." He bowed formally, which made his elbows stick out more than they already were.

"He's lying." A female Yarkoran entered the room, wearing a similar outfit to Kenny's, only the vast majority of her pockets had been torn off, leaving a ghostly patchwork of threads everywhere. She had a purple root vegetable in her hand with chew marks on it. "There is no such thing as the Kenny Night Clan, he made that up about an hour ago so he'd sound more important. I'm Piti, the pilot and navigator."

Kenny seemed not to mind that his genealogical cover was blown. In fact, he hardly even flinched at the correction. It must be a common occurrence, Gella thought.

"Isn't there usually a Jedi or two on your Pathfinder team?" Orin asked.

"Yes, but we split up with the Jedi and Padawan on our team to deliver this message since it was so urgent," the Yarkoran said.

"It's important we don't lose Axel Greylark," Gella said, her voice rising.

"We won't. The warden told me that he's got a tracker on him. It's in his clothing and right now, it's working," Orin said.

"Piti. That ship we're following . . . Can you tell where it's going?" Gella asked.

"Yes," Piti answered, waving her purple carrot. "It appears they are headed to Jedha."

Gella frowned. "Jedha?"

"Yep. Once we get an idea of where they're landing, we'll drop you off and be on our way."

Piti had to drag Kenny away to leave the two Jedi alone to think.

"Why would Axel go to Jedha? And who was that Mirialan who was with him? Binnot. Wasn't that his name?" Orin said.

"Yes. Jedha's not a great place to disappear. But considering what Creighton said about the battle there, it could be a chaotic place right now."

"But Gella," Orin said. "You can't go looking for him in your present state."

Gella looked down at her Jedi robes. They were the color of wheat, with a brown sash and brown boots. "I don't need to get dressed up to fight Axel."

"That is not what I meant. Although—you would look spectacular with a pair of Corellian boots. Or even a cute pet sheffi on your shoulder. But I digress. I mean—you're not in the right mindset right now. It's like when we first went to Pipyyr. You carried anger with you, though most wouldn't notice it. And the first thing in your mind is the inclination to fight him."

"Orin, he nearly killed us!" Gella said, exasperated.

"You're not focused. Or rather, you're focused on appeasing your betrayal. A fight is not what is needed. At least, not right now."

Orin was right. Gella's mind was a jumble, all glued together in an inextricable morass of frustration and betrayal. Anger, too. She wished she were inside a temple, water trickling nearby to ground her, to remind her about the flow of the Force. If only she could have a week, or a month, to meditate and concentrate. If she could only seek a way forward that harmonized with the Force. But she had no time.

Sitting before Orin, she closed her eyes. She recalled a lesson from when she was a youngling. She was so teachable then, so willing to acknowledge the gaps in her knowledge and skills. She felt the Force, flowing through and around her. Gella let her mind sink deeply into the darkness behind her closed eyes. She gently pried herself away from her fiery emotions, the facts, and saw herself sitting in the center of them—not divorced from them, but acknowledging her relationship to them, a complex orb with connections that thrummed like living things.

She opened her eyes. Orin caught her eye, and he tipped his head to the side.

"Well done, Gella. I sense the order collecting within your mind. What would you like to do now?"

"I would like answers," she said, in a measured voice. "From Axel. We'll follow him at a distance, gather information. We must find out why the original transmission to Pipyyr was wrong, and how it was corrupted. We'll inform the Jedi Council and anyone near Jedha to spread the word about what's happened." She raised an eyebrow. "And I'd like to get my lightsaber back."

"Excellent. I've already sent messages updating them. But I'll ask

Kenny to send out a second wave of transmissions in all directions regarding the news about his escape. And we'll follow him to Jedha."

"I appreciate your guidance, Orin. And your leadership."

Orin nodded and left. Gella said under her breath, calm as a windless lake, "And *then* I'll fight him."

ABOARD THE PIRATE CARGO SHIP, HYPERSPACE

"Are we being followed?"

Axel Greylark had his feet up on a table with a Shah-tezh board. He had knocked over the Counselor and the Beast pieces, and was entertaining himself by tossing the Imperator piece up in the air and snatching it repeatedly.

"What do you think?" Binnot Ullo was sitting across from him. He was examining an elbow-length glove on his right arm. As he flexed each finger, tiny needles protruded from the fingertips and palm of the poison glove. He looked at the slim vials in the sleeve that furnished the poisons. He removed one and checked that it was full. "Of course someone's following us. There was a Pathfinder ship very close by. I'm sure they used their Force powers to force the crew into following us."

"You said *force* twice," Axel said, tossing the piece again.

"I meant to."

QN-1 flew into the room and buzzed a little near Axel. He looked at his droid, grinned at it, and it whizzed away. But not quick enough to escape Binnot, who shot out his ungloved hand and captured the droid by one of its antennas. QN-1 bleeped in dismay.

"Binnot. I know you don't like droids, but this is not one that needs to be a target of your wrath. Let Quin go."

"Sorry. Old habit." He let go of the small droid, who whined in relief and returned to Axel, hovering close for safety. "I never grew up with droids on Dalna. We did everything by our own hands. I only sort of hate them. Technology disconnected from the life is disconnected from the Force—so the Path says."

"Quin feels alive to me," Axel said.

Binnot said nothing, only giving the small droid a sideways glance. For a moment, he almost thought Binnot's glance was one of jealousy, rather than disdain.

Axel dropped his Shah-tezh piece and put his hands behind his head, slumping deeper into the chair behind him. "This is definitely better than my jail cell on Pipyyr. Definitely worse than my residence on Coruscant."

"You're going to have to stop making comparisons if you want to succeed within the Path. Other things, too."

"I'm willing to do a lot for the Path, if it can do a lot for me," Axel said, a sly grin on his face.

Binnot stopped examining his poison glove and leaned forward. "For example, don't ever, ever, ever admit things like that out loud."

Axel's grin disappeared. He sat up straight, and looked left and right. Though they were alone, the other muscle that Binnot had brought to rescue him were nearby, no doubt.

"There you go again, always teaching me things."

"I'm not your guardian, Axel," Binnot said.

Binnot was more than that. They'd first met on Hynestia when his mother was making Republic connections there. Axel quenched his boredom by wandering around the hot springs and caves, slipping away from the watchful eye of her security detail. Binnot was a similar age, in that twilight between childhood and young adulthood. He had traveled there with the Path, evangelizing the message and bringing new followers to Dalna. They'd spent a whole afternoon making it a game to evade his guards—the most pure joy and exhilaration that Axel had ever experienced in his whole life. After that day, whenever there was a chance, through scattered messages, he'd meet Binnot on other planets where his mother's work happened to cross routes with Binnot and the Path.

Binnot was a kind of friend he'd never had. Kids on Coruscant always had treated Axel oddly, like he was a prize to be paraded around, or a means to something they wanted. With Binnot, there was none of that. Only the mutual warmth of two young people growing up too fast in a galaxy that wanted them to be objects of usefulness. They had whispered to each other back then about wanting greater things. To be greater people that surpassed a famous name or being part of a sea of believers in the Path. But as they traversed through adulthood, the Path solidified its hold on Binnot, and Axel continued listening to anything Binnot said. Axel already had a heart hardened against the Jedi. Binnot had made sure it stayed that way, and Axel was just fine with that.

"I know, Binnot," Axel said. "You're not my guardian." He meant more to Axel than that, which was the truth. "Still. The whole time things unfolded on Eiram and E'ronoh, before I went to jail, I always felt like somehow you were keeping an eye on me."

Binnot leaned closer, his eyes meeting Axel's. "And yet you still failed in your task to deliver that poison to the Mother. I had to find another to use in my glove."

Axel froze. He opened his mouth to apologize, but nothing came out. Perhaps an apology might somehow make Binnot's statement even more true. Or was Binnot looking for tear-dripping remorse and forgiveness? Or strength?

"What was it?" Binnot said. "Did that Jedi get inside your mind?" He stretched out his poison glove, a tiny drop of liquid glistening at one of the needle tips. "They're a little too good at that."

"Yeah," Axel said. "Very good, unfortunately." He was grateful that Binnot had perhaps inadvertently explained Axel's choice to turn away from the original plan. He tried to relax. Binnot tossed a game piece, the Disciple, at Axel. Axel reached to catch it midair, then placed it gently on the board.

"You disappointed me, Axel," Binnot said. "Disappointed the Mother."

"And yet you rescued me," Axel said.

"It's only a rescue if you survive," Binnot said. "If you can't right your wrongs, then no one can help you anymore. You'll be worse off than in that Republic prison cell. Or you'll be dead." He crossed his legs and placed his gloved hand casually on the table before him.

Axel looked at Binnot's hand. It was only centimeters away from his own bare hand, holding on to the game piece.

Enough. He couldn't keep playing it cool anymore.

"I'm sorry," Axel said, exhaling after the words left him. "Things got complicated. I don't like to let people down. That much is true. But I'm here now, and I want to be of use to the Path. You've taught me a lot, Binnot. There's more I can do if I can have another chance."

Binnot just watched him. He drummed the fingers of his bare hand. "You've got skills, Axel. You know how to stretch your good name to get you into places a person like me couldn't get a toe in. And you're an absolutely beautiful liar." Binnot leaned back, the dim light of the cabin making his pale-green skin even greener. "But you don't know how to navigate the Path."

"Then tell me how," Axel said, trying to keep the slight desperation out of his voice.

"You have to use what you have, what no one else has. It's an asset."

"I don't see what my good looks have to do with anything," Axel joked.

"Axel," Binnot said quietly. He leaned in over the Shah-tezh board. "I'm serious."

Axel's face lost its mirth. "Okay."

"You have to be smart. Useful. In every way. I've learned how to become every person that the Mother needs me to be. A farmer. A thief. A spy. A negotiator. A helpless transporter victimized by pirates. A survivor." He held up his glove and pointed it at QN-1. The small droid shook in the air. "I've got a droid poison, you know. A type of electroshock that causes an irreversible malfunction that incapacitates the entire behavioral circuitry matrix."

Axel sat up straighter in his chair. "Binnot," he began. He was sweating now at the thought of losing QN-1 again. It had been so painful to see his droid destroyed once.

Binnot withdrew his hand and stood up. He extended his fingers, which sheathed the needles back into the glove, and then placed the gloved hand on Axel's shoulder. All he would have to do to kill Axel was to squeeze. Axel knew Binnot was devoted to the Path and to the Mother. In fact, it was likely this devotion that controlled those deadly little gloved needles. Surely, though, their friendship had weight. He was counting on it.

Axel stayed motionless nevertheless, and Binnot laughed. He withdrew his hand from Axel's shoulder and sat back down. "And I've been other things, too. I am an extension of her hand."

"I can be more, Binnot. You know this." Axel had relaxed again, but he couldn't undo the tension in his shoulders. He felt ready to spring to action. Or his own defense.

"I know you, Axel. You're tired of just being a name. Only someone's son. Not a person. You don't have to be known as a negative balance sheet for what you owe everyone in the galaxy," Binnot said. "You don't have to owe anyone anymore."

"I'm ready to prove myself. I went to jail, after all. Faked an illness that fooled even the Jedi."

"Did you? Add that to your list of colorful lies!" Binnot said, clapping his hands.

"As a kid, it came in handy, being able to make myself ill on cue. It took years to train my body to fool the doctors and the monitors. The shakes, or the vomiting, or the high heart rates. It got me out of so many events and obligations my mother tried to drag me to. Sympathy is a powerful card to be played. I was hoping it would get me transferred to an easier life." One way or another, Axel was always going to get himself off Pipyyr. Now he had to stay alive.

"Yes," Binnot said. "Though it was our fake transmission that really got you out. It's a good thing we have our people in this sector, keeping an eye out for the Mother. But you did score sympathy points with those Jedi, that's for sure."

He had. He thought of Gella with a guilt he couldn't squash down. She had watched him with worry when he was retching, or whispered to Orin about a transfer when she thought he couldn't hear.

"But to what end? Did you even have an endgame with the Jedi? Remember what the Mother told you about trusting them. You play your cards wrong all the time, Axel. Let me guide you this time."

"What's our next move, then?" Axel asked, trying to sound relaxed. "What does the Mother really want from me? To be part of the Path?"

"Perhaps. Perhaps she's just angry, and wants to tell you to your face. She likes her plans to be successful, and . . . tidy."

Meaning, Axel was a mess that needed cleaning up.

"I believe the Mother thinks you can be a larger asset to her," Binnot went on. "More power than you could have ever imagined. More than Kyong Greylark and Orlen Mollo, combined. The Mother has her hands full. She needs a bona fide ally within the Republic." Binnot leaned closer, his hand grasping the Shah-tezh figure of the Imperator on Axel's side, a bent figure in a hood. He made as if to crush the figure, but instead placed it on the board in a position where it could not be cornered by the Knight or the Counselor. "You could make this happen. What say you? Who do you want to be, Axel?"

His mother had asked the same thing, so long ago. He remembered that day so vividly that he could practically smell the Coruscant rain hitting the ground. His mother had dragged him hours away from home, and now they were standing before a medical pavilion that sparkled with newness. His mother was in her usual regalia, a pearlescent gown with her jadeite headdress and bell sleeves so large, she looked like she might fly away in them. She was an inky blemish on the pale-gray rain and mist around them at the entrance to the pavilion.

"I'm hungry," Axel had said, pulling his hand away from his mother.

"You're not starving." She gave him a withering look. "This isn't about your comfort, Axel. It's not about you. It's about who you want to be. It is about duty."

Axel had pulled at his collar, and she gave him another severe glance that made him freeze in place. He instead daydreamed of running races in his speeder over the valley gardens near the enormous building where he lived. He would soon have an expansive dinner with iced honey cakes, rich breads, and roasted fowl, enough to feed three Axels. He'd be out of here soon.

But his mother brought him before several patients who were there to thank the Greylarks for their generous work in creating the pavilion. Axel bowed and shook hands with children his age who were blind, awaiting their new cybernetic eyes but still showing scarred sockets barely covered with a light gauze bandage. He saw a radiation blight in a family still recovering from when their mine exploded on a nearby moon. And more. So many stories of desperation, some coming from children even younger than Axel. Now they were here to spread the word of the medical opportunities on Coruscant. Axel felt useless in comparison, with his perfect clothing, his perfect hair, his perfect mother. None of the praise belonged to him, and somehow, even in the face of so much illness and despair, he was furious. Face-to-face with a little girl who was missing three limbs and sitting in a hover chair, he had spoken loudly to no one in particular.

"I am tired, and I should like to go home."

Home he did go, shortly after. The second they arrived at their grand residence, his mother had chided him severely.

"Where is your sympathy, Axel?"

Axel had spun around in their fine foyer, shining with cut Jelucani fogstone and glistening curtains painstakingly embroidered by ancient artisans on Tenoo. Shuttles and carriers whizzed by at a distance outside their windows. He was angry, angry to have to squeeze his heart on command. He could not.

"Where is yours, Mother?"

She had raised her hand for a moment, and put it down. Her face went from ire to disappointment. "You're right, Axel. This is my failure."

At first he was triumphant. He had won the argument. But right now, sitting in front of Binnot, having escaped prison, having thought he had left his mother's penetrating and judgmental stares behind for the rest of his life, he finally understood that he had never won that argument at all.

This is my failure.

Axel. Axel was her failure.

"What say you, friend? My brother?" Binnot hadn't moved at all, still leaning over the Shah-tezh board, awaiting an answer.

Axel had already worked with the Path and had thought he'd burned that bridge. With his escape, any reconciliation with his mother was in ashes. Gella would despise him more than ever. He told himself that in this new life, he would not care for such sentiments. Still, the guilt simmered in the back of his heart. But his mind knew this: The second he went with Binnot and turned away from Gella, he'd made an irreversible choice.

He still had other choices. Or did he? If the Path wanted him dead, Binnot wouldn't have come for him. That bridge was crumbling, but not completely destroyed.

This time, he'd succeed. No regrets, no hesitation, no judgment from anyone.

"I'm ready, Binnot. I want to be good at everything, like you. I'll do whatever it takes to change my fate." He rubbed his forehead. "My mother prepared me to be a diplomat. Prepared me poorly. I'll learn how to survive in a way she never thought I would need. She is so far removed from everything true and real in this galaxy, she probably can't even put her own shoes on anymore."

"Oh, you're too tarnished to be a diplomat. But it doesn't mean you can't move pieces on the board. Now, don't worry about the grime and grind of the day-to-day. You weren't born for that, and your place in the Path will be one that is far more important. You'll see."

"Even after the failure on Eiram and E'ronoh?" Axel said.

"Eiram and E'ronoh are back at war. The goal has been achieved. The Mother will enrich her coffers to keep the Path healthy and well supplied. If anything, what you did showed the galaxy that the Jedi and the Republic are absolute fools and even liars. They promise to broker peace, and what do they deliver? More war and more pain and more suffering. In the meantime, the Mother and the Path shall thrive in the chaos."

My chaos, the Mother called him. It was time to live up to the name and be what she wanted him to be. He would still be imprisoned without her, and his survival meant making himself useful.

"As will I," Axel said firmly. "What about the Herald?"

"That's for the Mother to decide. He's a true believer. But she is very unhappy with how things unfolded on Jedha. The battle certainly raged in her favor, but the way the Herald incited the riot—it was far less calculated and controlled than she wished. He had acted without her, on pure emotion kindled by Path sentiment."

"But isn't Path sentiment important to her?" Axel asked.

"The mind and the heart are equally important, but the Path's place in the galaxy cannot be achieved by sentiment alone. The Mother has the vision and the mind for our future. She is our leader, once and for all," said Binnot.

"What will we do on Jedha?" Axel asked as QN-1 reappeared and safely hovered behind Axel's shoulder.

"It's a stepping-stone. No one will look for us there, and we can easily change ships. And these nuisance Jedi will be lost in a sea of Force-lovers. Fools. The Force isn't to be loved, or hated, used or abused. They have no idea how to treat it as anything but a possession." He raised his eyebrows at a sudden thought. "Perhaps we may even have a chance to kill that Jedi who put you in jail."

"Yes," he said. He didn't love the idea of killing Gella, and he knew Binnot could tell.

"Well, if we encounter her again, we'll make sure you get your revenge. Her death would be your glory. It would be quite the turnaround for you, would it not?"

Axel smiled and raised his drink to his lips. He had abandoned his

Imperator playing piece, lying prone on the table. Binnot changed the subject to something regarding droids and rice and the San Tekka clan. How the Leveler—a precious new weapon that Binnot promised Axel would soon see for himself—would strengthen their fight against the Jedi. How they would harvest more bioweapons against Eiram, and create more lethal ones against E'ronoh that could scorch the land so badly that the water shortage would be even more devastating. Weapons would exacerbate the paranoia of each planet. And they were always the best tools for negotiating, after all. Kindness never changed wars; fear did. They would tip the war into a new balance, growing their wealth and power. The Path would be unstoppable.

Binnot hadn't noticed that Axel wasn't smiling anymore. Because Axel was too busy trying to extricate the thought of killing Gella Nattai from his mind.

Chapter Ten

GREYLARK RESIDENCE, CORUSCANT

It was late, and the work was never-ending for Chancellor Greylark.

More Pathfinder ships that needed to be approved for release in the Outer Rim. Talks regarding trade disputes between Castell and Shulstine, on the Perlemian Trade Route. Essential Coruscant meetings that seemed to increase in number no matter how many people she delegated to assist her.

Kyong's human assistant, Lia, was carefully removing the chancellor's headdress as Kyong sat before her dressing mirror in her bedroom suite. The headdress was heavy, and Kyong reflexively massaged her neck when her skull had been freed of its weight. The heavy earrings of Eirami pearls were removed, along with the collarette of fire amethysts.

A polished silver protocol droid, C-04L, came in with a steaming cup of floral tea on a tray and set it down before her.

"Chancellor," C-04L said, "I know you asked not to be disturbed at your bedtime. But there is an urgent incoming message."

"Can't it wait, Fourell?" she asked the droid. She was wiping off her makeup with a soft cloth. Looking down at the cloth afterward, the smudge of red and black makeup made it look as if she'd wiped off a bloody scowl.

"But it's from Pipyyr, Chancellor. A recorded transmission."

Kyong's heart fell in her chest. "Very well." She waved off her attendant and C-04L. "I'd like to take this in private, please."

They left her, and she stood in her dressing robe and sat on the edge of her circular bed. There was a small communications console at her bedside table. She pressed the button with her hands, bare of rings.

The holoimage of Jedi Gella Nattai appeared, her face serious.

"Chancellor Greylark," Gella Nattai said. "We have grave news. Your direct message about Axel Greylark was received, delivered personally by Pathfinder team Seventy-one-Beenine. We were accompanying Axel to the rehabilitation facility near Coruscant, under the false orders received by the prison on Pipyyr." She paused, her eyes flicking downward for a second. "It was my mistake to not verify the message. My judgment was clouded after seeing Axel apparently ill, which he wasn't. Before we could receive the message about the falsified order, our ship was attacked by what we believed to be pirates. Only too late did we realize the ship belonged to the Path of the Open Hand." She took a deep breath. "Axel Greylark has escaped."

"What?" Kyong growled, her hands grabbing fistfuls of the silken coverlet on her bed. "*What?*" she actually yelled. Kyong Greylark had not raised her voice to that level of loudness since she gave birth to Axel. It was a good thing this wasn't a live transmission.

Jedi Nattai's image was replaced with an unfamiliar Jedi. Kyong had not met him before, and was somewhat taken aback by his messy, ruddy hair and bushy beard. He had a mischievous expression, as if he were on the verge of saying something inappropriate.

"This is Jedi Master Orin Darhga. I will be accompanying Gella Nattai as we pursue Axel Greylark. He appears to be heading for Jedha, and we will stay hidden while we try to ascertain his contacts and plan. He seemed rather chummy with one of the Path members, a Mirialan male. Binnot, was the only name we caught. Do you know anything about him? Looked as if they'd known each other since they were in nappies. In any case, we'll report as soon as we have eyes on either one of them again."

Kyong turned off the transmission.

She stood up, but without the bed linens to grab, she instead balled her hands into fists. Escaped? Who was this Binnot? How could Axel do this, after knowing he'd been wrong, after knowing he deserved this punishment?

How could he do this to *her*?

Calm yourself, she thought. *Rage will not solve anything.* She had let out one angry exclamation. Luckily, no one heard it. No one trusted a leader who couldn't control her temperament, no matter the situation.

A normal person would grab the nearest object and throw it, perhaps descend into a puddle of tears. Kyong had other options. She merely stood up, took a deep breath, and went to the doors of her chambers, throwing them open.

"Chancellor!" One of the two guards outside her room started in surprise.

C-04L shuffled into view from down the hallway. "Why, Chancellor Greylark! Why, you're in your sleeping robe . . . outside your chambers!"

"Never mind that. Take note," she said in clipped syllables as she walked speedily down the shining marble hallway. "I need to know where the closest group of Jedi or Republic patrols might be near the exit of the hyperlane to Jedha. A Pathfinder team, if need be. Send a message and orders to put their current plans on hold; to arm themselves and recapture Axel and bring him back to Pipyyr. Alert Master Yoda and send this message along to him if he hasn't already received it. Get my transport ready."

C-04L could barely keep up with her master. "Yes, Chancellor! But—"

"I need my team with me, now. Summon them all to my council room at my office immediately."

"But, Chancellor! Your clothes. Your makeup!"

"To hell with my makeup, Fourell!" she growled.

Within the hour, Yoda sat before her in her council room. She was still in her sleeping robes, drinking cup after cup of an energizing tea to keep her concentration up.

"This Binnot person. Know him, do you?" Yoda asked the chancellor.

"No. I've tried to keep a close watch on Axel's social circle of late, but that name hasn't come up."

"An old friend, perhaps?" Yoda suggested.

"Axel never had close childhood friends. He spent a lot of time with his father, but then after his death . . ." She waved a hand, but it shook. "He was hard to keep track of. There were weeks when I didn't see him. So I don't know every person he's met. I wasn't able to always be there."

"Even in the best soil, a plant cannot grow unscathed."

Kyong turned to look at Yoda, tried to smile and this time failed. "I appreciate what you are trying to say. But I have failed him, in my own way. I think we both know that."

Yoda turned to face her. "No one, no galaxy, no Republic, no Jedi Order, no family, is perfect."

"You are right. As hard as I have tried, I've wanted the Republic to unite this galaxy, to spread out and reach civilizations that would benefit from our connectedness. Perhaps we are doing too much, too fast."

"You must continue. The greater good is a good vision. Fight for this good as well, the Jedi do."

She shook her head. "I know what you're about to say. That we sometimes forget we have the same goals. I think we have been sometimes fighting each other without fighting. But now the Path . . . I feel as if we've been moving through a fog lately. One we can't grasp, but it's been corroding everything good and important around us. Eiram and E'ronoh. Jedha."

"And now, your son."

"It heartens me to hear you consider my son something good."
Kyong smiled weakly.

"Good, he has within him. But bad influences, yes. Corroding his
integrity."

Despite the sinking feeling inside, Kyong had to hold on to hope.
Even Yoda affirmed there was something to salvage in Axel.

Yoda left her there, alone in the room. Outside, the morning was
bright, silvery, and shining as Coruscant was its usual bustle of activity. She briefly saw her reflection in the window. Her gray-flecked hair,
out of the usual tight swirls over her head. The dark circles beneath
her eyes. But her eyes blurred as she stared straight ahead and her
mind filled with thoughts.

She saw none of it. Not herself, any longer. Not the light, or the
brightness, or the future.

Only Axel.

She had wanted him to stay in prison. Perhaps she was a terrible
mother, but morality and motherhood were not supposed to be at
odds. Often, she had heard young parents cooing over their little ones,
murmuring, "I would do anything for my child. Anything."

Kyong Greylark, however, could not. In a position like hers, where
millions of beings could be affected by her decisions, such a murmuring could never be spoken. Kyong loved Axel with all her heart could
bequeath upon him. But she would never put others in danger for the
comfort of her child.

She had come close to doing so on many occasions—paying off
enough debts to fund a young country. Pulling him out of a night in
jail and enduring the embarrassment thereafter. Squashing a tempting
exposure to spice usage at an early age. The holo-tabloids loved Axel.
Likely they would go wild with glee over this latest news. This time she
truly didn't care.

Until now, he always needed and deserved another chance. Her
guilt in having a career that overshadowed her family drove many of
those chances. After the death of his father, she saw how devastating

the hurt had been. She saw it in every poor choice he made, reaching for some bright shiny goal that would not fill him with the happiness he so sought.

Axel must finally learn his lesson. And this time, he would truly feel the consequences of his actions.

THE ROOK, E'RONOH

Chancellor Orlen Mollo was seated in a plush velvet wing chair, a large bowl of lush, candied cactus flower—a pricey and rare delicacy on E'ronoh—and a carafe of Corellian wine at his hand. A handwoven carpet was under his muddied boots, and music played from E'ronoh's best string trio.

"Comfortable?" the Monarch of A'lbaran asked, seated across from him at a table of polished E'roni ironwood.

Mollo gritted his teeth. "Very," he lied.

"May we get you anything else?" he asked, waving an attendant forward.

"Good depths, no," Mollo responded, a little too quickly. What did he want right now? A jug of ale, maybe, and a joint of roasted diredeer would be nice. Burnt and crispy, the kind that threatened to permanently oil-stain your clothes. Or better yet, a freshly caught jawfish from one of Eiram's lagoons.

This was exactly the type of situation that Mollo despised. The coddling, the dancing around and not speaking frankly while lavish food and drink were pushed his way. He would rather dig a garden or a trench with a leader and sweat in the sun while talking about what really mattered. But the E'roni Monarch was aged and seemed to enjoy the confines of his palace. And he seemed set on keeping Mollo in the same environment.

This was where his co-chancellor, Kyong Greylark, excelled. Packaged up in finery, jewels, and makeup, fifth digit out while drinking, and talking around the uncomfortable topics in order to make deals. The first time he had to settle a fight among competing tradespeople over silicon ores he had just finished his schooling in interplanetary affairs. It was awful. He was so frustrated he nearly inked all over the carpet.

"How is Chancellor Greylark?" the Monarch asked, as if reading his mind. Mollo looked at him skeptically, and tried to avoid the question by sipping the wine. By the void, it was like syrup. He would so much rather enjoy a salted tea from Mon Cala.

"She is well, the last I heard." He put down the wine, which was immediately refilled to the top. A slight wave of nausea hit him at the thought of having to politely drink the rest of it. It would be worse than guzzling a glass of honey, straight up. "Your Grace. I wish to speak to you about the pressing matter of the communications buoys that you share with Eiram."

"We are working on it," the Monarch said, waving a hand dismissively. "I would rather talk about how joining the Republic could possibly ensure our success in this fight with Eiram."

"That is not—the Republic is not a means of winning wars. It's a means of keeping peace," he said.

"I can't imagine you said the same to Queen Adrialla."

"No. In fact, my last conversation with her was also about the broken buoys. And her son, who is evading her messages. How is Phan-tu?"

"I wouldn't know. I thought he was on Eiram, with the queen, recovering."

Orlen could tell the Monarch was being evasive. Why wasn't he more caring about how his son-in-law fared? Orlen crossed his legs and sank deeper into the velvet cushions. This chair was trying to eat him alive. "In any case, regarding the buoys . . . as I see it, there are Eirami and E'roni ships waiting to repair one buoy as we speak, but neither you nor the queen has given the go-ahead to do so. This is madness. You both need the buoy to communicate with the Outer Rim planets as well as several of the nearby systems. Not to mention the fact that it would help me communicate with Chancellor Greylark on Coruscant."

"We will only have one hundred percent control, otherwise it stays broken."

"You are spearing yourself in the foot," Mollo said. "Eiram has said the same thing to me, and instead, nothing gets done."

"Then there is the issue of the type of work that needs to be accomplished. Our people say this buoy only needs a repair; the Eiram technicians have asked for an entirely new buoy to be created and launched. Of course, to add in their own gadgets to taint it."

Mollo was inwardly rolling his eyes. It was like speaking to two children, pointing fingers at each other in fury.

The Monarch leaned in. "We have heard rumors that the Jedi have broken the buoys themselves. They are unfixable, and they do this to weaken us. Do you not think they are capable of such things?"

"Yes. I mean no. Actually, yes." Mollo despised double speak. "Let me be clear. The Jedi have nothing to do with this. It was shot down, mutually, by pilots on both sides. The Jedi are only trying to help."

"My father once told me to be wary of a people who had nothing but good intentions when the stakes were so high. Most people must survive on more than just good intentions."

"The Jedi are not like most people," Mollo countered. "And without your buoy in play, information dribbling into Eiram and E'ronoh could be spoken through the mouths of those willing to sing their own version of the truth."

The Monarch pulled both his shoulders back, as if chided. Mollo inwardly groaned. Straight talk didn't work well with leaders sometimes. For some reason, the voice of Kyong Greylark entered his mind. It had been a year or so ago, when they were arguing how best to resolve a territorial dispute between Voon and Wor Tandell. Orlen had wanted to patch things up. Kyong had wanted to tear up the agreement.

Sometimes you have to burn things before you build them.

He stared the Monarch down. "Very well. I'll fix this one myself."

The Monarch went red. "You and the Republic have no authority to do so!"

Mollo thumped his fist on the armrest. "You're so full of anger and the rules of war, you don't realize what's best for E'ronoh. I know what Princess Xiri would want. And she would want this."

"I must do what a father would do. Protect her." The Monarch's voice was rising quickly.

"And yet you sent her off to try to quell more violence before it erupts," Mollo said. "She has fought for E'ronoh, and has been a braver captain than most I have seen in my day. She wants peace. In your heart, you know this. Shed your garments of anger, Monarch. See the possibility of peace."

The Monarch stood, as did Chancellor Mollo. Mollo tried to keep his face neutral, but he knew he had spoken too brashly. Dammit. If only he had the sway that Kyong did. He was always better at showing how he could bring the simple folk into the fold, and work the influence from the ground up. He was already cursing himself in his head when the Monarch reached out a hand.

"Very well. We'll tell our people to go ahead and work on the buoy, in concert with the Eiram technicians."

"You will?" Mollo tried to hide his surprise, but failed.

"I know you despise all this, Chancellor Mollo. The trappings of diplomacy." He motioned to the wines and the sweets. "You're rather shallow that way. Can't hide your feelings. But it is that inability to hide your true feelings that tells me you speak from your heart, as Xiri always does." He smiled. "You're a better negotiator than you realize, Chancellor."

Chancellor Mollo bowed as the Monarch left, thankful that his shaking hands were hidden beneath his long sleeves. He couldn't wait to tell Kyong how the meeting had gone. He imagined her having mind-numbingly boring conversations over tea somewhere in Coruscant right now.

No doubt he'd be the one with the exciting stories to share once they finally spoke.

Chapter Eleven

THE PATH COMPOUND, DALNA

Aida Forte and Creighton Sun gave each other a once-over.

"You're standing too tall," Aida remarked, whispering, as they hid behind a large farming toolshed, rain pattering on their hoods.

"Is there another way to stand?" he asked.

Yaddle pushed her hood past one covered eye. "You look proud and confident. Like a Jedi Master. Look about, Master Sun."

Creighton barely peeked past the edge of their shed. The few Path members on the outskirts of the farm and the large meeting hall walked about, but there was a distinct slump to their posture. As if they were responsible for holding up something much greater than themselves, invisibly, on their shoulders.

"I see what you mean," Creighton said. He slumped over, ever so slightly.

"That's it. That's the look of someone with their eyes on the ground, doing what they've been bidden to do," Aida said. Her normally bright smile and expression had gone dimmer. "I don't like this place. It feels . . . wrong."

"I feel it, too, Aida. We will follow them, and see what we can find."

He turned to Master Yaddle. "Master Yaddle, have you thoughts on how to proceed?"

Cippa stepped forward, her white hair peeking out from her hood. "We ought to separate. Yaddle and I—"

"Youngling," Creighton said, not unkindly, but with a certain amount of irritation, "I am speaking to the *great* Master Yaddle. Your turn will come to speak your mind."

Aida whispered to Cippa. "I remember being eager to help at your age. Your enthusiasm is noted, Cippa." She winked at her. "But let us listen to the Jedi Master speak first, eh?"

Master Yaddle didn't seem annoyed by Cippa's interruption.

"We have come here to help," Yaddle said. "Cippa is proud of her talents and is willing to help." She turned to Cippa, looking up at her. Cippa beamed. "But pride is a powerful attachment to one's own actions, or others'," she said gently. "From pride comes an inability to use the Force in a pure way."

Cippa's self-satisfied expression withered. The lesson seemed to register, penetrate her being for a few seconds, before she pointed to the distance. "Look! A flutterbug!" She ran off a short distance to crouch and observe a native Dalnan insect with stubby wings. Yaddle's face was placid, watching her. Meanwhile, Creighton was trying not to ball up his fists in frustration.

"This is why you are one of the great teachers, Master Yaddle," Creighton said. "Your patience is an enormous sea compared with my puddle."

"Patience can be a learned skill, Master Creighton. Even in circumstances like this, where we fear for the lives of others who may come to feel pain, and death."

Aida frowned. "So you feel it, too, Master?"

"I do. We have much work to do." Master Yaddle motioned to Cippa, who returned to stand behind her. "Cippa is correct. We should separate. A group of four cannot blend well. Jedi Forte and Master Sun, you should head over there." She motioned her three-fingered hand to an area in the distance. Several huts were scattered there. Creighton watched two Path members walk beyond a grassy mound and abruptly disappear.

"There must be an underground structure, or cave," Creighton said. "No one going over that small hill has returned in a while."

"Cippa and I will stay aboveground and check out the buildings," Yaddle said. "Master Sun and Jedi Forte—if people recognize you, convince them otherwise. But when necessary, tell them you have come from Jedha and have information to report. It may open doors you otherwise cannot."

"What about us?" Lu said, with Priv nodding. The two soldiers' Path disguises looked particularly ill fitting.

"I think it would be best if you protected the *Lazuli.* We may need a quick getaway and your backup. Keep your comms at the ready," Master Sun said.

They all nodded.

"May the Force be with you," Master Yaddle said before she and Cippa walked out into the light rain and toward a grain shed.

As Creighton and Aida headed for the hills where Master Yaddle had pointed, Aida exhaled audibly.

"I know what you're thinking," Creighton said.

"That I am worried about what we're going to find?"

"No. That you're relieved Cippa didn't come with us."

Aida smiled mischievously. "It probably doesn't take a Jedi to read that thought, Master Sun."

He tried not to smile as they walked forward. There were sun opals embedded into the ground in waves. Normally they'd be beautiful under shining suns, but now they were smeared with mud. The area before them wasn't much to look at, with overgrown gardens tangled with weeds. Most of the agricultural fields were farther way. But even at a distance, it seemed like they were poorly kept, with grain dying in the sodden ground.

"I heard that the Path had been nurturing a very simple life here on

Dalna. Living off the land . . . in better weather, I'm sure it's very bucolic," Aida said.

"Yes."

"Well . . . they sure aren't taking care of their crops much. It appears to be late summer here. This Dalnan corn is starting to rot on the stalks. Seems like they're distracted."

"I agree. But distracted by what, I wonder." Creighton pulled his hood a little closer to his face to shield it from the rainfall. The structures here were also not well kept. They cautiously opened a door or two, and found living quarters that seemed uninhabited for the moment, with tipped-over bottles and containers. A rain barrel stood outside, overflowing onto wet dirt. "Aida. Turn off your comlink. We don't want any messages coming through and exposing us. We'll contact Yaddle as soon as we're done."

Aida nodded.

"Hey! What are you doing here?"

Aida and Creighton spun around to see a Togruta Path member, a male, standing some distance away. He was carrying what appeared to be a pretty heavy bundle, but its contents were obscured in cloth.

Creighton's hand had already gone to grasp his lightsaber hidden under his cloak.

"Do I know you? What's your name and assignment?" the Path member asked, taking a slight step backward. Like Creighton, he had put his hand inside his cloak. He could be holding some sort of comlink.

Creighton could sense the paranoia emanating from the Togruta, his heart beating a mite too fast. He relaxed and pressed his own thoughts toward the man, enveloping him inside another consideration altogether. One that felt irresistibly true.

"We are your brethren in the Path. We are on your side. And you will help us," Creighton said, calmly.

Aida stayed silent and Creighton leaned on the man's consciousness until, rather easily, he accepted the new thoughts as his own. The man's demeanor morphed into one of patience and almost chemically induced relaxation.

"Where is everyone?" Aida asked.

"In the caves," the Path member said.

"Why?" Creighton said.

"I do not know."

"How do we get into the caves?" Aida asked.

"Over there." The man tipped his head just behind him toward the mound they had seen so many others disappear over. "There's an entry code. And a sentry droid."

"Take us with you. We are working together, after all," Creighton said, and the man nodded.

Creighton and Aida followed the Path member, who walked ahead unsteadily, as if slightly lost. They followed him toward several rolling hills, past an octagonal building and some other structures, including one that looked like a simple cottage.

As they crested over a rise, several Path members awaited entrance at a security door tucked between two small hills.

"Moora," Aida heard a Path member say to a young child leaning on her arm, "nearly there. You can rest soon."

"What about grandfather?" the child said.

"He's coming later," the Path member said nervously. "Maybe he's already there."

Another Path member just inside the door instructed them to head to a room down the corridor.

Aida grabbed Creighton's arm. "It looks like elderly and children are inside somewhere. C'mon, Creighton. You just aged fifty years."

"I am not that old, Aida. We could as well reverse this charade. Your mind is strong enough to fool them."

"Yes, but as my master once taught me—it is easier to let water run downhill than it is to push rain back into the clouds."

He groaned. "I see your point but it would be nice next time if you threw in a compliment about wisdom and the years, to soften the blow." He bent over, leaned on Aida, and began to hobble. The Togruta Path member took his turn entering the code, and the sentry droid opened the door. They followed him in.

"My grandfather is feeling unwell," Aida said to the Path member just inside, a short woman who peered at them as they came closer. Creighton could feel Aida manipulate her vision of Creighton's form.

"Grandfather?" Creighton growled quietly. "Am I your grandfather now?"

"You see, the rain makes him feel ill." She smiled and patted Creighton's hunched back.

"The elderly are to stay aboveground. In the huts," the woman said.

"In the huts," Aida repeated, her face questioning.

"To keep them safe. They are our shield, as the Mother says."

Shield? Against what? Creighton wondered with disgust.

"Please. Just for a short while," Aida pleaded.

The woman sighed. "Very well. Head to the chambers on the right. Stay until you are summoned."

"Summoned for what?" Aida asked, pressing the Force through the woman, loosening the kept secrets in her mind.

"You'll know when I know."

"Thank you," Aida said. She and Creighton hobbled past her. Under the lip of the cave entrance, the temperature dropped ten degrees and a cool clamminess emanated from beyond. Their wet robes left trails of water on the ground, already slick from water trickling in from the cave entrance. Small lights illuminated the way, with colored markings on the wall. To the right were several passages that opened to larger rooms. They walked by, noting there were mostly children within them, playing quietly.

Beyond these caves, the passageway was abruptly blocked by a set of three burly guards. Unlike the other Path members they had seen on Dalna, these wore bandoliers of ammunition, with blasters holstered at their sides.

"For a peaceful group of people who believe in keeping the Force free for all, they sure are decked out with a lot of firepower," Aida said. "How are we going to get past them? We can influence a few, but we can't take on that many people at once."

"Let's wait. Next time someone comes by to pass them, we'll add ourselves on as if they miscounted how many are in their party. It's easier to mildly sway many by influencing their thoughts than changing the set mindsets of a few."

Aida and Creighton ducked into one of the rooms and waited. Some of the older children were bringing water and food to the youngest children. A few had broken off from the rest and were playing in an alcove together.

Two little ones, half Creighton's size, were kneeling, one hiding behind a cave rock.

"Pew pew! I got you!" said one before she leapt over the rock and pounced on the one hiding. She pummeled him hard with her tiny fists and the other one defended himself with kicks.

"No, no! They said not to fight like that," said a slightly older boy, who had been crouching with his hands holding a pretend blaster in the form of a crooked stick. "Shoot them in the back! Haven't you learned anything?"

"That doesn't sound like lessons in farming," she said to Creighton, her face devoid of her usual general mirth.

"No, indeed."

A shadow grew near the entrance of the chamber. Creighton saw a group of three Path members, dragging another person in ropes behind them, a Teevan man with telltale silver-tinted skin. The man looked ill, his Path clothing torn and bruises on his face. Though Creighton and Aida were hidden in the shadows, the man's head swiveled and Creighton was shocked to see the Teevan's blue eyes immediately find his own.

The look in his eyes was plaintive: *You see me. Please help me.*

Creighton sensed the Force about him, disturbed, stronger than most, but weakening. Creighton pulled back into the shadows out of the eyesight of the captured man. Aida put her arm on Creighton.

"That prisoner. Is he a Jedi?"

"I don't think so. He's dressed like a Path member. But he's Force-sensitive, there's no doubt about it."

"Please," the Teevan man wheezed. "Please don't do this. I don't use the Force, I swear, it's just a gift—"

"Silence!" A human guard turned and punched the prisoner in the face. The Teevan's whole body went slack. "The Force is not something to be gifted. It is neither given nor taken. And you have *used* it. There are witnesses. You do not have the right to call yourself one of the Path any longer." Blood fell from the mouth of the prisoner with dribbles of saliva. They dragged him forward.

Creighton nodded to Aida, and they pressed their intentions not to be noticed onto the three guards, as well as the ones heading deeper into the caves. Quietly, they slipped behind the group of four as they passed the guards, who blinked and shook their heads as if cobwebs had descended upon them.

The prisoner let his feet drag harder, slowing the guards down. Creighton could feel the Force emanating from him, an unfocused beacon calling out in distress. Glancing at Aida, he saw her concentrating hard but also likely sensing the prisoner reaching out to them. For help. And yet right now, they couldn't help him.

Another guard kicked the prisoner for slowing the pace as he was dragged ever downward. They didn't notice Creighton and Aida following close behind. It was painful for Creighton to see his bloodied ankles and feet dragging in the cave dirt before them. With a few swings of his lightsaber, Creighton and Aida could easily incapacitate the guards, save this man, and escape. But to what end? They were here to prevent the possible slaughter of countless more. Why would the Path choose to imprison this man instead of simply kicking him out of the compound? And what else existed in these caves? If all went well, they would save him, too. But not yet.

"Concentrate, Aida," Creighton said. "I know what you feel. We must stick to the plan."

There were several offshoots of tunnels that went left and right.

Some led to more storage areas; some were full of Path members sitting, eating, talking; others who were reviewing plans on holos the Jedi could not get close enough to see. The Path weren't acting like people readying for a cold winter ahead. They were planning something. But what?

The guards and the prisoner reached a circular metal door flanked by more guards with blasters.

"The Mother in there?" asked one of the guards holding the prisoner.

A tall, muscular human guard at the door nodded. Creighton and Aida gave an imperceptible glance at each other.

"The Leveler, too?" asked one of the prisoner's guards.

"Where there's one, you'll find the other," said the other door guard, a Weequay woman. She lowered her voice. "I heard it could kill hundreds. Maybe more."

"It'll change everything," the prisoner's guard said. "Well, let's get a move on. I've been told to feed it."

"Be quick about it. We've been ordered to assemble. Everyone is gathering," the Weequay woman said.

The prisoner sagged nearly to the floor, as if exhausted by the exchange. The Force was emanating from him in fitful bursts. His energy was waning. Aida frowned deeply. Creighton, too, was upset by the prisoner's attempts to reach out for help in the only way he could.

The heavy blast door to the chamber was meant to keep out armies, not genteel farmers. Was the Mother going to kill this person? Why? Creighton wondered what they meant by the Leveler. Was it a tool? A weapon?

Feed it, one of them had said. As if speaking about an animal of some sort. One guard punched in a code to the door. It opened, and a puff of air escaped, washing over Creighton and Aida, fluttering their robes.

Creighton was closer to the door, and he felt a bizarre sensation wash over him immediately. He stumbled and reached out to steady himself against the wall. Aida wavered at his side, and he grabbed her arm. But there were seven guards now clustering around the door, plus the prisoner. And then he felt it again, even stronger.

A sense like he was trapped, like fingers were rising up out of nowhere and clawing his legs, pulling him downward. Down to what? There was no water to drown in, no mire below. And yet that was the overwhelming feeling. He didn't know why. None of it made sense. He saw Aida squeezing her eyes shut, hands shaking. He had never seen her like this. He pulled her to him, and they slowly backed away from the group. The prisoner was being dragged inside the place past the blast door, and was now screaming at the top of his lungs, a devastating sound.

But there was another voice, too, an unrecognizable, chillingly soothing voice that reached to his core like a dagger.

You're doomed, Creighton. You don't matter. Nothing you do matters.

Creighton backed away. He would have staggered drunkenly but he forced himself to appear unaffected, taking all his strength to do so. Pulling Aida along with him, they headed in the opposite direction and dashed into a simple entryway. He shook his head, trying to focus and use the Force to crush the lock on the door. He pushed it open. It was dark inside, and he shoved Aida ahead of him. Before he shut the door, he saw several Path members rushing in the passageways, all collectively heading somewhere. Creighton shut the door behind them. The scent of something rotten surrounded him.

The slithering voice in his head became fainter.

You're nothing, Creighton.

In the dark, he gasped and fell to his knees. The terrible sensations were like tendrils twisting around his limbs, sticky and impossible to push away. Giving up would be so easy. The voice was growing fainter, yet still so inviting, coaxing him to succumb.

Aida, too, fell down on all fours. She must have been holding in her panic, because she began to suddenly hyperventilate and whimper— truly whimper, like a tiny child in severe pain. Creighton clenched his fists, intermittently pushing away a nonexistent presence. It was as if the darkness had become a sentient thing, attempting to trap him in an indescribable, inescapable mire. It didn't make sense.

And what was worse was knowing in his bones, in every cell of his being, that there was a terrible disturbance in the Force, and part of that disturbance was affecting him and Aida.

The more he reached out to the Force to gain control and clarity, the worse it became. As a child, he remembered being attacked by other children, well before he was a Jedi youngling—and being filled with so much fear. The terror he felt now was similar—a pure, cold emotion. But as a child, there had been another emotion that came alongside the fear and replaced it. Rage. He had ended up fighting hard with gnashing teeth and nail gouges and dirty punches, overwhelming his attackers until they lay around him with broken bones and raggedly bitten skin. A similar anger filled him unexpectedly now, an almost primeval instinct.

Inside his head, Creighton roared.

The relentless tendrils pulling at him began to dissipate. Creighton breathed, inhaling the stench within the room, a stench that could've been real or a hallucination—he couldn't tell. But the horrific sensations mercifully faded, slowly at first, but then more quickly the longer they stayed in the dark.

Creighton lost all sense of time as he and Aida recovered. He wasn't sure if they had been in this room a minute, or an hour. The voice of the prisoner was gone inside their heads. The absence of his voice chilled Creighton. Finally, Aida spoke, her voice shaking.

"By the stars. What happened to us, Creighton? Are you okay?"

"I am, now. But I can't . . . explain what happened. I've never felt anything like that before."

"Me neither. It felt like my mother was dying in front of me. And I was the one killing her. It couldn't have been real, but it felt real. I have never felt so much fear in my life. It didn't make sense. I never even knew my mother! But it was so horrible." Aida put her hand to her chest, as if to feel the rise and fall of her breathing to be sure she really was alive.

"I felt like a thousand hands were trying to drown me," Creighton said. "Inviting me into oblivion. It was fear, true fear, the deepest and worst I've ever encountered. And nothing I told myself could convince me otherwise. Until I got angry."

Aida's eyes opened wide. "Creighton, I've never seen you angry."

"It was instinctual. I had no control. And then . . . it weakened. What would have caused such a thing?"

"A chemical?" Aida said. "I felt it when they opened that door. It smells odd."

"No. There's something in here that smells strange. We feel better and I can still smell it."

"Maybe it was that Teevan prisoner, in a last-ditch effort before whatever befell him."

"That would explain the disturbance in the Force I felt. But that would be an odd Force effect. And I don't think it was an attack by someone else. How would they know we were there? Why not attack us outright?"

"I don't think anyone really knows we're here. Whatever just happened to us was inadvertent."

There was a commotion outside in the hallway. Creighton and Aida opened the door a sliver, grateful that the Path had some old-fashioned doors. All they could see was a pair of dusty feet lying on a rough tarp. Bare feet, bloodied and scarred. It was the feet of the Teevan Path member.

"Are you ready to go back out there?"

Aida nodded. They readied themselves. Creighton exhaled, found his sense of self again, and prepared to use the Force to sway any guards. But no one was near the prisoner.

Aida whispered. "We can save him now, before any other guards show up. I just hope it's not too late."

He nodded.

They stepped outside their door. *Please,* Creighton hoped. *Please may he not be dead.* He certainly didn't look different than before—no gouges or lacerations. Only unconscious, but covered nearly head-to-toe in a grayish powder, like he'd been dipped in dust. Curiously, there was a similar telltale dark, powdery stain on the tarp that he lay on like it had been used to haul person-sized masses of charcoal. They heard a group of guards' voices from around a corner.

"Quick. We need to hide," Aida said.

They pulled on the tarp, dragging the unconscious prisoner into the room they had just left and shutting the door firmly. They heard the guards walk by, and Creighton exhaled in relief. Aida turned on her lightsaber. From the greenish glow, they examined the prisoner. She reached for his face.

"Hey. You're safe now. We're here to help." She patted his cheek, but the Teevan male didn't respond.

Creighton put his hand on the prisoner's neck, and felt his chest to see if it would rise.

"He's breathing, but barely," Creighton said.

"What happened?" Aida asked. "Why did the Path do this to you?"

The Teevan's eyes fluttered. "They punished me. Because I used the Force." His lips were so dry, flakes of gray came off in powdery bits.

"What happened behind that door?" Creighton asked.

"It con . . . con . . . me." The Teevan's eyes were rolling into his head.

Aida took her hand away from the man's cheek and gasped in shock. There were chunks of ash clinging to her skin. Pieces of his face looked like they had been burned. Not blistered, or charred. But turning straight to gray ash. She wiped her hands on the dirt floor, the bits of the man's face crumbling to dust on her fingertips and smearing in a dark streak.

"Creighton! What's happening?" she said, her voice rising in a panic.

"Con . . . con . . ." the Teevan kept muttering. But now his ear had fallen off in a crusty mass, and his chest spasmed. His hand fell off in a whole, gray, dusty piece. Creighton backed away, as did Aida, afraid that whatever blight had touched him would infect them, too.

There was one last breath within the Teevan's chest. He exhaled one last time, with ashy flakes from his lips and tongue rising into the air as he spoke a final word.

"Consumed."

Chapter Twelve

THE PATH COMPOUND, DALNA

If Cippa opens her mouth one more time, Master Yaddle thought, *just one more, I might actually have to rethink this entire plan.*

Yaddle wasn't annoyed by questions from Cippa. In fact, Cippa wasn't asking any. Aside from the one that wasn't really a question, when Cippa had casually looked down at her master and said, "I'm doing very well, aren't I?"

Master Yaddle and Cippa were walking together deeper into the center of the compound, past the meetinghouses and the many abodes where she assumed the Path lived. The plan had been to try to integrate into the Path and learn what they could, but there weren't many Path members around. Some were bringing the ill or the elderly southward toward the hills, and the others began following as if they were gathering for some purpose. From a distance, they saw an ancient cruiser land inside the compound, but they couldn't see who was disembarking, or what cargo they had. Shortly after, an elegant ship flew over, probably landing in Ferdan.

Once, Cippa had bungled an attempt at speaking with a lone child, attempting to fill a basket full of rain-sodden grain. She helped scoop the purplish kernels alongside him. Within a minute, she complained, "This place is boring. I surely hope the Jedi Temple won't be this boring, too."

Yaddle was able to manipulate the thoughts of the child so he perceived Cippa as saying *This grain will be good to eat. I surely hope the people will think it's good, too.*

"I think the best place for us to investigate is the buildings, since everyone is leaving."

"Shouldn't we go where everyone else is going?" Cippa asked, gesturing to the hills where people were disappearing after they crested a rise in the ground.

Yaddle imagined Cippa in the middle of dozens of Path members. No. That would be a terrible idea.

"Let's take advantage of everyone being gone. Come, Cippa."

At first, there wasn't much to see. There was the washing house where she had stolen garments; a building that fixed farming equipment; multiple small stone living quarters. There was a central garden with green-blue vines and flowers that probably looked lush on sunny days but now were waterlogged and drooping. Cippa wiped the mud off a sun opal embedded in the ground, one of many, and turned her head this way and that to see the multiple colors in the stone.

"I wish it wasn't raining," Cippa said.

As if to chide her, the rain began to intensify.

"Let's go into some of these shelters," Yaddle said. At that moment, Yaddle felt a disturbance in the Force that made the hair on the back of her neck stand up. Even Cippa had noticed her change, as Yaddle froze for almost a minute. Cippa put a concerned little hand on Master Yaddle's clawed hand.

"Master Yaddle," Cippa whispered. "What's wrong?"

But Yaddle could not escape the feeling. It was close by. A flare, and then an absence in the Force. A death. She reached out, and could tell that Master Sun and Jedi Forte were safe, but they were affected, too.

"I'm all right," Yaddle said. She squeezed Cippa's hand.

"I heard about these," Cippa said as they walked forward toward a small pink granite hut. "My momma called them *doddery moments*. I guess you're a lot older than I realized."

Yaddle harrumphed. "If you think I'm old, wait until you meet . . . never mind." Master Yoda was firmly middle-aged—probably past that—and his wisdom was manifesting in his commentary of late. But she didn't want Cippa to meet him and immediately spew out how Yaddle called him *old* once.

They entered the small hut, pushing aside a door. Inside there was an extinguished fire, cooking pots by the hearth, and two chairs by a bare table. A door on the far wall indicated another room.

"I can't imagine they're hiding weapons in such a place, but let's check," Yaddle said, pushing open the door.

"Oh!" Cippa said, unable to hide her surprise.

There was an elderly human Path member lying on a pallet. The rain was dripping through a crack in the roof, and the floor was glistening from water.

"What are you doing here?" the man said. His voice was hoarse. "You should have gone with the others."

"I came for you," Yaddle said, improvising.

"I am to stay here," he said. "All of us are."

"I think I missed that message, tending after this little one," Yaddle said. "What do you mean by all of you?"

"The eldest of us all. We are a shield. Our one last gift, given freely," he said, smiling. Many of his teeth were missing.

Yaddle and Cippa looked at each other. "But surely you need help being looked after," Yaddle said.

"I require very little," he said, pointing to a small basket near the bed, with some crusts of bread. "As for water, the sky takes care of that." Rain was pattering on the edge of his blankets, darkening them with moisture.

Yaddle leaned gently on the elderly man's thoughts. "I have been trying to teach this young one the value of listening to the wisdom of those who came before. It would be helpful for this child to hear, from you, why we must go with the others," she said.

"A gathering. A great work to be done by the Path. Our beliefs brought to reality. A weapon that will make even the mighty Jedi cower in fear. The Force is free, and must not be used like a tool," he reiterated, eyes closed.

Cippa found another blanket on a table nearby to cover him, and together Yaddle and Cippa stopped up the leaking roof with spare slats of wood.

"Gifts given freely. Thank you," he said. "May you receive them in turn."

Yaddle nodded and put a hand on Cippa's shoulder to leave. As they exited the small home, the man croaked one last time.

"Death to Force-users!"

They closed the door behind them and stood in the rain. Yaddle could not speak for a moment. Leaving the elderly behind meant one of two things: either abandoning their weakest members, or incapacitating the ability of any morally sound fighting force to attack the place, knowing the infirm and elderly would be killed first. Both were unconscionable.

They visited several huts, finding other elderly Path members waiting, their faces contented, awaiting their fate. Each of them waved Yaddle and Cippa away, telling them to go to the caves, but not knowing why everyone was being ushered there. Everyone else had apparently descended below the compound. The last older person they found was a Pantoran woman. She had broken her hip and could not leave her bed. When she saw Cippa, she whispered to her.

"Come here, child. I have a gift for you." Cippa looked at Yaddle uncertainly until Yaddle nodded. Cippa went to her and the Pantoran woman pulled a blaster from beneath her bed linens. "For you. It's never too early to follow the teachings of the Mother. To do the bidding of the Path."

"Thank you, but this should stay here with you." Yaddle pulled away

Cippa, who was speechless for once. After they closed the door on the Path member, who was clearly disappointed her gift was not heartily received, she and Cippa scurried around the central gardens, back toward the forest west of the compound.

"Why are these mats around?" Cippa said.

There were bowls of water sitting out in the open air, filled with long soaking wheat straws. Nearby, the straws had been braided and sewn together in mats of various states of completion. Yaddle spotted something a way off—a yellow mat, draped over something large. It appeared to be a vehicle of some sort. She approached another mat-covered item. She pulled up the braided straw to reveal machinery—a ground-to-air missile launcher.

"What kind of farming equipment is that?" Cippa said.

"It's not," Yaddle said, trying not to show her surprise. Why had she not noticed the machinery before? And then she realized. The straw camouflage looked like a haystack from a distance. She now saw there were "haystacks" everywhere, dotting the area around the farmland.

She had to tell Creighton and Aida.

And they had to tell everyone.

"Master Yaddle," Cippa said.

"Yes, child."

"You say you sometimes bring younglings on your missions," Cippa said, wiping rain off her face.

"Yes."

"Why me?"

"Because, you have needed extra training. If I left you in the training classes with the other younglings, they would have gone very poorly."

"Because I'm so much better at using the Force than anyone else my age?" Cippa said brightly.

"No. Because the Force is nothing but a meaningless tool unless you engage this." Yaddle stopped and pointed to Cippa's forehead. "And this." She pointed to Cippa's heart. "Do you know what those children in the Path could be up against?"

"They are telling them to fight. Like soldiers," Cippa said, fear in her eyes.

"Do you think they truly understand what it means to kill another being?"

"Yes. And no."

"If I told you your abilities could save those children, or kill them, what would you choose to do?"

"Save them, Master."

Yaddle was relieved that the answer came so quickly. "Now, if I sent you back to your regular training, you'd be spending your time showing how much better you were than all the other younglings, instead of learning a deep understanding and respect for the Force, and how it can save the lives of innocents."

Yaddle continued to walk forward. They were now clear of the buildings on the Path compound, and luckily no one had followed them. In the distance was the forest, inside of which their ship was hidden. When they got closer, they saw Lu and Priv standing near the entrance to their ship. At the sight of Cippa, they ran inside.

Cippa frowned at them hiding from her. Yaddle noticed and tried to hide a smile.

"How do you know you did a good thing," Cippa said slowly, "if it was in fact, a bad thing?"

Yaddle prepared herself. "What did you do, Cippa?"

"Back there, you said not to use the Force. I'm sorry, Master, but I couldn't help it."

"Cippa, tell me. What did you do?"

"I broke that blaster before we left. That weapon won't ever be used by a child like me," Cippa said.

Yaddle said nothing. In her mind, she could imagine the Path member shaking the nonfunctioning blaster in confusion.

During their quiet last minute of walking toward their ship, Cippa continued to cling to Yaddle, even though there was no longer a reason to. When they were closer to the *Lazuli,* Lu and Priv continued to stay hidden within the confines of the craft.

"It appears you really startled our guards, here," Yaddle said.

"Or maybe they don't like the rain. I'll make it up to them. I'll only flip them over once this time," she said, letting go of Yaddle's hand to run toward the ship.

Yaddle followed her with her eyes. The little one had much to learn, but hopefully this lesson was over for now. They would meet with Creighton and Aida soon, and see what information they could take back to Yoda and Chancellor Greylark.

Her thoughts were suddenly jerked away to the disruption she sensed on the ship. She could see Cippa nearly there, steps away from the boarding ramp. Steps away from something gone terribly wrong.

"Cippa!" Yaddle called, but it was too late.

Two Path members, heavily armed, appeared in the doorway of the *Lazuli.* Cippa held up her hands in defense, but one of them shot her, stunning the child. Cippa dropped limply onto the boarding ramp.

Yaddle only had a split second to think. Either fight, win, and invite more attention to their secret mission, or pretend to be a Path member and manipulate the guards into working with her. She sensed Lu and Priv inside the ship, their minds quiet, likely unconscious.

Hide, or fight?

Cippa lay motionless, her thin legs sprawled at an awkward angle and her head on top of a bent arm, as if asleep. She was Yaddle's responsibility. And she had failed to protect her.

Yaddle would not make the same mistake again.

"You there!" The guards trained their blasters on Yaddle, but she knew she was a touch too far away to be hit accurately.

She continued to walk toward them, her hands up. "An explanation is at hand," she said.

When she was just close enough, she paused.

Hide, or fight?

She could already see a faint bruise forming on Cippa's temple where she had fallen.

Yaddle looked almost sorrowfully up at the two guards, one human male and a Weequay woman.

"Who are you? Is this your ship? You do not have clearance to be on Path grounds," the Weequay said, her leathery face frowning deeply.

"When I said explanation, I meant you, not me."

She lifted a hand, and the blasters from both guards were immediately wrenched out of their fists, flying onto the grass at a distance. She lifted a second hand, and both their bodies flew into the air as they began to holler in protest and shock. Master Yaddle flipped them upside down, Cippa-style, and knocked their skulls together so painfully hard, it sounded like an ax hitting wood, enough to render them unconscious.

Yaddle dropped her hands, and the two guards fell hard to the boarding ramp, a few meters away from Cippa.

"I choose to fight," Yaddle said. She gently picked up Cippa with the Force, levitating her into the ship. As she passed the two guards, she said, "That is what you get for shooting a child."

Chapter Thirteen

Xiri had her legs up on the table in the central cabin, reading a datapad. She had found a century-old tome on diplomacy. She was skipping through it, sweating the whole time. There were chapter headings like "Culture Immersion" and "Mastering of Languages of the Mid Rim" and "Preventing Imminent Death Through Conflict Resolution."

That last chapter didn't actually exist, but it might as well have.

She read a short passage aloud. "The key to diplomacy is not always to push your own agenda, first and foremost, but to find common ground. Imagine, with true feeling, the hopes and fears of the other party. You must balance the needs of the many and avoid blunt statements that indicate your unwillingness to compromise." Xiri groaned.

"Sounds like the groan of an ambassador," Master Char-Ryl-Roy said from a far corner of the room, where he was sitting with his legs crossed and eyes closed, his tall forehead nearly touching the low ceiling. Enya was on the floor nearby, making some final adjustments to 4VO-TG. The legs were finally attached, but the droid still couldn't quite maneuver smoothly. Xiri thought Master Roy had been meditating. Maybe he was still meditating. Perhaps Jedi could talk and meditate at the same time?

Phan-tu's voice commed in. "So. What's the plan on approaching the Path?" he asked.

"Phan-tu, you should be resting instead of checking in on us," Xiri said.

"My wounds are healing pretty quickly thanks to the juvan the healers used on me. You're avoiding the question, though."

Xiri's relief was soon replaced with a touch of irritation. She was still trying to figure that out, wasn't she?

"We're handling it, Phan-tu," Xiri said.

"Then what's the plan?"

At this point, Master Char-Ryl-Roy opened his eyes. Not so much at the words, Xiri mused, as at Phan-tu's tone of slight irritation.

"Well," Enya said. "When we're close, I guess we'll contact the Path. Whoever's in charge. Ask to land, and have a chat."

Xiri cringed. It sounded like they were going to ask the Path to come have a drink and a snack together.

"I mean, it'll be more formal than that," Xiri said. "When we speak to them, we'll ask as carefully as possible if they know of any rogue members who might have been dealing in biological weapons, with respect to our planetary conflict."

"Well, what if they say they don't want to talk to you?" Phan-tu asked.

Xiri started pacing. "Phan-tu. Shouldn't you be resting?"

"I did rest."

"You sound tired."

"You sound annoyed," Phan-tu said.

"I am not annoyed!" Xiri nearly yelled.

At this, the two Jedi exchanged glances. Enya pointed her thumb at the door, and Master Char-Ryl-Roy nodded. They left the room faster than a beeping thermal detonator could empty out a tavern.

Xiri turned around in the empty room and sighed. "We cleared the room, Phan-tu."

"Huh?"

"The Jedi didn't want to listen to our marital squabbles. They left."

Phan-tu was silent for a moment. "We're not having squabbles. I'm sorry, Xiri. I'm just . . . feeling useless. I want to be helping you."

"You should enjoy staring out over that beautiful ocean of yours while you recover," Xiri said.

"*Our* ocean, you mean."

"Huh?" Xiri said.

"Our ocean. Eiram is your home now, too."

Xiri held her breath. She was still adjusting to thinking of their worlds in that way. She'd always seen her marriage with Phan-tu as the link between Eiram and E'ronoh, not her actual self. But he was right. The "yours and mine" mentality wasn't good for anybody.

"I never think about it that way, to be honest. See, Phan-tu? You are helping. Plus, you saved my life. Again," Xiri said.

"I guess so, but I still want to do more. The queen and the Monarch were going to work with Chancellor Mollo, but it feels like nothing is moving fast enough."

Xiri laughed. "Now you know why I like to fly ships. At least I can do that fast."

Phan-tu laughed, too. "Let me start over." There was a long pause. "Be careful."

"You mean don't be my usual impulsive self?"

"I would never try to change you, Xee. I don't want to tell you what to do. But I don't want you to tell me what to do, either."

Xiri felt stung. There was a way to do things. A right way. Was it so wrong to insist that everything and everyone in your life followed it? The lives of millions were at stake. Phan-tu's voice had commed out as she stared at nothing, her mind swirling with thoughts.

No one could truly tell Xiri what to do. She had to do that herself, but . . . like diplomacy, her actions had to take into account all those she loved. It meant change, painful as it might be. It meant being braver than she'd ever been, defending E'ronoh.

She imagined seeing the Erasmus Sea, thinking of how utterly heartbroken she would be if the creatures beneath the waves were driven into extinction. If those little, green-freckled kids of Eiram grew sick and died as a consequence.

No. When it came down to it, she would fight for both Eiram and E'ronoh. Whatever happened, she would stay true to both her worlds.

ABOARD THE PIRATE CARGO SHIP, NEAR JEDHA

Binnot Ullo and Axel Greylark were in the cockpit of the raider ship. The Klatooinian pilot sat in the main seat, while Binnot and Axel spoke behind him. A viewport showed that they were passing by a purplish and pink planet, NaJedha. Jedha, its cold moon, was not too far away.

"Are they still following us?" Binnot asked.

The Klatooinian pilot, Grus, nodded. "Here." He pointed to a screen that showed the rear view of the ship. There in the distance was a small, irregular, brown dot amid the darkness and bright stars.

"That's it. The same ship that was nearby when we found you. They're going to either attack us now, or attack us when we land," Binnot said. "The sooner those Jedi are dead, the sooner we can focus on the future."

"We can fight back, can't we?" Axel asked. He couldn't hide the fact that he wasn't terribly excited about the prospect.

"We would crush them," Grus said, punctuating his words with a growl.

"The sloppy way to do it," Binnot said, and Grus growled again. "At this distance, they have plenty of time to gather help and turn this into a larger battle than we need it to be. Why even give them that chance?"

"What do you have in mind?" Axel asked.

"We're approaching Jedha. We'll aim to head for the far side, and when they're out of sight, we'll accelerate and hide on the bright side of the moon, waiting. The sunlight will obscure us when they're visible. We can power down and hide in the noise of NaJedha's magnetic field. And then we'll attack. It'll be a perfect, clean kill."

Axel nodded, but internally, he doubted. Surely Gella might suspect their maneuver. Gella and her Jedi powers might twist their stealthy attack into an advantage somehow. Next thing he knew, Axel would be back in prison before he even had a chance to do something with his newfound freedom. Spending time with a bunch of occasionally inebriated pirates didn't count.

"Here we go," Grus said. He began to accelerate, and the ship began to pass the dark side of Jedha.

"Go faster," Binnot said. Grus mumbled something, and Binnot slapped his hand on the back of the pilot's chair. "I said, faster!"

Grus leaned forward, making some adjustments to the engine, a low rumble in his throat signaling that he didn't appreciate being bossed around. The cargo ship began trembling once it hit its maximum sublight speed. It took a few minutes, but soon they were curving around Jedha to the bright side, decelerating quickly and turning.

Grus shut down the engine and they waited. With the sun at their back and the noise from the planet, they would be difficult to find. Binnot picked up binocs since their own scanners were off, searching for the pursuers. And finally, the small, irregularly bulbous ship emerged from behind the dark side of the cold moon.

"There they are. We only have one chance to make this work. On my mark, power up the ship and accelerate," Binnot said, leaning forward. "Three, two, one . . . engines on! Go! Keep the sun behind us."

The small bulbous Pathfinder ship was heading into the sun, and it didn't seem to realize anything was amiss until it was too late.

"Fire," Binnot said, calmly.

Their laser cannons shot out directly at the coming ship, which immediately began to swerve, turning around toward Jedha. The shots missed the Pathfinder ship, but their cargo ship had the advantage of speed and arms, and quickly fired again. The Pathfinder ship had shields, began to accelerate, trying to evade them. It had some rear guns, but the ship was clearly not built to fight.

"Our shields are too good for those little guns," Grus said, a low laugh in his chest.

Just then, a bright blast of light flashed toward their ship and hit them hard. Axel lost his balance, hitting the side of the cockpit, and Binnot cursed.

"What was that?" Axel said.

"What is a ship of that size doing with an ion cannon? It took out our shields!" Grus yelled.

Grus didn't complain for long. He turned the ship around, maneuvering to avoid the repeated cannon fire, hitting the Pathfinder ship on the side until a ball of fire spit out one of the engines.

Axel gripped the wall of the cockpit. Gella's ship was seriously hit. It wouldn't last long. He imagined her on that ship, probably firing the ion cannon or piloting. Their cabins were probably filling with smoke. Their engines failing.

The pirate cargo ship fired their laser cannons at the small Pathfinder ship in quick succession.

"Got it!" Grus yelled, his fist in the air in triumph.

Axel's mouth opened in surprise. The ship was listing to the side when Binnot spoke in a calm, almost lazy voice.

"Finish them," he said, simply.

Grus fired his cannons one more time. A direct hit to the other engine, and the entire ship exploded in a ball of fire.

It was done. Gella Nattai was no more.

Axel thought of the first time he'd seen Gella on the *Paxion,* during the talks between Eiram and E'ronoh. The way she hadn't acted like he was anything special, so unlike how he was used to being treated. She'd seen him. When they were on Pipyyr, she had worn a look of relief and, dare he say, happiness, when he had told her how sorry he was.

That hadn't been a lie. He had been sorry he hurt her. He would have liked to have said more. And now she was gone.

Binnot was clapping him on the back, saying something about Jedha, and their need to board a different ship. But Axel could hardly fake the smile that was expected of him, and the words entered his mind like a cloud he could hardly understand. He would have to pretend he was happy about her death, about their success in the moment. He had to clear her out of his mind.

He would mourn Gella someday, with the time and space she deserved.

"You ready to land, Axel?" Binnot said as they left the cockpit.

Axel turned to face Binnot. He knew his eyes weren't tearful. His face was not suffused with grief. In fact, he probably appeared perfectly fine. He even smiled.

"Better than okay. Why wouldn't I be?" He flashed one of his holonet smiles and slapped Binnot on the back. "Let's go."

But he saw, out of the corner of his eye, Binnot pursing his lips, something he always did when he was unsure of the truth. He had worn that expression when they had talked only hours ago. Axel would have to be more careful. He remembered Binnot telling him a few years ago—something he'd kept within himself with pride—*Oh, Axel. You really are a beautiful liar.*

It was only beautiful when the lies worked.

Gella watched herself die a fiery death from a far, far distance.

It's done, she thought.

"The Pathfinder ship has been destroyed," Orin said.

They stood watching from a cabin on an antiquated Republic ship. It was so odd, planning your own death, seeing the pirate ship hide in the electromagnetic field, firing on the Pathfinder ship when it had come around from the dark side of Jedha into the light. Piti, the pilot and navigator, had a trick up her sleeve—the ability to control the Pathfinder ship and her weaponry remotely. It had come in handy on their Pathfinder missions when Kenny had taken ill with a violent bout of spacesickness, and Piti—the only one who could pilot the ship—had to be in two places at once.

Kenny and Piti had their hands on each other's shoulders. Kenny started to bawl at the sight of the distant fireball that was once their ship.

"My baby."

Piti patted his tall, bony back. "There, there, Kenny. We'll get a new ship. These Jedi promised us the Republic would compensate us."

Gella nodded. She knew that the Republic would balk at the expense, but it was worth it. It was her idea to comm the *Alliance,* which had been near Jedha since the battle. They had done a quick transfer while out of visual contact with the pirate ship, guessing that they'd be attacked.

And now the pirate ship was landing in Jedha City. Gella, Orin, Piti, and Kenny landed a small shuttle at a distance. But as they'd flown in low over the bare plains and rocky terrain, Gella had clutched her chest in distress, seeing the enormous, grand statue of the Jedi that had fallen and was now broken, nearly embedded into the ground beyond the holy city. Though the Battle of Jedha was over, the scars would stay forever.

Once her feet were on the ground, she refocused and her resolve was there, steady as gravity. Having Axel and Binnot think they were dead would make them less suspicious about being followed. They would let down their guard. In fact, they already had. With their binocs and the tracker, they saw Axel and Binnot already out of hiding, heading right through the middle of the market.

"Do we follow him?" Kenny asked. "I've never been on a mission like this before!"

"No, Kenny. Piti, you too. The next steps are up to us. You stay safe, find the rest of your Pathfinder team. They said they'd meet you here to regroup."

Piti nodded, being someone who seemed to enjoy sensible plans, but Kenny's lower lip protruded in a pout.

"But we can help!"

"Kenny, you know how to code and fix buoys," Piti said. "Spying is not your thing. Besides, at the sight of your ship exploding, you practically laid an egg, you were so scared."

"I'm human, I don't lay eggs," Kenny said indignantly.

"Exactly."

Gella smiled at the two. "Thanks, you two. May the Force be with you."

She and Orin pulled their hoods up so their faces were shaded as they strode into the heart of the city. Normally, Gella expected to see a busy bazaar, merchants, and various priests, scholars, and others who surrounded themselves in all things related to the Force. But she was shocked at the piles of rubble, smoke arising from a pit full of burning refuse, and buildings that were now piles of masonry and stone and caved-in roofs. The streets were choked with debris, and dust was everywhere.

"The place is a mess," Gella said.

"Which they'll use to their advantage," Orin commented. "Come on."

Binnot and Axel had slipped behind a group of merchants carrying large baskets of goods. QN-1 buzzed near Binnot, and Binnot swatted at him. Binnot pointed a finger at QN-1, as if he were a child. They lost sight of him for a few minutes in the swirl of people ahead of them.

Gella's shoulder throbbed a bit, but she ignored the pain and kept her speed up.

"Where did they go?" she asked. "Orin. Do you have Axel's tracker in sight?"

Orin shook his head, looking at a small datapad in his hand. "Not anymore. He must have found it and gotten rid of it. But we know which direction he went in. This way." He pointed to the left.

Gella looked in the direction Orin indicated, but somewhere inside her body, she felt the pull—a gentle but irresistible sense that something far outside of herself was almost calling to her. It was as if a string were being plucked somewhere with a unique frequency, and Gella could feel the resonance within her own self. Her head turned in the opposite direction of where it seemed Axel had gone.

"What is it?" Orin asked.

"That's not where Axel is." She pointed her chin. Beyond the stalls, messes of debris, and the brown buildings, there was nothing much there.

"Are you sure?"

"Yes." She pulled her cloak aside and showed Orin the single lightsaber at her belt. "Axel stole my other lightsaber. When it's close enough, the kyber crystal tells me where its sister is." She looked to her right. "It's singing to me. Axel, or at least my lightsaber, is in that direction."

They abandoned following the crew and instead wound their way around buildings, a smokehouse, and a small fenced-in area and tiny barn for spamels, until they encountered a long line of low, wide hangars at the edge of town. Before Gella saw Axel, she saw his droid.

QN-1 was zipping about, as if gleeful in his ability to fly. He was zipping between two buildings before diving down and hovering. A person walked out from behind one of the buildings, and QN-1 had flown to circle his head.

Axel.

Axel seemed to speak to the droid before QN-1 dived into Axel's backpack. Gella could see her stolen lightsaber hung at his waist, and she tried to quell the anger she felt seeing her weapon in his possession.

"There's the other one," Orin said.

Binnot spoke to Axel. He led them to a fairly large transport that had large crates being loaded by what looked like Jedha locals. They boarded the ship.

"What's in those crates?" Orin wondered.

"Weapons? Food? Could be anything," Gella said.

"Could be dozens of Kowakian monkey-lizards," Orin said.

Gella only stared at Orin. His smile disappeared.

"Fine, I'll amend my guess to crates of sunberry wine. And only two or three Kowakian monkey-lizards."

"Or maybe they're just hitching a ride to their next destination. Smart of them to ditch their last ship. And those pirates, too."

"Shall we hitch a ride, too? I always wanted to know what it felt like to be a smuggled item of importance," Orin said.

"Let's do it."

The last crate had been carried into the cargo hold of the ship, and the engine began to rumble with activity. Gella and Orin moved closer, hiding behind other cargo in the area. At the last minute, Orin reached out and knocked over a large metal sensor dish near a pile of junk. It clanged and sent other pieces of broken metal rolling away. The porters turned to the noise, and Gella and Orin took the opportunity to hide in the kicked-up dust and slip into the cargo hold, sliding between crates and ducking down. They stayed stone-still, and soon the hatch closed.

The transport hummed louder and vibrated, and they could feel they had taken off. No one on the ship was venturing into the cargo hold. After a time, Gella stood up and stretched, as did Orin. She lightly rapped her knuckles on one of the crates.

"Curiosity killed the tooka-cat," Orin said. "But I'm not a tooka, so." He ignited his lightsaber and carefully broke the latch on one of the crates with the glowing green blade. Gella lifted the lid.

It was filled with purple rice. The next crate was filled with green rice.

Gella shrugged.

"If only we had some water. And a fire. And some spicy pickled vegetables," Orin said.

"Maybe they're headed to Dalna. Bringing food to the Path," Gella guessed.

"Maybe, but don't they farm their own food there?" Orin was letting the green rice slide through his fingers.

"Perhaps they don't have time to farm, when they're all meddling in the business of other planets," she said. Gella sat down between the crates, keeping her hand on the hilt of her sole lightsaber. Orin started to go on about his favorite foods and made no less than four jokes about rice. But she was hardly listening.

All she could think of was Axel. Whether he liked it or not, he would soon be seeing Gella rise from the dead.

Chapter Fourteen

THE PATH COMPOUND, DALNA

Jedi Aida Forte and Master Creighton Sun stared at the smudges on their hands, frozen in surprise. The ashes of the dead Tee-van man were on their fingertips.

Aida, holding her lightsaber aloft to see by its green-colored glow, surveyed the body in shock. What had he died from? His body hadn't completely turned to ash, but parts of him had, as if the outside of him had been burned. But he clearly hadn't looked like that when he'd been dumped behind that door.

"Whatever happened back there, something killed him. We can't ignore the fact that he was Force-sensitive, either, and being punished for it. They despise people like him. Like us."

Creighton was trying not to be angry, but Aida could tell he was struggling. Normally, he controlled his emotions well, but after what they'd just experienced—Aida could feel her own emotions fraying. Tears were at the edges of her eyes. They'd had the chance to save him, and they hadn't. The regret would not leave her for a long time, if ever. But it also meant they were alive to see the consequences and alert the others.

"This happened on Jedha, too. Remember what Silandra said? She'd been overcome. It affected her connection to the Force. Her words were, *The worst thing I've ever felt*. It was the same for me. She'd said Jedi were left as husks, but we never found out what caused it. And now it's happening here—both instances are connected by the Path. This is irrefutable evidence that this weapon—whatever it is—is here on Dalna and they used it to murder this victim."

"She'd said she felt a horrible hunger coming from whatever it was. Creighton—that guard had said something about feeding time." Horror blossomed in Aida's mind and a prickling sensation raised the scales of her arms.

Creighton and Aida locked eyes, fear reflected between them.

"We've got to tell people what we know," Aida said. "Now."

"Let's get out of here," Creighton said, turning to the door.

Aida nodded and took a deep breath. "Ugh, what is this smell?" she said.

Creighton and Aida began to walk around, realizing they were in a fairly large room. It was dark, but their eyes were growing accustomed to the low light. There were several tanks running around the periphery of the space, along with wall shelves of different-colored liquids in containers. Testing equipment cluttered a table nearby.

"The smell is coming from the tanks," Aida said. "That faint blue glow, too."

They found another chamber connected to it, and even another. All full of blue tanks, all carrying that slight stench that smelled like seawater gone rancid. Careful not to touch anything, they searched the rooms until Aida stopped in front of a shelf.

"Creighton. Look."

The shelf held several different containers, all labeled.

KLYTOBACTER SPECIES AIGU, SAMPLE 010

KLYTOBACTER SPECIES BIRU, SAMPLE 014

KLYTOBACTER SPECIES VIBRIO, SAMPLE 003

"I've heard of this. When we were on Eiram."

"A poison?" Creighton said. "Is it the same poison that the queen had manufactured?"

"No," Aida said. "Totally different. This one is a bacterium. It kills off the smallest species in the ocean and waters, and the effect moves up the chain of life. It's an ocean killer," Aida murmured, her hand covering her mouth.

"You kill an ocean, and you kill the people and the life that depends on it."

Aida turned around, afraid to get too close to any of the tanks. "It could be a planet killer, if it gets into the wrong hands."

"I think it's too late for that, Aida. The Path has it. There is absolutely no reason for someone to be making vast quantities of this unless they're planning something terrible."

"You were right, Master Sun. About your fear that the Path was up to something else, that Jedha was just a small piece of a larger puzzle."

"One of the guards had mentioned the Leveler. Remember what he said? *It could kill hundreds.* It's got to be the new weapon."

"Or the Leveler could be what husked that prisoner. What's the fight for? Here, or elsewhere?" Aida asked.

"Maybe. Both are a catastrophe in the making. We have to inform everyone about this. The chancellors. The Jedi, anyone who will listen."

"If we can get out of here. We'll have to regroup with Master Yaddle and leave immediately."

They went to the door, and Aida reached to open it, but her hand shook. Her lightsaber, in her other hand, also shook. It made their shadows look like they were experiencing a groundquake.

"Are you all right?"

She shook her head. "I feel a little weak, but I'll be okay."

"Me too. We have to concentrate and leave unnoticed."

She opened the door. The corridor was empty, aside from the ash stain that trailed into the room. They listened; it was quiet. Creighton vaguely remembered hearing some Path members saying something about a gathering. The passageways might be fairly empty. They exited their hideout and headed back down the corridor that led to the outdoors. It was winding and confusing.

"Are we going the right way?" Aida asked.

"I think so."

But Aida had sticky cobwebs in her brain. Was it left or right at the next turn? The farther they got away from that thick metal door and whatever was behind it, the better she felt, but it was slow going.

They ventured along a long curve of passageway, noting corridors that went left and right. It was an absolute maze down there. They had taken a pretty direct route downward when they had followed those Path members. But one wrong turn, and it would be incredibly hard for anyone to find anything down here.

"We should be mapping this place out," Aida said.

"We should. But there's no time."

The corridor turned left, and they were stunned to see two Path members ahead. Creighton froze, as did Aida.

"Concentrate," Creighton said, seemingly more to himself than Aida.

Creighton began to move forward, probably knowing their hesitation would cause more suspicion. Aida focused. When she was close enough, she would reach out and offer the only message the Path members needed to know:

These are fellow Path members. Nothing to notice.

Their cloaks would do the rest of the work, at a distance. But as they approached, Aida could see confusion on their faces.

"Creighton. They're already suspicious," Aida said.

"Be calm. Be ready."

She saw Creighton perspiring. He was fatigued, as she was. They weren't completely themselves. Concentrating was a huge effort. But once they were only three meters away, the faces of what looked like two armed guards suddenly looked collectively less suspicious and relaxed into a placid calm.

They nodded at Creighton and Aida as they passed by. Aida was trying to keep her hands from shaking as she walked. A breath or two later, they had passed.

Aida felt relief wash over her, but it lasted only a moment, as a voice called out from behind them.

"You! You're not supposed to be here right now."

She twisted her head. The guard had a hand on a blaster now.

Aida tried to concentrate again, but it was too late. The guard had started running toward them.

"What do we do?" Aida whispered hurriedly.

Creighton looked back at her. "We run."

Chapter Fifteen

ABOARD THE PATH TRANSPORT SHIP,
NEAR DALNA

Axel Greylark sat in the forward compartment of the transport ship, near the cockpit. Somewhere in the rear of the ship were countless crates of precious cargo headed for Dalna. QN-1 was nestled in his lap, and he was enjoying the comfort of his droid in the same way he had when he'd been a child and longed for a moment of quiet. He didn't ask anything of him. He was just there. His time in prison without QN-1 had been far more difficult than he'd anticipated. He'd thought he didn't lean on the droid much as an adult. Incarceration proved him wrong.

In the cockpit, Binnot was instructing the pilot how and where to land on Dalna. Soon, they would have the reunion of a lifetime, one that would make or break Axel's future. He was hoping for all make, no break. But uncertainty nagged at him. He couldn't stop thinking of Gella's ship exploding. He was usually good at keeping the negative consequences of his choices shuttered away, but this time, it was impossible. He worried he was walking into a disaster. He shook his head. *No, Axel. You're going to make this work. No matter what.*

Binnot entered the compartment and sat down across from Axel.

"Look," Binnot said, pointing a green hand to the viewport. Axel leaned forward. Against a backdrop of a gray, cloudy sky covering a large portion of the brown-and-green planet of Dalna, he saw a large ship in orbit. It had a teardrop-shaped body with a tapered end. Unusual, and quite large for a fairly ordinary farming planet like Dalna. "It's the *Gaze Electric*. The Mother's ship."

"I hope that the Mother is ready to speak to me." Unlike his mother, the chancellor, who always seemed ready to talk *at* Axel. It felt like they were always looking in opposite directions when it came to Axel's life.

"We sent a message ahead that we were arriving," Binnot said.

"How do you know they received it?" Axel said, trying not to sound nervous.

"The communications buoy in this sector is under complete Path control. Nothing comes in or out without our deciding if it goes through. Which means we have the ability to intercept messages and act on them before problems arise."

Axel smiled. "Is that how you got that counterfeit message through to Pipyyr, to have me transferred?"

"Of course. Our people are in the shadows in more places than you realize." Binnot leaned forward, his knees bouncing. He looked like a kid getting ready for a party. "Things are going to happen soon, Axel. Big things."

"Tell me, Binnot."

"That's not my place. The Mother will explain everything, and your role in it." He turned to Axel and clapped him on the shoulder. "It's all coming together."

The pilot called from the cockpit. "We have clearance to land."

Axel tried to breathe slowly and steadily, calming his nerves. The truth was it was hard for him to focus. He kept replaying the vision of that bulbous ship carrying Gella, and seeing it explode. There was no way even a person gifted with Jedi powers like Gella could have survived that. It left an impact in his mind that seemed to bruise every thought he had.

Enough, Axel thought. *Enough of the past, and of Gella. It's time to make my future.*

He looked through the viewport and saw the familiar snowcapped volcanoes and the river valley with purple and red trees. Normally, opals glinted in the waterways and the riverbed, but the skies were a block of gray clouds, and there was no shimmer to greet him. Rain spattered against the viewports. The ship veered closer to the town of Ferdan and landed at the docks. Their ship was too large to land at the new landing pads on the Path compound, apparently.

Soon, they were in a speeder, in a light rain, on their way to the compound. They passed through the main entrance. Every time he'd seen the compound, even when lush and verdant with its gardens and agricultural fields, he'd wondered if the Path truly possessed the capability to be the shining kingdom he wanted to be a part of. A people that couldn't even bear to use droids in farming because it messed with the Force, somehow.

But since his last visit, there was now a wooden wall surrounding the footprint of the compound, instead of just the small pink boulders that had dotted the edge of the planting fields. There were shuttles on the landing pads and speeders near the outer buildings; the gardens and fields seemed to have been abandoned. And they'd just delivered a huge shipment that would change everything, when the time came.

"Will we be going into the caves?" Axel asked. Most of the compound here was underground. Axel knew that all of the Path members could hide there if they needed to.

"We'll be meeting the Mother in the Crystal," Binnot said. "It's a recent addition, and rarely used, but her favorite now. And she knows she can get to the *Gaze* quickly if she's in danger." There was something about how Binnot spoke that made it sound like danger was already on its way.

They walked through the main part of the compound. The smell of wet soil was probably welcoming to some, but not Axel, whose boots were already irritatingly muddy. He saw the familiar barn at a distance, various pink-stoned huts, and one of the gathering halls.

They soon entered an octagonal structure, wide and low, named the Crystal for its faceted shape. There were guards posted near and far around the building, and the nearby shuttles, for the Mother's safety. Nothing spoke of importance and influence like a battery of guards and a getaway ship. It was unlike the usual calm, farming atmosphere of this place. He squinted and noticed several Path members carrying packages of various sizes into the shuttle. *She sure did pack heavy for theoretical getaways,* Axel thought.

He marveled at the building. It was simple, made of smooth round stones put together in a beautiful array. Inside, the walls were fortified with durasteel, the kind that could withstand the force of a cannon-sized blast from a starship, and easily handle blasterfire and small explosives in a ground battle. The Mother had planned out her safety well in advance.

They passed a closed door in the corridor where he heard two voices arguing. They were so loud, you could hear the conversation clearly.

"He had no right. He is *my* Herald. He never should have acted without me."

"But Mother, he claimed that you do not do as the Path beliefs say. That we are to follow the Path. Not a person."

Something crashed inside the room. Like a glass object was thrown.

Binnot put his hand on Axel's shoulder as they passed the door. "Never mind that. Any organization with power has its own petty arguments."

Axel wondered. It didn't sound petty. It sounded like a major power struggle. But he soon was thinking of something else, when Binnot corralled him into another room.

It was beautifully laid out, with carved chairs fitted with shimmer-silk and satin embroidered cushions, pricey marble trays with tumblers of carved crystal. There was no one there, and Binnot and Axel sat down and waited. Binnot seemed uncomfortable in such lush surroundings, but Axel helped himself to a crystal tumbler and poured himself a fingerful of spirits. QN-1 hummed a warning, but he ignored his droid. He sipped his drink.

"Not bad," he said, raising his glass to Binnot, whose head turned to the door suddenly.

Axel hadn't heard anything at all, not even a faint vibration of a footfall. But at the movement, he, too, looked to the door expectantly.

It opened and the Mother entered, trailed by two attendants. She looked completely unperturbed by the intense conversation that Axel had overheard moments ago. At the sight of her, Axel stood, still holding his glass.

Unlike the other Path members, the Mother had robes of a finer, silken material, edged in blue and cinched with a finely wrought belt. She bore the typical blue marks of faith over her forehead. He was always surprised into silence at how youthful she appeared, and how small. But now, she seemed to have aged markedly since they'd last spoken. She leaned heavily upon a cane, and her dark hair was interspersed with more gray. Her medium-brown skin was more deeply lined than before, and she was almost gaunt. Even her eyes were sunken into her skull, but they quickly surveyed the room and took in everything at once—Axel holding the drinking glass as if the room belonged to him, his little droid hovering near his shoulder, Binnot appearing nervous. Those eyes still shone with intelligence and quickness, not unlike the eyes of Axel's own mother, Kyong Greylark. They made Axel nervous.

Her apparent aging didn't soften her ability to intimidate. Some might look at her and think she'd entered a complacent time of life; Axel found it frightening. People still had the fire of youth smoldering within, an ever-evolving definition of hope, and the calm of growing wisdom, but they were unpredictable. You didn't know what would ignite action. Decades of life could soften some; in others, it intensified their viciousness and sharpened their ability to deliver pain.

The Mother smiled as she approached Axel. "Ah. Axel Greylark. My Chaos. It is a pleasure to see you again." She saw QN-1 hovering behind his legs. Unlike Binnot, she was not as perturbed by the presence of a droid. "I trust you didn't suffer too much on Pipyyr?"

Axel was tempted to ask about her health, given her marked change in appearance, but he decided against it. He decided to give no indication that he might be concerned about her abilities in any way.

Axel tipped his chin downward, and put down his glass in the same movement. "Looking like the queen of the galaxy, as always. The pleasure is all mine. I am in your debt for helping me to escape Pipyyr. And Binnot's, as well."

"Yes. Binnot." She cocked her head, as if she'd forgotten he existed. Axel noticed his friend's discomfiture. Was this a gesture to keep Binnot off balance?

"Mother," Binnot said, bowing deeply, his poison-gloved hand out in a respectful flourish.

A rumbling whine that sounded like an embodied groundquake came from the door.

"Ah. My little Leveler. Come." She waved to the door, and a beast that Axel could have only imagined in his nightmares entered.

The creature was a meter and a half high, four-legged, but the forelimbs ended in curled claws ready to open and disembowel at a moment's notice. It was muscular, and yet oddly, its bones protruded, as if it was being underfed. It had a gray, almost silvery sheen to it that changed with the light, and its face had inscrutable eyes and a mouth of tendrils that dripped with saliva. The Mother didn't seem to mind it staining the luxurious carpet in the room. As it breathed, its tendrils swayed inward and out, like a curtain rippling in a poisonous wind.

At the sight of it, Binnot reeled back and appeared nauseated. He bowed and left the room. It was disgusting, and with such a vicious appearance, it was hard to understand why the Mother clucked and doted on it. She made a motion with a gnarled finger, and it settled on the carpet, eyeing Axel.

"He won't leave my side," she said fondly. Her bony fingertips ran along the spiky ridge on its spine, the way some people might lovingly touch a blade to check its sharpness. "So. Axel. Here you are."

"Yes. Here I am, and I'm all yours, in whatever capacity you need," he said. Axel was trying to stay relaxed, despite the Leveler's close proximity. He needed to appear as if he absolutely belonged in this room. As if he were doing the Mother a favor, when they both knew it was absolutely the opposite. But he knew she wouldn't want to see him groveling. He'd seen how she treated such people.

The Mother motioned to have her crystal tumbler filled by one of the lingering attendants. She sipped the liquid and closed her eyes for a moment. For someone living in the middle of nowhere on such an ordinary planet, she seemed an anomaly among the Path. But perhaps that was why she was their leader. She had a vision.

She folded her withered hands on top of her lap and stared at him. An unblinking stare, as if she weren't sure exactly what she wanted, or who Axel really was to her. If she should kill him right there on the spot, or invite him to dinner.

Finally, she shifted her gaze and glanced about the room. "Do give us some privacy. Everyone out."

The attendants and guards didn't hesitate to leave at her order. The door shut with a click.

"Ah," the Mother said, smiling at Axel. "Sometimes it's very nice to have a room to oneself. As someone who has been surrounded by sycophants and servants and guards, you must know what I mean, Axel."

Axel nodded. He did, but the Mother seemed almost greedily to admit that she, too, had to deal with such trappings of power and wealth.

"I do. And I also understand the opportunities that being in this position affords." He leaned forward. "I would like to know how I can be of service, after my last act."

"Yes, your last act. Helpful, you were, though you failed utterly." The Mother hid her face by sipping her drink.

"I paid my dues by going to jail."

"In the Path, many die to pay back their failure. What say you, Axel? Do you deserve the same treatment?" she said.

Axel's heart beat rapidly. And he thought even quicker.

"If you wanted to kill me, you had ample opportunity. You know I can be useful. That's why I'm here, isn't it? I am forever grateful for you giving me a second chance," Axel said, bowing his head and keeping his voice as smooth as possible.

She stared at him with an unnerving gaze and that wizened face. As if waiting for him to slip up somehow. Or perhaps trying to figure out her next move. He felt like a tip-yip, with its owner pondering if he ought to be food or a pet. Or both. After almost a full two minutes of silence, she broke it, and Axel was inwardly relieved.

"I do have a proposal for you, Axel."

She stood, and the Leveler watched her walk around the octagonal room with her cane. Though it seemed to always have a faraway look on its monstrous visage, as if listening or trying to sense something beyond the walls that Axel could not hear or know.

"I had grand plans for you once. I thought you could be a chancellor of the Republic. My Chaos, with so much power! But regretfully, you've sullied your record beyond repair."

Axel swallowed nervously. "But—"

"I'm not done speaking," she said icily. "You've sullied your record, as I said, but only for the moment. We can get you your freedom back. A title. Money. Power and standing in the Republic. You can still be as powerful as a chancellor, without being a chancellor."

"How?" Axel asked.

"Stars, you're a beautiful man, but sometimes you're not so clever." She leaned forward on her cane and smiled. "There is something more powerful in this galaxy than money. More powerful than weapons, or cunning. It's love. You know what the most dangerous thing in the world is? To love someone. Because you hand the most breakable, precious thing over to this person. You willingly give them your living, beating heart, and it's theirs to crush at their will." She leaned back slowly. "I'm talking about your mother, Axel. She will do what you ask, if you say you are in danger."

Axel couldn't move. His mother? The one who wanted to keep him in prison without any chance of allowing him a second chance?

"I don't think she will," Axel said, realizing too late that he wasn't helping his own situation.

"Even you cannot see it! But I can. You will ask her to come to Dalna and let her know your life is at stake. When she arrives, it will be clear that in order for us to spare your life, we shall influence her decisions as she leads this ever-expanding Republic. Those decisions will favor the Path. And over time, you will gently be led back into the public sector after an appropriate period with evidence of, shall we say, *personal rehabilitation.* You'll be free. You'll get your life back. And Chancellor Greylark will know her son is safe. It's perfection."

"Wait . . . you mean right now?" Axel said, his mouth staying open in surprise.

"Yes. This way, you will have more influence than you ever dreamed. No waiting for crumbs at your mother's table." She turned to Axel, her eyes sparkling. "And with that influence, the Path can be meaningful to more than just a handful of believers. It can be a foundation of the entire galaxy. Balance the thoughtless might that the Jedi have wielded. The Jedi, who have been answerable to no one, who have no accountability. By pulling the strings of the chancellor, you can truly bring greatness to this galaxy, not hold it back. *You* will share this vision with me."

Axel shook his head. "My mother will never agree to this." A small voice seemed to enter his head.

Axel. You could actually do good on your own terms. I've seen you do the right thing. This isn't it.

Axel wanted to growl, *Get out of my head, Gella.*

"She's a chancellor," the Mother said. "A diplomat. A politician. She'll talk. That's what they all do. So invite her here. Let her know you're in danger. How could a mother say no? And just think. In time, we can push our influence upon those who don't believe in you," the Mother said, taking another sip of her drink. "The Path has many friends."

Axel ran his hand through his hair. "But what about Chancellor Mollo? My mother doesn't work alone."

"Orlen Mollo lives a dangerous life in the Outer Rim. Things happen." The Mother smiled and came to sit at his side, clasping his hand in her thin, bony palm. Her eyes were large and when they focused on him alone, it felt as if there were no other beings for kilometers around.

"Axel. Do this, for the sake of my ultimate purpose, and for your future."

"The Jedi may come and stop us," Axel said. "They disrupt everything." He thought of Gella yet again. If not for the Jedi, his father would still be alive. His anger strengthened him.

"If they do," the Mother said, "they do at their own risk and will pay with their death. The Jedi will create more havoc. We are ready to fight them, in ways they cannot even fathom. And we will win."

Axel thought. He could not imagine his mother ever agreeing to anything of this. The Mother seemed to sense his hesitation.

"You're wondering if we will kill her," she said, putting her hand on his. "We need her. And you're our leverage. We are not bloodthirsty, Axel." She laughed. "Our quarrel is with those who abuse the Force for power, or try to control it. We have no reason to hurt Kyong Greylark."

Axel wanted to yank his hand away from beneath the Mother's but he dared not move. His thoughts came quickly, as they tended to do when he felt cornered.

He had spent so much of his adult life rejecting everything having to do with his mother's chancellorship. The endless politicking, the glossy lifestyle with the trappings all done for the sake of playing a role. A life of service to others, never for yourself, or, the stars forbid, for your son. He had rebelled, with all of his being, against everything his mother had stood for. And now he could be a shadow of power behind the chancellorship itself. And to be truly free to chart his own future, wasn't that what the Path always promised?

He now examined the opportunity not with disgust, but a clear eye. The Mother saw possibility in Axel. No one really had before. It shattered a mindset that had been set in stone for so long. He felt lighter, freer, just considering it.

Of course, Axel would not endanger his own mother. But the Mother was right. Surely Kyong Greylark could be convinced to do this. Or at least, to come and speak to him face-to-face. To work with the Path, and the Mother, and in doing so help Axel do something purposeful with his life. He could turn the cogs of influence in this galaxy. It was time for Axel to step into the light and take the power for himself. Whatever it took, he'd do it.

"Don't worry," he said, with a sudden burst of confidence. "I'll be sure she comes here."

She was at the door, and the Leveler was by her side, its hulking presence still disconcerting to Axel. QN-1 had been quiet the whole time, and finally rose to hover near his shoulder, but he pushed the droid away. "The fight is coming here, Axel. To Dalna. You have to be on the right side when we win. And this may be the single most important thing you ever do in your whole life. You have no choice but to succeed."

And with that, she was gone.

Chapter Sixteen

THE PATH COMPOUND, DALNA

"We've arrived," Xiri said.

Dalna was in view. Browns, blues, and greens, with cloud cover over half the globe. It was a fairly ordinary-looking planet. On the surface, at least. It was the ordinariness that made Xiri nervous.

Master Char-Ryl-Roy and Jedi Enya Keen entered the cockpit to survey the terrain.

"If we're close enough to bypass any interfering comms and buoys, perhaps we can announce ourselves," Enya said.

"Very well," Char-Ryl-Roy said.

"Is that a good idea?" Xiri asked. She thought of a line from the enormous book on diplomacy she'd been reading. *Imagine, with true feeling, the hopes and fears of the other party.* "I think it best that I open the conversation. They may feel uncomfortable speaking directly to a Jedi at first."

"Well. It's time we announce ourselves. Shall we, Xiri?" Char-Ryl-Roy asked, motioning toward the cockpit.

Xiri led the way and began landing procedures.

"We're on an open, general frequency. Anyone in the Path of the Open Hand compound will hear it," Char-Ryl-Roy said.

Xiri cleared her voice. "This is Princess Xiri A'lbaran of . . . Eiram and E'ronoh. I am accompanied by Jedi Master Char-Ryl-Roy and Jedi Enya Keen, here on a diplomatic mission to open a dialogue about a recent occurrence regarding our planets. We wish to hear your full perspective on the matter."

She held her breath and waited. She whispered to Char-Ryl-Roy, "Do you think it was received?"

Char-Ryl-Roy nodded. "Nothing to do but wait."

Minutes later, a voice came through.

"This is Elder Yulon Onning. Senior council member of the Path of the Open Hand, thanks be to the Mother. We have received your request. At this time, we do not see the usefulness of such a dialogue, as you call it."

"It would be quite useful, I assure you," Xiri said. "We have much to discuss—" She could hear her voice rising with irritation. She took a breath to pace herself. "We recognize the importance and the influence of the Path of the Open Hand in this galaxy. We wish to hear your wants and needs with respect to our great planets."

"I see," said Elder Onning. "And how would you propose to show your good faith in opening this conversation?"

Xiri muted the comm. "What is he talking about? I don't understand this diplomacy speak!"

Master Roy rubbed his chin. "I believe he's talking about gifts, Xiri. A token of faith."

"Gifts? Tokens?" she whispered. She nearly said, *I didn't get to that part of the diplomacy book!* She patted herself down, as if searching for a blaster without a holster. At her waist was her ever-present bane blade. Xiri never wore jewelry, or anything else of consequence.

Elder Onning spoke again. "We believe in gifts given freely. A tenet of how we see the Force, and a measure of our sense of selves within this universe."

"Gifts given freely," Xiri repeated. "And yet you request a gift to simply open up a conversation?" She'd spoken without thinking and saw the result in Enya's wide eyes of alarm. Master Roy put a hand to his substantial forehead. Oops. Perhaps that was the wrong thing to say.

"If that is how you feel," Elder Onning said, a clear chill in his voice.

Come on Xiri, she said to herself. *Step up. Be a diplomat. Do something.*

"I offer you a cherished personal item, my bane blade, carried with me since I was a youth," Xiri said, trying not to rush her words. "They are priceless on E'ronoh, as they cannot be bought or sold. We never, ever part with them, not until death." She caught her breath. "I offer you the bane blade of a princess of E'ronoh as a token that our discussion is offered with the best of intentions."

"Princess Xiri," Elder Onning replied. "I thoroughly appreciate your vision of our peaceful community. We are but a simple folk, not ones to accumulate shiny little trinkets for the sake of a teatime conversation."

Xiri threw up her hands in frustration.

Enya reached forward to mute the comm. "He's bluffing!" Enya said. "I think he's salivating at the idea of receiving gifts. You can practically hear his hands making grabbing motions."

"What about Teegee?" Xiri suggested.

At this, Enya jumped up and unsuccessfully suppressed a squeal. "Not Teegee! I only just got him together in one piece!"

"Okay, okay!"

Xiri looked over her shoulder and saw Enya exhale with relief and pat 4VO-TG, who was at her side. The droid also made a noise of relief that sounded slightly like a human passing gas.

What else did they have, Xiri wondered. They couldn't give up their ship. The astromech wasn't up for grabs. Her own precious bane blade was rejected outright.

"But I believe," the Elder continued, "in a true show of an . . . *open hand* of friendship, there may be something aboard your ship that would prove how deep your good intentions truly are."

"Here we go," Char-Ryl-Roy whispered. "Let the bargaining begin."

Xiri opened the comm. "Please do speak. We are all here to listen."

"I believe you said there were two Jedi aboard," Elder Onning said. "Given our differing views on the Force, the very presence of a Jedi is an affront to everything we believe in."

Xiri watched Enya and even Char-Ryl-Roy stiffen at the remark. She didn't know what to say to that. The Elder broke the silence, finally.

"As a show of faith, as you expressed so eloquently, we would accept a gift that was sincerely important to us, as well as those in your party."

"Yes?" Xiri said.

"A lightsaber. The Jedi's killing weapon. After all, it is the embodiment of how the Jedi use the Force. And the Path believes it ought not to be used. Giving us a personal lightsaber would be the ultimate show of respect to our people."

The two Jedi couldn't hide their astonishment. Xiri muted the comm once more, and Master Roy put his hand on his lightsaber.

"We cannot do such a thing. It has never been done," Master Roy said. "It is a part of who we are. A lightsaber is a dangerous weapon in the wrong hands. It would be reckless to give it away."

"I agree," Xiri said. "Surely they can choose something else." She turned the comm on again. "I am afraid a Jedi lightsaber cannot be gifted."

"Then we do not believe you truly choose to talk to us in the spirit of diplomacy. We would see this as an affront to the Path, for it is clear that the people of Eiram, E'ronoh, and all Jedi look upon us with disdain. We have every right to see you as a threat, given your inability to offer a gift given freely. That is all."

The transmission went dead.

Xiri muttered to herself. "I can't believe we came here for nothing," she said.

"Wait!" Enya interjected, standing up. Her dark eyes shone as she held out her lightsaber. "I . . . I'll give them my kyber crystal."

Char-Ryl-Roy faced Enya, holding her shoulders. "Enya. Do you know what you're saying? Finding our kyber crystal is a sacred part of our training as a Jedi. It has chosen us. We cannot give it away like a mere jewel or gem of worth. This is non-negotiable."

"I understand. But I have a feeling that what's happening here is larger than me and my lightsaber, or even my kyber crystal. I'll be okay, Master." Enya smiled. "And who knows. I might get it back, if the talks go well. When they realize we truly are here in the spirit of peace. There are lives at stake. I think it's worth it."

Xiri put her hand on Enya's shoulder. "Are you really sure?"

"I am," Enya said, nodding.

"Okay then." Xiri hailed the Path frequency again. "This is Xiri A'lbaran again. Elder Onning, though we cannot gift a Jedi lightsaber, we offer instead the personal kyber crystal belonging to Jedi Enya Keen to open our discussion together."

They could practically hear the Path Elder smile with satisfaction. "That is satisfactory. Excellent. The Mother will very much appreciate your gift. We are transmitting coordinates to your ship. You may begin landing procedures. We will meet you on the landing pad of our compound shortly."

There was a pall cast upon the party as they prepared to enter Dalna's atmosphere. Enya sat behind the pilot's seat from which Xiri steered the ship. She held her lightsaber in her lap and stayed quiet, as if communing with the crystal in their last moments together. Enya touched the grooves and switch, as well as the various pieces of metal that had come together to make a lightsaber that resembled no other.

"Thank you for doing this," Xiri said. "I know what it must feel like to lose something so precious." She held her bane blade out. "I gave this up once, too. But it found its way back to me, in the most unexpected way. Maybe it will be the same for you."

Enya smiled sadly. "And yet, you offered it again, because you believed in this mission. Maybe I'll get my kyber crystal back, maybe not. A good Jedi does not let their emotions overcome them. It does feel like a piece of me will be lost forever. But a Jedi is more than their lightsaber. As long as the Force is with me, I am still a Jedi. The Force is always with me."

"I think I felt the same way about Phan-tu. And then I almost lost him." She smiled. "I know, it's not the same to compare such things—people and crystals. But I suppose you're feeling like you're losing a piece of yourself. Something irreplaceable."

"Phan-tu is okay, isn't he?" Enya asked, her face frowning with worry.

"I think so? But I can't be sure." Xiri knew he wasn't quite okay, but she didn't know how to fix it. She saw the rainy sky above Dalna in the viewport and watched the rivers, forests, and farmland speed by. "We're nearly there."

Enya carefully dismantled her lightsaber, removing the slightly glowing yellow crystal from the focusing mount. She held it in her hand and smiled.

"It warms to me."

"Are you sure you want to do this?" Master Roy asked once more as their craft landed with a slight bump on the landing pad at the Path compound.

Enya's eyes were shiny, but she was not crying. Her brown cheeks grew duskier for a moment. She stood, her hand gripped around the crystal.

"Yes."

Xiri led the way, exiting the ship, followed by Master Roy and Enya. Master Roy had an odd look on his face. He seemed to be searching in the distance for something.

"Everything okay, Master Roy?" Xiri whispered.

"Yes. I have the feeling—are there other Jedi here?" he wondered quietly.

"I sense them, too," Enya whispered back.

"Now is not the time to ask that question too loudly. Elder Onning certainly didn't mention it. It'll have to wait," Xiri said as she walked forward.

The landing pad was actually one of several large, oval uprisings of compacted soil, with connecting pathways that made the landing pads look like a cluster of spiders from high in the air. There were a few shuttles resting nearby, an old cruiser, and in the distance, planting fields and buildings of all shapes and sizes. On a sunny day, it must look peaceful, but with the rain, it looked almost abandoned and sad. Still, Xiri hungered at the sight of so much greenery and rain, compared to E'ronoh. The moisture in the air was something nonexistent on her home planet. On the watery planet of Eiram, the thickness of the humidity nearly overwhelmed her.

They had landed the *Andesine* on one of the peripheral landing pads and were now being led by a Path member to a central oval set with chairs. An older Sakiyan in khaki robes stepped forward. His robes were marked with blue lines at the hem, and like the three armed Path guards behind him, three wavy vertical lines shone on his light-grayish forehead. A necklace of simple but large brown beads hung from his neck.

"I am Elder Yulon Onning," he said. His black eyes were unblinking, and his large cranium of gray skin was bare. "Welcome to our modest home here on Dalna." He bowed.

"We thank you for your generous welcome," Xiri said. "I am Princess Xiri A'lbaran, of E'ronoh." She added quickly, "And Eiram."

"Jedi Master Char-Ryl-Roy," Char-Ryl-Roy said.

"Jedi Padawan Enya Keen." She held out a hand. Her dark-brown Padawan braid fluttered in the breeze. "We freely offer the gift of my kyber crystal, taken from my lightsaber. Thank you for welcoming us today."

Elder Onning held out a hand, his eyes glistening at the sight of the irregularly faceted yellow kyber. Enya dropped it into his palm, and he very quickly closed his thin, gray hand around it and shoved it into a pocket of his robes. Enya visibly contracted at the almost greedy disappearance of her crystal.

"Let us sit and speak," Elder Onning said. He motioned to a set of wooden benches set out on a bare landing pad.

Xiri balked. Would they not be led indoors to a private place? The landing pad seemed like a hasty, last-minute decision, and not terribly appropriate. Xiri was so used to having official visits and talks with delegations of various planets and organizations visiting E'ronoh. There was always a welcoming banquet or a party with the most illustrious guests on the planet. They'd have plush sleeping quarters ready for the guests and their many attendants, prepared food and drink, and walking tours of the grounds and parts of the capital city to show off. Even at the height of the war, when resources were most scarce, her father insisted on the protocols.

Xiri had a weird feeling their conversation would last five minutes, and then they'd be back on their ship, shooed away, minus a very important kyber crystal. They all settled into their seats, and the Elder opened his hands.

"Please, speak freely," he said.

Xiri couldn't help but wonder if he would allow himself to do the same. She calmed herself for a second, building up her confidence.

"An event has occurred on the small moon in the neutral space between my two planets. As you know, Eiram and E'ronoh had been observing a cease-fire at the time and awaiting the signing of a formal peace treaty. That is, prior to hearing the news about the failed signing on Jedha."

At the mention of Jedha, the Elder turned his head and fixed his gaze squarely upon the two Jedi. "The failure was grave, indeed."

"Yes," Xiri said. "We have been thankful for the ongoing help from the Jedi during this difficult time." She cleared her throat. "In any case, two people claimed to be hauling goods from Skye to Shuraden and alleged that they were attacked by pirates. Their incapacitated ship ended up on our moon. Upon boarding their ship, a supply of klytobacter was found, in a volume that amounted to a bioterroristic threat against Eiram. The two people claimed to have nothing to do with it. However, upon questioning, one of the survivors, Goi Ganok, declared himself a member of the Path of the Open Hand and swore allegiance to the Mother. He then killed himself while speaking words usually spoken by the Path. The other, Binnot Ullo, escaped."

"I see," Elder Onning said. "And you think we take responsibility for these two criminals?"

Master Roy and Xiri exchanged uncomfortable glances. "Any information you may have about them would be greatly appreciated," Xiri said.

"Your accusation," the Elder said, his fingers gripping his robes, "shows your false allegiance to diplomacy itself."

"We make no accusations," Xiri said, trying to keep her voice level and failing. She could practically hear the voice of Phan-tu in her head telling her to be calm. In fact, her wrist comlink buzzed. He was trying to communicate with her. *Not now!* She discreetly hit her communicator to disregard the message. "We would never accuse a people who are so set upon spreading their peaceful message in the galaxy. These people could have framed you, which would be atrocious on many levels. Any information you have would be helpful." A new idea popped into Xiri's head. Might as well try. She sat back, saying, "We would certainly be happy to speak to the Herald, or the Mother, if this information is too sensitive at this level. We understand that everyone has limitations of power, no matter who they are."

The Elder heard her words, and clearly understood her challenge. Was he important enough to even be discussing this?

"I can assure you, I am a direct representative of the Mother. As for the Herald, he reports to her. It is not my place to speak for him."

There was a very abrupt way he spoke of the Herald that implied an unsteady relationship with him.

Char-Ryl-Roy whispered to Enya, but Xiri could hear them. "Yoda told us from Master Sun's report about Jedha that the Herald was responsible for the riots. Perhaps the Path was formally a part of this, but he could have been working alone."

Enya nodded. "Sounds like a power struggle to me."

There was a beeping at a distance: 4VO-TG had rolled out of their ship, heading for her. Enya gave a warning gesture for the droid to halt, but it kept coming anyway. The astromech was starting to show a stubborn insistence on being useful.

The Elder saw the droid headed their way and balked, standing up and waving his guards forward.

"What is this? An assassin droid?"

"No! Forvio-Teegee is a regular astromech droid," Enya explained. "He's very friendly, and somewhat attached to me."

"I see," the Elder said, his face still quite suspicious, as 4VO-TG wheeled its way to Enya's side.

"As I said, any information about Binnot Ullo or Goi Ganok—any at all—would be useful," Xiri continued.

"As I said, we know nothing of either name," the Elder said.

"Please," Xiri said. "Are you sure? Do you know if there are, perhaps, ex-Path-members that might be working with their own agenda separate from the Mother?"

The Elder's face suffused with anger. "Are you accusing me of *lying*, Princess?"

"No! I just . . ." Xiri backpedaled, but wasn't sure what to say. Smooth talking could only go so far. And it wasn't like both Jedi could suddenly give up their kyber crystals to soothe the tension. This was going horribly. To make it worse, her comlink buzzed again, and she hit it distractedly to disregard the message, but instead, accepted it.

Phan-tu's voice was suddenly loud and clear. "Xiri! Watch your back."

Master Roy gave her a severe look, and the Elder stamped his foot. Why would Phan-tu say that, now of all times?

"Are there other undisclosed parties listening in on our meeting? How dare you! This is a disgrace and an affront!"

There was a sharp cry, followed by a shout in the distance. Everyone stood up. The Elder was furious. Xiri was trying to shut off her comlink, and Char-Ryl-Roy and Enya had turned to the noise, their bodies ready to spring to action. Which the Elder's armed guards took as a threat to them, as they swarmed toward the meeting with their blasters and pikes held aloft.

Xiri wanted to start over again, which was impossible.

How could things possibly get worse?

Chapter Seventeen

DOCK FOUR, TOWN OF FERDAN, DALNA

Gella Nattai and Orin Darhga had been hiding for some time inside the cargo hold of the ship when it landed. As the crates were taken off one by one, Gella and Orin managed to keep to the shadows and slip off the ship, seeking refuge in the darkness of the storage building they were now in. She heard one of the Path members say something about transporting the crates to the compound soon, as if it were urgent. And then they waited for the Path members to leave.

"Orin," Gella whispered.

"What?"

"Why did you help me? This isn't technically a Council-sanctioned mission. You've helped me every step of the way, even though I never asked for it. Even though you could have done other good things, like help Jedha recover, or, I don't know, teach younglings not to use the Force to steal sweets, or something."

"Who says I won't still do that? Though I would take some sweets as a token of my teaching, after they'd stolen it all." His grin softened. "Even fellow Jedi with pure minds and hearts need guidance."

"Well, in case I forget, thank you, Orin. For everything." She smiled.

She knew it wasn't quite like her to suddenly blurt out words of emotion and reveal that sometimes, even Gella Nattai needed to lean on others. And Orin seemed to know this was unlike her as well, and that what they were about to do was not straightforward or easy. That they were in more danger than they'd been in until now.

Uncertainty prickled her skin. She took in Orin's friendly face, as if she might not see it again. She had a terrible feeling that she was going to die soon and leave Orin to carry on this mission without her.

Orin's smile wasn't nearly as grand as hers, but he put his hand warmly on her shoulder and squeezed. Did he feel it, too?

"Let's take a look, shall we?" Orin suggested. Gella peeked out from behind a row of crates to look around.

"There were probably three dozen crates on our ship," she said.

"That's a lot of rice," Orin said. "Enough carbohydrates to put a few banthas to sleep."

"I don't think this is about the rice," Gella said. "Maybe it's poisoned?"

"Perhaps. I think it's time we did some serious cereal surveillance."

Gella had gotten quite used to Orin's quips, and didn't mind them anymore. In fact, she found them oddly comforting. A tiny speck of humor in a usually humorless world.

When it seemed like the Path had left the area after unloading all the crates, Gella and Orin used their hands to pry off the side of one of them. Gella expected a heavy mass of rice to flow out. But there was merely a loose cascade that fell at her feet.

The crate wasn't full of rice.

It contained a droid, sitting in a crouched position, ready to be deployed. She could tell it was taller than her by half a meter. It had an expanse of featureless and smooth black shielding for a face, with arms thick with weapons, and sturdy bipedal legs. The droid looked brand-new, the shiny metal body glinting in the low light.

"That's an enforcer droid," Orin said. "It's built to massacre. Not for farming."

"There's a battle coming here, on Dalna," Gella said. "Otherwise, they'd have shipped them somewhere else. We have to tell people."

"How? We have no ship. No access to comms."

Gella shook her head. "There's only one person here on Dalna who could help us."

"Who?"

Gella shrugged and gave him a look.

"You're not talking about Axel, are you? I think maybe I've had the wrong kind of influence on you, Gella. Because that is truly a terrible joke."

"Look. He thinks I'm dead. I know him well enough to know it probably upset him. A lot. He's probably feeling incredibly guilty. He's made some terrible choices, but I don't think he truly enjoys hurting people. I might convince him to do the right thing. And if I can't, I can at least snare him into helping us get a message out."

"Sounds like an awful plan." Orin smiled. "All right. Let's go and see if that scoundrel Axel has any good left in him."

"Let's blend in and find out where the leadership of the Path is. That's where he'll be. He's probably already getting elbow-to-elbow with anyone important here."

Gella and Orin shortly managed to render unconscious two Path members who were outside the huge shed with the enforcer droids, put on their clothing, and wipe the blue paint from their faces then smear the residue onto their own foreheads. They surreptitiously followed some Path members, occasionally hiding behind purplish trees, on the hour-long walk to the Path compound. The skies were gray and a light rain dampened their robes. When they arrived at the compound, it was strangely devoid of people. Gella wondered if the rain prohibited them from working.

They walked past a large meeting hall and past a flat area that was paved with wavy lines of sun opals. Over a rise of land, they saw several Path members making their way toward the huts around the compound. They were carrying people on stretchers.

"Is there some hospital here somewhere?"

"No, Gella. The only ones on stretchers are the elderly. I think they're being evacuated for some reason."

Gella and Orin immediately pivoted when one of the stretchers passed them by.

"Please. Let us help," Gella said, her hand on the arm of a woman who looked fatigued from carrying her human load.

"Thank you. We are already late for the gathering."

"How many are there?" Gella asked.

"These are the last ones. And then we will be ready."

Orin said, "Ready for what?" He pointed to his ear. "I don't hear so well."

"They're coming," the woman said, looking fearful.

"Who?" Orin said, cocking his ear toward her as if partially deaf.

"*Everyone,*" she said, as she turned around and ran back where she'd come from.

Gella and Orin stood, confused, when the other person holding the stretcher said, "Let's get a move on! We have to get this lady to shelter, quickly."

Gella nodded. She took one and Orin offered to take the other one as the tired Path member accepted the help and also ran back over the hills.

"Where are we going?" Gella asked the older lady. She was so frail, nothing but bones and wrinkled skin under her robe. The blue lines on her forehead hadn't been redone in a while, and the paint was cracking and flaking off. She had no teeth, and lisped her answer.

"To my home. My last home."

Her words gave Gella chills. The old woman pointed with a gnarled finger. There were a group of huts on the far side of a field studded with stunted-looking gourd plants. The rain pattered down upon Gella, Orin, and their charge as they quickly brought her to an empty hut and gently laid her down on a bed of straw. There wasn't much else in the hut, just a stale pitcher of water and another straw bed.

"Is there anyone here to take care of you?"

"No. They have other responsibilities now," she said. She waved her hand. "The Force will be free."

Gella nodded, frowning. Orin pulled her sleeve. "We have to go," he said.

They made their way back from whence they came, over the rolling hills beyond the planting fields. The compound was completely deserted now. They headed in the direction where the last Path member had gone, when Gella stopped.

She reached out with the Force and listened. A slight hum called to her from beyond the area, as if a song wished to resonate within her very self. She felt the kyber crystal in her remaining lightsaber, hidden behind the folds of her robes, echo the feeling coming toward her. The twin kyber crystals were close to one another now.

"No. Axel isn't there. He's there." She pointed to an octagonal structure east of the underground entrance.

They walked toward it, eyes searching out the area from beneath their hoods. A single Path guard stood before the entrance, and he tensed at Gella and Orin's approach. Orin motioned with his hands.

"You will let us through the door, then leave us."

They nodded and stepped aside. As Gella reached for the door, Orin hesitated.

"Gella. Be careful. I sense a great deal of danger here. Do not let your feelings confuse you. Think this through."

Gella felt almost as if she were a young Padawan from years ago, looking to her master for guidance. What was it about Axel that sometimes disoriented her, and made her feel like she didn't know what she was doing?

"Yes, Orin. I'll be careful."

They proceeded inward, out of the rain, which had intensified. The structure seemed to be built with concentric hallways. As they made their way through the outer passageway, they noted alcoves with what looked like priceless crystal formations and sculptures made of precious metals, glowing with lights above them. The tiles beneath them were handcrafted and ancient, and the walls intermittently decorated with fine textile art with ropes and tassels of silk.

"Pretty fancy for a people whose robes are all in tatters at the edges," Orin noted, looking down at his own disguising robes and the threads falling off them.

Gella heard a voice, and her skin prickled. Axel. There was a door around the next curve, and they stood outside. Orin gently slid the pocket door open by only a few millimeters. Gella and Orin spied inside, listening.

It *was* Axel. He was standing before a holorecorder, which was recording him. He wore a new set of clothing, no longer in his prison wear. He was fidgeting with his collar, murmuring under his breath about missing his Coruscant tailor. QN-1 was buzzing around him, gently clicking and whirring, attending to his nervousness.

"I'm fine. Yes, Quin." He spoke to the holorecorder. "Start over. Delete last recording." He sighed deeply, composed himself, and began to speak.

"Chancellor. Mother. I am speaking to you from the Path of the Open Hand compound on Dalna. I am sure you have some choice words for me about my leaving Pipyyr."

Gella tried not to snort. *Leaving?* Didn't he mean "illegally escaping"?

Axel went on. "And when I did, I left many things behind me. I'll no longer take the blame for a wrestling match between parties in which I was a pawn. I will no longer be told what to do instead of orchestrating change myself. Until recently, I did not question my true place in this galaxy."

Axel looked down, and QN-1 was circling his ankles, unseen by the holorecorder. Axel showed QN-1 his palm, instructing the droid to keep out of the recording. Gella knew he wanted to look like a grown man in charge, not a perpetual boy with petty anger. He looked up again, squaring his jaw.

"I know you always hoped that someday I would take my place at your side in leading this galaxy. That I would learn the meaning of leadership, and what enormous sacrifices it would take to bring this galaxy together. I am ready now. My first action is to ask you to come to Dalna. To speak with me. To speak directly with the Mother of the Path. To fix what is broken."

What? Gella mouthed, nearly shouting the words. Orin, too, seemed to hold back an exclamation.

"I do not speak for the Path," Axel continued. "I speak for myself. No one else knows them as I do, and their purpose in this galaxy. And I can tell you this. If you and I don't fix this right now, the lives of many people are in great danger. Including my own."

Orin gripped Gella's arm, knowing she would intrude before they heard everything first.

"Yes," Axel said. "I'm tired of us being broken. After all, who can trust a chancellor that cannot even save her own family?"

Axel's gaze had dropped back to the floor for a moment. A perfect moment of drama. He pushed his shoulders back and stared into the holorecorder. "I know how ashamed you are of me. But you happily live with that, as you did when you threw me into prison on Pipyyr. But what I know in my bones is that you loathe being ashamed of yourself more. This is your chance to rectify mistakes."

He stopped the recording and exhaled. His shoulders fell, and even watching him from this rear angle, Gella could see the immense exhaustion weighing him down. Because he knew what he was asking. Kyong Greylark would be in serious danger if she came. He was about to send the transmission when Gella yanked her arm away from Orin's hand and burst into the room.

"Stop!" she yelled.

Axel's hand pulled away from the holorecorder as he turned in surprise. At the sight of Gella, Axel's face was one of pure shock.

"*Gella?*" he said in disbelief. "You're alive? I thought—I thought—"

"You thought you killed me?" she finished for him.

Orin stepped into the room. "Don't forget about me. You thought you killed a bonus Jedi, for points perhaps? Didn't work."

"I just—no—I wasn't trying to kill you, Gella. Or you, Orin." He shook his head. "You can't know how glad I am that you're alive." He approached her, as if wanting an embrace or to possibly poke Gella to make sure she was truly and actually alive, when she took out her lightsaber, lighting the purple blade with its familiar hum. Axel put up both his hands, QN-1 swinging behind him. "Hey. Listen. I was just trying to get my freedom. Surely you know what that feels like."

"You were running, Axel. That's what you've always done, what you're good at. Running away from responsibility, from your potential. You could be better than this, and you know it, but you keep looking for the easy, wrong answer. When will you grow up?"

Axel leaned against the console behind him. "Can we take a moment here? Stop trying to sound like my mother. You don't understand, Gella. You have no idea how people have to work together to make things function in the Republic. As a Jedi, you travel the galaxy, but you have no home in it. You visit world after world as part of some grand purpose. But all you do is sit in judgment of others."

The words stung. Because there was a time when Gella had felt uncertain about her place in the galaxy. But then she remembered who she was, and what she believed in.

"No, Axel. That is a child's understanding of being a Jedi. Figures someone like you would dirty up a pure and good thing because it doesn't fit him like a tailored suit."

"You're wrong, Gella. This is what I was meant to do. I get it now. I didn't have the ability to see this, but it all makes sense. I've been a shadow in my mother's life for decades. I've actually learned a lot about diplomacy and negotiation."

"And now you're ready to fill her shoes? Perhaps let her casually die at the hands of the Path?"

"They are capable of that, you know," Orin said quietly. His face was grave. "Murdering her. That may be the plan, and you may be the pawn once again."

"Oh, and they'll probably time it with an enormous battle they'll blame on the Jedi again," Gella added.

"What are you talking about?" Axel said.

"Those crates of grain that you and that Mirialan fellow brought over here from Jedha? Don't you know what's in them?" Gella didn't wait for him to answer. "Enforcer droids. The Path doesn't need to defend itself on that level, according to the way it claims it's been behaving. It's readying itself for a battle. Can't you see that?"

"So what? If you believe in something, you should fight for it. Isn't that what we both helped Xiri and Phan-tu do?"

"You are so lost," Gella said, "You have no idea how deeply disoriented you are. And speaking of lost things—hand over my lightsaber, thief."

Axel looked down. He pushed aside his long jacket, where Gella's lightsaber hung. "You know, I've cherished this as a remembrance of you."

"Axel," she said again. "Look at me. You don't have to do this. You always said you wanted to burn through the galaxy like a supernova, but look what damage you're leaving in your wake. Innocent people, and people who care about you. You're incinerating *yourself.* There's another way to do good in this galaxy, to be the person you want to be. Not your mother. Not the Path's Mother. Not me. You need to follow your heart, not the hurt that's been trailing behind you for years."

QN-1 clicked and hooted. Axel shook his head, but uncertainty flickered across his features. "Stop it, Quin."

"Quin knows I'm right," Gella said quietly.

"Son," Orin said. "You need guidance. And real friends. Bringing your family into a slaughter is not the way to make peace with yourself, or anyone. You think she can just hand the chancellorship to you? It's not how things work. Can't you see that bringing the chancellor here puts her in terrible danger? They'll frame her presence here to suit them, you know. The chancellor brought the war with her. It'll be far too easy for them to kill her in the melee. Or perhaps torture her for some other goal."

Axel seemed to hesitate. His hand was still on the console, a second away from sending the message to Chancellor Greylark.

The doors opposite the room opened. Binnot Ullo stepped in, along with three guards.

"We saw you enter the building," Binnot said. "You and your Jedi mind tricks. You think they're a free pass to get whatever you want. The same way you use and abuse the Force. You take and take. Over and over again. Well, it's time for us to do the taking for a change." He wore a long black leather glove on his right hand, and closed his hand into a fist.

"We are one with the Force," Orin said. "It is no beholden relationship. That is what you misunderstand."

"And that is what you make yourselves believe," Binnot said. He looked to Axel. "Did you send it?"

"Almost," Axel said, reaching for the console button.

In one quick thrust, Gella swung her lightsaber so it was between Axel's reaching fingertips and the button.

"No, Axel. This is the wrong decision." She looked at him. Somewhere, he must know. *He has to know,* Gella thought. *Don't do this. Please.*

Axel looked between Binnot and Gella, wavering.

"Goodness, this is worse than babysitting," Binnot said. "Kill them," he ordered the guards.

They were large, these Path guards, and they immediately launched forward. Blaster bolts lit up the room as Gella and Orin deflected them, trying not to kill Axel with a ricochet in the close quarters. Binnot pulled out a blaster and began firing, but Orin deflected four shots before he used the Force to throw a chair in the room straight at Binnot, who dodged it at the last second.

Gella lifted her empty hand, trying to push Binnot hard enough to throw his body against the wall, when Binnot stared at her hard. She felt a resistance that surprised her, but Orin had lifted the chair up again, throwing it against Binnot, who was concentrating on repelling Gella's Force assault. The chair hit him hard against his head, and Binnot fell limply to the ground.

Burn holes sizzled into the fine furnishings and wall hangings in the room. Gella blocked the blaster bolts of two of the guards, until the deflected shots hit them one after the other—in the head, and in the chest—killing them both instantly.

Binnot lay on his back upon the floor, unmoving.

Axel pulled out Gella's lightsaber, igniting it and stepping in front of Binnot. "Get back!"

"You'll defend him?" Gella said. "You don't deserve to hold that lightsaber and you never will."

Orin was just behind her. "He's cornered. He knows it."

"I won't go back to prison, Gella. I don't belong there!" Axel yelled, taking a slight step backward.

"What, you think you're better than everyone else?" Gella said.

"No, because I won't have a chance to redeem myself there."

Gella shook her head. "You had your chance! And you keep making the wrong choices!"

"Son, put down that lightsaber," Orin said. "Before you hurt yourself."

"Stop calling me *son!*" Axel said, his voice cold with anger.

Orin had walked closer to Axel, and Gella knew he was on the cusp of disarming him with a simple movement of his own lightsaber. It was something they'd learned as younglings, a basic defensive maneuver. Push down with your lightsaber on your opponent's, use the momentum of a twisting motion to weaken their wrist so the blade flies out of their grasp.

Gella could practically see it in their future when a different sensation suddenly intruded. A terrible sensation.

"Orin!" Gella yelled in alarm.

He felt the danger, too, and held up his lightsaber in defense, but that was not where the danger was. He had stepped too close to Binnot's unmoving body. Binnot shot out his gloved hand, and Orin sprang out of reach in the fraction of a second after Binnot reached for him. Orin flipped upside down and back, landing near the back of the room and out of harm's way.

Gella looked at him, saw him safe, and then pulled with her free hand using the Force. The lightsaber in Axel's hand yanked free and went sailing across the room into Gella's palm. Back where it belonged.

Axel held his hands up.

"Don't surrender, my friend. We've just won," Binnot said, getting to his feet.

Gella looked at him, confused. She heard a soft thudding behind her and turned.

"Gella," Orin said, wheezing.

He'd fallen to his knees. It was then that she saw his face turning a shade of greenish-purple as tendrils of poison spread up his neck. She ran to his side.

"Orin!"

He gasped, holding his neck. He was suddenly breathing so fast. "I can't get enough air, Gella," he said as his body fell backward. She couldn't hold him up. She saw Binnot standing triumphantly next to Axel. He held up his dark-gloved hand, and only then did Gella see the light reflecting off the minute needles protruding from his gloved fingertips.

"He'll be dead in minutes, if you don't surrender," Binnot said. "Only I have the antidote."

Gella froze, unable to think. Orin, dying? No. It simply couldn't be happening. She looked at Binnot's face, so calm and confident. "You're lying. You're just going to watch him die," Gella said.

"Are you going to bet his life on your guess?" Binnot said, leaning against the wall.

Orin was panting, but he was still clutching at his neck and chest, as if trying to will the oxygen into his body. She couldn't take that chance. She deactivated and dropped her lightsabers so her hands could clutch Orin's face.

"Orin! Stay with me! Orin!"

He already looked exhausted, his chest rising and falling so fast. He was looking at Gella, but it was clear he couldn't focus on her face.

His hand now clutched at her wrists. No matter how hard he tried, oxygen wasn't getting into him. By the stars, he was drowning in front of her.

"Gella," he said, between tiny gasps of useless air, "when you remember how to laugh again . . . think of me."

"Stop it. Save your energy. You'll be okay. You will." She didn't care if she was lying, she needed to believe the words herself.

Binnot made a motion, and Axel opened the door behind them. The room flooded with more Path guards, who picked up Gella's lightsabers and began to bind her hands behind her.

"Orin! It'll be okay. You'll be okay," she screamed at Axel, grunting as they twisted her arms hard. Orin's breathing had become quieter, slower. She knew that was bad. "What have you done? Help him now, please!"

"Axel," Binnot said. "Send the transmission already."

Axel walked to the communications console, touching it. "It's sent."

"Our new chancellor!" Binnot grinned at him. Like a skull.

"Not yet, Binnot." Axel didn't look nearly so happy. He was watching Gella, unable to look in Orin's direction as the Jedi Master's mouth foamed with pink froth.

Gella closed her eyes. "Please. Just bring him the antidote." The guards hauled her to her feet, painfully so. Orin's breaths were coming in irregular gasps now. The purplish-green discoloration, like a bruise, had spread through Orin's face. "Please!"

Binnot casually walked over and glanced at Orin's unmoving body. "Too late. He's already dead." He smiled at Gella. "Not that it mattered. No antidote anyway."

Gella roared at him as she was dragged out of the room.

Chapter Eighteen

GREYLARK RESIDENCE, CORUSCANT

Chancellor Kyong Greylark was in the hothouse of the Greylark residence. The top floor of the building was enclosed in a double layer of transparisteel, perfectly temperature- and humidity-controlled to grow a bounty of scarlet queen's heart flowers, purple musk rose, sweet nannarium, and more. Transplanted from all over the galaxy, the blooms were an homage to the Republic's ever-growing reach. Aside from decorating the residence, they were often brought to Kyong's meetings so that distant ambassadors could enjoy the local blooms they loved. It proved how detail-oriented the chancellor was in catering to members of the Republic and, by proxy, the Republic itself.

Normally, she was too busy to visit the hothouse. But waiting for news about Axel had proven so frustrating that she'd been canceling appointments left and right. She couldn't bear to be in meetings, doing nothing but talking.

Axel still had not been found. His haunts on Coruscant, like Raik's Parlor, the Hesperys station, and many others, had come up empty. He could be anywhere. What was his next move? She knew him well enough to know that he didn't like hiding. Soon enough, his face would show up and be recognized by a Republic-friendly scanner somewhere. Kyong would have jumped into her own Longbeam to search herself, but knew it wouldn't help. So instead she mercilessly deadheaded flower after flower, needing to do something. Anything.

The head gardener had balked when she had appeared in her yellow satin gown, rolling up her bell sleeves. When Kyong snagged her skirt on a thorn, she yanked it away and yelled, "Get me some pants!" After the delivery of the clothing, the gardener had wisely left the hothouse to the chancellor.

C-04L was at attendance by the door while the chancellor's aides flitted in and out with various messages. Her shears, after cutting through many tough stems, had grown dull.

"Fourell," she said, wiping the sweat from her temples, "I need a whetstone, or a new pair of shears."

"The gardeners carry the extra shears," the silver droid responded. "As for a whetstone, I can have one fetched from the Heirloom Room."

Kyong paused. "The Heirloom Room?" Why was there a whetstone in the room where her collection of Greylark jewels was kept?

"Shall I retrieve it for you, Chancellor?" C-04L asked.

"No, thank you. I'll get it myself."

Kyong put the shears in the gardener's tool belt at her waist and left the hothouse. She took the lift down to the floor where the family heirlooms were kept. Usually, she went to the illuminated wall display behind glass that held her jadeite headdresses, the bracelets so long they were almost wrist guards, collars encrusted with gems, and more. But the opposite wall was where cabinets that she had all but forgotten existed.

She opened one to find several daggers and a long sword. There were even blasters that were over a hundred years old, held by her great-grandfather during the Procopian Crisis. In a drawer, she found one of many whetstones. They were ancient.

She picked up a black stone, oiling it and sharpening her shears until they were razor-sharp, then returned the stone to its drawer.

"Well done, Chancellor," C-04L said brightly. "I didn't know you had that skill."

"I'd forgotten myself. Everyone thinks of me as a fancy woman of means who isn't in touch with anything or anyone." She tilted her head. "I had some pretty intensive training in the Coruscant Academy before I decided on a life in diplomacy. I used to get my hands dirty. It's just been far too long."

Yet another aide swept into the room. "Chancellor. A message incoming from your son, Axel."

"Axel!" Kyong said. "Call Master Yoda immediately."

She hurried to her meeting room upstairs, shooing away her attendants who urged her to change, or at least wash her hands. She settled before the holoprojector where her home desk was. Yoda's image appeared and they nodded to each other. Yoda's eyebrow ridge twitched at the sight of her, plainly clothed and grease stains on her hands.

"Play the message," she ordered.

Yoda's image disappeared and instead Axel's appeared as they listened simultaneously. There he was, her beautiful, clever son, doing everything she loathed. He took no responsibility, nor showed any regret over his escape. He was not trying to create an honest future for himself. He was trying to steal it. His words stabbed her, but she felt not his betrayal so much as her own regrets and failures.

Every word, a cut. Sharp and deep.

"I am asking for you to come to Dalna," Axel said. "To speak with me. To speak directly with the Mother. To fix what is broken."

Her body didn't feel solid but another form altogether. Liquid. Vapor. The rest of Axel's demands came into her mind, poisoning whatever goodwill she felt toward him. He mentioned the danger he was in, and she knew it was far worse than even Axel realized. She had zero doubt that her one and only child could die if she did not go.

She reached out and clung to the edge of the table. Axel's image disappeared. Yoda's holoimage replaced it. He waited a long time before speaking. "What will you do, Chancellor Greylark?"

She finally let the weight of her body take over and leaned forward, her head in her hands. She wondered if her voice worked anymore.

Finally she whispered, "I don't know. I don't think I have a choice." She looked up at Yoda's image. "I have to go to Dalna."

THE PATH COMPOUND, DALNA

Creighton Sun and Aida Forte were running, but it felt like they were in a bad dream. Though nothing truly impeded them, it was as if their limbs were mired in mud. The effects of whatever had caused them to feel so terrible deep within the caves—and whatever had killed that Force-sensitive Teevan man—had not fully left them.

Still, Aida's mind felt clearer and clearer with every pump of her legs forward. Which meant Creighton, too, must be recovering. There were at least two Path members running after them, and soon two more joined. There was nowhere to hide this time.

"I see daylight!" Aida said. Creighton was running at her side.

"We have to stop this now, before we're out in the open. Everyone will see and attack us. We'll hardly have a chance to escape."

"Turn and fight?" Aida said.

"Yes."

They stopped running, and the Path members behind them yelled in alarm. They ignited their lightsabers and turned to face their pursuers. There was a sudden spray of blasterfire that Enya and Creighton deflected easily. They took a step forward as they tried to push the fight backward. Creighton's eyes were shining and sharp, and whatever fog had been in his brain seemed to be melting away. He used the Force to yank away two blasters as one Path member fell from a shot to the leg. Then another fell.

Aida felt more confident and clearheaded. They pushed the Path members back farther until only one was standing, and she turned and fled.

"We're good. Come on," Creighton said. "We could hide for a while before leaving, or—"

The small lights studding the tunnel walls every other meter went from a placid white to blinking, angry red, paired with a beeping warning siren.

Ten Path members, armed, rounded the corner blocking their way to the exit. Some held blasters, and some held clubs, swords, even a whip.

"Are these the Jedi?" one of them said.

"Must be. Kill them," said another.

Were there other Jedi here? Aida wondered. Running footsteps sounded behind them. She twisted her head to see no less than eight new Path members, similarly outfitted with blunt weapons, spears, and blasters, sandwiching them in on the other side.

"Force-user!" one screamed.

"Vile Jedi," another hissed. "Kill them."

"Or we can fight. Again," Aida said, holding up her green blade.

This time, the fight was ten times worse. The passageway was narrow, and Aida was too busy fending off blasterfire, thrusting her lightsaber, and being bludgeoned. She pushed one way, only to have a whip wind around her wrist. She twirled toward her attacker and freed herself with a slash of her blade.

At one point, her back thudded against Creighton's as they fought back-to-back. The sound of their lightsabers humming and parrying, the smell of burnt clothing and sweat, would have overwhelmed a normal person. But Aida had been taught well, and she was focused as her master had taught her. She felt the Force flowing through her, anticipating the strikes against her, knowing when Creighton was swinging his lightsaber and she needed to duck down. She jumped against the side wall of the cave to strike a Path member down with her own lightsaber and kick another in the chest on her way down.

Four more Path members showed up to replace the four she had brought down.

"Master Yaddle!" Creighton said, turning on his comlink. "Come in! We're being attacked. Have the ship ready—"

There was nothing but silence.

"Where is she?" Aida said, between parries with a Path member.

"Maybe it's the caves. We'll have to try again when we're out of here."

"Creighton," she panted, parrying blasterfire away from hitting the Jedi Master's taller head.

"Yes, Aida?" He wasn't panting, but he spoke in staccato beats.

"I think we may be in trouble."

"I believe you're correct," Creighton replied as he flipped forward to engage five new Path members blocking the way. Their enemies kept coming. And coming.

"Creighton," Aida said. "Have you ever opened a bottle of Alderaan sparkling wine on a hot day?"

"What?" Creighton was yelling, deflecting blaster bolts that were coming faster and faster. "Yes, but what's your point?"

She gestured toward the cave tunnel that led to the exit. "Some of the Path are carrying explosives on their belts." She planted her feet. "We're about to shake that unopened bottle."

Gella's arms were bound behind her back. She had been dragged out of the octagonal building and into the pouring rain, across the rough ground, over stones and thick mud. Gella should have fought. She should have used the Force to knock out her captors, snapped her bonds free, run away. But she could not.

She could only see her failure. She could only see the dead face of Jedi Master Orin Darhga. Orin had done nothing but be at her side in the last few days of his life. Giving her guidance when she needed it. Helping her. Allowing her to make choices but being a sounding board for her thoughts—even when she didn't ask for it, yet needed it. And he had been cheerful the entire time, as if this was everything he wanted. In his nonexistent future, he could have helped rebuild Jedha City, or reached out to civilizations far beyond the Inner Rim and Core planets to bring people of the galaxy together. Instead, he decided, on an apparent whim, to accompany a Jedi he had just met because he sensed she was in need. He trusted the Force and stayed with Gella when she impulsively went to Axel Greylark, her anger clouding her mind.

For all those choices, he had paid the ultimate price.

At some point, her captors dragged her through dark, damp, ever-descending tunnels before throwing her into a room. Beneath her was hard-packed dirt, and around her were walls of what seemed like thick clay and stone. She was on her knees, as if meditating or praying. She felt like doing neither. For the first time since she could possibly remember—she truly felt alone. Her eyes smarted, and a tear crested over the edge of her lashes and fell to the hard-packed dirt with an audible little *pat*.

Intrusively, Orin's voice sounded in her mind, her imagination churning out the words before she could stop it.

Ah, you're in a pickle, aren't you, Gella? But then if you were a pickle, you'd need a lot more vinegar in that cell with you. And some herbs. But no hot peppers. And no salt. You're spicy and salty enough.

Against her will, the edge of her mouth tipped upward in a minute, lopsided grin. The mirth mixed with her grief and failure.

"Orin," she said aloud, knowing he couldn't hear her, knowing he was no longer at her side, alive. She had heard of the possibility that spirits of deceased Jedi could commune with living Jedi. But that was a fairy tale. This was not that. This was her imagination trying to fix things she had broken. "Oh, Orin. I'm so sorry."

And she imagined his next words: *Eh, I've eaten so many dubious foods from so many dubious places that it was only a matter of time before poison found me. Took away my ruddy good looks, though, that's a shame.*

Gella smiled again, but this time it was a real, true smile. She even chuckled aloud.

She knew, from her understanding of the Force, that Orin wasn't truly gone. That the Force was in him before he died, and afterward, he was one with the Force in a way that was anything but corporeal. But he had left a part of himself in her memory. He had affected her and, in turn, all her future actions. And that part of him was alive, very much alive.

Gella sniffled. She stumbled to her feet and shuffled around, taking in her surroundings for the first time. The room was actually a small one. She bumped into the walls and could tell they were quite thick. The door was metal, but there was an opening with short, thick bars. The ceiling had a ventilation shaft, but it looked to be very narrow. Already, the air was stale in here. She stamped on the floor. It was hard clay, with no layer of wood beneath the dirt.

She backed into the stone wall behind her, her fingers searching until she found an edge that was rough and slightly sharp. She pulled her bonds tightly, and carefully rubbed the rope against the sharp edge. Concentrating, she was able to break the ropes before too long.

Gella's first thought was to jump into the ventilation shaft, but it was too small anyway. And what would she propose to do? Find Axel, and make him pay for what he'd done? Perhaps stop the Path from whatever larger ill intent they might have? But then she thought of Orin, and stopped.

Once again, Axel was pushing her to act, and she was tired of being subject to that pull.

It was time to stop reacting. If Gella wanted to act, it had to be on her terms.

Gella gently went to her knees, closed her eyes, and began to meditate. The faint sounds around her came to her like ripples in a stream, intermingling with her existence. There were people nearby, not imprisoned like her. She sensed a guard outside her door, his nervousness, his elevated heart rate thumping the pulsations of anxiety into the air around him. Something was about to happen, or was already happening. She smelled the air, wet from the loamy ground beneath her. But there was also the faint metallic tang of weapons being sharpened, of explosives being prepared. And finally, a twist of two emotions that made the Force feel like a turbulent flow in what should have been a Force-respectful, peace-loving settlement.

Anger. So much anger.

And the other sensation—a yawning, vicious hunger emanating from somewhere nearby. A terrifying disruption in the Force that frightened her.

The anger, she surmised, came from the Path members around her. But the other feeling was inexplicable. Nevertheless, she had to clear her mind to guide her way. She must simply exist within the Force, with all its ebbing and flowing, all its nearby turbulence. With much effort, she allowed her emotions to melt away, leaving her to exist so there was nothing but Gella, and only Gella, listening with every atom of her being to the Force.

She waited. And she listened.

It told her to be still. Not to escape.

Something, or someone, was coming for her.

Chapter Nineteen

THE PATH COMPOUND, DALNA

Master Char-Ryl-Roy was a good listener, but right now there were voices coming from all directions, going in all directions, and amounting to nothing but pandemonium. In the rain and on the large oval landing pad that rose several meters above the ground and had served as their diplomatic meeting place, Elder Yulon Onning was yelling at Xiri. She was trying desperately to turn off the comlink at her wrist, from which came Phan-tu Zenn's voice loudly and clearly asking if they needed armed backup.

"Liars!" Elder Onning hissed. "Look at you, pretending to be peaceful, and yet you cloak yourselves in falsehoods! How dare you!"

He seemed less angry than Roy expected. There was a disconnect between his words and his face. Elder Onning actually appeared pleased, as if he had expected this all along.

But something else caught his attention. A noise that rumbled from a distance under the gray clouds, beyond the buildings and farmland that spread out east of the landing pad. Something outside of the chaos of this diplomatic meeting had gone awry. Along with the patter of rain, there were distinct cries of distress.

In the distance, farther south where swells of land rose beyond the largest planting field, smoke arose from a nondescript hill. Several people wearing the blue-streaked cloaks of the Path were running from what appeared to be an entrance into the hill. There must be an underground structure there, Char-Ryl-Roy thought. Caves perhaps.

"No! This meeting is officially over!" Elder Onning was heard. "Leave now, Princess Xiri. To attack us with nothing but accusations and spies listening in—unacceptable!"

One of the Path guards with Elder Onning whispered something hurriedly. Several other guards had come to the landing pad, some with blasters in hand and two with large pikes. Char-Ryl-Roy found his hand touching his lightsaber at the sudden appearance of more guards.

"What Jedi? They're right here." He pointed at Char-Ryl-Roy and Enya Keen, who were intensely watching the spark of chaos in the distance that no one else seemed to be noticing.

"Not *them*," the guard said, her face pale with anxiety. "*Them*." She pointed behind the Elder's back, toward the smoking hill.

A string of small explosions suddenly sounded. Smoke and fire billowed out from the entrance to the underground caves, along with the bodies of half a dozen Path members that flew out like wet rags. Children and adults screamed as other Path members began streaming out of the smoking hole.

Despite the rain, Char-Ryl-Roy clearly saw bright blue- and green-colored lightsabers within the melee. He wiped the moisture from his face with a sleeve and peered into the distance. The unmistakable face and beard of the human male Jedi and the young Kadas'sa'Nikto female at his side made Master Roy's eyes open wide.

"It's Creighton Sun! And Aida Forte! Well, that explains what I sensed. What in the stars are they doing here?" he said.

"Running away, from the looks of it," Enya said.

"It's an ambush! Kill them! Kill them all!" the Elder yelled, immediately scrambling backward. He shoved away an aide, who fell right off the platform onto the hard-packed dirt six meters below. Two Path guards nearby took direct aim at Xiri.

"No!" Enya yelled. She ran forward, knocking Xiri out of the way as a guard pulled the trigger. With two swift parries with his lightsaber, Char-Ryl-Roy sliced the end off the blaster. The guard turned on his heel and ran, trailing the Elder who was far ahead of him.

"My crystal!" Enya gasped, as Elder Onning disappeared down an embankment behind four more bodyguards. 4VO-TG bleeped in distress and rolled quickly away from all the chaos, toward their ship.

"You don't need a lightsaber to be a Jedi," Master Roy reminded her, his body already in a fighting stance. He swung his lightsaber toward three guards with pikes who approached them. He grabbed one of the pikes, twisting it out of the hand of the guard and kicking him off the landing pad. He tossed the pike to Enya, who caught it easily. "Protect the princess. The *Andesine* is not too far off. We have to reach Creighton and Aida and get out of here."

"Yes, Master!" Enya was already parrying with one of the guards, who had both a pike and a long knife. She ducked and jumped, easily evading the weapons of the Path member, who stabbed and swung. With one well-timed jump, she landed on his pike and snapped it in half, kicking backward with her leg to strike the Path guard in the chest. His knife went sliding away on the slick plateau, and she pulled it into her grasp with the Force as she struck the guard in the temple with her pike to render him unconscious.

"Sweet dreams!" she said, spinning around at the sound of a shriek behind her. She swiveled her head. "Teegee? Where did you go?"

Xiri had picked up a pike from a fallen Path guard and was battling another, who was pushing her closer and closer to the edge of the landing pad. One of the Path members came up behind her and was about to strike with a long knife when Enya used the Force to shove him right off the edge. His body hit the turf with a splash and a thud.

Xiri disarmed the guard before her, sweeping her leg underneath him. He, too, rolled off the muddy plateau to fall far to the ground below. She pushed the wet hair out of her eyes and looked over at Char-Ryl-Roy. She yelled, "Master Roy! Time to go!"

"Back to the *Andesine!*" Char-Ryl-Roy hollered back. More and more armed Path members were starting to emerge from . . . where? They seemed to be rising right out of the ground, as there were no buildings near them. It had been four, then seven, now almost fifteen of them attacking from all sides. As Char-Ryl-Roy fought, pushing back their attackers, they were able to get closer to their ship.

But what were Creighton Sun and Aida Forte doing here? He couldn't see any Jedi or Republic ships anywhere nearby. He saw the two Jedi, closer now, as they fought off attackers chasing them at a steady clip from the cave entrance. Another small explosion went off several meters away from the landing pads, obscuring Creighton and Aida for a moment. When the smoke cleared, three Path members were facedown on the ground and Creighton and Aida were running at top speed toward them. In two large bounds, they jumped right up to the high landing pad that Roy and their whole party were on.

Creighton looked slightly ill, with a pasty complexion evident even though his face was obscured by his beard. Aida's green, scaly skin was covered in dust, with the rain cutting clean paths down her face. She was breathing hard. As soon as they appeared on the landing pad, Xiri looked relieved, then suddenly angry. Xiri shot at a Path member right behind Creighton, who had run up with an ax in hand.

"Thanks for that," Creighton said, leaning over and resting his hands on his knees. "What is going on here? Why are you here, Master Roy? I thought you were being sent to E'ronoh and Eiram?"

"I should ask the same, but perhaps when there's more time," Master Roy said. They ran, with blaster shots being deflected here and there, but the fighting Path members on the landing pad had suddenly decreased in number. Perhaps they had won.

As they ran across one connecting bridge to another landing pad where a decrepit ship lay on its side, Creighton explained. "I'm here with Master Yaddle, who brought a youngling in tow along with two of Chancellor Greylark's guards. We came to secretly gather information to prove the Path's involvement with the catastrophe at Jedha."

"Secret?" Master Char-Ryl-Roy's considerable forehead moved upward. "I don't think it's much of a secret anymore."

"I know, I know. But listen. They have a whole klytobacter laboratory in there. It's not good."

"What?" Xiri yelled, her face livid.

"Yes. Tanks and tanks of it," Aida hollered as she ran past the group and deflected blaster bolts coming from below the landing pads.

"We've got to tell our people," Xiri said. "They have no idea how much danger they're in!"

"We suspected as much," Char-Ryl-Roy said. "But not to this extent. Ours was supposed to be a diplomatic mission—"

Creighton threw him a reciprocal look. "I don't think it's a diplomatic mission anymore, Char-Ryl-Roy."

"What can I say? Today is the day of failed missions and a big mess," Master Roy said, still running.

"It gets worse!" Aida said, now at Char-Ryl-Roy's side.

"How can it be worse?" Char-Ryl-Roy said. Xiri and Enya were far ahead of them. They were all running from landing pad to landing pad, all linked by narrow walkways to the *Andesine,* which was close by now. Luckily, they were no longer being trailed by Path members. Perhaps they would escape after all.

"We saw a Force-sensitive Path member in trouble," Aida told Char-Ryl-Roy. "A few minutes later, he was killed by something. Something that turned him to ash, and had a tremendous effect on the Force. Master Sun and I felt the effects, and it was like what Silandra had described there. They've got to be connected. Jedi there were turned to ash, too. We have to tell Master Yoda and the chancellors what's going on. The Path is not on a mission for peace. They seem to be preparing for a war."

"A war against the Jedi?" Char-Ryl-Roy asked, his face horrified.

"Maybe," Creighton said.

"Whatever they're planning, we'll be in the middle of it if we can't get off this planet," Aida said.

They'd nearly reached the ship when Creighton stopped them. "Wait. Master Yaddle and her youngling and the other two guards are hidden with our ship a kilometer away, in the forest beyond the outskirts of this compound. We have to let them know what's going on. For all we know, they're still hiding with the Path, pretending to be one of them."

"Don't you have a comlink?" Xiri asked.

"I tried to contact her when we were in the caves. She didn't respond," Creighton said. "But I know where the ship is."

"We'll get you there." Xiri looked around. "It's strangely quiet, isn't it?"

"What . . . are those?" Aida said, peering into the fields.

The tall grain, wet from rain, was bent over, giving the planting fields a messy, wavy appearance. But that wasn't what Aida was pointing at. Figures were arising out of the fields, dozens of them, as if sprouting straight from the ground. Droids, rain spattering on their silver heads. Their faces were a dark mask, with three red lights shining from them—one light slightly bigger than the other two.

Collectively, they began marching through the tall grain toward the landing pads. The nearest ones raised their arms and began firing red lasers. Chunks of dirt flew into the air from blasts hitting the landing pads.

Master Roy yelled, holding his lightsaber aloft. "Enforcer droids! From the fields!"

Aida and Creighton began shielding the others from the blasts as they continued to head toward the *Andesine*.

"Look out!" Aida yelled.

There was the sound of an engine, but no one could tell where it was coming from. A repulsorlift skiff rose from behind one of the higher landing pads. There were no less than twenty Path members shooting at them. As they came closer, some of them jumped off and blocked their way to their ship.

Char-Ryl-Roy started blocking blasts to the group, while Aida and Creighton continued to fight off the blasts from the droids on the other side. Enya began fighting hand-to-hand with the Path members raining down upon them. Xiri threw herself into fighting two Path members that blocked their way to the *Andesine.*

Char-Ryl-Roy and Creighton were soon separated from the others by a wall of Path members. This was going terribly, and he knew that in order to get away, there would be a horrific amount of bloodshed. He seemed to watch in slow motion as Xiri tried to fire at a Path member with a bludgeon, but her blaster wouldn't fire. She threw it at the Path member's face with perfect aim, as it hit him square in the forehead. He staggered back.

Xiri pulled out her bane blade from the sheath at her waist, looking for another weapon, when a stray blaster bolt grazed her cheek. She cried out, cradling her face as the brute with the bludgeon laughed at her.

"A princess! My kill today will glorify the Path!"

Master Roy watched in shock as the bludgeon came swinging down at Xiri.

Xiri barely had enough time to duck. Before the guard's bludgeon could strike the killing blow, a blaster bolt struck the weapon, knocking it out of his hands. Another shot hit the guard in the belly, and he went reeling backward, screaming in pain.

A blaster twirled and slid on the wet surface of the landing pad, thudding against Xiri's feet. She grabbed it, realizing it had come from the figure that had shot her attacker. The figure was crouching in the shadow of the *Andesine.* He stood, and Xiri saw black curls waving on his head and a spray of faint green freckles on a very familiar face.

"Phan-tu!" Xiri shrieked.

"Are you okay?" Phan-tu asked, seeing the blood smearing down her left cheek.

"I'll be fine."

He shot over her head, and a shriek followed. "I guess the diplomacy didn't work?" he yelled.

"Not at all. How—why—how are you here?"

She ran over to him, shooting at Path members as he ducked red laserfire from the droids as well.

"I was stowing away on your ship," he said.

"But you were hurt!"

"I still am," he said, holding his chest. "But I rested on the trip over. I've been in a storage compartment near the sleeping quarters the whole time, and let me tell you, I have some muscle cramps that may never go away." He grinned. "I may not be able to tackle anyone, but I can point a blaster. I wanted to help, and no one forbid me to come, so I just . . . did."

Xiri kissed him quickly. "The queen is going to be furious with you!" Before Phan-tu could speak, Xiri lifted a finger. "But we'll talk about that later! We've got to get on this ship and take off. Phan-tu, the Path has tanks and tanks of klytobacter. Who knows what they were going to do with it."

Phan-tu was speechless, his face livid.

"Save that sentiment for the fight." She looked for the Jedi. They were fighting extremely well, the Path around them thinning quickly. They could all be on the *Andesine* within moments. Enya, Aida, and Creighton had managed to fell the remaining Path members. Brown-cloaked bodies littered the landing pad. Just as Xiri stepped a single foot onto the boarding ramp of the *Andesine,* a whistle sounded in the air.

"*Incoming!*" screeched Aida.

Everyone ducked, covering their heads. A ground missile whizzed overhead, squarely hitting the *Andesine* in the left engine. The explosion rocked the entire platform, and Xiri felt it in her bones. Her ears ringing, she felt Phan-tu's hand on her back pushing her hard.

"Run!"

Another whistle heralded a second missile that struck squarely on the *Andesine*'s body. Thick black smoke issued from the wounds of the ship as Xiri, Phan-tu, and the Jedi ran.

"Teegee! He might be on the *Andesine!*" Enya cried out.

"We have to go," Creighton said, pulling her backward.

"Teegee's a smart droid," Xiri said. "He'll take care of himself. But if we go in after him, we'll be dead."

"Where did they get ground missiles from?" Aida said, sprinting away from the ship. "What happened to them being a *simple folk?*"

"Simple folk with missiles and enforcer droids," Creighton yelled back. "We have to find Master Yaddle. She has another ship. Follow me."

The Jedi easily jumped off the platform. Phan-tu and Xiri had to scramble down a narrow stone staircase slippery with mud. She could see the forest in the distance through sheets of rain, far from the buildings. Maybe half a kilometer away or less.

"Everybody okay?" Master Roy said as they began to run as a group. He did a double take when he saw Phan-tu.

"Absolutely not," Phan-tu yelled, running while he cradled his chest. "If we can't get off this planet, we're doomed."

Axel Greylark was sitting in the same room he'd met the Mother in earlier. He sank into one of the plush sitting poufs, with a single Path servant standing motionless and emotionless at the door. Binnot had been in to check on him, but other Path members (apparently higher up) kept shuttling him away to do different tasks. They were told to leave Axel alone.

QN-1 buzzed near Axel's legs, but he put his hand out, not wanting the droid to act up. QN-1 had been buzzing at him that way since the death of Orin Darhga and Gella's capture, knowing how much it would upset him. Though his knee bounced with anxiousness, he didn't want to be soothed right now.

Axel would rather imagine his mother's reaction to his message. He could practically see her pacing in whatever fancy room she was currently in—probably back on Coruscant. Fretting over his health and his safety. Knowing, very well, that she had to come to Dalna. But then immediately, the voice of Gella would enter his head.

The Path is capable of more than you know. Murdering her. That may be the plan, and you may have willingly, ignorantly, acted as the bait. Why can't you think past your ego and do the right thing?

Axel shook his head. That was the Jedi fearmongering, and they were so very good at that. He wouldn't be played by them. But his knee kept bouncing with irritability anyway.

The sight of Orin's dying, purpling face entered his mind. He could hear Orin's air hunger and frantic gasps growing weaker by the second. Axel squeezed his eyes shut and balled his fists, pushing them against his legs to keep them still. *No. Don't think about it. That wasn't your fault.* Axel needed to focus on the future. His future.

His own mother hadn't believed in giving him a second chance. But the Mother of the Path of the Open Hand had.

But again, his attempt to concentrate failed. He had a vision of Gella, bound and locked up somewhere on the grounds, and he squeezed his eyes shut again. Quin whirred a consoling whine next to his legs. Axel patted his droid.

"I'm glad you're here, Quin. Wine, please," Axel said, eyes still shut, waving his hand.

The servant left to fetch the drink. When the door opened a good ten minutes later, Axel was looking at his cuticles. He made a sound of exasperation. "Took you long enough," he said.

"Did I? Apologies. I had no idea I was on the clock."

Axel snapped his head up to face the Mother, leaning heavily on her cane, next to a Path member holding two tumblers of wine. He immediately turned his irritated face into one of smooth relaxation.

"Of course you aren't. Welcome back," he said without missing a beat.

She handed Axel the tumbler of wine with shaky fingers. Her wrinkled face looked flushed and animated.

"Is everything okay?" Axel asked.

"Of course," she said, holding up her glass. "Not everything in my world happens as I expect, but I make it all work, no matter what." She smiled. "I have some good news. A transmission from Chancellor Greylark has just been received."

"It has?" Axel said, his throat suddenly dry. He took a hasty sip of wine, thankful for something to keep his voice from cracking.

"Indeed. Let's watch it together, shall we?"

"Absolutely." Axel hesitated. "Only—I would appreciate it if Binnot Ullo could watch it as well. He has, after all, been quite an asset. I think he ought to be here."

The Mother smiled, but the smile did not extend to her eyes. "How loyal of you. Of course." She snapped her fingers at the attendant. "Fetch Ullo. He's in the armory, I believe."

They sat down near each other, and she sipped her wine. "You've had wine from all over the galaxy. How does it compare?"

Axel glanced at her. For the leader of such a simple folk, the Mother sure seemed to have some grand ambitions. He noticed that unlike all the other Path members, she wore jewelry—discreet, but there, peeking out from beneath the curls of her hair and the sleeves of her robe. She liked finery. And she had a slightly hungry look on her face as she waited for Axel's response.

The wine was average. Certainly not the best he'd ever had. He decided to answer diplomatically.

"It has a good essence of moonberry. Not too acidic. I like my wines smooth," he said, taking another sip.

"Mm." The Mother raised her glass. She took another sip and sighed. Apparently, Axel's words had been the right ones.

The door opened, and Binnot Ullo walked in. Like the Mother, he looked energized and excited. He certainly didn't possess the relaxed friendliness of before. Of course, the Mother was here. Most everyone was tense in her presence. Everyone but Axel.

"We have a recorded message incoming from Chancellor Greylark," the Mother said. "Binnot, Axel especially requested that you be here for the viewing."

Binnot bowed slightly. The bow was more toward Axel, which was odd. They never had such formalities with each other.

The Mother began to play the holovid. Axel's mother appeared on the screen. Axel audibly gasped when he saw her.

Kyong Greylark was wearing a pale-brown tunic, smeared with what looked like soil. Her hair was not in her ornate hairstyle, dripping with pearls or Greylark family heirloom gems. It was in a tidy bun, with gray hairs slightly frizzed around her temples. She looked tired. Exhausted, actually. And she wore pants, the cargo type often worn by the ship workers preparing transports, filling fuel, and fixing things.

Yes. She looked like she had been fixing things.

With her bare hands.

"This message is for Axel Greylark, and the Mother of the Path of the Open Hand," Chancellor Greylark said, her voice formal as usual, but without that regal edge that usually punctuated her words. "Your message has been received, Axel," she continued, and it sounded the way she used to say his name as a child. Not with disappointment, or anger, or frustration, but gently. Softly. "I believe I understand exactly what you're trying to say. And I am sorry, truly sorry, for never having heard you clearly before. I know you have a strong desire to do good. To be a leader. To be taken as seriously as a chancellor would be."

At the word *good,* Axel tried not to cringe. There she was, trying to criticize him again somehow. But the Mother glanced at Axel and smiled. She even reached over and patted his hand. Binnot, however, was staring straight at the holovid, looking somewhat angry.

"I wish to support you in your endeavors," the chancellor went on. "In a way that I never have and, perhaps, is a little late coming. For that, I apologize as well. But love is love, no matter how late it shows up." She closed her eyes for a second, and when she opened them, her eyes shone glassily from a film of tears. "And so I wish for Jedi Master Yoda and my two closest aides to be witnesses for this."

Behind her, the wizened, green face of Master Yoda appeared, his head reaching well below the chancellor's waist. His expression was neutral and unreadable. Two of the chancellor's closest aides also appeared behind her, ones whom Axel had seen so perpetually at her side over the years that they were more consistent and present than her actual shadow. Their clothes were usually a muted version of the chancellor's own choices, but now, they looked like princesses next to her grubby clothing. His mother spoke again.

"I shall voluntarily come to Dalna to speak with you and the Mother of the Path of the Open Hand. But I shall be there as a support for my one and only child, Axel Greylark. As a parent. That shall be my only title in this regard. I formally and officially hereby renounce my chancellorship, beginning now."

"What?" the Mother yelled. Her wine splashed onto the carpet.

Axel froze. Out of the corner of his eye, he could have sworn that Binnot was silently laughing.

Master Yoda and the aides nodded and exited, leaving Kyong Greylark standing alone, tired, dirty, as resplendent as a ship technician.

"I shall arrive as soon as possible." She smiled uncertainly. "See you soon, my son." The holovid ended.

"What just happened?" the Mother said. She knocked over her cane, and an attendant hastily handed it back to her. The Mother stood up and turned to Axel. "You said she would come as a chancellor to see me. How dare she give up her position? Replay that transmission! Perhaps we missed something?"

"No," Binnot said. "She was clear as day. She's a nobody now. No power to do anything." He turned to Axel, a slight sneer on his face. "Which means Axel has zero chance of doing anything worthwhile now. He has no bargaining power. None at all."

"You did this!" The Mother pointed at Axel.

"Did what? I promise you, I did what you said to! I asked her to come to Dalna. To speak to us."

"And relinquish her chancellorship?" The Mother's beautiful face contorted into something ugly, terrifying. She was no longer yelling, and that was so much worse.

Axel held his hands up. He was trying not to panic. QN-1 immediately rose in alarm, bleeping at him and his apparent distress. "I swear . . . I did exactly what you asked me to. I had no idea she'd do this."

"Why? Of all the foolish choices! She had all the power. Why give it up? It's nonsensical." She started to pace the floor before Axel.

Axel watched her, the Mother, a title that meant so much but was technically artificial in that regard. He knew the answer to her questions. Kyong Greylark had given up power because previously, the title had always, always come first, before her love for him. For the first time since he was born, she was trying to put Axel first. Now, of all times. She was trying to show the depths of her love. The Mother could not fathom such a thing.

"I know why," Axel said, but she cut him off.

"Enough. I don't need petty explanations from a rich nobody with no influence," she said quietly. Viciously.

"What are your orders, Mother?" Binnot said, bowing slightly.

"Take him out of my sight," she said, waving Axel away.

"And?"

"I couldn't care less. Make him useful in some way," she said. She looked at Axel briefly, her face suffused with disgust. A faint boom sounded, its reverberations felt beneath Axel's feet. "Look at him. He has no idea what's happening outside of these walls, at this very minute." She glanced back at Binnot. "When the chancellor—I mean, when that Greylark woman arrives, kill her on the spot. It saves us the trouble of holding her hostage, after all."

"What? No!" Axel yelled. QN-1 bleeped in concern over Axel's rapid rise in blood pressure and heart rate. Axel's face was hot as fire. The Mother never intended to barter with her over Axel's life. She had planned to keep them both hostage.

"My pleasure, Mother." Binnot bowed.

As the Mother marched to the door, Axel could see that great, hulking beast waiting for her in the corridor, rumbling its pleasure at being close to her again.

"Put him to work, Binnot," was her parting goodbye.

And with that, the Mother was gone.

Axel could barely breathe. What had happened? How had his mother, in one fell swoop, once again destroyed everything that Axel was trying to build for himself? She ruined everything. But no. Even Axel couldn't deflect blame anymore. Axel had done this, and Axel alone. And his actions may have just cost him his life.

"I've waited a long time to do this," Binnot said, raising his hand, ready to strike.

Axel put his hand up to shield his face. "Binnot! No, don't—"

He couldn't stop Binnot's arm as it swung down with great force, swishing by Axel's face. It came down firmly on QN-1's shell of a body, making a crunching sound as the droid hit the floor. Axel shot out a hand to stop Binnot, who punched him and sent him falling to the floor. All the while, Binnot's foot stayed upon the droid as QN-1 whined and bleeped in distress.

It was the sound of pure pain. Axel knew it. It was the sight of Gella's stricken face, seeing Orin Darhga die before her. It was imagining his mother being slaughtered the second she set foot on Dalna. It was Binnot's boot coming down hard on QN-1's body as he pleaded with his master, and his master cried out uselessly for Binnot to stop.

It was the sound of Axel losing everything in his life that mattered.

Chapter Twenty

Master Yaddle cradled Cippa in her arms. Which was an awkward thing to do, given the child was bigger than Yaddle herself.

She was still recovering from being stunned by the Path soldiers while they had waited and waited for Creighton and Aida to return from their investigation. When Yaddle reached out multiple times via the comlink and they didn't respond, Yaddle knew something was wrong.

They were inside the main hold of the ship. Nearby, Lu Sweet and Priv Ittik, the chancellor's security detail, were nursing their aching chests where they'd been struck by stun bolts. The child appeared to be resting, but not peacefully. Cippa's eyebrows drew together in consternation, as if dreaming about what had happened. Or perhaps, being visited by unpleasant memories.

Yaddle sighed. It was difficult to teach younglings, who often had experienced so much pain at such an early age. Many didn't understand their gifts, along with their caretakers, who reacted with a spectrum of emotions. It was not easy to have Force abilities before someone was around to teach them about control, and limits, and how lethal they could be. Yaddle knew that Cippa would have difficulty reconciling that being extraordinary didn't mean you were worth more than any other being in the universe. Dealing with the pain would be a harder task. It could make or break a Jedi, no matter how dedicated they were to learning the ways of the Force.

Cippa looked so innocent, so very breakable right now. It would take some time for the stunning effects of the attack to wear off. The girl's white braids were dirtied with broken leaves, and her ill-fitting Path clothing hung on her awkwardly.

"She going to be all right?" Priv asked. One of her curved horns had broken off at the tip, and she seemed even more glum than her resting glum face usually was. Lu sported a large bruise on his face that was swollen, and held a compress against it. He stooped next to Cippa and Yaddle.

"Little fighter, she is. Strong as a Sweet," said Lu.

"She is strong. And she has much to learn," Yaddle said. "But for now, she has to rest. The stun seems to have affected her more because of her size."

"Master Yaddle, we need to prepare ourselves," Lu said, standing. His hands went unconsciously to touch the blasters holstered at his thighs. "There will be more coming when these Path members don't return," he said, motioning to the Path members that Yaddle had knocked out. They were tied up and gagged in the corner of the hold, still unconscious. "Our ship is not very well hidden, even within this forest."

A large boom sounded far in the distance, but everyone felt it under their feet. There was the sound of blasterfire, too. Yaddle put Cippa gently down and stood to peer into the distance. Priv stood up and held a pair of macrobinoculars to her face.

"What is it?" Lu asked.

"I don't know. But it's not good. There's some sort of activity going on at the edge of the Path compound where the landing area is," Priv said, adjusting her binocs.

"There are people fighting," Yaddle said. "I sense Jedi fighting, too.

I could swear that there's an E'roni ship with smoke coming out of it, but maybe I'm imagining things."

More small booms sounded in the distance. Closer than before.

A tiny voice spoke. "Who's fighting?" They all turned around to see Cippa propping herself up on her elbows, squinting into the light. "Ow. My head hurts."

"You were stunned, little one. Rest," Yaddle said.

"I don't want to rest. I want to fight. Like you, Master Yaddle."

"I do not fight unless it is absolutely necessary. That goes for you, too, youngling. You are recovering, and you are not trained for battle. Not for years to come."

"But I want to be a Jedi now," Cippa said.

"Not all Jedi do battle. Some are guardians of knowledge, or teach, like me."

Lu and Priv had squatted behind her. Priv's large hand descended on Cippa's shoulder. "If you ever do, small one, I'd rather be on your side, if you don't mind."

Cippa raised a finger, and a stray piece of dead leaf was lifted from Priv's shoulder and flew away.

"Come, child. Let's close up the ship and bring it to a more hidden location," Lu said.

Master Yaddle helped Cippa to a standing position. Together, they walked deeper into the ship. When faint shouting could be heard, Yaddle left Cippa on a seat and hurried back to the ship's ramp.

Yaddle gazed toward the Path compound. Lu came up next to her, peering through the macrobinoculars handed to him by Priv.

"Oh no," Lu said. "There's a group of people headed this way. And fast."

Somewhere out there, Creighton Sun and Aida Forte were still gathering information. Yaddle knew that if they fled, they would abandon Creighton and Aida. She thought of contacting them right now, but worried it might make their situation worse somehow—especially if they were concealing themselves. Already in the distance, they could see a group of twenty or so running toward them, most wearing the gray-colored clothing of the Path.

Except they weren't all members of the Path. Shots were being fired, and Yaddle saw the unmistakable bright dashes of three lightsabers. Creighton and Aida were not the only Jedi here. There was at least one more. And they were being chased.

"There are more Jedi," Yaddle said to Lu. "Be ready to take off as soon as they arrive. They're not coming here to bring the fight to us. They're trying to escape."

"Yes, Master Yaddle," Lu said, disappearing into the ship.

"Priv," Yaddle said. "Turn this ship around so we can fire on those who are attacking our Jedi. Try to hold them off, not kill."

Priv nodded. "What are you going to do?"

"What I must. Make sure Cippa doesn't go anywhere. She's still recovering."

Yaddle saw a streak of white out of the corner of her eye. She was quick enough to run to the edge of the door and caught Cippa, who had been trying to dash right out of the ship.

"Cippa! What do you think you're doing?"

"I was going to help!" she said, her eyes wide.

"You don't even know what's going on."

"I do. I was listening to you the whole time."

Yaddle turned to Priv and said, "Please. Take her. Keep her safe."

"But—" Cippa began.

Yaddle looked up at the youngling. "Cippa. You nearly died on my watch. I cannot risk your life. I have to protect you."

"But Master Yaddle. Who will protect you? Because Lu and Priv are, you know." She wiggled her hand in a gesture that clearly meant "mediocre."

"Hey," Priv said. "I'm right here."

Lu's head popped into view from deep within the ship. "I'm going to move the ship. Everybody who needs to be on board, be on board. I'm closing the hatch."

Yaddle activated her lightsaber and looked at Cippa. "Take care of Lu and Priv, then. Stay on this ship!"

Cippa nodded with disappointment as Yaddle bounded off the loading ramp. She could now see that indeed Creighton and Aida were leading the group fleeing the Path, with Master Char-Ryl-Roy and his Padawan, Enya Keen, right behind them. Enya was missing her lightsaber and had a blaster in her hand. She kept twisting around to fire at the group of fifteen or so Path that were chasing them. Behind the Path were several droids shooting red laserfire at the fleeing Jedi and their group. It was hard to see all of them in the worsening rain. They were all nearly at the ship, which had risen off the ground and was turning toward the fight.

In two long bounds, Master Yaddle landed in the middle of the melee, deflecting blaster shots and pushing a line of Path members back three meters as her assault confused and disorganized the front line.

Creighton was at her side seconds later. "Master Yaddle. We need to get on that ship. They're going to kill us all unless we can get out of here."

"Understood. We need to hold back this line long enough for everyone to get on board. What are Master Roy and Jedi Keen doing on Dalna?" Yaddle asked.

"Another long story. And Princess Xiri of E'ronoh and Prince Phan-tu from Eiram are here, too."

Xiri and Phan-tu were fighting hand-to-hand with two Path members swinging pikes at them.

"To me!" Yaddle hollered as she led the way back to the ship. It had turned completely around and was starting to fire over their heads into the group of Path members well behind them when Yaddle commed.

"Lu. You need to land so we can board."

"Copy that."

The ship landed and a side port opened up. Xiri and Phan-tu were the first to make it aboard, followed by Aida and Enya. But just as the three Master Jedi, holding back blasterfire, were able to board, a low craft rose over the hills behind the entire group. It was squat and not terribly threatening looking, until Yaddle saw the turret on the top.

"Cannons!" Yaddle yelled in warning.

The cannon fire came fast and quick. Everyone, including the Path, ducked as the shots blazed above their heads. The small ship couldn't possibly have much firepower, but the cannon fire was brutal, hitting the ship squarely in the belly.

"Hurry! We're too exposed while people are boarding!" Lu said.

Their ship was firing back, and she knew Priv was probably operating their cannons, but the smaller Path ship was far more maneuverable, evading the shots. Plus, it was concentrating all its power, over and over again, on the same wound in the belly of the ship.

"Go!" Yaddle yelled, and Creighton, Char-Ryl-Roy, and Yaddle boarded the ship quickly and closed the hatch.

An enormous boom rocked the ship, again, and again.

"Lu! Shields up!" Yaddle yelled.

"I have good news and bad news," Lu hollered back.

"What?" Yaddle said.

"Our shields are down, and we're taking on more damage by the second."

"And?" Creighton asked. "The good news?"

"I don't think this ship can fly anymore."

Yaddle closed her eyes. "That is *all* bad news, Lu."

"I know!" he said, grimacing. "I'm trying to be optimistic!"

"By lying?" Aida said, eyes wide.

"Never mind that! It's just not the flying we need. It's the comms," Creighton said. "Patch me into a channel that will send a message out to any ship in this sector and beyond that is friendly to the Jedi or to the Republic. Anyone on this planet, for that matter. We need help."

"Hey!" Lu called from the cockpit. "I think I can get this ship to fly. Priv bypassed the power converter. Hold on."

They felt the ship rise, still getting knocked about from the cannon fire. Char-Ryl-Roy growled, "That cannon fire has changed. Did they switch over to new weapons?"

Yaddle looked out of the viewport. "There's another ship attacking us. Nope, make that two more."

The *Lazuli* rose into the air, still taking on heavy shots from below and around them. Creighton had run to the cockpit with Yaddle and was opening comm channels far and wide, both planetside and beyond, asking for help.

"This is Jedi Creighton Sun. Several Jedi and personnel from the chancellor's guard are on the Path of the Open Hand compound on Dalna, taking on heavy fire. We have representatives from Eiram and E'ronoh with us. Anyone in the area, we are asking for your urgent help."

"Master Sun," a voice immediately answered. "This is Master Ela Sutan. We are under heavy fire in the cave system beneath the Path compound."

"There are other Jedi here? How many? Why—how are you here?" Creighton asked.

"We were sent just after you left for Dalna, but haven't been able to contact you. Three other Jedi, and some Temple guards." There was a pause, and blasterfire could be heard in the background. "I'm sorry. We can't help you."

"We'll try to send for help, as best as we can." Creighton paused. Master Yaddle and Aida looked at him, their faces uncertain with worry. "May the Force be with you."

"Send the message out again," Master Yaddle said. "We'll take all the help we can get."

"How do we know it's going to get farther than a parsec?" Aida asked.

"We don't. We wait for help to show up," Creighton said, helplessly.

"I have my ship," Yaddle said. "It's deeper within the forest, if we need to abandon this one. It's small but fast."

The *Lazuli* was turning in the air when an explosion sounded. Yaddle looked out the viewport to see smoke and flames rising from half a kilometer away in the woods.

"And . . . it looks like they just found my ship. The *Lazuli* is our only way out now."

"We can keep fighting on the ground," Creighton said. "But the Path could have hundreds or thousands underground, ready to fight. Aida and I saw them stockpiling bioweapons against Eiram. We're in over our heads."

"Over our heads is accurate," Lu said, sweating profusely. He turned to Yaddle. "Because our ship is about to crash."

The ship groaned and lurched. From the viewport, they saw black smoke emerging from part of their own hull, and the smoke began to fill the cockpit. They had risen about a hundred meters or so above the ground, flying askew. Lu had been trying to steer the ship away from the Path compound, but one of their maneuvering thrusters was out, which meant they were now twisting in a circle right where they didn't want to be. Lu coughed into his sleeve, choking on the black smoke. He tried to steer the ship into a descent that would slide into the ground, instead of a stone-dropping-out-of-the-sky scenario.

"Lu. You and Priv stay with Master Sun and Jedi Forte. Watch your backs." Master Yaddle touched his sleeve. "I'll keep Cippa with me. May the Force be with you."

Yaddle ran back into the body of the ship. Enya and Aida were already running to Creighton and Char-Ryl-Roy, trying to stand upright in the rapidly tilting vessel. Yaddle soon found Cippa, eyes wide and gripping the harnesses on her seat. Xiri and Phan-tu had flanked the Arkanian child, their arms around her.

"We're crashing, right into the center of the Path compound," Yaddle told them. "It'll be mayhem when we land. I'll take this youngling. We are going to have to emerge fighting. Right now, we'll be overwhelmed if we stick together. Stay in pairs, and scatter. Help is hopefully on the way."

"This is suicide," Phan-tu said. He and Xiri were holding hands, clasping Cippa in their arms like human harnesses. They were gripping each other so hard it was blanching their own skin.

"No," Yaddle said, taking Cippa's hand in hers. "It is fighting for life. And light. Good luck. May the Force be with you."

Chapter Twenty-One

THE PATH COMPOUND, DALNA

Axel Greylark was lost. The caves beneath the Path compound were dizzying and never-ending. Shouts were echoing up and down the hallways. Binnot Ullo walked behind him, not at his side. Their positions weren't lost on Axel.

"I don't know what happened," Axel said. "My mother has never done anything like that."

"You mean make the worst decision of her life?" Binnot said. He held Gella's lightsabers and was now prodding Axel's back with one of the hilts. "Faster, Greylark. This isn't a leisure tour."

Ahead of him, a group of Path members threw their fists into the air.

"To the Path of the Closed Fist!" several chanted, followed by a roar of voices.

"What does that mean? What are they talking about?" Axel asked Binnot.

"You wouldn't know, would you? While you were in the Crystal being useless, we moved on without you. There you were, waiting for the future to be handed to you. Now we'll take our future. The Path of the Closed Fist is us."

Axel still didn't quite understand. But then again, Axel had never been a believer like Binnot and the others. As always, he was somewhere on the outside of where he really wanted to be. But clearly, something had changed. The Path members were acting like they were at war, and there were booms and blaster shots distantly in the passageways that told him the war was here. Whether he liked it or not, he had a feeling he would be right in the middle of it soon.

Axel forced his legs to move faster, but he had no energy, no hope. There was a tiny glint within him, arising from one thought: Had his mother truly given up her whole life, the chancellorship, for Axel? Was it a power play of some sort? A gesture—or rather, a sacrifice? It felt like a dream. It felt like—not something his mother would do. He wondered if there might have been a trick played on him.

But there had been something in her voice, her eyes. A rare glimpse that he'd seen before. For once, there existed raw emotion that wasn't being carefully hidden and crafted with her chancellor's communication skills. That felt real. And it was, to be honest, astonishing.

But it didn't matter. His mother may come to Dalna to face her inevitable death. Or she may regain her senses and turn around, abandoning Axel for the failure that he was. That was much more likely. That made sense. It would be what he would do. Wouldn't it?

A hard poke shoved his right shoulder. "Faster, Greylark."

They reached their destination, which was a large cave lined with arms—blaster pistols, rifles, projectile launchers, swords, staffs, daggers, pikes, axes. Even handheld explosives. Axel recognized some as farming tools that had been repurposed for weaponry. Many of the blasters and other higher-grade weapons were new, but many looked old, as if they'd been handed down from owner to owner, time out of mind. The room was filled with Path members. Some were choosing weapons, others simply being given them and ushered right back out of the room.

Binnot was holding Gella's two lightsabers. He tucked them into his belt and turned to Axel.

"I have a feeling that you'd lose your head immediately in hand-to-hand combat."

"At the Coruscant Academy, there is a basic training for combat," he said. "I did fine in hand-to-hand fighting. But my mother got me out of the other lessons so I could travel with her instead."

"Hand-to-hand combat in the face of blasters is useless. Like I said, you're basically an unskilled lump of meat."

Axel gave a lopsided smirk. "C'mon, Binnot—"

Binnot turned a little and swung back with a resounding slap against Axel's face that had him seeing stars for a moment. Axel bent over, cradling his throbbing cheek. His eyes were wide as he stood up, livid.

To which Binnot struck his other cheek, hard. This time, he didn't give Axel a moment to say anything. He shoved his gloved finger in his face.

"Shut up, Greylark. Be thankful to the Mother that you are not dead."

Axel opened his mouth, but when Binnot raised his hand again—the one clad in his poisonous glove—Axel shut his mouth and waited, trying not to whimper. Like a kicked dog.

"As I was saying, you *are* basically an unskilled lump of meat. Ever use these?" He walked by a whole wall full of old blasters, rifles, and electrified pikes.

"No, but—"

"As I figured. Which means you get this."

Binnot went to another wall with long sticks, knives, and swords, and removed a stout bludgeon. It had several metal spikes embedded in the heavy end. He handed it to Axel, who grasped it gingerly. He felt sick just looking at the weapon.

"I have no chance surviving against a blaster attack," Axel said.

"You kill one Jedi with that and you can come here and get whatever you want."

"But—"

"Greylark. It's simple. Fight. You've got one job now. You're not to be trusted with an endless supply of ammunition."

"But we'll be fighting together, right?"

At this, Binnot took several steps back. He looked at Axel from head to toe, and back again. It was not unlike being a child waiting to be chosen for a game of grav-ball and wondering if he'd get chosen at all.

"I'm far higher ranked than you. You'll be with the unskilled fighters. The farmers. Who, to be honest, are more skilled than you are, since they have to deal with Dalnan bears and beasts stealing their crops and cattle."

Axel looked around. It was true: Most of the Path members trying out weapons in this room looked burly or wiry from years of hard work. They looked askance at Axel, the outsider, before going back to the weapons racks.

"Are these all of the weapons that the Path has? They don't have much," Axel said.

"That's for me to know, not you. You have no true idea what we have in store for those who oppose us. We have weapons far beyond the imaginings of the Republic. The war has come here to Dalna. Just as the Mother had planned."

"Who's come to Dalna?" Axel could feel the blood in his face drain away.

"You think that those two Jedi—Gella and that dead one—are the only Jedi sneaking around this place? There are other contingents here. There's an aboveground assault going on right now. Jedi being attacked in the caves right now. All your Jedi friends are being killed, one by one."

Axel went quiet. He gripped the bludgeon, which felt unpleasantly heavy in his hand. A slight boom sounded from far away, causing pebbles and dust to rain down lightly onto Axel's head.

"Oh, and just so everyone knows exactly which side you're on." Binnot went to the corner of the room and pulled out a shapeless piece of cloth. He threw it at Axel, watching as Axel pulled it over his head. It was dusty and dirty and smelled of rodents. Axel closed his eyes for a mere second, thinking how far he'd come from wearing golden satin jackets meticulously embroidered with costly crystal and silver thread. The Path garment went over his shoulders basically like a blanket with a hole for the head. The edges were marked in wavy blue stripes. As he looked up, Binnot shoved his fingers against Axel's forehead, wiping downward in a zigzag motion.

Axel touched his forehead, looking at the blue paint on his fingertips.

"You're one of the Path now. And if you're lucky, you'll do something useful with your life. Kill some Jedi. Maybe die in the service of the Mother."

There was a holler from outside the armory room. And then a few more, from harried voices running their way.

A human woman's face appeared in the entranceway. Her skin was shiny from sweat, and her blue streaks looked blurred.

"They've taken down the Jedi ship. This is our chance! Everyone to their positions!"

Binnot clapped Axel on the back. "Finally. Time to get off your ass and do something useful, Greylark."

The other Path members yelled collectively, with spirited "For the Path!" and "For the Mother!" as they poured out of the armory into the caves. Binnot pushed Axel hard with the blunt lightsabers again. Axel had no choice but to let the river of fighters push him toward a battle he didn't want to fight.

Gella could hear the activity in the caves. She could feel it in her fingertips, which lay gently against the cool, dirt floor. There was excitement, fear, and anger, cresting in a wave that was coming ever closer to her.

Now it was at the door of her prison.

"Well, hello there, filth."

Binnot Ullo's face appeared in the tiny window to her room. Gella was leaning against the back wall of the small space, one knee up, one leg down. She looked at the Mirialan's face placidly.

"Coming to gloat?" she asked.

"Yes, as a matter of fact." He ignited both of her lightsabers, regarding their glow. "These feel good in my hands. I may keep them forever." He turned them off and stared at Gella.

"The reason why they feel so good in your hands," Gella said, standing up and slapping the dust off her fingers, "is because you are Force-sensitive. I noticed it when we fought."

"Shut your mouth, Jedi. You throw out lies to everyone. It must be second nature."

Gella slowly walked toward the door. "I'm not lying, and you know it. I'll bet you've felt it since you were a child. Maybe you hated it. Maybe that's why you like the Path so much. Because they despise you as much as you despise yourself."

"You are good at making up stories, aren't you?"

"I'm not lying when I say you're a hypocrite," Gella said, staring at him evenly. "You use the Force when it suits you. Now we all know what the Path would do to such people. You're an enemy in their midst, aren't you?"

"I said shut your mouth!" Binnot said, moving slightly. She knew he had positioned the lightsabers so that if he turned them on, they'd go right through the door, impaling Gella. That is, if Gella were a hair closer to the door. She knew he was tempted. A blood vessel throbbed at his temple, and he was clenching his jaw.

"Where's your little friend? Axel?" Gella asked.

Binnot relaxed, visibly relieved that the subject matter had changed.

"Doing his job. Fighting, the way he should be."

"Not being the right-hand man to the Mother? I thought he had grand plans."

Binnot laughed. "Grand plans. Well, yeah, those fell through."

Gella blinked. So Axel's plan had disintegrated. This was what he chose, and now his choices had come to nothing. She wondered how he felt right now. She wasn't even sure what she felt right now. Sadness, mostly. Looking at Binnot's face, the satisfaction was probably hard for him to hide. "You're happy about that, aren't you?" Gella cocked her head. "How does it feel to be a little closer to your boss? A little more important?"

"I don't need her to tell me that I'm important."

"He says to himself," Gella added. "Why are you here, Binnot? To kill me?" She continued to stare at him, knowing she looked like she pitied him, rather than challenging him. "I doubt you took a stroll just to tell me that your friend Axel's plans all went poof, dissolved into nothing?"

Binnot shifted his feet. "Axel told me you're a Wayseeker."

"I will be."

"What does that mean?"

"It means that someday, I'll pursue my own direction to become more attuned to the Force."

"So you don't listen to the Jedi Council. You're your own boss."

"That's not exactly how it works, but for this conversation, let's say okay. Is that what you want, Binnot? To not have to do whatever the Mother or the Herald says?"

He said nothing, which said everything.

"Ah. So you're not happy taking orders. Interesting." She frowned and put her hands on her hips. "Let me give you a word of advice. Living the way of the Jedi is nothing like living in the Path."

"I disagree," Binnot said. "They always want you to do what they want. They always want you to live by other rules. Even if you believe in the same core principles."

"Ah, but there's one thing you keep forgetting," Gella said, moving closer. She was almost nose-to-nose with Binnot now, despite the thick door between them. "If you leave the Jedi Order—which I haven't, by the way—the Jedi don't try to murder you because you're a traitor. Can you say the same for the Path?"

Binnot's face morphed into fury. She sensed his movement before Binnot probably felt it in himself. He immediately ignited Gella's two lightsabers, which burned two holes right through the thick metal door. The odor of melting metal permeated the air.

Smoke obscured their view of each other. When the small window cleared of the haze, Gella was again leaning against the back wall of the cell, arms crossed casually. She watched the smile on Binnot's face disappear as he could see she was, disappointingly, unimpaled.

"Know this, Binnot Ullo. You and I are nothing alike."

With that, Binnot turned off the lightsabers and walked away wordlessly. Gella noted the holes in the door, which was otherwise still thick and intact. She was still trapped. But not for long.

Chapter Twenty-Two

THE PATH COMPOUND, DALNA

The *Lazuli* was at a forty-five-degree lurch when it skidded straight into a field, snapping off the tops of a cluster of purple-leaved trees before it finally came to a crunching, grinding halt. The smell of smoke was strong inside the ship. Phan-tu and Xiri were still holding each other and sheltering the little Arkanian girl in their arms when the crash occurred. But after a few seconds of being motionless, they looked at each other.

"I'm okay. You?" Phan-tu asked.

"Yes," Xiri said, her eyes wide.

"I'm all right, too," Cippa said.

Phan-tu and Xiri let go of each other, and Cippa undid her harness buckles.

"Shields are down. Everything is down. This ship is trash," Lu yelled over the speakers. There was a pause. "Good luck everyone."

Master Yaddle unstrapped her harness and stood on the angled floor. "Come, Cippa. Stay with me."

Cippa immediately took her hand again, her white eyes large and frightened. Yaddle looked up at Xiri and Phan-tu and nodded. There was a light coming through one of the doors down the crooked corridor. The rain was coming down at a steady clip. Cippa looked back at Xiri and Phan-tu, in that particular way children do when they sense they're never going to see you again. Yaddle and Cippa jumped through the open door into the rain and were gone.

Phan-tu and Xiri could already hear yelling and blaster bolts hitting their felled ship. Somewhere, in another direction, the Jedi were leaving via different exits. Those other two chancellor guards, too, whom they'd barely had time to meet.

"Ready?" Xiri asked.

"Not really, but what choice do we have?"

"Fight until more help comes. We have to hope that Creighton's message got out to someone. Anyone."

Phan-tu gripped his blaster. Xiri did as well. They had one each, plus Xiri's bane blade. That was it. Xiri kissed him suddenly. "I'm glad you're here, Phan-tu. I wouldn't want anyone else at my side during a battle."

"That may be the most romantic thing you've ever said, Xee."

They walked along the lopsided interior of the ship, feeling more blaster bolts rock the walls. Outside there was yelling, and the swooshing sound of a spacecraft.

They peeked out the door. Yaddle and Cippa were nowhere to be seen. But Path members were everywhere. There were two or three groups of them, flanked by enforcer droids, slowly advancing toward the fallen ship. One group kept shooting at the door, probably hoping it would keep them from leaving so they could be cornered.

A small ship whizzed overhead. Narrow wings, and guns beneath it, but not firing. It looked like it was scouting out the area of the crash. Xiri scrutinized it.

"That's a starfighter. An old one, probably a BT-40 from Rendili." She looked at Phan-tu. "Are you thinking what I'm thinking?"

Phan-tu nodded. On the ground, with Phan-tu unable to fight well, they were at risk of being overrun by too many Path members. In the air, Xiri and Phan-tu had a chance.

"We know where the landing pads are. But I don't remember seeing any other starfighters," Xiri said.

"They wouldn't have them out in the open. They could be in Ferdan."

Xiri pointed. "When we flew in, I swear I saw a hangar just north of here, beyond this big field. If we can't find anything there, we'll go to Ferdan and steal a ship."

"Let's go."

They jumped off the *Lazuli,* the rain immediately drenching their clothes. Nearby was a large field full of tall grain grasses that were almost shoulder height. They ran through it, nearly getting hit. A moldy scent rose from the grain, which had been suffering from too much moisture in the ground. Phan-tu could feel the energy of the bolts whizzing past, singeing his skin. When Phan-tu and Xiri stopped for a brief moment to return fire, they managed to fell at least three or four Path members.

"Keep going!" Phan-tu yelled. They'd almost reached the wooden fence and pink boulders that edged the compound when Phan-tu's leg struck something hard and he tumbled head over feet.

"Ow!" he yelped.

Xiri ran back to him. "What happened?"

"Tripped. On that." He pointed at a cylinder of reddish metal in the grass.

It bleep-booped at him.

"Forvio-Teegee?" Xiri said, ducking under the tall grasses. "How did you get all the way over here?"

The droid, shiny with rain, was lying on his side. He whirred a response.

"Ran away from the blasterfire, eh? And now your mech wheels are tangled in grass. Hold on," Phan-tu said. He reached over and yanked out knotted, tough grasses from the bottom of the droid's legs. "There you go, buddy. Come with us. We'll find a safe place for you to hide."

Xiri and Phan-tu continued running. The grain field ended, and they were about to climb the wooden barrier that surrounded the compound when 4VO-TG whistled at them. He wanted to get beyond the fence, too.

Xiri crouched down next to the astromech. "Wow, he really doesn't want to be anywhere near this battle."

"Smart droid," Phan-tu said. "Look. The rain has loosened the soil where some of these posts are dug in." Together, they were able to shove two posts forward to make a small space for the droid to be pushed through. Half of him got dragged through mud, and they wiped him off as best as they could when they were on the other side.

They ran forward, passing through a meadow full of shoulder-tall, waving grasses of yellow and green. Every time any kind of ship flew over, they fell deep into the meadow, smashing wet lompop flowers as they lay hiding, knees and hands getting muddy. Their trodden path made way for 4VO-TG, who followed behind steadily. Finally, they reached the hangar. There was a small private farm surrounded by a stone wall, with scattered equipment on the planting field. The lights were out inside the stone house.

"There's nobody guarding it," Xiri said.

Phan-tu pushed open the gate to the stone wall, then snuck over to peer into a tiny window of the hangar, wincing as he held his chest. "Well, that's disappointing. It's just junk."

"Really?" Xiri said, despondent.

"Take a look." Xiri wiped at the window to get a better view. Inside there were parts of starships littered all over the place. An aged Forward ReCon fighter was partially covered by a sheet. It was one of the old classes, maybe an FRC-40.

"It's in pieces. Junk," Phan-tu said. "We'll have better luck in Ferdan."

"Wait. Let's get a closer peek," Xiri said. They easily broke the lock to the door and walked around. Xiri whipped off the sheet, and a cloud of dust made them both cough.

The ship was smaller than the current class of FRC fighters and sported several holes, some of which went right through one of the triple wings. The cockpit was open, and the canopy was practically opaque from dirt. The entire tip of the nose was missing, and one of the wings was minus a panel section. It was a medium-sized two-seat fighter with an astromech socket and was equipped with forward guns on its larger middle wings and a single dorsal tail cannon. At least half of the ship was taken up by its hybrid hyperdrive sublight engine. But by the stars, it looked decrepit.

"The owner must make a hobby of fixing these ships," Phan-tu said, kicking away a cylinder of metal.

"I can fly that, if the engines are functioning," Xiri said.

"You've gotta be kidding. I bet even the Path won't fly this piece of junk!"

"I doubt they have pilots worth their salt that can handle it," she said, scanning the belly of the ship.

"Don't. There's got to be another way."

"And I say, it's the only way." She stood up and frowned at Phan-tu.

"What about Ferdan?"

"Ferdan is probably crawling with Path members," Xiri said, crossing her arms.

"We're supposed to be a united front, Xiri. We're supposed to be on the same page."

"Marriage doesn't mean you always have the same opinion, Phan-tu."

"It also doesn't mean that you keep making unilateral decisions for us."

"Says the guy who stowed away on a ship without telling his partner."

He pinched the bridge of his nose. "Good point."

"Okay," Xiri said. "I admit, sometimes, I do make unilateral decisions, too. But I know what I'm doing."

"Do you?"

"Yes."

"How would I know, if you don't tell me?"

This time, Xiri said nothing for a while. "You're right. I don't tell you. But you can't assume we have to agree on everything. Works for peace agreements. Not for marriages."

Phan-tu smirked. "Even my mothers don't agree on everything, but they make it work." He looked at the broken ship. "All right, Xiri. If you can prove that this thing will fly, then we'll fly."

"You've got a deal. First things first. We have to find out if the electronics are functioning." Xiri ran over the ship and patted it affectionately. It had metal panels of different shades of tiered gray, from all the past repairs. "Hi there. I bet you miss the flying," she said. She climbed into the cockpit. Phan-tu could hear switches being turned on and off. The ship stayed quiet.

"Engine dead?"

4VO-TG bleeped loudly. They looked over to see the astromech rolling through a far door. It paused to expel a squirt of dirty rainwater from a seam near its head, then rolled toward a long hose, pausing and looking directly at Xiri.

"Teegee! Wow. Can you help?" she asked.

The droid bleeped and whirred, once again rolling near the hose.

"His programming seems to be intact. Lucky! I think he's saying we need to prime the engine. Here, plug that in, Phan-tu."

"Will it work?" Phan-tu said, his face full of doubt.

"Probably not," Xiri said. 4VO-TG whirred. "Hm. He seems more optimistic than both of us. Teegee, can you check the engine? Run some diagnostics and see what needs fixing?"

The astromech spun around, rolling beneath the belly of the ship. It unfolded its utility arms and opened the engine panel, humming almost merrily. Small nuts and bolts began falling from the open panel, bouncing off the droid's dome.

Phan-tu cast a worried glance at Xiri. "He's going to put those back, right?"

"I sure hope so," Xiri said. She left the cockpit and rummaged through some old tools piled up along the wall. Xiri found the pneumatic hammer and a drill, and went immediately to fixing the hole in the wing. Phan-tu kept an eye out, and saw a group of Path members in the meadow, between the Path compound and the farm. When Xiri dropped the drill, the clanking sound went far. The Path members in the distance turned their heads toward the hangar.

"We're going to have company soon," Phan-tu said. "Hurry."

It took a little while, but soon Xiri dusted her hands off and surveyed her work. "I'm done," she said. The hole in the wing was covered with a piece of scrap metal. It wasn't smooth or pretty, but it was patched. Hopefully it would work.

"Teegee? How's it going?"

The droid was shutting the door to the engine. It rolled away and bleeped, circling beneath the astromech socket. Xiri turned on the lift mechanism, and the droid ascended into place on the ship.

Phan-tu ran to the end of the hangar and pulled the door wide open. The light was dimming. The suns must be getting low behind the clouds, and the rain was only getting worse. He could still hear blasters firing at a distance. Somewhere out there, the Jedi were fighting a ground battle with not a whole lot of ammunition and zero backup. He ran back to the small ship.

"There's room for two, you know," Xiri said, strapping on a helmet. The blaster wound on her cheek throbbed, but wasn't too bad. She held out another helmet.

"I knew you were going to say that," Phan-tu said. He jumped into the copilot's seat, which was back-to-back with Xiri's and shared a canopy.

"I need you to be my eyes in the back of my head," Xiri said, her voice coming through the comm of the helmet, which thankfully still worked. "And run the rear cannon. If it works."

Xiri went back into the pilot's seat and tried the switches again. Nothing.

Through the wide-open doors of the hangar, Phan-tu saw the group of Path members running toward the hangar. "Hey!" one of them yelled. "Hey!"

"Dammit!" Xiri said, stamping her foot hard against the floor of the cockpit. "Work!"

4VO-TG's head swiveled left and right. There was a hiss and a zapping noise, and suddenly the engine sputtered again. But this time, the sound turned into a low rumble and a whir. The ship hummed to life. The triple wings on each side began to bloom open.

"You did it!" Phan-tu said.

The droid whistled triumphantly.

"What? I just needed to *pinch* it awake? What does that even mean?" Xiri shook her head. The canopy began to close, and 4VO-TG tried to wipe off a circle of dust so Xiri could see forward.

She touched various controls on the ship, and it began to hover. She maneuvered the starfighter forward just as the group of Path members reached the hangar. They started to shoot at the small ship, but Xiri had already gotten it into the air. The canopy finally closed, making a vacuum noise as it fitted securely into its seams. Rain hit the canopy in sheets, rinsing the dust off.

The sky was darkening the edges of the horizon where the twilight threatened to expand. The other ship that had flown and hit the *Lazuli* was in the sky, too. It swung around and began heading straight toward Xiri's fighter. Their comm crackled.

"G-2, this is Path Captain Jep Gri. You are not authorized to fly," a voice came in. "Identify yourself."

Xiri held down the comms button on the console. "Hey, Phan-tu, should we announce ourselves?"

"Whatever you say, Xiri."

"This is Captain Xiri A'lbaran of E'ronoh. I'm seizing this fighter on the grounds that we were having a pretty civilized conversation before you starting shooting at us."

The other ship immediately fired at them. Xiri curved her starfighter down low and swooped in a long arc to avoid the attack.

"Well, that's one way to do it," Phan-tu said.

"Well, they *did* shoot first," Xiri said. "Let's see if these guns are working." She squeezed the triggers on the forward guns and heard them click uselessly. "Mine are dead. What about the rear guns?"

The rear cannon shot out like a quick heartbeat. "We're good there, but this is a problem."

"One set of guns is better than none."

"I'm not talking about that." Phan-tu pointed to the eastern sky. "There are six ships coming in. No, seven. Four on our starboard side, three from above, passing through the atmosphere."

"Friendly or not?"

"No idea." Phan-tu frowned as he polished more dust off the inner canopy so he could see better. "But we got to assume they're not. Xiri, how are we going to win dogfights with rear guns only?"

"I don't know, but I'm always up for a challenge."

The astromech bleeped helpfully. "Finally where you want to be? Looks like our droid is hungry for a fight." She glanced back at Phan-tu. "All right, everyone. Let's hope we've all got strong stomachs and circuits, because this is going to get rough."

Inside the soggy grain fields, no one could see Master Yaddle and Cippa through the rain. It was a good thing sometimes, being short. As they ran through the stalks, explosions sounded both far and near. It was impossible to tell how the other Jedi were faring. A droning noise sounded overhead. She motioned to Cippa to duck down.

A chunky ship with bilateral cannons beneath its wings flew by, one she didn't recognize. It meant more were on the way to join this battle. Yaddle needed to hide Cippa, quickly.

"This won't do," Yaddle said. Cippa was crouched down, looking left and right down the rows.

"I don't like this. I want to fight!" Cippa said. "Not hide."

"No, Cippa. We need to find you cover." Yaddle looked up and down a row of grain, then up and down the next row. "There."

She led Cippa to a brick-and-clay structure at the edge of the planting field. It was made of sunbaked bricks, and dug deeply into the
ground. Yaddle went inside and popped her head out.

"It's as I thought. An underground storage for root vegetables. It's
weatherproof and pretty dry in here. You'll be safe. It'll shield you from
any fighting overhead."

"I'm not a root vegetable," Cippa said, crossing her arms. Her braids
were waterlogged wet cords on either side of her head.

"You'll stay here. I'll come and get you when it's safe."

Yaddle began to walk away. She knew Creighton was fighting somewhere near the landing pads, probably trying to find another ship to
use. The suns were starting to set, which was not good. When it grew
dark, the Path would have their knowledge of the grounds on their side.

Yaddle closed her eyes, listening to the Force, trying to decide where
the Jedi were most in need. She reached out and sensed distress in
many directions. She opened her eyes. This battle was not going to end
well. They were vastly outnumbered, and who knew if Creighton Sun's
message had gotten out to anyone?

"Master Yaddle," Cippa said.

Yaddle turned around. Cippa peeped out from the entrance to the
vegetable storage structure, three meters behind her.

"What if you don't come back?" Cippa said, her white eyelashes
almost glowing in the low light.

Yaddle never knew exactly how to answer such questions. She could
not foresee exactly how this battle would end. She could not know if
she would survive or not. Yaddle did not believe in pressing unfounded
optimism into her younglings; reality was part of their training, as was
dealing with the injustices and whims of fate. So she said what she
believed, no matter how the outcome ever seemed.

"Trust in the Force, Cippa. And stay out of sight!"

With that, Yaddle bounded away into the sodden grain field under
the dying light, clenching her three-fingered fists, readying for the
battle ahead.

Chapter Twenty-Three

THE PATH COMPOUND, DALNA

Creighton Sun and Aida Forte had left the *Lazuli* before it ever hit Dalnan soil. They had opened a port and jumped off into the pouring rain, landing in the area of outbuildings west of the planting fields. There were knots of Path members there, all rushing toward the area where the *Lazuli* was about to crash. No doubt they were going to attack any survivors and squash this fight before it could gain any steam.

"We have to keep them at bay," Creighton said, running toward the Path. "Long enough that help can come."

"*If* help comes," Aida corrected him, running slightly ahead of him. "Creighton, this is beyond just a skirmish arising from a misunderstanding. They're trying to obliterate us. Like using a torch to kill a fly."

"For a so-called peace-loving group, they're shockingly ready to fight."

"Like they expected this all along. Hey, watch your back!" Aida yelled.

A Path member had jumped out of hiding in the tall grass and swung an electrified lance at Creighton's head, rain hissing on the point. He dodged it, swinging his lightsaber and splitting it in two. Blaster shots whizzed toward them, and Aida blocked a few with her lightsaber. Beyond them, she could see at least five other Path members, some shooting at them, others vying to get closer for a full-on physical attack. The enforcer droids were scattered around, their red lasers adding to the blasterfire.

Aida thrust out a green-scaled hand, pushing hard with the Force. Three of the Path went flying back three meters along with a droid. The droid regained its footing and fired directly at Aida, who blocked the blasts. A nearby Path member screamed out.

"The Force will be free!"

Aida blocked two more blaster bolts before pulling the weapons out of the hands of the Path men. But in her effort to fling them far away, she was slightly off balance. A Path woman came up behind her, bashing the back of her knee with a club. Aida fell, and saw a knife in the woman's fist thrusting toward her chest. Aida blocked the thrust by holding the woman's wrists, her lightsaber still in her hand between their faces.

"Abomination!" the woman hissed at Aida, spitting on her.

She looked at the woman, who was struggling to push the knife closer to Aida's body. Aida gathered her strength and twisted out of the way, letting the woman's momentum cause her to fall forward. The woman's knife embedded deeply into the dirt. She yanked uselessly at the hilt, and Aida struck her over the head with the butt of her lightsaber. The woman lay unconscious.

A low roar sounded over her head.

Aida blinked into the falling rain to see a small, older FRC starfighter fly over. It was seemingly patched up with random pieces of discolored metal. Its engine was far too loud, like it was not too far from failure. It flew in front of a similar craft, firing from its rear cannons as it spun upward in a high-g twirl. The ship behind it took a direct hit, exploding.

"That's Xiri!" Aida yelled.

The starfighter flew over their small group, once again firing from the rear guns as it passed overhead, destroying two droids and making several of the Path members halt their attack and cower for cover. A ground missile shot out from what appeared to be a haystack, but was clearly a camouflaged artillery weapon. The missile followed Xiri's ship as she curved over the vast field of the central compound, evading a chunky Path ship. Xiri suddenly broke left, twisting beneath the enemy. The missile hit the Path ship in a brilliant-yellow explosion.

"Excellent," Creighton said. Another roar sounded overhead, but it wasn't Xiri's ship. "Oh no. Spoke too fast."

Up in the sky, near overhead and approaching from the east, were four transports of varying sizes. And more from above, entering from space.

"Friends, or foe?" Aida asked.

"We'll see if and when they start shooting at us," Creighton said. One of the largest transports circled above them, its landing feet unfurling as it approached the ground. The door was open before it had even touched down, with three dozen Dalnans dropping out of it, armed. A Togruta Jedi came forward, bowing quickly before Creighton and Aida.

"Master Sun. I am Jedi Master Fliss Woora. We were in the system very close by when we received your message. We dropped down to the city of West Platt and gathered those who were willing and able to come."

"Master Woora. I am very grateful," Creighton said, wiping his forehead.

"I'm afraid this is all the help you'll get. Most Dalnans are either too afraid of the Mother to fight, or are sympathetic to the Path of the Open Hand."

"How many have come?" Aida asked.

"About a hundred. Some on this transport, the others coming piecemeal."

Creighton looked at Aida. Creighton knew what Aida was thinking: They would feel better about the help if they could quantify what they were up against. But with so many in the Path situated underground, and no idea of exactly how extensive the underground cave system was, there was no knowing how many Path members were around. It could be a hundred; it could be thousands.

The other three transports that had followed this one also landed, full of Dalnan citizens. And the ships were not built for fighting. It was a ground force. Xiri was the only aerial help they had, and who knew how long her ship would last.

"Look!" One of the Dalnans pointed up at the sky.

There were three more ships descending, likely having come from orbiting Dalna or another nearby system. These were moderate-sized but rather ugly, with tow hooks, folded-up scavenging arms, and bulky storage areas.

"Scavengers," Master Woora said. "We've seen them around this system. They usually show up after any sort of skirmish, but they're early. And maybe pirates. What are they doing here?"

"The Mother probably asked them to come," Aida said. "Why else? Even if they're planning on scavenging this place after the battle is over, they have enough firepower to wreak some havoc."

One of the scavenger ships flew low and swooped over their group, firing upon the Dalnan transports that had just landed, setting one on fire. Another flew past, targeting the new landing party that had arrived from a smaller transport. The explosion rocked the side of the vessel, and to Aida's horror, she saw bodies flying. Cries and screams of pain punctuated the chaos.

Aida cursed, so unlike herself. "So much for passive scavengers," she yelled, running away from the line of blasts being shot. "We've got to get the injured to the edge of the fields."

"Get out! Get these transports out of here!" Creighton yelled. "They're going to come around and fire again. They're trying to keep us stranded on the ground."

"Creighton," Char-Ryl-Roy commed him. "I'm at the south edge of the compound, near the cave system. We're taking heavy fire and need backup."

"Sending help your way. How many are you talking about?"

"Fifty and growing. They keep emerging from the caves. There's a good number of droids, too, and it's hard to get close enough to destroy them. We need ground reinforcements at our back, so we can head into the caves to stem the tide."

"Master Ela Sutan is already fighting down there. If we can, we'll try to help, but we need to keep control aboveground for now."

"Will do. But there are children and elderly about. We have to be careful. It's definitely making it harder for us to fight," Master Roy said.

"We'll send a message around. We have to try to fight without harming them." He looked to Aida, but she had already run away to help with the injured on the now growing battlefield. He said to himself: "Having the elderly remain in these huts—it was a horrible move on the part of the Path, but it's working in their favor. We'll be blamed for their slaughter if they get hit by crossfire. This is a disaster. It's like fighting with one arm behind our backs."

Master Roy heard him. "We don't have a choice."

Creighton ducked as one of the scavenger ships began another pass while shooting at them. "Maybe our message will get out farther than Dalna," Creighton said.

"It won't," Master Woora said, shaking her head. "The one communications buoy in this system seems to be malfunctioning. None of our own messages have gone out beyond this system while we've been in the area. We may be the only other Jedi that heard your distress signal."

"But we must have more help," Creighton said. He commed Xiri. "Xiri. Can you hear me?" He looked up at the sky, holding his hand up to shield his eyes from the rain. There was Xiri's small starfighter, zipping around the scavenger ships, flying away from one that had turned to pursue her past the fields.

"I hear you. I'm after these junkers," Xiri said. "They're well armed but they're slow."

"Listen. We need more help beyond Dalna. You're the only ship on our side with a hyperdrive."

"I don't even know if this ship is spaceworthy!" Xiri said.

"If it's not," Creighton said, "you'll know before you make it past the atmosphere. Then come back and fight. But right now, what we have is not enough to survive."

"Okay. After I do this one thing."

Xiri's ship swooped back closer to them, maneuvering to chase one of the scavenger ships that had just fired on their party. The chunky ship didn't turn fast enough. Xiri got in front of it and shot it down, backward, as it had been doing.

Creighton lifted a fist. One by one. That was all they had to do.

"Thanks, Xiri. Now go!"

"Copy that."

Xiri's starfighter pulled up and flew away from the battle. Creighton hoped she wouldn't encounter even more of the Mother's supporters out there, coming in to join the fight. If Xiri couldn't get the message out, the Jedi and their friends here would be dead in the water.

Creighton knew people were looking to him for leadership, for help. For hope. What he couldn't tell Aida or anyone else was that there was a dampened feeling in the center of his being, like when you threw a stone into the water hoping it would float, but knowing the reality.

Creighton knew in his very marrow that this battle might never be won.

Binnot had no less than seven Path members swarming him, all speaking at once. He was in a corridor that led from the planting fields to the cave system, in a room usually used by the Mother for some meetings. He'd been trying to comm her, and couldn't find her. That was why he was here, to look for her. It was the same reason why everyone had come, for answers and direction. And all they found was Binnot.

"They've brought in more Jedi!" said one woman, her face livid.

A Pantoran man who worked directly with the Elders grabbed Binnot's shoulder. "I need to speak to the Mother. Where is she?"

"We don't know where she is," said another woman. "Where are the Elders?"

"What about the north fields? They're completely unprotected! The elderly can only shield so much."

At some point, Binnot couldn't match up the voices with the people around him. They needed answers and guidance. As did he. He had started by giving people directions that seemed blatantly obvious. Protect the cave entrances. Attack in small groups and take down any newcomers who join the Jedi. Fight viciously, to dishearten them and frighten them. With fear on their side, they could win.

But he had been running out of things to say. Leadership and warfare were skills he had not had time to master.

He pushed people aside and shut himself into an inner room with a fine table and wall hangings. A decanter was half full of wine on the table, and he tipped his head back and drank thirstily. He lifted his wrist comlink to his face.

"Mother. This is Binnot. We must speak."

He waited.

"Mother—"

"I am here, Binnot," the Mother's voice came in, slightly hoarse and with an edge of irritation.

"Everyone is looking for you. They need orders. They need a plan."

"They're looking for you, Binnot. Guide them. Better yet—fight with them. Keep the caves protected. You have the upper hand. Fight outside and show them what it's like to be a leader."

He couldn't answer for a second. This was what he wanted, wasn't it? He swallowed his nervousness, and his face warmed from drinking the wine.

"Where are you?" Binnot asked.

"That doesn't matter," she said. Her voice sounded distant, and he couldn't help but wonder if she was even still on Dalna. "I'm here. More important, I'm with you all in your hearts. But I have other larger issues to deal with. You understand. The Path needs you now, Binnot. Lead them. Fight. Show them your courage, and you'll be rewarded tenfold."

"Mother, I—"

The comm went silent. She was gone.

For several, precious minutes, he stood in the room alone. He could almost feel the anxious fear on the other side of the door, and the desperation. The anger. The Jedi were trying to destroy everything the Path had built. But he felt acutely alone, and it took all his effort not to crumple up and hide from the violence that was seeping toward him.

He stretched out his poison glove, extending and then retracting the needles. He needed not to be afraid, but to see this moment for what it was. The moment he dreamed of. This was what he wanted. The light of fortune was on him now. It was time to shine. For the Path of the Closed Fist to take what it deserved.

He opened the door and the group of Path members stopped talking and hollering and stared at him.

"I've spoken to the Mother. And I know what to do. You, you, and you," he said, pointing to three different Path members. "Gather thirty people each and circle around to the east, by the landing pads, west to the field, and north by the hangars. Attack the Jedi simultaneously when you can. We must overwhelm them with numbers. You," he said, pointing to a Trandoshan man. "Get ready to release the droids in Ferdan. On my command. Everyone else—keep the caves closed and send out parties to keep the Jedi and their forces at bay. Attack in groups, especially where you see weakness. Strike to kill. If you have a chance to kill a Jedi, let nothing get in your way. Nothing."

"Where are you going?" a young Path man said as Binnot pushed through the throng of people who were dispersing to their missions.

"I'm going to fight," Binnot said, grabbing his blaster.

Axel was being pushed down the corridor by a sea of Path members, all chanting, "Death to the Jedi!" and "The Force will be free!" He held his bludgeon, mortally afraid he'd get trampled on the way out.

The corridor split into a Y. Up front, one of the leaders—a human man—halted the incessant flow of people to holler instructions.

"I want some of you to guard the opening to the caves and remain here. The rest—" He pointed at the group surrounding Axel. "—I want you up on the ground fighting. For Mother!" He raised his fist, holding a long knife that glinted from the corridor lights.

"*For the Mother!*" the group roared, so loud that Axel felt it reverberate in his chest.

Axel's hands shook. This wasn't what he wanted. He didn't want to fight. He didn't want to kill. And yet, a voice in his head that sounded very much like his mother told him, *You wanted to be in charge. You wanted to be a leader. When you lead, you have to be willing to do what everyone does with your guidance.*

Axel's mouth was dry. If he had wanted a leadership role in the Path, and he'd told them to fight, then Axel had to be willing to do the same. That was what this was. Only he no longer had power. He could only follow.

The mass of Path members around him pushed forward into the darkening light of the late afternoon. Emerging into the open air, Axel was quickly drenched by the rain, which was already flowing along the ground and straight into the cave's entrance. There were several buildings aboveground here, including the Crystal. Chunky ships flew overhead, shooting into the masses of people fighting on the ground. The smell of smoke and wet soil filled the air. Axel blinked in the fading light, eyes blurred by raindrops, disoriented. Around him, there were clusters of Path members hollering and yelling. Their marks of faith were smearing and running in blue rivulets down their faces. Some were running (away? Toward something?) and others were fixed in place, fighting a group of people he didn't recognize. They weren't wearing uniforms, or unified in any way. But they were clearly not the Path, lacking the blue lines on their heads or clothing with the blue markings. But he did recognize the hum and buzz of lightsabers. There were Jedi in the crowd, fighting.

"You three, come with me," a Path member yelled at him.

"Who—who are we fighting?" Axel asked.

"The chancellors and the Jedi have come to attack us. They've called for more reinforcements," a Path woman next to him said. She grinned, though it was more of a grimace. "They'll never get the help they need. We have prepared for this."

A group of regularly clothed people plus a Weequay Jedi were being attacked on all sides by the Path.

"For the Closed Fist!" the woman screeched, holding her pike before her and plunging forward. Axel held back, watching in shock as the woman stabbed one of the humans who had turned to defend himself against two Path members shooting at him from the side. He cried out as he was impaled, and fell down. The Path woman jerked her pike out of his torso before throwing herself toward another group fighting beyond them. Before she could stab another person, a blaster bolt hit her in the head. She fell like a stone to the ground.

Axel gasped. Everywhere around him, he was surrounded by fighting. A Dalnan citizen fell forward at his feet. But when Axel didn't strike him with his bludgeon, he simply got back up and ran past him to assist a Twi'lek Jedi who was fighting off five Path members, all trying to hit her with their blasters at close range.

Suddenly, a blaster bolt whizzed by Axel's head close enough to nearly singe his hair.

He couldn't just stand here. He had to hide, or—

"Axel!"

Binnot's voice shocked him. He turned to see his friend clenching his teeth and his brown tunic smeared with purple blood, clearly not his own. "Follow me."

Binnot led the way, shooting past members of the Path in his way, taking out one, two, three people as they made their way across the hilly area around the cave entrances, flanked by a row of plain little huts. Still, Axel had yet to engage in any fighting with his weapon. There were five Path members with Binnot, some grim-faced, some looking frankly frightened, including a blue-skinned Pantoran who barely looked like he was over eighteen years old, his face still youthfully boyish. He stood with them under a line of dying fruit trees, where they had some shelter from the rain.

"There's a contingent of attackers trickling in from the north planting fields," Binnot said. "You're to hide here since none of you are very strong." He didn't even try to disguise the sneer directed at Axel. "Stay hidden, and kill every non-Path-member that comes by."

Axel nodded, but he was thinking more that it would be easier to steal away and hide once Binnot left them.

The young Pantoran youth froze with fear. Binnot stepped up to him.

"What's wrong with you?" Binnot asked sharply.

The youth was holding the blaster with his fist, his finger nowhere near the trigger. He was shaking his head. "I don't want to."

"This is what you were trained to do. This is how you will glorify the Path, and the Mother."

At the word *Mother,* the boy looked up at Binnot with sorrowful eyes. "My mother just died. I don't . . . I can't . . ."

"If you can't fight, then you're no good to anyone. You disrespect your mother's memory."

The youth started to silently sob, dropping his blaster to the ground. His face was wet, from tears or rain. Probably both.

Binnot looked up at the sky, his face suffused with irritation. "Surrounded by incompetence. Always."

Binnot looked up at the group of Path members cowering around him. "You either fight, or you're useless. This is what you are needed for. This is what the Path asks. The time of peacefully growing crops and letting the rest of the galaxy step all over our beliefs is over." He stepped up to Axel. "And the time has come for you to finally do something useful, Axel."

Axel frowned. What did he mean?

Binnot put his hand on the Pantoran's slim shoulder. "So. You can't fight? You won't fight?" he said softly. Almost sympathetically.

"No," the youth whispered back. He wiped his face with his sleeve.

Binnot nodded. He picked up the discarded blaster, examined it briefly, and handed it to Axel, who gladly dropped his bludgeon. "Now kill him."

"What?" Axel froze, holding the blaster.

"You heard me. If he can't fight, he's worthless, and he endangers our work."

The youth looked up at Binnot with pure shock.

"But—Binnot. You can't be serious."

Binnot took a deep breath, looking at the youth, then looking at Axel. He turned around, the sounds of fighting, screams, and explosions all around them beyond the brush and trees.

"I have been fighting to do everything for the Path since I was younger than him," Binnot said. "Since my parents encouraged me to misuse the Force, and since the Path gave me purpose. A life with the Path is not for everyone."

Axel's hand on his blaster was shaking. He couldn't believe what he was hearing.

"You know what you have to do, Axel. Show that you deserve to be alive, here, among the Path. Show how everything you've done, every choice you've made, has brought you here. You have to start somewhere to build your future. And no one is going to just hand that to you anymore."

Axel stared at him. He knew if he didn't do this, he was as good as dead, like this kid.

"Earn it," Binnot yelled. "Do it. Now."

Axel gripped his blaster. The youth's mouth was still open in shock, his eyes red-rimmed and tearful. Axel put his finger on the trigger, but his hand was shaking. He couldn't bring himself to raise the blaster up. The Pantoran youth was only a year or two older than Axel had been when he first encountered Binnot, all those years ago, when he was so angry for being dragged all over the galaxy and being abandoned with babysitters. Feeling like he was orphaned when his own mother stood at his side. Feeling like a pretty, done-up, polished accessory. He'd asked for death when he was that age. It was all drama of course. *I'd rather be dead than go with you on another stupid diplomatic mission, Mother!* Axel remembered saying. Because he'd said it more than once.

He could hear Gella's voice in his head, pleading with him. *There's another way to do good in this galaxy, to be the person you want to be. Not your mother. Not the Path's Mother. Not me. You need to follow your heart.*

How wrong Axel had been. About absolutely everything.

Before he could think, he raised the blaster and fired at Binnot.

The trigger clicked uselessly.

Binnot laughed down the barrel of the gun.

"Goodness, Axel. You are so utterly predictable." Binnot pulled a blaster cartridge from his pocket. He must have removed it before he handed the weapon to Axel. "Now you decide to have a conscience? How precious. I thought you once called me a brother."

"Brothers don't ask brothers to kill innocent people," Axel said, dropping his useless weapon.

Binnot quietly took a step closer to Axel, staring him down. "You were *never* my brother. You're a soldier. Like me. And not a very good one at that."

Binnot raised his own blaster to Axel's chest. Axel thought back to all those times he and Binnot had run around together. Shared tables at his favorite cantinas, run around to escape the watching eyes of his mother's guards. Laughed at themselves, and at the world around them. None of that friendship meant anything to Binnot.

And so this was it. This would be how he would die, so ingloriously. So utterly wrong about everything.

A nearby explosion threw Axel off his feet. He flew into the air, the light in his eyes white, and a heat like a burning fire all around him. His body impacted the ground with a crunching noise, his head bouncing so hard and painfully that he saw more white sparks. He couldn't breathe for seconds. His injured ears rang with a high-pitched tone. And he couldn't move at all, his body hurting with an exquisite pain he'd never felt in his whole life. One pain in particular bloomed viciously compared with the rest. His hand went to his chest, where he felt a piece of sharp shrapnel sticking out of his flesh. He raised his hands in front of his face, ears still ringing loudly, and saw sticky red blood on his fingertips. He was shocked at how very red and bright the color was, before it diluted to pink from the rain. At how beautiful it was, like the color of one of his mother's hothouse flowers.

His vision began to narrow as darkness flooded the edges of his view. He let his lids fall and his fingertips went numb.

"Damn." He heard Binnot's voice somewhere above him, and the muffled sound of feet crunching toward him. "New airborne enemy. They must have come beyond Ferdan. Looks like the Jedi and the Republic have more friends than we realized on Dalna."

A stiff boot touched Axel's head, roughly rolling it back and forth. Even though he vaguely knew it was his head being pushed about, it felt like it was all happening to someone else. Axel kept his mouth slack, his eyes closed as the dizzy darkness clouded his mind.

"Looks like my work has been done for me," Binnot's voice said. "Good riddance, little prince." The feet crunched away.

Axel had one bell-clear consideration as he spiraled at the edge of unconsciousness. Binnot had been 100 percent correct.

You have to start somewhere to build your future. And no one is going to hand that to you on a silver platter anymore.

Everywhere around him was smoke and screaming and death. But Axel would try to survive this. He just had to have a plan, he thought, trying desperately not to pass out. Just one step at a time.

Step one. Don't die.

Step two. Find Gella Nattai.

Chapter Twenty-Four

THE PATH COMPOUND, DALNA

Cippa Tarko did not like root vegetables.

For one thing, they were always very mealy when cooked. When raw, they tended to taste like dirt. Or slightly sweetened dirt. Didn't matter if they were red or orange or white vegetables. On Arkania, they were one of the food staples of their people, but she relished the more interesting fare from offworld. She couldn't quite understand why Arkanians thought they were lesser civilizations when they made such tasty dishes.

The only thing worse than being forced to eat root vegetables was being *trapped* with root vegetables. As was Cippa's plight at the moment.

Master Yaddle had told her to stay in this root cellar until she was fished out again at the end of the battle. The whole point of having Master Yaddle as her special mentor was to learn. How was she to learn in this mud hut?

She peeped out of the doorway above her. The suns were almost completely set now, and darkness was flowing across the agricultural plain of the Path compounds. The rain had become very heavy, and a nearby ditch was flowing like a tiny river that gurgled in her ears. She liked this better. Her vision was sharp, sharper than most other species, and she relished the fact that she could see in the infrared spectrum. In the far distance, she could see the orangish-colored bodies of people moving around, fighting. Glowing areas where blasters were being held, cannons were being primed on ships, and engines burned hotly in the sky as ships flew by. Some ships were big junkers fighting smaller, scrappy fighters. It wasn't clear who was on what side.

She thought of everyone fighting there that she knew: Priv. Lu. Master Yaddle, and the other Jedi she had only briefly met before the *Lazuli* had crashed. The couple who clasped her tightly when they landed, as though she were their child. Cippa had hardly any memories of her parents. She vaguely remembered them being tall and proud looking, and her mother having elegant hands. That was all.

Mostly, she remembers Master Yaddle always being nearby. She was always so kind. So short! And very, very patient. Every gentle admonishment from Yaddle was a lesson in disguise. Cippa thought it ridiculous. How would she learn like this? Instead, she practiced her Force abilities, as she was particularly gifted with the levitation of objects. Yaddle had taught her patiently about that, too.

"Your strengths can be your greatest weakness," Yaddle had said. "When you do not practice what you do not know, it is like inhaling, and never letting your breath out."

"That makes no sense, Master Yaddle."

"Which is why you have much to learn."

Cippa knew she was right. There would be lightsaber training, and learning how to reach out with the Force and sense it around her, to understand if there were disturbances, harmonies, and discordances near and far. Cippa found this particularly frightening. She had a tendency to like facts and mathematics. But the Force was not data, and she could not quite understand why, or how, she was able to do the things she did. Cippa would never admit this out loud, however.

As she watched the orange and reddish infrared bodies glowing like coals in the distance, she knew Master Yaddle was there. No one would be able to see in the growing darkness the way Cippa could. She had a distinct advantage. She could help. She wanted so much to prove to Master Yaddle that Cippa was worthy of being at her side. But she was also so afraid to make a mistake.

Trust in the Force, Yaddle had said, when Cippa had asked whether or not her master would ever come back.

Cippa looked behind her at the piles of root vegetables, her nose curling in disgust. "Enough of you. I'm getting out of here." She stepped out of the root cellar and began to run through the rain toward the battle, where bodies glowed like coals in the twilight.

THE MOON BETWEEN EIRAM AND E'RONOH

Chancellor Mollo was currently in a makeshift office on the moon, within the waystation. He eyed the blue and red planets of Eiram and E'ronoh from his window and grimaced. Usually, he preferred his boots to be solidly on planetary ground, but he was up to his very high ears in the bureaucracy of both planets. At least on the moon, no one was yelling at him.

Queen Adrialla was frantically trying to locate her son, as Phan-tu had simply disappeared from the E'roni hospital without any word about where he'd gone. She immediately thought the worst, thinking that there had been a cover-up when E'ronoh's hospital wing took care of him. Orlen had tried to get the queen and the Monarch to talk, but they dug their heels in and went on accusing one another of terrible things. The war was still raging hotly, and it was becoming infrequent that Orlen looked into the sky and didn't see cannon fire between starfighters. With Phan-tu's disappearance coinciding with Xiri's mission, Orlen let his suspicions be known to the queen and the Monarch. Without better communication to Dalna, his hunch could not be verified. And yet still, they refused to fix the buoy.

"Chancellor," one of his aides said, knocking on the door to his tiny office. "We just received an Ee-Ex droid that came from Coruscant. There's a recorded message from Chancellor Greylark. We've transferred the message to your office."

"About time," Orlen said. "It's been nothing but chaos, trying to speak with her. In the future, we have to do better. Two chancellors is a headache sometimes." He touched the holoprojector and tented his fingers in anticipation, his tentacles twitching slightly.

Kyong Greylark's image glowed before him. She was dressed in the plainest of clothing, unlike her usual formal regalia. No makeup. No jewels. It was a shocking sight.

"Orlen," she said. Also a worrisome thing. She rarely called him by his first name. "This message brings . . . tidings of change. I have news that you may or may not like." She smiled uncertainly, which was unusual given that Kyong Greylark rarely smiled at all. Even at the end of a vastly successful mission, bringing in an entire sector to join the Republic, or having heard that twenty new hyperlanes were just prospected. Never a smile, only a nod of approval. "There is no good way to say this, so I'll just say it. I have decided to step down from my chancellorship."

Orlen yelled. "What? Kyong . . . *What?*"

"I know this must be shocking," Kyong went on. "Let me try to explain the circumstances. My son, Axel, escaped from Pipyyr due to that corrupted message of ours. He has been working in concert with the Path of the Open Hand. Probably for months or longer. Instead of facing the consequences of his betrayal to the Republic, and to me, his own family, he has embedded himself deeper into the Path. Just now, I received a request from him that I come directly to Dalna. He wants a chancellor there—me—for a reason. It isn't a good reason, and it breaks my heart to know this."

"No," Orlen gasped. "Don't go. It's a trap, Kyong."

"I know it's a trap," Kyong said, as if she were conversing with him in real time. "I know that if I go to Dalna, I will most likely die. Or be held hostage. But much of Axel's and the Mother's potential to hold sway in this galaxy with respect to the Greylarks is through my power as a chancellor."

"Oh, Kyong. No," Orlen whispered.

"So I am going. As a mother. I've already officially relinquished my chancellorship. It's done. But this galaxy is not without a leader. It has you, Orlen." She held up a hand. "I know what you're thinking. We were always a good pair, because we both had our weaknesses and our strengths. We complemented each other. And how will that work when one hand of a pair is missing? The answer is . . . it will work. With loss and change come adaptation and new strengths. You are a skilled diplomat, wherever you are, Orlen. I will always be around to lend you my ear and my counsel. That is, if I survive what is to come."

Orlen noticed, for the first time, that Kyong was a very slight woman without all her dazzling costumes and fanfare. Her cheeks were carved and angled, her body wirier than he realized. From one perspective, she looked frail. From another, dangerous.

"But I believe I will. And I believe you, Orlen, will succeed. What the Republic needs now is you."

Kyong looked down, but when she spoke back through the holovid, there were no tears in her eyes. Only resolve.

"We have not been able to converse openly at all in the last week, save for these scattered messages. I am asking you now, Chancellor Orlen Mollo, to bring Eiram and E'ronoh together once and for all, and to see the Path of the Open Hand for what they truly are. There is more going on in Dalna than anyone realizes, and I fear that more direct action is necessary there. The Jedi need you. The galaxy needs you. And as a citizen of Coruscant and a friend . . . I need you."

The message ended.

Orlen felt gutted. He was alone. There was no way right now, given how delicate things were with Eiram and E'ronoh, that he could magically make them come together to join a battle across the galaxy.

But he also knew something that Chancellor Greylark—that is,

Kyong—didn't. She didn't know that he had already sent a diplomatic mission with Jedi Char-Ryl-Roy, Enya Keen, and Princess Xiri to Dalna. If Axel was asking his mother to come to Dalna to broker peace, then that must mean the diplomatic mission had failed. Otherwise, why wouldn't Axel have mentioned it? Why would he even need Kyong there?

Orlen had received not a single message from the Jedi or Xiri. It was as if they'd gotten swallowed up into a void. Where were they? What had happened? How would he convince the two planets to send troops for a hypothetical coming war that he was only guessing at?

If he did what Kyong asked, it would mean the end of Axel Greylark. And yet this was what she was asking for. Even after renouncing her chancellorship, Kyong Greylark wanted what was best for the galaxy's peace.

Sometimes you have to burn things before you build them.

Those had been her words. Even if they meant seeing her only remaining family die as a result.

He stood up and stormed out of the waystation, his boots crunching on the salt-crusted ground. He glared at the planets. They held so much beauty. And so much stubbornness. If their leaders wouldn't listen to reason, then Orlen would show them reason. He pushed his sleeves up and called to his aide.

"Ready my ship. We're going to fix that buoy. Right now."

Chapter Twenty-Five

ABOVE THE PATH COMPOUND, DALNA

Captain Xiri A'Ibaran was used to flying old ships, but this was ridiculous. She and Phan-tu had escaped two scavenger ships that chased them for several kilometers, away from the Path compound, before Phan-tu was able to shoot them down over a large northern lake.

Now if this ancient FRC starfighter could only survive passing through Dalna's atmosphere, they might have a chance of getting a message out.

As Xiri pointed her nose toward the sky, she slowed her acceleration.

"Why are you slowing down?" Phan-tu asked.

"Because, first, we need to talk. I don't know if this ship is actually going to make it if we leave the atmosphere."

"For the record, I did say that flying this wreck was a terrible idea. It seems to only have two speeds," he complained. "Fast and stalled."

"Just be glad it doesn't have one speed. Zero," Xiri said. "But aside from that . . . we're taking a huge risk, Phan-tu."

"I know."

"If we make a jump to lightspeed and our navigation is off, we could be stranded in deep space. We may run out of oxygen," she added.

"I know."

"Our astromech has also just been patched together."

Here, 4V0-TG bleeped an acknowledgment.

"I know," Phan-tu said, yet again. "But we have a better chance with you as the pilot. I trust you."

"Do you, really?" Xiri went quiet for a beat. "Then why didn't you tell me you were stowing away on the ship?"

"I . . . I don't know."

"You're the son of the queen and the consort," Xiri said. "You've been counseling them on political and domestic matters for years. And you're telling me you didn't know what you were doing?"

"When it comes to you, no. I don't," he said. "It was a knee-jerk re-action. I was lying in bed doing nothing and I wanted to help. I knew there was no way you or anyone else would let me come, so I hid."

"You took a risk, Phan-tu," Xiri said.

"I know, but it was worth it. Kind of like our situation now," Phan-tu said. "Whatever we do, let's do it together."

"Even if we burn to a crisp?" Xiri said.

"Without us, the message for help won't get out. We're the only hope the Jedi have, aside from the Force. Plus, the Path has done so much to harm Eiram and E'ronoh. This is how we save our homes."

Their seats were back-to-back, and Phan-tu reached over his shoulder, his fingers barely grazing Xiri's head. She reached back, and they clasped each other's hands, squeezing their assent.

"Then let's go." Xiri let go of Phan-tu's hand, slipping her fingers back around the control yokes. She accelerated upward and the blue sky darkened to the blackness of space. Warnings began to beep inside the cockpit.

"Are we holding, Teegee?"

The droid whistled a confirmation.

"Oxygen levels stable. Hull is intact, though we're pretty rough around the port middle wing," Xiri said.

The second they fully left the atmosphere, 4VO-TG made a noise that sounded distinctly like a droid cuss. The FRC starfighter stalled again as the ship cruised forward and stopped accelerating. 4VO-TG then went into a flurry of more droid curses.

"This droid is trying pretty damn hard to show it's useful," Xiri said. The engine kept changing sounds as the astromech continued to try to improve its function.

"I know how it feels," Phan-tu said. "After I was orphaned, I did the same."

"Aren't Queen Adrialla and Odelia going to be pretty mad that you left without telling them?"

"I don't want to talk about it," Phan-tu replied. "Parents will be parents. All right. Where are we going?"

They were silent for almost a minute. Phan-tu reached behind him, and Xiri's hand rose to meet his. They squeezed each other's hand.

"You thinking what I'm thinking?" Xiri said.

"Yes," Phan-tu said. "Xiri, let's go *home*."

It was a very, very odd thing to have two brains making decisions instead of one. But it was also a great feeling for a change. Xiri restarted the engine, and miraculously, it hummed to life after a cough or two.

"Let's head for the hyperlane to the Eiram-E'ronoh system," Xiri said. The ship sped off away from Dalna and its suns, stalling yet another time. When they had reached the entrance of the hyperlane, Xiri took a huge breath. "Here goes nothing. Teegee, are we ready?"

The droid made a small squeaking noise. It sounded like he was nervous. Xiri engaged the hyperdrive, and the stars around them stretched like linear lines as they entered the hyperlane. Phan-tu whooped in triumph, and Xiri exhaled in relief.

"We should be there in about—"

The ship juddered, banging Xiri's head against her seat. 4VO-TG let out what sounded like a scream and a yelp. The plasma lights of the hyperlane began to morph back into starry lines, and the FRC fighter suddenly found itself spinning gently into space.

"What just happened?" Phan-tu said, panicked.

"We just exited the hyperlane. I thought I put in the right coordinates! What?" Xiri read the readout in her cockpit. "Teegee says our hyperdrive broke!"

"Is it fixable? Where are we?" Phan-tu asked, his hands up against the canopy. "Ugh, this spinning is going to make me sick."

"We have worse problems than your stomach contents," Xiri said. "The engine is fried, and we aren't anywhere near Eiram and E'ronoh."

"What?"

"Teegee, what about the life-support system? How much time do we have before we run out of oxygen?"

The droid was silent, and Xiri's readout was also paused.

"Just tell us, Teegee," Xiri said.

A readout in the cockpit read *3.35 hours.*

"A couple of hours," Xiri whispered.

"Can't we get help?" Phan-tu asked. "Maybe there's someone nearby . . ."

But Xiri looked out of the cockpit and saw nothing but stars. Beautiful, unhelpful stars. "We can send a message out, but no one on Dalna could possibly help us, even if our transmission gets through. And the communications buoys on Eiram and E'ronoh aren't working." Her breath caught in her throat for a second. "Phan-tu, this is my fault. I shouldn't have let you come with me. I'm the pilot. I shouldn't have flown this ship, knowing it was this dangerous."

"No, Xiri. It was both our decisions. We co-piloted this terrible idea. But you know what? Being here with only you, a million stars and a few precious breaths to share . . . I'd do it again."

"I would, too. A hundred times." Xiri sniffled. "I love you, you know."

"I love you, too, Xiri," Phan-tu said.

4VO-TG made a long, warbling *wooing* sound.

Phan-tu chuckled. "Love you, too, Teegee."

"That's not what Teegee said," Xiri said, wiping her nose. She tapped on her console. "Hot suns! Teegee says there's a functional Eiram and E'ronoh communications buoy that's receiving!"

Phan-tu clapped his hands. "That's better than an *I love you!*"

Xiri touched her console and opened a communications channel. "This is Captain Xiri A'lbaran with Phan-tu Zenn, of Eiram and E'ronoh. Our starfighter is stranded at these coordinates. Are you receiving us?"

They waited two minutes, before a familiar voice spoke inside their cockpit.

"Xiri? Phan-tu? It's Chancellor Mollo. Thank the depths you're all right! We are receiving you loud and clear. I have your coordinates. I'll alert Queen Adrialla and the Monarch of your position, and we'll send help immediately. Hold tight."

"Wait!" Xiri said. "We aren't requesting just our rescue. We need you to send a message directly to my father and the queen. The Path of the Open Hand is waging a battle with the Jedi on Dalna. We have evidence that the Path was responsible for bringing the klytobacter to the moon and are manufacturing klytobacter in enormous quantities. They've unleashed enforcer droids, and the Jedi and the Dalnans are hopelessly outnumbered. So many have died already, and it's only getting worse."

Xiri's voice shook, and Phan-tu reached behind to hold her cheek in his hand. When Xiri squeezed his hand, he spoke.

"This is Phan-tu Zenn. The people of Eiram and E'ronoh must recognize, once and for all, that our planets are stronger together than apart. We've been so busy following the blueprints of our mutual destruction that we can't see the obvious. That *we* can be the architects of good. Together." Phan-tu took a precious breath. "The Jedi have only ever wanted peace between our planets. For once, this is their time of need. And it is our time to fight for the truth—and what the Path has always known. If Eiram and E'ronoh were to unite, there would be no tidal wave, no groundquake, no storm, and no Path that could *ever* shatter us."

GREYLARK RESIDENCE, CORUSCANT

Kyong Greylark had dismissed her aides and the many personnel that normally swarmed her on a daily basis. After sending her message to her son, Axel, Kyong had switched off the holotransmitter. Soon, Yoda and her aides had left the room, and she was alone.

She had stayed like that for a long time—standing there. Unmoving. She was still wearing her dirty clothing from working in the hothouse. It had felt good to use her mind in a way that was direct, as minor as the task had been. So unlike diplomacy, where her actions had to trickle down complex cogs in the engines of governments and cultures as varying as there were stars in any given sky. It had felt good to get her hands in the dirt, her fists around tools. And then Axel's demands had dropped into her lap.

Axel.

Where had she gone wrong? She wanted to laugh, but instead, had stifled a cry. She knew the answer. She had gone wrong in so many ways, as a leader. As a parent. As a friend? No. She had never been her son's friend. But she could try. She could try to undo the damage. The one thing that always stood between her and her son was her job. It had always come first. She knew it. He knew it, too. In fact, the whole Republic knew it. The job had demanded it from her, and she had allowed it to consume every minute of her day. Even before she was chancellor, when she had been crafting her career moves toward that apex. And throughout that time, Axel had grown up in the environment of prominence, but never being the center of it. She had seen other ambassadors and politicians who had somehow found the ability to stay attuned to their family's needs, no matter what culture or species they were. She had often found herself feeling superior, as if they could not possibly be as dedicated to their work as Kyong had been. Now she knew how ignorant that pride had been.

At first, after the message was sent, Yoda stayed with her wordlessly, to offer his support. The old Kyong would have wondered why he stayed, if there was more to discuss regarding Jedi and Republic inter-actions. But now, she recognized Yoda's quiet offerings for what they were. Kindness. After her husband had died, she had not blamed the Jedi, but had not spoken to Axel about it, either. In that gulf, Axel's anger toward the Jedi Order tightened like a vise around his heart. Yet another mistake. But Kyong was not able to speak about her failures to Yoda. Not yet.

Messages were sent far and wide with her formal declaration step-ping down as chancellor. In places where communications were patchy, EX droids were deployed, including the one sent to Chancellor Orlen Mollo—now the only chancellor. She wondered how he would feel once he received this message. If he received it.

She and Orlen had always had a formal relationship that worked.

And now, whether he liked it or not, Orlen would have it all to handle himself. She hadn't wanted it to be this abrupt, but it was. She was also acutely aware that to help her son, she could not bring the one valuable thing that would put the entire galaxy at risk: her chancellor-ship.

After all the messages had been sent, she'd allowed herself a single hour of silence and solitude before she went into her suite, shedding her gardener clothing and washing off the grime from the hothouse. In her vast closet full of museum-worthy gowns and capes, she dug out her old academy clothes—the fireproof and blade-resistant military-style pants and jacket. She pulled them on, shocked to find they still fit. She went to the Heirloom Room, ignoring the wall of priceless jewels, instead turning to the cabinet of weapons. There were old knives, swords, and blasters that no longer functioned. Too old to use. She left the room, thinking.

Her personal Longbeam had the defenses she'd want, but she no longer had the Republic crew, and anyway, she wouldn't want to put them at risk. The other Greylark ships didn't suit her needs. She needed a small craft, a fast one, with some good weaponry. And she no longer had the Republic fleet at her beck and call.

All her aides were gone. She spoke to C-04L, who waited for her outside the room.

"Fourell," she said. "Contact the armory. I need to call in one last favor."

It didn't take long. A small *Beta*-class shuttle, trapezoid-shaped, well armored, and equipped with weapons, was soon docked on the roof of the Greylark residence. It couldn't have come a moment sooner. It had now been hours since she'd dispatched her response to Axel, and nothing had come back. She had hoped that he would be happy to hear she was on her way to Dalna. But there had been silence.

When Kyong boarded the shuttle, alone, she was happy to see a set of several blasters, rifles, and some knives of varying sizes waiting for her. There was also a voice memo from the administrative head of the armory.

"Call it a security courtesy, for domestic Coruscant use only. At least, that's what I reported," the administrator's voice spoke. "Chancellor— I mean, Kyong. Please be careful." There was a hesitant pause. "May the Force be with you."

"Yes," she said to herself. "We'll need all the help we can get."

She smiled and let out a huge sigh, giving the inside of the empty ship a once-over. It was strange not being swarmed by attendants and aides watching her every move. *Enough was enough. It was time to go.*

She entered the cockpit, only to find it occupied.

"Master Yoda!" Kyong said, surprised.

Yoda nodded. "Go with you, I will," Yoda said. "Axel's message shows much is happening on Dalna. Much that has been hidden from us."

"You still haven't heard anything from Master Sun, or Master Sutan?"

Yoda shook his head. "Not since either entered the Dalna system. The silence is troubling."

"Yes. The fact that Axel's message could come through but nothing else means the Path is likely blocking outgoing messages from Dalna. It's a black box there." She looked apprehensively at Yoda. "I mean to go alone. I no longer have authority to call for more support. I don't wish to get anyone else hurt, including you, Master Yoda."

"We will go together," Yoda said, nodding in the affirmative. "Chancellor you may not be anymore. Friend, you still are."

Kyong smiled gratefully. "Thank you, dear friend. I appreciate it."

As they left Coruscant, Kyong saw a larger ship following them, a medium-sized Jedi Longbeam.

"Master Yoda, are we being followed?" Kyong asked.

"Not followed. Accompanied. Danger, you are in. Prepared we shall be."

"What have you heard?"

"Murmurs in the galaxy, there are. Factions heading to Dalna. I sense a great disturbance."

Yoda's words sent a chill through her. She was grateful for the Jedi escort. At least there would be more witnesses to what might be happening on Dalna. They left swiftly, leaving behind the bright, bustling, city-covered planet for the darkness and silence of space. They entered hyperspace in one of many jumps to get to Dalna. Throughout the short stretches of time, they spoke little, Yoda no doubt sensing that she had a mind full of thoughts that needed the silence. But once they had exited the last hyperlane, Kyong received an urgent message. She motioned to Yoda as she clicked on the console in the cockpit.

It was a distress call from Xiri and Phan-tu. They listened, in shock to hear how the battle was raging on Dalna. Every word coming from Xiri and Phan-tu felt both terrible and hopeful. For all that the Jedi and the Republic had done for Eiram and E'ronoh, perhaps it would be these unifying voices that finally brought peace. Phan-tu's words struck her particularly hard.

We've been so busy following the blueprints of our mutual destruction that we can't see the obvious. That we can be the architects of good.

Kyong could tell Phan-tu was speaking of his two planets, but Kyong could only think of her son. A second message came through, almost immediately after the first.

It was Orlen Mollo.

"Kyong!" he said, breathless. "We need to talk."

"What's going on?" Kyong said.

"Chaos," Mollo said. "The queen and the Monarch heard the message from Xiri and Phan-tu. And they aren't listening. They're fighting, about who lost Phan-tu, and who's going to rescue them. Not about coming to Dalna."

Kyong stayed silent.

"They aren't seeing the big picture. They're disintegrating back into petty arguments."

Still, Kyong said nothing.

"Are you going to say anything?" Orlen said, exasperated.

Master Yoda cleared his throat. "Closer to Captain A'lbaran and Phan-tu Zenn, we are. Low on oxygen, they must be. Rescue them, I will," Yoda said. He nodded and left to speak with a tall Jedi who entered the cockpit.

"Kyong?" Orlen said.

"You already know what to do," she said gently. "You don't need me."

"But they can't see—"

"Then help them see. Show them what they cannot fathom. And let Xiri and Phan-tu's words inspire them." She paused. "Why did you become a chancellor, Orlen? To see new worlds? To flee the confines of Coruscant and get your boots muddy?"

"Of course not." He, too, paused. "It was enjoying a meal with someone whose world was wholly different from mine. It was finding that raising children was joyful and difficult, no matter what world you lived on. It was shared laughter, across the galaxy." Kyong could already hear him breathing easier. "I know what your next question is, Kyong. 'And what does Eiram and E'ronoh share, aside from conflict?'"

Kyong smiled. "And the answer?"

"Xiri and Phan-tu. And they share a future—two intertwined worlds that have a larger consequence in this galaxy than they ever realized."

"I feel a speech coming on. One that will change the foundations of Eiram and E'ronoh, forever," Kyong said. "I told you, you didn't need me."

"I'll always need you, friend."

"It's not my usual sign-off, but I think this is apropos," Kyong said. "May the Force be with you, Chancellor Mollo."

THE PATH COMPOUND, DALNA

Enya could tell at a distance that Master Char-Ryl-Roy was exhausted. He had just used the Force to push three Path members away, and had stepped backward only to get hit hard on the back with a mace. He reeled from the blow, slipping in the mud. The fact that he hadn't anticipated it meant he was growing truly fatigued.

"Master!" Enya called out. She ran toward him, wiping her face of rain. It had gone from heavy to torrential, and made fighting ten times as difficult. They'd been able to take down a good number of enforcer droids, but every kill took a huge amount of effort because the laserfire came fast and intense. They both had splatters of blood on their clothes, and her feet were heavy with mud. She flipped over her shoulder a Path member who was holding a club. "Are you okay?" She knelt by his side.

"We need more help."

"I know. More help is coming. Look." She pointed.

In the distance, two small ships had landed. Twenty or so Dalnans—a mix of humans, Pantorans, and Theelins—came running off the ships, blasters firing. The Path members that were forming a circle around Char-Ryl-Roy and Enya broke up and ran to meet the fresh onslaught. Master Roy and Enya looked around with dismay at the bodies lying immobile on the ground both far and nearby. Only a few meters away lay a Jedi she had met years before—Pom Gornay—who had died when a Path member tackled him and set off an explosive.

"They're more than willing to die, these Path members," Enya said.

"And there are more coming." Char-Ryl-Roy shook his head.

"Master," Enya said. "There are untold numbers of Path members in that cave system. Every time we get a handle on keeping things under control, more emerge. We have to block off those entrances. It is one way to stem the tide."

"Sounds good. I'll go meet our new friends who just arrived and let them know what we're up against. Meet me at the southernmost cave entrance in fifteen minutes."

Enya nodded.

As soon as she turned around, four Path members stopped her. An Ongree male held a lit green lightsaber. It chilled her. What Jedi had fallen so that their lightsaber could be taken? Could it have been Aida?

Enya held up her blaster. "That lightsaber doesn't belong to you."

"Look! A Jedi without a lightsaber. You must be a terrible Jedi to lose it. Or perhaps, like all Jedi, you don't deserve to hold such an implement of the Force?"

"Look who's talking!" Enya yelled.

"Come and get it, trash," the Ongree Path member said, spitting on the ground.

She shot at him with her blaster and missed. But he was just a decoy. The other three Path warriors with bludgeons and blasters had spread out and begun to attack her from all sides. She pushed one away, dodging a blaster bolt, while shooting at the other three. But one of them, wielding a bludgeon, had swung it so quickly that she'd been knocked off her feet. She fell hard onto her shoulder, her blaster falling out of her hand.

Enya could feel panic rising in her chest. She saw the lightsaber in the Ongree's hand go high above his head, readying for a death blow. And the other two aiming their blasters straight at Enya's head.

If I only had my kyber crystal, and my lightsaber, Enya thought, feeling the bitterness in her throat. But it had been her choice. A gift given freely. Even with the anger she felt, she could imagine Master Char-Ryl-Roy's voice in her head. Tired, but true.

You said it yourself, Padawan. As long as the Force is with you, you are still a Jedi.

In moments when she had just milliseconds, she took that fraction of time, stretched it to a thousand breaths. Enya relaxed. Felt the Force around her. Felt the Dalnan soil beneath her fingertips. The fury of the four attacking her. And she exhaled.

The two blaster shots released missed her head as she quickly rolled on the ground. The lightsaber came down, missing her, and she responded with a scissor kick to pop his knee joint. He dropped the green lightsaber, screaming in agony. Enya rushed upward with her hands as her fists met the Ongree's bulbous eyes. He cried out, staggering back and shielding his face.

Enya reached out and the lightsaber flew into her palm. She felt the energy pulsating within it, feeling it within her own body and palms. It was not hers, no. But it seemed to recognize her as a benevolent extension of the Force. It felt warm in her hands.

With the lightsaber, she quickly dispatched the blasters of the two Path members. One woman withdrew a knife from her tunic, charging Enya with a scream. Enya swung her lightsaber down, slicing the tip off the blade, and brought her free fist forward to knock the woman out squarely on the jaw. The other two went running away.

Enya dashed around groups of Dalnans fighting the Path. She could see Master Woora and two Togruta Jedi Knights—Meya Wuk and Den Harrit—at the center of knots of Path members attacking relentlessly. Several droids, with the three glowing red spots on their faces, shot their red lasers into the deepening darkness of the twilight. Cries and screams told Enya that the blasts had found their mark. Somewhere near these rolling hills was the southern entrance, for she had seen Path members arising from behind a hill where no buildings or ships existed. Enya walked cautiously forward. The suns had already set, but their burning light was still on the northern horizon, making this part of the fields dark and bluish in color.

There were no voices, no activity ahead of her, but something was there. She could feel it. As if an army of malevolent beings were about to rise up out of the ground and tear her to pieces.

Enya shook her head. What was she thinking? That was a bizarre fear, out of proportion to what was really before her.

A growl sounded from somewhere nearby. Were there wild animals on Dalna? Surely there must be some dangerous native species here. Enya held her lightsaber aloft, and the growl resonated even louder, closer.

"Stop! Help!"

A cry sounded from her left, over the hill. She started to run toward it when she saw a blurred figure—no, a creature—bound out of the darkness in the distance, heading straight for the cries of help.

The hair on the back of her neck stood up and goosebumps erupted over her arms.

"What in the stars was that?" she muttered. It was too dim to see, but she thought she glimpsed something low to the ground. Small. Grayish, or possibly purple. Or black. She didn't even trust what her eyes were telling her. And now, from wherever the cry had come from, an anguished scream.

The person sounded like they were being tortured. Gurgling, choking wails of agony.

Enya couldn't move. Her mind wanted to help, but her body was frozen, shaking, as if something had taken every gram of bravery from her and stolen it. She sank to her knees, shivering.

Instead of moving or escaping, she curled against a boulder, unable to help anyone nearby who was fighting. When she had finally caught her breath, and her pulse had simmered down to where she could stand upright without passing out, she went back toward the southern entrance of the caves.

Whatever she had seen, it wasn't there anymore. She knew it. She could feel its absence, in that her inability to think rationally, the fear, had slowly trickled away. As she ran forward, she saw an ashen log burned to the ground, and went to leap over it, when she stopped.

She looked down. It wasn't a burned log. It was in the shape of a person, a human woman, her hands still curled like claws as if trying to hold off whatever had attacked her. Enya recognized the outlines of a Jedi cloak, and a lightsaber had fallen only a few meters away from the figure. But it wasn't a Jedi anymore. It was nothing but a gray, crumbling material. The Jedi's eyes were cloudy and swirled with specks of black and white soot. She touched the arm of the fallen Jedi, and the entire body within its clothing collapsed into a pile of ash.

"What is this?" she whispered.

Master Char-Ryl-Roy was at her side, out of breath. "Enya. I thought you were following me. Why—where did you get that lightsaber?" Then he looked down, where another lightsaber was partially covered in gray ash and muddy silt. He reached down to pick it up. "I know this lightsaber. It belongs to Werla Cayn. A Jedi Knight. She came over with that first group of Dalnans when our ship crashed." His face dropped to look at the pile of watery ash. He knelt, his hands touching the gray substance. "I remember when she was a youngling at the Temple on Coruscant." He looked up at Enya, his face aggrieved. "What happened here? I didn't see a fire . . ."

"I don't know, Master. I can't explain it. I felt something terrible— and I thought I saw—" She shook her head. "I don't know what I saw. A blur of something running. I never felt such fear as when it was close by. And then I heard her screaming." Her eyes watered. She felt such horrible loss, and she'd never met the woman. "I don't know what happened."

"Master Sun had mentioned a Path weapon of some kind."

"There was the klytobacter they had that Aida Forte saw. Enough to kill a planet."

"We have to be careful. We're up against more than we know."

"Yes, Master." Enya wiped her eyes, and Master Char-Ryl-Roy got to his feet. He took Werla's lightsaber and hooked it to his belt. "Where did you get that lightsaber? Another fallen Jedi?" he asked, gesturing to the weapon in her hands.

Enya held it up. It felt heavy in her hands. Odd. But also—comfortingly warm. "I was fighting some Path members, and one of them had it. I don't recognize it."

Char-Ryl-Roy took it from Enya, and his shoulders fell. "It belongs to Master Orin Darhga. I had no idea he was here." He gave her back the lightsaber and closed his eyes for a moment. She couldn't tell if it was from grief, or for meditation. Enya felt too many things at once—the lingering fear, the danger surrounding her, her exhaustion. She felt the heft of the lightsaber in her hands, and it calmed her.

Enya watched her master, his face lined with worry and concentration. Finally, he spoke. "There are more Jedi here than we realized. Somewhere nearby."

"Where?" Enya asked.

Master Roy opened his eyes. "I don't know. There are so many people in pain right now. The Jedi are fighting hard and well, but we're hopelessly outnumbered."

Just then, a ship flew overhead, cannon blasts hitting the ground on either side of them. Clods of soil and turf flew into the air. They dove next to a large boulder and some shrubs, the smell of singed grasses arising from the soil nearby where small fires broke out from the shots.

"We still have to block that cave entrance," Char-Ryl-Roy said. "Let's go."

"What about the other Jedi?" Enya said as they began running over a ridge away from the fields, lit up with blasterfire and the laserfire from ships flying overhead.

"Right now, they're on their own. May the Force be with them."

Chapter Twenty-Six

THE PATH COMPOUND, DALNA

It should have been a beautiful night, Aida Forte thought.

The rain never bothered Aida. She thought it was lovely when the skies reached down to try to touch the ground in this way, and it always was refreshing on her scales. Overhead, the clouds were thick, making the darkness even more intense, as if the world had been washed in ink. It was cool but not biting. The wind rustled in the fields.

It should have been beautiful. But instead, Aida was surrounded by death.

Master Creighton Sun and Aida were in the middle of the same field where the *Lazuli* had crashed. Their backs were against the hull, which meant they could only be attacked from 180 degrees, instead of 360. It didn't make it that much easier. The number of Path members coming at them seemed relentless. Already, bodies of both Dalnans and the Path lay in the field around them. Broken and sizzling droids were scattered everywhere. Creighton had suffered a severe wound to his right arm, and it hung useless as he wielded his lightsaber with his nondominant arm.

Aida and Creighton had fought the Path on Jedha, but that had been vastly different. Dry and cold, with a bright sun that hid nothing at all. But here, in the early evening on Dalna, it was what she could not see that frightened her. In truth, it terrified her. Whatever affected them in the caves was still out there, and every now and then, a wave of icy dread washed over her, immobilizing her for seconds at a time. Seconds she didn't have. Meanwhile, after one Path member would fall, another would emerge from the darkness with a different weapon and a different approach to attacking them. And yet the same look was on their face, always. Bloodthirsty hatred.

Aida's arms were so tired even her lightsaber felt heavy. She took a moment to catch her breath.

"Aida, look out!" Creighton yelled.

She had zoned out for just a moment, and the next thing she knew she was on the muddy ground, her ears ringing. She looked up, trying to orient herself, and saw an enormous man nearly two and a half meters tall expertly swinging a metal lance and ready to impale her in the chest. Creighton jumped forward, his lightsaber catching the lance in the air, and it went flying away, hitting the hull of the ship.

Aida got to her feet, wiping the rain out of her eyes. She scrambled to pick up her lightsaber where it had fallen. She shook her head, and bent her knees and hips in a fighting stance. Creighton grunted as two Path members began fighting him with vigor, as if freshly dropped onto the fighting fields, one with a blaster and the other with another metal staff.

"You will lose, little one," the Path member said, his beard barely hiding his grimace. He pulled out a small blaster from his waist. "We are more than you. And there is no more help coming for you. The Mother made sure of that. They will call this the Great Night of the Jedi's Defeat."

He fired at her, and Aida blocked each shot as the man crept closer, step by step.

When he came close enough, he pulled out a long, thin blade from his waist and jabbed forward, catching her in the upper thigh.

Aida crumpled to the ground.

"Creighton!" Aida yelled, but Master Sun was nowhere to be seen. He could now be fighting on the other side of the *Lazuli,* out of view.

The Path member swung his blade, but Aida's lightsaber did not swing fast enough to catch it. She saw the next milliseconds as if they were being dragged through tar, slow and inevitable, waiting for the blow to land on her. Aida knew it was a killing stroke coming her way, but she refused to close her eyes. The defiance in her eyes would be fighting, too, at the very last moment of her life.

The blow did not come. At the last moment, the Path member seemed sucked backward into the darkness. She heard him land with a wet thud far away. Through the fighting Path members and Dalnans nearby, she saw a small greenish figure, its three-clawed hand raised.

Master Yaddle. Her lightsaber moved like a bright blur in the rain as she fought attackers before her. With her free hand, Yaddle moved left and right, and Path members nearby went flailing into the sky, landing on others with cries and thuds. Aida thought Yaddle looked like a small boat impossibly cutting through wave upon wave that tried to sink her.

When she was close enough, Master Yaddle lowered her hand and knelt at Aida's side.

"You're hurt," she said to Aida. Yaddle touched Aida's leg. Aida felt a calm emanating out of Yaddle and her touch, and the pain lessened. Every time a Path member approached them to attack, Aida would startle, and Yaddle, without even looking behind her, would lift a hand and push hard, and they would fly five meters away, forced to renew their attack from another direction.

"On your feet now, Jedi Forte. Where is Master Sun?"

"Creighton is . . . somewhere. He's hurt, too. Master. How much longer can we sustain this?"

"That question is not one we can ask, since the answer helps us not. The more important question is . . . oh, what's that?" Yaddle looked off into the distance.

"What?" Aida asked.

Not a hundred meters from them, deep in the growing darkness, they saw a Path member lifted into the air, spun, and thrown some distance. Then another, thrown in a different direction. And another. Whatever was throwing them, it was coming their way.

"Oh no," Yaddle said, sighing. "I have to go take care of something. In the meantime, keep up the fight, Aida. Your body is not the only thing that battles the darkness. The Force is with you, and it is limitless. Rest tomorrow. Fight now."

"Yes, Master Yaddle."

With that, Yaddle crouched down and sprang high up into the air and forward, in the direction of the bodies flying here and there, almost haphazardly. As Aida fought off two more Path members, she wondered what terrible creature or being Yaddle was about to encounter.

She found out rather quickly, as Yaddle bounded right back into the cover of the ship, next to Aida, along with the Arkanian youngling, Cippa Tarko.

"I was just trying to help!" Cippa was arguing.

"You were supposed to be hiding!"

"Let me help! I can't do anything helpful in a cellar full of vegetables. I hate radishes!"

Yaddle wheezed a sigh. She stepped forward several steps, ignited her green lightsaber, and felled two Path members who had evaded Aida. Then she turned off the blade and went right back to chiding Cippa.

"I gave you a command as your master, and you directly disobeyed me. This is why I am tutoring you. This is why you need more instruction."

"I want to help."

"Now is not the time. It's too dangerous, youngling!"

Cippa suddenly raised both her hands. Yaddle spun around to find two Path members with axes held high over their heads, now dangling uselessly in the air. Cippa raised them higher then dropped them, screaming, back to Dalnan soil. They struck the ground and lay unconscious at Yaddle's feet.

Aida shrugged. "She could be useful. Right?"

"I'm not even tired!" Cippa yelped.

Yaddle frowned. "Never in my years of teaching . . ." She put her hand on her face and wiped the frustration away. "All right, Cippa. You will stand here next to Jedi Forte. Anyone who tries to attack her while she is already engaged, you levitate them, high enough to render them unconscious when they fall. That is all."

Cippa beamed.

Yaddle turned around, pushing her wet hair out of her face, and reignited her lightsaber. "It's going to be a long, long night."

Axel Greylark didn't know how long he'd been unconscious. Rain was pattering on his face and his clothes were soaked to the skin. He was still lying on the wet ground—at least he thought he was on the ground, his body shoved against some sodden sacks of cloth. Sacks of something.

As he became more awake, he noted a headache pounding behind his eyes. Good. That meant he wasn't dead. He wriggled his fingers and toes. All working. But something in his chest hurt more than everything put together. He raised his hand to gingerly touch his chest, the movement making him gasp in agony. He felt it. The piece of metal still impaled right through his shirt and the thick tunic overtop.

He noted the sticky blood that had congealed around it. He took three quick, successive shallow breaths, and pulled.

"Gnnnnnrrr!" He tried not to utter a sound, but it was impossible. The pain was awful, but the piece of shrapnel was finally out. His ribs had prevented it from penetrating further. He pressed his hand over the wound, feeling new, warm blood there. Hopefully he would live. Whether he deserved to live was another question he wasn't ready to answer.

Under the dark, cloudy sky, ships of various sizes were flying back

and forth, laserfire brightening the sky in streaks. He could hear fighting from a short distance. Axel got up onto his elbows, trying to push
away the sacks or whatever was enclosing him on both sides.

It wasn't until he had sat up that he realized he hadn't been thrown
on top of sacks of grain, or even rubbish. He'd been thrown onto a pile
of dead bodies.

Axel stifled a cry, scrambling off the corpses. There were Path members, the blue streaks on their heads faint from being rained upon.
Gashes and wounds lay open and raw and strangely bare of blood,
having been washed relentlessly by the ongoing storm. Some of their
eyes were open. Some were young, too young, like the youth that Binnot had asked Axel to kill.

But Axel was miraculously still alive. Step one complete. Now time
for step two.

"Gella," he whispered. He got up, tripping over ankles and elbows
and other body parts that threatened to make him retch. There were
trees around him and the pile of bodies scattered haphazardly, not in
any way placed here out of respect. He looked around, dazed, and tried
to find his bearings. To the north were the fields where the fighting
appeared thick, and dense ropes of smoke rose, only visible when the
sky became illuminated from an explosion or more ground missiles
firing. He turned around. The caves were behind him, and somewhere,
Gella.

He stumbled into a run, slipping on mud. Good thing he was still
wearing his Path clothing. Path members were coming at him, running in the opposite direction, some looking fresh to the battle while
others looked exhausted. As he reached the cave entrance, the look of
him made the heavily armed guards pause.

"You look more dead than alive," one of them said.

"Anything for the Mother," Axel said. "And the Closed Fist," he
added, remembering the words from Binnot. The lies came all too easily. He looked down and removed his hand from his bloodied chest.
"They took my weapons. I need new ones. And something to dress this
wound."

"Go to the armory." He looked at the palm-sized bloodstain on Axel's chest. "You're on your own for that. No time for the wounded."

Axel nodded and limped into the cave entrance. Rainwater was flowing into the entrance in a stream and down the steep hallway. Alarming, but no one seemed to care. The place was swarming with activity. More Path members suiting up with weapons, and some lying in the corridors, dead or wounded. Some were being dragged into larger rooms where they had been left. Like the guard said, there was no one to attend to them. He pressed his fist to his chest, hoping it would stanch the bleeding, and walked deeper into the caves. How deep did they go? How many Path members were actually in here? It occurred to him that these bits of information were crucial to the battle, and he'd never thought of asking. Because he was only ever thinking of himself.

How would he find Gella? He wandered around but was getting deeper and more lost. And then he stopped. *Use what you have,* he thought. *Get it together, Axel.*

He straightened up, despite the pain it caused him, and walked with purpose. He saw a human guard nearby, looking weary. Axel stopped him.

"You there. I have word from the Mother herself. There's a Jedi imprisoned down here. She wants them taken to her, immediately."

"Then get them yourself," the guard said, trying to pass him by.

"You want me to tell the Mother that you refuse? What's your name?"

"Lumbo." He didn't look that afraid, but he'd stopped trying to walk away.

"What do you think is going on up there? A party?"

"No, I—"

"I almost died up there, and I'll do it again. For the Path. Get your priorities straight. The Mother says she wants this captive Jedi. Now."

Lumbo looked at him, and truth be told, Axel must have looked horrific and furious, because it worked. He sighed. "For the Leveler?"

"Yes," Axel said, not knowing exactly what that creature had to do with anything. The guard turned around and went back where he came from. He took a sharp left turn, then took a bunch of descending tunnels down, spiraling until they came to a dimly lit corridor full of alcoves.

"There are only a few rooms here capable of holding a Jedi."

"Which one?"

Axel walked down the corridor. Inside the alcoves were different entrances, but one or two had thick metal doors set with tiny barred windows.

"It's about time," a woman's voice said from the darkness. Gella's.

"This one," Axel said.

"Are you sure?" Lumbo said. "She's dangerous."

Axel gave him a withering stare, and the guard tapped several buttons on the side of the wall. The door rose. The guard raised his blaster and stood back. He handed manacles to Axel.

"I'd advise you to use these."

"Thanks, brother," Axel said as Gella walked out of the cell.

She looked at Lumbo and smiled. "I'll take that." She lifted her hand, and Lumbo's blaster immediately left his grip and flew into Gella's hand.

"Stop!" Lumbo yelled, but Gella had already stepped toward Lumbo, striking his head hard with the butt of the blaster. Lumbo fell.

"Sweet dreams," Gella said.

"I'm so glad I found you," Axel said. "You have no idea what I've just gone through."

Gella slammed her hand against Axel's throat, shoving him hard against the corridor wall. "What you've gone through? You? Orin is dead because of you. But that doesn't matter, does it? Because it's always about you, Axel."

Axel's hand scrabbled against Gella's iron grip on his throat. He was having trouble breathing, and it occurred to him that maybe, just maybe this was what he deserved. He wanted to fight. But he didn't want to fight Gella. Not anymore.

So Axel let go of Gella's clawing hands, looked her in the eye, and let her go ahead and stop the blood going to his brain.

His resignation shocked her into letting go.

"What is *wrong* with you?"

Axel fell to his knees, wheezing hoarsely. In between breaths, he answered. "Every . . . thing . . . is wrong with . . . me."

"Wow. I think we agree for the first time ever." She stood back. "Talk. Quickly."

Axel fell over, sitting on his side. His hand went to his chest, pressing again. He took it away and saw that the bleeding had slowed. He looked up at Gella, but decided he couldn't meet her eyes, and stared at the dirt floor instead.

"Binnot. He wanted me to kill someone who wouldn't fight. Execute this innocent young Path member, after he'd lost his own mother. I couldn't do it." Axel covered his face. "I can't do this anymore, Gella. I can't keep pretending to be something I'm not. I can't be a leader, or change the galaxy, or eclipse my family, or make you respect me. I can't play this game. I'm tired of bluffing."

Gella said nothing for a long time. Finally, she sighed. "I don't believe you."

"You shouldn't. I don't really deserve it."

"So why did you set me free?"

He looked up, daring to finally glance at the intensity that was always in those dark, all-seeing eyes. "Because it was the right thing to do. For once."

She took a measured breath. "Like I said, about time." She motioned to his chest. "What happened to you?"

"Some explosion, and I was too close. It was a piece of shrapnel. I pulled it out."

"You know, you're not supposed to do that, but I'm impressed. Sounds painful."

"Not nearly painful enough."

Gella crossed her arms. "What's going on out there? There's a lot of activity in the corridors, but I can't hear anything. I can sense a lot of Jedi nearby."

"It's a war, Gella. I've never seen anything like it. Some Jedi and people from Eiram and E'ronoh came to talk to one of the Elders. But apparently there were other Jedi here as well. The Path went crazy, trying to kill them all. So they called in help, and it's just . . . exploded. The battle is enormous. So many have died already."

"It's like they were looking for a reason to stir things up," Gella said. "Those enforcer droids that Orin and I found in those crates. Those aren't destined for another planet or place, are they?"

Axel shook his head. "They're already on the battlefield."

"I have to help," Gella said. "I just don't know what to do with you."

"Do whatever you want. You know you can kill me at any time. Let me at least show you how to get out of here."

"I would never kill you, Axel." Gella said. "But—"

"Look. Things can't get any worse for me. I'm sorry. I am. There's a lot to make up for. Let me do something good before you get rid of me forever. Please."

He'd never really been so sorry, or begged so much. It was an odd feeling, and strangely freeing.

"Fine," Gella said finally, though her face remained stolid. "But wait. We can't just walk out of here. You lead me out. I'll pretend to have the manacles on."

"Good idea."

He loosely left the manacles on her, and put his hand on her back as he led her out of the cell block. A few people looked at them askance as they walked upward in the passageways, but Axel kept that look on his face—sheer confidence and the sheen of authority. It worked about 60 percent of the time. He hoped it would work now.

Luckily, the activity belowground was so hectic that no one paid attention to them as they walked hurriedly ahead. A few people gave Gella withering looks when they passed by, knowing what she was. Once, a Path woman, half Axel's size, reached out and slapped Gella in the face.

"Filth!" she yelled, and then she walked on.

"If that's the worst we get, I'll take it," Gella whispered, smarting from the blow.

They managed to exit the caves into the darkness of the night. As soon as they were beyond the hectic activity of the cave entrance, Gella threw off her manacles. She looked at Axel.

"Are you going to get rid of me now?" he asked.

"Not yet." She looked around. "Where can I find Binnot?"

Axel blanched at the thought. "Why do you want to find him?"

"Because he has my lightsabers!"

"I have no idea where he is. Knowing Binnot, he found a transport and left this place."

"That actually sounds like an Axel move," Gella said drily. "Really, though. Think like Binnot. You know him. What would he do?"

"He'd be making decisions. Trying to force himself upward in the ranks and taking advantage of the situation to make himself known. And important."

"Then we need to find a central location. Where he'd be calling the shots."

"We have a problem, though," Axel said, pointing.

Up in the sky, a small trapezoid-shaped shuttle was circling with a spotlight on the ground, as if searching for someone. Once in a while, it took on heavy fire from other craft, and it would pitch upward to the sky and circle around, shooting the offenders, sending them careening into the night sky trailing smoke behind. But then it would be back to circling the fighting on the ground, taking on blaster bolt fire from the Path on the ground.

Axel looked at the shuttle. "We'd better take cover—"

A moment later, the shuttle's spotlight landed on the two of them.

"Run!" Gella yelled.

She and Axel ran as quickly as they could away from the area where the busiest fighting was happening. An explosion happened right at Axel's left—he recoiled, covering his ears, which rang from the blast.

"That ship is shooting at us!" Gella yelled.

They ran toward a group of trees, where they had some cover, if only for a few seconds.

"Take off your Path clothing," Gella said, hurriedly. She yanked the dirtied, bloodied cloak from over Axel's head. "There. You're officially on the right side. Now which way do we go?"

"We need an aerial view. Maybe we can find a ship and locate Binnot that way. Shoot the Path down along the way."

A spotlight from above shone upon them both. Again, from the same shuttle.

"Oh no," Axel said.

Just then, a group of Path members emerged from the darkness. Panting and covered in trails of blood, they saw Gella and Axel. Without missing a step, they lifted their weapons and grimly headed their way through the rain.

"Oh no," Gella said.

"I said that already," Axel said.

The shuttle above them fired. Gella and Axel ducked away from the group of attackers just as an explosion blew the dirt nearby several meters around. The impact threw Gella and Axel, who landed face-first onto the ground, mouths full of muck and water. The only good news was that the group of Path members nearby were blasted away, too, lying unconscious or dead nearby.

"We're never going to get away from this ship," Gella said.

"It's landing," Axel said.

"Convenient. Maybe we can take it, search for Binnot." She groaned. "I would have an easier time with my lightsabers," she added, gritting her teeth. "Grab a blaster from that guy." Gella pointed to one of the fallen Path.

Axel did. His ears were ringing again, his chest still hurt so badly he wanted to constantly scream in pain, and his legs were shaking from the last blast. He was so weary, so drained. *If whoever's on that ship tries to kill me, I don't think I can fight back.*

"Fire the second the door opens. Don't even give them a chance for an offensive," she said.

Axel nodded.

The ship was fairly small, only large enough for ten people, so they wouldn't be facing too large an assault.

The second the door began to crack open, Axel and Gella got to their knees and began firing.

The door kept opening, but smoke obscured the entranceway.

"Hold your fire!" Gella said. "We're wasting shots. They're holding back, whoever they are."

They waited a few seconds for the smoke to clear. A few seconds that felt like a few years.

A single voice broke the silence.

"Axel Greylark! Will you please stop shooting at your mother?"

Gella and Axel lowered their blasters, mouths open.

From the edge of the door, a figure emerged, walking down the gangway, followed by five tall, imposing Jedi. The person in front had a slim figure of medium height, and wore brownish pants and a jacket with red markings of Coruscant military make. It was a woman, her hair in an untidy ponytail flecked with gray.

"Mother?" Axel croaked.

"Chancellor Greylark?" Gella said. She bowed awkwardly.

"No, don't," she said to Gella, holding up her hand. "Not necessary."

"She's not chancellor anymore," Axel said.

"What?" Gella's mouth fell open.

"He's right," she said. "I'm just a citizen of the galaxy. Here to help the Republic and the Jedi. And I brought some friends."

Axel shook his head. "I can't believe you came."

Kyong Greylark tried to smile and failed. "I don't always keep my promises to you, Axel, but this time I did." She held up a hand, and spoke into her comlink. "Master Sun? Are you there?"

The comlink crackled to life. "Creighton Sun here."

"This is Kyong Greylark."

"Chancellor!" Creighton said, his voice sounding relieved.

"Just Kyong. Not chancellor anymore. It's a long story. Master Sun,

I brought only a small contingent of Jedi with me. I was already on my way here when we received the message from Xiri and Phan-tu. Master Yoda is aware of the situation. More help is on the way."

"Thank you, Chancellor."

"Just Kyong," she repeated. "Good luck."

She turned to the five Jedi behind her. "Contact the other Jedi here on the ground. Be careful, and may the Force be with you."

One of the Jedi, a tall Zabrak, placed his hand on Kyong's shoulder. "We can stay with you."

"No, Master Vaqqi. They need you more than I do," she said, gesturing to the darkness. He nodded and disappeared into the battle along with the other four Jedi.

"So . . . why were you shooting at us?" Axel said.

"Well, this feels more normal," she said with a smirk. "Starting off a conversation with criticism." She looked around, the rain already soaking her clothes and hair. "I was shooting at the Path. Can't you tell the difference?"

"In this battle, it's hard to tell," Gella said grimly.

"In life, it's hard to tell," Axel said, raising his eyebrows.

Kyong pinched her finger and thumb together. "Can we focus? We received a message from Xiri and Phan-tu. They're on a starfighter, adrift, somewhere between Dalna and the Eiram system. Master Yoda went to help rescue them with some other Jedi because we were so close."

"What were they doing?" Gella asked.

"They were here with Creighton Sun, trying to help. They left Dalna on a stolen ship, trying to get aid." His mother turned back to the ship. "Come on. We're safer in the air. We can try to contact the other Jedi here and see where we're most useful."

Together, Kyong, Axel, and Gella boarded the ship, quickly closing the ramp behind them. The second it was shut, they could hear blasters hitting the hull. Kyong ran to the cockpit and started flicking switches, readying the ship for flight. She narrowed her eyes at Axel and Gella, who were strapping in on either side of her. "You're hurt, Axel."

He put his hand to his chest. "I'll be okay. I can still fight."

Axel's mother looked at him with surprise. "You? Fighting?" She pulled the control yoke toward herself, and the ship began to rise off the ground.

"I didn't say I was good at it, but I'm doing what I can."

"I thought you were on the other side," Kyong said. "What happened?"

"When did you learn how to fly?" Axel said, watching his mother guide the ship high in the air.

"Oops. Enemy coming ahead. I'm going to fly around and give them a chase to survey what's going on," Kyong said, tilting the ship and accelerating upward. "I learned the basics at the Academy. It's probably been, I don't know, thirty years since I piloted anything. Some things you don't forget."

"You never told me," Axel said.

"You never listened."

"Hey, how about we figure out our next step?" Gella said.

"Of course. How can I be of help? I have a limited number of weapons on board. The ship has some low-grade ion and laser cannons. Either of you know how to operate those?"

Gella and Axel looked at each other, shrugging.

"I thought you took basic starfighter maneuvers at the Academy!" Kyong said.

"Hooky," was Axel's reply. "I have regrets. There are many."

Kyong shook her head. "Fine. Okay. Gella, you control the forward guns. Axel, head to the back where the ion cannons are. Keep the square focus on your target, and wait until you get a targeting lock for at least a full second before firing, or we're wasting power. Spinning around, you'll get dizzy. Keep your eyes on a fixed object. The triggers tend to be really touchy. Be careful."

"Got it," Axel and Gella said simultaneously. Gella ran to the forward guns.

"Wait, Axel." Gella looked at him. "Tell me the truth. About how bad it is down there."

"It's uneven. The Jedi may be able to hold things for a while, but without help—they're hopelessly outnumbered."

"Is that the worst?" she asked.

"No. The Path has other weapons, not just the droids. But . . . Binnot didn't tell me everything. It's what he didn't tell me that scares me the most."

She exhaled loudly. "Got it. Now go. We're losing time."

Axel nodded. But before he left, he turned back to look at his mother. With her ponytail and no makeup, she looked simultaneously older and younger than her usual self in her chancellor regalia. He hardly recognized her. She seemed to notice that he hadn't left, and turned to him.

"What?"

"Nothing. I'm just . . . glad you came. And I'm sorry."

"About what?" She had freckles across her nose and cheeks. He'd never noticed that. She usually had so much makeup on.

"Too much to say right now. All of it, I guess."

"How about we survive this, and then we talk after."

"Not sure which will be harder, to be honest," Axel said.

She smiled. "I was thinking the same thing. One step at a time."

He nodded and left. The ship lurched as his mother evaded yet another set of ships coming their way. He had the vaguest sense that he was not going to survive this battle. But he was strangely at peace with that knowledge. He ran to the back of the ship, finding the rear cannon well where he sat down in the swinging, gyroscopic seat and strapped himself in. He flicked on the two cannons and the targeting program.

"I may die, but for the first time, I'll live on my terms," Axel said, gritting his teeth.

Gella's voice commed in. "Fight first, die later. Also, everyone on the ship can hear you right now."

"Copy that," Kyong said.

Axel slapped his forehead. At least he no longer had anything to hide. Embarrassing as it was, it still felt better than whatever life he was living only a day ago. He gripped the controls, spinning around as enemy ships came into view, and began firing on them.

"Okay," he said, aiming his cannons at the ship in pursuit. "I'm ready to fight."

Chapter Twenty-Seven

THE PATH COMPOUND, DALNA

Padawan Enya Keen and Master Char-Ryl-Roy had managed to gather a group of fighters, a mixed group of Republic supporters who had heard the local call for help, all fighting near one of the main cave entrances. Thanks to Kyong Greylark's arrival, there were five new Jedi fighting on the ground. Why Greylark was here was still a bit of a mystery, but the news was spreading well beyond Dalna that they needed help. And help they needed. A score of bodies obscured the ground between the Jedi and the Path.

"It's working, Master," Enya said. "We're keeping the bulk of the Path in the cave. They haven't been able to get any parties out for at least half an hour. And we've destroyed a huge number of the enforcer droids."

"Don't speak too soon, Padawan," Master Roy said grimly. He was bleeding from a wound on his long forehead, and was constantly comming the other leaders of the groups nearby.

"How is Master Sun faring?" Enya asked in between blaster shots. Aida and Creighton were behind a rise of stone and soil, dense enough to protect them from the blasts coming from the caves. For the time being, those fighting on the side of the Jedi and the Dalnan citizens were finally pushing back in a meaningful way. Not without grave losses, though.

"Creighton's group is holding steady. Three of the new Jedi are with him, and having fresh fighters has helped. The Path has not been able to renew their ranks out on the fields. They had far more ground weapons and missiles stockpiled than we ever anticipated, but they seem to have exhausted most of them. We've taken out more of those flying junkers than we expected. A lot of those ships belong to prospectors. They're not equipped to defend against starfighters. We only have two that joined us from south of the capital city."

"With the droids out of the way, we might win this after all," Enya said. She had been shooting steadily, when she stopped.

"What is it?"

"Listen," Enya said.

Char-Ryl-Roy looked up. Or rather, he listened. The sounds of blaster shots had halted, along with the cries of the newly wounded and the detonations from the makeshift explosives that the Path had been throwing—chaotically, but nevertheless with brutal effect.

For a moment, the Jedi Master actually heard Dalnan sylbeetles chirping among the knotted weeds and grasses at the end of the field where they had trenched themselves. The rain pattered heavily all around him. He looked over the edge of their trench—a dangerous thing for a Cerean, given his substantial cranium. The cave entrance had gone dark. As if the Path were shielding themselves.

"We're looking in the wrong direction," Char-Ryl-Roy said, suddenly filled with foreboding. He spoke into his comlink. "Watch your backs! All free hands on defense to the north!"

Enya and Char-Ryl-Roy spun around. Behind them in the darkness of the field, a tiny clustered trio of asymmetric red lights glowed. And then six, nine, then countless, all blinking like a spray of blood droplets glowing against black. The lights were bobbing slightly over the terrain, marching through the torrential rain.

More enforcer droids. Dozens of them. Lightning illuminated the smothering darkness for a moment, showing a flood of shining metal droids in the planning fields, coming ever closer. The thunder followed, along with roars and cheers from the Path fighters throughout the compound.

"Where did they come from?" Char-Ryl-Roy muttered. "We're in trouble." He dropped the binocs and spoke into his comlink. "They've released another wave of enforcer droids. Twice as many as before. Creighton, do you read?"

"I see them. They're coming our way, too. We're—"

The comm was disconnected abruptly. From the far distance, the sounds of laserfire and yells reached them, like a chorus of distress and destruction.

"Enya. Let's go. The rest of the group doesn't have the defenses or the firepower to fight well."

"Yes, Master." Enya lifted Orin Darhga's lightsaber. Once again, it felt heavy in her hands, as if reminding the Padawan about what was to come.

Enya hesitated, nevertheless. She had been eager to fight at the cave entrance, hoping she would have an opportunity to enter the subterranean network. Somewhere in there could be Elder Onning and her kyber crystal. She knew she wouldn't fight her best without it. She still remembered as a youngling, stepping gingerly through the Crystal Caves on the ice planet of Ilum, listening with her whole body until a particular glowing crystal embedded deep down a three-meter chasm had spoken to her. She had wedged her body into the crevasse, creeping her way down, cutting her palms and elbow and knees against the almost knife-sharp edges, until she pulled the crystal free. In her hand, it seemed to shine an almost golden-yellow compared to the rest, as if to say, *I've been waiting for you to find me, Enya. Now we can begin together.*

Begin what? she had wondered. But she didn't need to answer the question. It was there to help her as a Jedi, and help her commune with the Force in a way she hadn't before. So when Char-Ryl-Roy said to turn around, away from the caves, she thought—*It's over. I can't look for it anymore. That's not where the Force needs me right now.*

Orin's lightsaber warmed in her grip. Reminding her that she was needed. That this crystal, orphaned as it was, needed her. She turned it on, the green light glowing in the storm, a talisman against darkness.

"Let's go, Master."

She ran forward at the side of Master Roy, faster than any of the troops behind them. Looking left and right, she saw four other Jedi running with them. Two Jedi Knights, one Jedi Master, one Padawan. Toorin, Woo, Riponjonang, and Equaa. Keen, and Roy. The six light-sabers glowing in the night, dashes of hope in the gloom.

The enforcer droids fired as soon as they were within range. The red laserfire was so much more powerful than standard blaster bolts. Every time that Enya deflected one, she felt the impact of the blow deep down into her elbow and shoulders. It was worse because she was tired after so many hours of battle. She had to push harder, concentrate more, to keep her strength from withering.

The deflected laser shots hit some of the enforcer droids, but they were well protected with strong armor. Enya inhaled deeply, gathering her strength and attuning her body with the Force all around her. For her next step, she took a high, bounding leap, deflecting shots as she tumbled in the air, landing in front of the closest droid.

The droid before her turned to fire. Enya swung her lightsaber down, hitting the droid in the torso. It staggered back, smoke rising from the blow that glowed red from melted metal. Still it fired on Enya. She deflected the shot, striking the droid again, and again. Finally, it fell. Enya was breathing hard as another droid aimed at her.

Master Roy ran to her side, covering her as she fought another droid nearby. Once again, it took several blows, and several long pauses while they deflected blows long enough to get in a strike. After a few minutes, two droids lay before Char-Ryl-Roy and Enya, the glowing red dots on the face shields winked out.

Enya hung Orin's lightsaber at her waist and backflipped, landing behind the nearest droid. They weren't terribly nimble, these droids, and not made for hand-to-hand combat. But they were heavy enough to resist a single body slam or lightsaber strike. She swept her leg at its ankles, felling it. Enya thrust her hand toward the back of the droid's head, gathered up a fistful of wires that connected the torso to the head, and yanked unmercifully.

It went dead.

"Enya!" Char-Ryl-Roy yelled.

She turned around. The rest of the line of enforcer droids had gone dark, realizing that their red dots were serving to mark them. At least fifteen other droids had scattered into the darkness, their existence evidenced only by the red laserfire hitting people left and right.

Enya ran to her master, who had raised his wrist. Voices erupted in panic from his wrist comm.

"Master Roy! We can't hold the droids off! We need your help. On the west side of the—"

The voice went silent, followed by another taking its place.

"Where is Creighton Sun?" said the other voice. It sounded like Master Woora. "We need his help! We are overrun by droids. Our blasters aren't getting through their armor easily."

"Master Roy!" Another voice came, this time from behind them. It was one of the Dalnans, a human female. "The cave entrance. They're renewing their attack. We're getting pummeled on all sides. We are losing people every second!"

Char-Ryl-Roy looked around, and Enya's heart sank. Even taking them out one by one, the Jedi would not be able to keep up.

"Destroy every droid you can, Enya. It's the only way." He started heading toward the cave entrance, but Enya stopped him.

"Master!" Enya said. "Are . . . are we going to survive this?"

He said nothing, his face awash in exhaustion and grief. "It's time to fight, Padawan. Not ask questions. Go. And may the Force be with you." He squeezed her shoulder and then bounded off into the night.

Enya looked around, spinning, the dizzying sensation of despair coming to her from all directions. She touched the lightsaber at her belt, but it had gone cold for the moment. Orin's lightsaber would fight with her, but it would not end this bloody battle.

A droid approached her, and she parried with it before flipping behind it and yanking out its wires viciously. She felt anger at the droid, though she knew beneath her fury that it was only following a program. That it had been built by its maker to destroy. If only she could attack its maker. Or at least, the one in charge. Fighting at the cave entrance would only do so much. What if there was a way to stop the droids and the battle entirely?

She looked up and around, not at the carnage nearby, but scanning the horizon far away. She ran back toward the rise where they had been assaulting the cave entrance, destroying another two droids along the way. She found the binocs that Master Roy had dropped, and began searching the edge of the compound. She saw fighting everywhere except for one area. The landing pads.

There, faintly visible in the darkness, was a row of Path members, quietly walking onto a shuttle. Their clothes were unstained, unwrinkled. They had not been directly touched by the fighting.

It was the leadership, leaving. The only ones that could end this battle, right now.

Enya dropped the binocs, and ran.

Binnot Ullo was in a deep cavern, the only one of its kind, fifteen meters beneath the Crystal. Despite being well-fortified, the Crystal had not survived when a pirate ship had crashed into it, exploding on impact. It wasn't the only building that had been decimated. But here, in the dirt cavern with a few whitish stalactites hanging from the ceiling, Binnot was finally where he wanted to be. In charge of the ground forces for the battle.

A tall human male entered, saw Binnot, and immediately knelt before him.

"Sir. You asked for me."

Binnot raised his hand. "I did, Sevi. As I have been asking for all the faithful."

Sevi nodded. His right hand gripped an electric rod, his weapon. Binnot reached over, bringing close to him a pot of blue paint. Sevi watched him warily as he held the clay pot with his leather glove. He had made it known to all that he wore poison on his glove at all times. A casual pat on the back or a handshake could kill if he wished it. Sevi exhaled with relief when Binnot reached into the pot using his bare fingers. He withdrew them dripping in bright-blue paint.

He touched the top of Sevi's forehead. Binnot let his three fingers shake erratically, dragging jagged lines down the forehead of the scout.

"Long live the Path of the Closed Fist," Binnot murmured.

"Long live the Path of the Closed Fist," Sevi repeated. When he looked up, he smiled. He had several teeth missing, knocked out recently from the fighting. The bloody sockets showed shiny and beefy in the dim light, and Sevi's cheek was slightly swollen and bruised. His brown hair was stained with dark blood.

"What news?" Binnot asked. "How are the caves holding up?"

"Holding steady. But there are skirmishes happening in some areas of them. We have not completely eradicated the Jedi underground. I'm trying to get more information."

"And the other creatures?"

"Feeding, and growing rapidly."

Binnot nodded. Sevi grinned again. "The enforcer droids are killing by the dozens. The tide is turning. The Jedi are taking out some of the droids, but they cannot keep up with the carnage. It is beauty itself, sir."

"I wish to see this with my own eyes. The glory of the Path—the true Path. And the bitter downfall of the Jedi and the Republic in our presence."

Binnot rose and Sevi led him out of the cavern, down a narrow and serpentine corridor and upward. He opened and closed his gloved fist, anticipating the view. With his other hand, he touched two of his prized possessions—the twin lightsabers of Gella Nattai, who was still locked uselessly in a holding room so far below the surface that no one would find her. For all he knew, she'd already been killed by his own people. He cared less what had happened to the fallen, than about what was to come. Glory, through the Closed Fist. The Mother had never appreciated Binnot. And now she wasn't here for him anymore. Forget the past. Marda Ro had seen the future.

When they emerged from the entrance, hidden by the fallen wall of a barn that opened like a cellar door, Binnot turned around to survey the scene as a few of the Path stood protectively around him.

It was beautiful. Starfighters, only two now, were being chased mercilessly by the ragtag group of treasure hunters and prospectors who were hoping to cash in on the destruction and take their anger out on the people who kept trying to make more rules for them. On the ground, he could see the enforcer droids with their telltale redlaser blasts laying waste to the few pockets of people still standing. And there were precious few left.

"Look," Sevi said, pointing with his electric rod.

Nearby, a pile of sodden ash lay. It was oblong, and one part of whatever it used to be was still in its old form. A hand, clutching the air. Part of a head, too, eyes open with the voiceless mouth already crushed into dust.

"A Jedi. They will litter the battlefield soon enough."

"Excellent."

A gorgeous sight to behold, Binnot thought.

Binnot preferred to watch the skies, however. It was up and away where his future lay, not here on Dalna. Dalna would soon be dead to him, like all who opposed him.

He saw a scavenger ship, well laden with towing gear and cannons, and a blackened prospector ship pursuing a small angular shuttle. Binnot could have sworn it was a Republic shuttle, compact and equipped with ion cannons and a hybrid hyperdrive. It had been hit and was now trailing a ribbon of smoke from one of its engines, unable to avoid additional hits from the pursuing prospector and scavenger ships. The shuttle lurched with every blast. It must have lost its ability to shield itself. But instead of flying away or trying to shake its pursuers, the ship was slowing itself and turning around in the worst possible maneuver, as if *trying* to get hit.

"Foolish Republic lovers," Binnot said. He wished he had a drink in hand to enjoy this.

"Uh, sir. It's coming this way."

Binnot's casual demeanor began to melt away as Sevi's words sank in. That Republic shuttle, still taking on cannonfire from its pursuers, wasn't trying to get hit. It was trying to crash.

Into Binnot.

"Run, sir!" Sevi yelled. He and the guards around him began lifting the door to the underground corridor, ushering Binnot inside. But Binnot wanted to see who was piloting the ship. He had to know.

"Your binocs!" he yelled at a guard. "Give them to me!"

"There's no time, sir! You have to take cover!"

Binnot snarled at him, grabbing the binocs out of his hands. He stood there as the rest of their party began scrambling under the hidden door. The binocs were blurring and sharpening, in and out of focus, as the ship rapidly accelerated toward him. He got one good view of the cockpit before he threw away the binocs and dived into the underground passageway, cursing the sky.

It was Kyong Greylark.

Enya ran as fast as she could, her feet splashing the ground with every footfall. She headed west toward the very landing pads where she had first arrived at the compound. There, in the storm, three shuttles quietly awaited their passengers of Path Elders trying to escape the chaos they had created.

Whenever she came within range of an enforcer droid, she fought with it until it was destroyed, catching her breath before swiftly moving forward. More bodies littered the drenched ground, several with mortal wounds from the enforcer droids. But something made her pause. Some of the dead bodies that had been felled by the droids were wearing Path clothing and traces of the blue markings on their lifeless faces. The droids were killing their own, too.

Enya ran even faster.

By the time she reached the landing pads, one of the three shuttles had already taken off. She walked along the base of the largest pad, several meters below where the Elders were arguing with one another. She ran closer to a shuttle, jumped up on the landing pad, and hid behind a wing of a shuttle, watching and listening. One of them, a tall gangly Elder with four eyes, spoke to a Sakiyan.

"Elder Onning. You're on this one."

"Yes, Barbatash," Elder Onning said before shuffling quickly toward his transport.

Enya ignited Orin's lightsaber and ran forward, making an enormous leap and landing between Elder Onning and his shuttle. The other ship with Elder Barbatash lifted off quickly, escaping. A guard immediately yelled, running off the remaining shuttle. He shot at her with a blaster. It ricocheted off Enya's blade and hit him square in the chest. He crumpled onto the gangway of the ship.

"Stop this," Enya said, speaking to Elder Onning. "Call off the enforcer droids."

Elder Onning's eyes bulged. "No."

"Please." Enya extinguished Orin's lightsaber, holstering it at her waist. She raised her hands. "For your own people. Those droids are killing your followers. Do you know that?"

"If we call them off, then we lose." He shrugged. "Now, if you don't mind, I have a shuttle to catch."

Enya stood before him. The other two Elders scurried around him, stepping gingerly over the fallen guard and into the ship. Disgust filled Enya.

"You don't care, do you? About your people?" Enya gestured to the fields of battle to her left.

"They're not my people anymore," Elder Onning said. "I represent the Path of the Open Hand. What you see around you?" He motioned to the vast battlefield to their right, the sounds of destruction coming ever closer. "That is something else entirely. Glory on your own terms. Fight for your own survival."

Enya shook her head. "What? What does that even mean?"

"It means, I have no authority here anymore."

"Where is the Mother?" Enya said, so close that she could see the beads of perspiration on Elder Onning's grayish skin.

"I have no idea. Now if you'll excuse me." He tried to walk past Enya, who extended a leg. Elder Onning tripped and fell to his knees. She grabbed the Elder by his robes, yanking him back to his feet. Enya stared straight into his eyes.

"Call them off!" she yelled.

"I cannot. They won't listen to me anymore." Behind him, the fighting was drawing nearer. Enya could see laserfire coming closer. "I see you have another lightsaber. Let me go freely, and you may have the kyber crystal that you so graciously bestowed upon me back in your hands."

Enya shook her head. "No. What I want is for you to comm your next-in-command and shut down the droids."

"It's like talking to a child!" Elder Onning said, laughing. "Very well. If you don't want the crystal, then I shall take matters into my own hands."

He reached into his robes, and Enya sensed the danger. She pushed him away as he pulled out a blaster. Enya's hand went for Orin's lightsaber, and found it wasn't there.

Elder Onning had filched it from her belt. He held it in one hand before him, and the blaster in the other.

"Goodbye, Jedi filth," he said simply.

A loud blast sounded. Enya sprang backward as quickly as she could. She landed on her feet and saw Elder Onning still standing several meters away, his large eyes fixed, and his mouth open in surprise.

A sizzling hole had pierced the middle of his body. Behind him, an enforcer droid was shooting up toward the shuttle that was preparing to take off. Enya ran forward to the lifeless body of Elder Onning. He dropped to his knees, and the lightsaber and blaster fell from his fingers, before he dropped down on the tarmac.

Enya reached for Orin's lightsaber and found it to be burning hot with a large scorch mark on the upper end. The laser bolt that had killed Elder Onning had glanced off the lightsaber in his hand after going right through his body. If it hadn't, it probably would have hit Enya, too.

She wrapped the edge of her tunic around the lightsaber and picked it up. Lying next to Elder Onning was a shiny yellow thing, something that had fallen out of his pocket.

Her kyber crystal. She squeezed her fist around it for a brief moment before placing it in a hidden pocket of her Jedi robes. She could fight with it, or without it, she knew now. Orin's lightsaber was still hot to the touch but cooling rapidly. Behind her, the last shuttle with the two remaining Elders rose into the sky. As it took off, it received hits from several enforcer droids on the ground. She did not watch to see if it got away successfully.

She squeezed the lightsaber and held it to her chest. She could feel the metal's warmth through her robes. "Thanks, Master Darhga," she said. "I need your lightsaber to keep fighting. Until the end of the battle, come what may."

Enya looked ahead. She rushed at the enforcer droid at the edge of the landing pad that was shooting off to an angle. Before it could even fire at her, she turned on Orin's lightsaber and decapitated the droid in one smooth movement.

It was time to find Master Roy. She would not stop fighting, no matter what.

Kyong Greylark gripped the control yoke, her arms shaking as she tried to keep the shuttle on course.

"Brace for impact!" she yelled to Gella and Axel, who had left their gunning positions to join Kyong in the cockpit.

Missile fire hit the back of the ship, making it pitch hard to the left.

"Gella, you sure this is where Binnot is?" Axel asked.

Gella was strapping herself into one of the copilot's chairs, as was Axel.

"Right there." She pointed to a dot on the grid screen before them. "I saw a group of Path members just hide under some fallen rubble. It's him."

"Well that's where we need to land. I mean, crash," Axel said.

"Our fuel cells have been hit. We've got about twenty seconds left. Remember what I told you."

"Nose up, thrusters down, landing gear down. Everyone strapped in. I think it's weird that you're teaching me to crash a ship," Axel said.

"See one, do one, teach one," said Kyong. "The next time, it'll be you piloting. Gella, you okay?"

"I'm ready," she said.

The ground came up to meet them. They passed over groups of people fighting, with enforcer droids dotting the fields shooting red laser blasts everywhere. The ship caught a few treetops as they scraped against its belly.

"Hold on!" Kyong said.

Kyong kept her eyes open. She never braced herself, never shut her eyes. Perhaps it was the ex-chancellor in her, but in every bad encounter she'd ever had, Kyong had never hid from any of the damage. She watched it unfold so she would learn exactly how not to repeat her mistakes.

The ship hit the dirt, a terrific cacophony of thuds, screeching metal, and one single loud bang that sounded like a building had fallen over. Kyong's head and torso jerked forward as they rapidly decelerated, the crossed harnesses on her torso digging into her shoulders.

And then there was silence.

"Everyone okay?" she asked.

"Yeah," Gella said, gasping.

Axel nodded, eyes wide. They ran to the aft of the ship to the small cabin that held weapons. Kyong took two knives for herself, plus a blaster with a thigh holster and a laser rifle.

"Take this. They're light and the aim is true," Kyong said, handing Axel two blaster pistols. "Short range only, but that's all you'll need to fell Binnot and capture him."

Axel nodded.

She shoved the knives into sheaths at her waist. "Don't shoot indiscriminately. Be purposeful in your aim."

"This is not the kind of life experience I thought you'd leave me with," Axel said, examining one of the blasters. "I always thought we'd be talking about things like how not to insult a Hutt, or which course to eat with a two-tined fork."

"Well, it's never too late to get a lesson in how not to die." Kyong tightened her ponytail and looked at Gella. "Once I get my bearings, I'll try to contact Master Sun and let them know we're here. Ready?"

Gella herself had taken two medium blasters. "Axel. Stay behind me and your mother. You're injured, so you won't be able to handle the hand-to-hand combat."

Axel inhaled, as if about to complain, but looked at the two women before him with their grim faces.

"I'll cover your backs," he said, nodding.

"It's been a long time since I trained for this at the Academy, but I remember a few things," Kyong said as she touched the hatch to open the ramp. The ship was partially embedded into the deep mud at an angle, and the ramp only opened wide enough for a single person to shimmy through at a time. "The only reason to shoot with a goal of maiming is to get information that will turn the tide of this battle. I'm talking groin shots and limbs, so they can keep talking."

"All those in nicer Path robes are going to be higher-ups," Gella said. "Though I doubt we'll see any on the ground right now."

Kyong checked the sharpness of one of her blades. "For everyone else? We are looking for a quick and merciful death."

As Axel gripped both his blasters, he thought, Chancellor Greylark had always seemed a formidable person to have as an enemy.

But Kyong Greylark was pretty terrifying.

Thank the stars they were finally on the same side.

Chapter Twenty-Eight

THE PATH COMPOUND, DALNA

Creighton Sun had lost sight of Aida Forte. She was fighting somewhere deep within the south fields, with Master Yaddle and her youngling, trying to destroy as many enforcer droids as she could. Creighton was doing the same, but for every droid he took out, there were bodies lying on the ground nearby that he hadn't been able to save. And all the while, the sky vomited rain unrelentingly, blurring his vision and keeping his feet mired in gluey, sticky mud.

He was breathing heavily, his limbs exhausted. Who would have thought that when they decided to sneak onto Dalna to get information, it would come to this? He had known in his heart that the Path was to blame for everything that happened on Jedha, and that they were up to something larger.

Creighton cursed himself for not realizing he had walked into a trap that set off the conflagration.

A laser shot whizzed by his head, and he snapped his head in the direction of the next enforcer droid moving in his direction. He dodged another shot and sprang toward the droid, knocking its body down as the arms kept shooting into the air. One of the shots hit a person, and he heard a mangled cry of pain.

Another one he couldn't save.

How, after all his years as a Jedi Master, could he be failing so terribly?

Creighton smashed his elbow into the face of the droid, which buzzed and sparked from the insult. Damaged, the droid backed away as Creighton sliced its torso in half.

Something at a distance caught his attention, making a noise that was so different from the sounds of battle that he stopped to look for its source. The sound was feral and unidentifiable. Creighton looked left and saw the distant blur of an enormous animal—or was it a misshapen human running on all fours? He couldn't tell. It was dark, and whatever it was had scant fur, with spikes along the spine. A faint glow in the chest.

He shook his head. When he looked again, he saw nothing, but felt a deep, harrowing fear within him. A version of what he'd felt inside the caves.

The weapon the Path guards had spoken about. The nameless thing that Silandra had spoken of that had affected Force-sensitives on Jedha. Whatever those creatures were, they were out there. Enormous, and feeding.

Crouching over the inert droid, he looked up. He longed to be fighting shoulder-to-shoulder with Master Yaddle and Aida. Where were Char-Ryl-Roy and Enya? How were the Jedi and the guards in the caves faring? He was alone on the battlefield. Perhaps they were all dead. He didn't have enough awareness or quiet within his self to reach out and sense where they were, what they needed.

"I'm here, Master Sun," a voice said from nearby. He looked over his shoulder.

Master Yaddle, her clothing stained with dark shades of blood, was walking toward him. Her face was calm but serious.

"Master Yaddle! Are you okay? Where are the others?"

"Fighting. All of us."

"There's something out there killing off the Jedi who have come to fight. Have you seen the corpses? All ash."

"I haven't. It's been a mess, with the rain and mud," Yaddle said. "We have to trust our senses and protect ourselves."

Creighton shook his head. "I haven't been able to sense even Master Roy or Aida."

"If you listen, you can hear them. You are filled with doubt, Master Sun. The turmoil outside has become your very self. You must separate them. Remember to trust in the Force."

"There's no time, Master Yaddle. We are losing badly."

"There is no losing, until there is nothing worth saving. And there is much to save, Master Sun. Even when we feel most alone, there is always something to save."

His comlink crackled. "Master Sun. This is Master Vaqqi. We just got word that the communications buoy is no longer under Path control. We are sending out distress signals. More help is coming."

Creighton clenched his fists. Even with the buoy up and running properly, the battle would be over and countless Jedi would be turned to ash before reinforcements arrived.

Cippa ran toward them, dodging a blaster bolt. She crouched at Yaddle's side.

"I was helping Aida, but she had to go help someone else. She told me to hide, but Lu and Priv are still fighting over by the *Lazuli*. I want to go help them."

Yaddle turned to her. "No, Cippa. They can take care of themselves. You must stay by my side, like you promised."

"But—"

"Stay close, youngling," Creighton said. "She knows more than all of us. Listen to her."

Cippa turned away, staring at the fighting beyond them. Creighton remembered when he was a youngling, wanting to do more than he was allowed. Thinking he knew more than his master. He wished, for a moment, that he could go back in time and ensconce himself in studies and training sequences, when all the galaxy's problems were not his, where his only duty was to learn. It seemed so simple then.

Cippa's face, though turned partially away, was clearly filled with discontent. She had no idea what she wanted to experience. Even this battle was a game to her. The difference between Creighton and this youngling was in some ways vast, but in other ways not. They wanted to be the best Jedi they could. They wanted the Force to work through them in ways that seemed fantastical, almost magical, to others.

They wanted to make a difference.

Creighton pushed away from the nonfunctioning droid beneath him, and Yaddle gave him room.

He turned on his comlink. "Master Roy. Enya, and Aida. The buoy is communicating messages again. We have reinforcements on the way. I repeat, help is on the way. Hold your ground, and keep fighting. Use every trick you know to succeed. The Force is with you. *I am with you.* And we will not give up."

Yaddle looked at Creighton and nodded before reaching for Cippa's hand. "Let's go find Priv and Lu," Yaddle said, and Cippa nodded. They ran impossibly fast, bounding away from clusters of the Path, occasionally pausing to throw an enforcer droid so high into the air that it crashed into pieces when it hit the ground.

Creighton picked up his lightsaber, looked about, and saw a group of Dalnans nearby being besieged by two enforcer droids and several Path members.

"I am with you," Creighton murmured before running back into the fray, his glowing blue lightsaber held aloft like a torch in the night.

Cippa and Master Yaddle ran in a zigzag fashion, killing what droids they encountered, trying to assist the Jedi and Dalnans that had come to the Path compound to battle. Cippa saw a large, silvery creature running into the darkness, and for a moment she froze, unable to breathe. Her infrared vision, evolved for survival on frigid Arkania, saw a spiked beast on all fours, pouncing upon a Jedi. Pinning down the Jedi, the beast shuddered as the Jedi beneath it struggled then quickly stopped moving. The bright warmth emanating from the Jedi body began to dim, far too quickly to make any sense. And then the Jedi disappeared from her infrared vision, like a candle snuffed out.

Cippa fell to her knees, shutting her eyes. At first, she replayed the horror of seeing the light of the Jedi wink out, but what filled her heart next was a different vision—her parents screaming in torment. Arkania, her home, on fire. Master Yaddle's hands slipping away from her as Cippa fell endlessly into a chasm that swallowed her whole, tightly strangling her.

It was fear, the worst she'd ever known.

"Master Yaddle!" Cippa cried out.

Nothing answered her but the yawning dread inside her as she continued to squinch her eyes shut. After an eternity, a clawed hand, warm and familiar, gently touched her shoulder. It was real. It was warm.

"I'm here, Cippa. Do not be afraid. Open your eyes and see the truth."

Cippa reached for Master Yaddle, and she clung to the tiny Jedi Master, shaking. "Something's here. It killed a Jedi."

Master Yaddle stroked Cippa's head. "Yes. Terrible dangers. We must be careful."

Cippa nodded, trying to orient herself to what was real. She saw their downed ship, the *Lazuli,* now pockmarked from incessant blaster-fire, and pointed it out to Master Yaddle.

"Lu and Priv. They were there."

"Let's go."

In seconds, they were near the ruins of the ship. A group of Path members were shooting toward it, focusing their firepower on a group of Dalnans, where Priv was also fighting. Cippa saw Priv's telltale wide face and downcurving horns as she concentrated on her blaster rifle. She was shooting from behind a downed speeder, with the *Lazuli* wreckage behind her. Cippa and Yaddle were by their sides.

"What are you doing here?" the Iktotchi said, her face sweaty in the darkness. Her arm was bleeding, though someone had managed to wrap a bandage around her enormous biceps. She was shooting with her good arm.

"What happened to you?" Cippa said.

"I got shot, that's what happened!" Priv said, exasperated. She pushed Cippa's head down. "Stay down. Your white hair practically glows in the dark. It's asking to get shot."

"I'm fine now," Cippa said, pushing her large, tan hand away but staying low nevertheless. "Where is Lu?"

Priv said nothing, shooting several blasts into the darkness. A droid started firing laser shots at the speeder, and Priv ducked for cover.

"Master Yaddle," Priv said. "The enforcer droid. None of our blasters can get through its armor."

"I'm on it," Yaddle said, slipping past the speeder wreckage and into the darkness.

"Priv. I said, where's Lu?" Cippa asked again, this time tugging on her sleeve for emphasis.

Priv wiped the sweat off her face and eyes. Cippa noticed her eyes were reddened. Maybe from the smoke.

She looked down at her blaster, checking how many more shots she had left. But Cippa's little white hand was on hers now, and she couldn't continue. She looked at the young Arkanian and shook her head.

"He's gone," Priv said.

"Gone where?"

Priv shut her eyes, shook her horned head, and then went back to checking her blaster. "Lu Sweet is dead. One of the enforcer droids got him."

Cippa let her hand drop. She stared at Priv's arm, and the red blood that had seeped through the bandage, the way she was keeping it close to her torso, because it probably hurt to move. Priv was injured, and Lu was gone.

No. Not gone. Dead.

"You should have waited for me," Cippa said in a small voice. "I could have helped."

"You're a kid," Priv said. "Kids shouldn't be in wars."

"I wanted to be here. To help."

"You can help by not getting in the way. And by staying safe."

"No."

Priv slipped down lower and yanked Cippa's tunic so she had no choice but to slip lower to the mucky ground, too. Priv's face was so close to hers. She hadn't realized before that Priv had golden-brown eyes. She was younger than Cippa had originally thought. It had been hard to tell. Iktotchi were a bit scary looking, and she'd only ever seen a few. Priv looked old enough to be fighting. But too young to die.

"Listen, kid. You're talented. The way you threw me and Lu up in the air like we were pebbles! You're going to be a great Jedi someday, just like Master Yaddle. But you've got a lot to learn and if you die now, you're no good to all those thousands of people you're going to help someday."

"But I could have helped!" Cippa said. Her eyes were blurring. She didn't know what was wrong with her eyes. Her throat constricted. "Master Yaddle! Where did she go? She said I should stay by her side."

Cippa scrambled to stand up, looking for Yaddle's small, green face and auburn hair in the rainy darkness beyond their shelter. Priv tried to pull Cippa down, but she wriggled free of her thick, clawed hands and ran out into the dark.

Cippa looked left and right, wiping the rain off her face. A droid twisted its waist and saw her, lifting its arm to fire. Cippa raised her hands, using the Force to pull the droid into the air. The laser shots zinged above her head into the night sky. She hefted it high enough, then released it. Its torso broke from the legs upon impact.

"Master Yaddle!" she screamed. Her eyes were blurry and wet, her nose running. A flash of the terrible fear she felt before—the echoes of her parents' screams, Master Yaddle's hand slipping away—paralyzed her for a moment. She could see Lu in her mind, his broad shoulders and serious face, and the funny way Lu would grimace when Cippa teased him. Lu was dead. Lying somewhere on this battlefield. She imagined a hole burned right through his forehead, above lifeless, hazel eyes. Hands open and beseeching the night sky.

"Halt," a voice said behind her.

She spun around. Two enforcer droids, next to a Path member holding a blaster rifle trained on Cippa's body. Cippa pushed her hands out, and one of the droids went flying backward.

"She's a Force-user!" the Path member yelled. He and the droid fired at her. She tried to jump away, avoiding several of the shots. But one of the blasts hit her in the foot.

The injury was like nothing she'd ever felt. Burning and searing, so vast in its pain that her vision went dark for a moment. She fell over, unable to stand, unable to understand what was happening.

"Cippa!" a voice called out. She looked up and saw Priv running toward her with her blaster, shooting at the Path member, who was shooting back. One of the blaster bolts hit Priv in her bandaged arm, and she fell to her knees, mouth open, unable even to cry out.

"No! Priv!" Cippa screamed. "Priv!"

The remaining droid had turned toward Cippa, ready to fire. Cippa raised both her hands in defense, but nothing happened. She was crying so hard she could see nothing but blurred darkness and blossoms of infrared light from bursting explosions around her.

Her vision was dimming at the edges, and vaguely she realized she was fainting. How awful and weak of her. But maybe this was her body's way of being kind, of sheltering her from the coming pain.

Lu was gone. Priv, too, any second now. She let the darkness take her, along with all her regrets.

"Not yet, you're not passing out. Come on, Cippa."

Cippa blinked, trying to shake away the fog threatening to take over her mind. She looked up to see Master Yaddle standing over her, arms akimbo. With one gesture, two droids aiming for them were snapped in half. With another gesture, the Path member with the rifle was pushed so far out into the darkness that there was a full three seconds before Cippa could hear him thud hard against something metallic.

Yaddle leaned over and grabbed Cippa by the torso, picking her up.

In two bounds, they were back behind the protection of the downed speeder. Priv was already there. Her eyes were closed.

"Priv? Priv!" she shouted, prodding her good arm. Cippa's foot throbbed something terrible; she ignored it.

"Ow. I'm alive. Don't poke me." The Iktotchi opened one exhausted eye. "Don't do that again, kid."

"Okay," she said, nodding. "I promise."

"Tell you what. From here on out, we don't move unless Master Yaddle says so. Got it?"

Cippa nodded. Around them, the fighting continued on with its orchestra of blaster shots, screams, and yells. Cippa saw the blood smears against the hull of the *Lazuli,* the bodies of a human and a Weequay woman lying nearby, their eyes open and unseeing. A blast hit the speeder protecting them, rocking them both. They would only be able to hold the Path off for so much longer, even with Master Yaddle doing her best.

Cippa curled under Priv's arm and kept her eyes shut. But she could not stop seeing the blood and bodies around her, and the image of Lu's lifeless form on the battlefield. The rain fell incessantly, like the sky itself was sobbing. Her chest hurt terribly, as if she'd been shot, but she knew she had no injury there. Someday she would understand. If only she was lucky enough to see another day.

Chapter Twenty-Nine

THE PATH COMPOUND, DALNA

"Aida!"

Creighton hollered with relief. He saw the Kadas'sa'Nikto's eyes light up when she saw him. He had fought his way back toward the entrance of the caves, letting the Force guide him here where he was needed. And there she was.

"Creighton!" Aida's chin was streaked with blood. "I'm glad you're okay! There are Dalnan fighters here who can barely hold off the fire-power from these droids. We have to help."

"Got it."

Creighton and Aida covered each other's backs, trying to evade la-serfire and destroying every enforcer droid they encountered. But at some point in what was feeling like an endless battle, Creighton paused, resting his hands on his knees. He had to catch his breath. Aida had just rushed toward a group of Path members who approached her. She deflected their blaster bolts, but Creighton saw that she had her eye on a group of droids nearby. He began to run toward her to help when an elderly Path member suddenly stumbled before him, white hair bedraggled with rain, face bruised and looking dazed.

"My granddaughter!" She reached out with knobby fingers. "Where is she? I left her in my hut an hour ago . . ."

How the old woman was still alive was beyond him. An enforcer droid in the distance raised its arm, pointing directly at the old woman's back. At that same moment, a Path member driving a speeder was bearing down upon them. Creighton's mind was scattered, his body beyond exhaustion. It was too many things at once. Dodge the speeder. Save the old woman. Kill the droids. Help the Dalnans. Cover Aida's back.

Everything had converged into a cataclysm of violence.

He pushed the old woman into the mud, below the level of blaster-fire. The speeder clipped Creighton's body, snapping his femur with a noise that utterly surprised him. As he fell, the blaster shots tore through his left lung, and then his right abdomen.

He landed on the ground, feeling pain that was indescribable. He was broken. Dazed, and eyes unfocused, he vaguely saw Aida now pulling the wires from droid after droid at a short distance away, mindless but for one task. Kill the droids. Save the people.

Save the people.

Bring light back to the darkness.

Fight, until you cannot fight anymore.

He reached out, pushing two approaching Path members away that were trying to shoot Aida. And Aida pushed more away, too, even as the droids descended upon her from behind. When she fell, she was close by Creighton, her eyes wide open. Those beautiful Kadas'sa'Nikto eyes, always so full of bright optimism, now full of tears and raindrops.

"Aida," he rasped, feeling his own life energy flowing quickly away from him.

Aida looked at him and smiled, actually smiled, though blood began to trickle from her mouth and nose.

"I am with you, Creighton," she said quietly. "My friend." Her smile brightened for one quick moment—a supernova in the darkness—before it faded and her eyes closed.

Chapter Thirty

THE PATH COMPOUND, DALNA

Axel Greylark exited the downed Republic shuttle behind his mother and Gella. The crash of the ship had left a deep gouge in the mud. They each held blasters at the ready, gingerly stepping outside onto the battlefield and into the pouring rain.

The crash had scattered the fighters, and no one seemed to be a threat at the moment. None of the enforcer droids were nearby. The only sound was the rain drumming the ground and the shuttle.

"It's too quiet," Kyong said. "Keep your eyes open."

"Gella?" Axel said.

Gella had collapsed, her arms shielding her face. From what? She began to make a strange sound, the kind you make when you're in so much pain you can barely breathe.

"Are you hurt?" Axel dropped to her side, but Gella wasn't wounded. Her eyes were closed, and she was crying—this brave Jedi who seemed to fear nothing—shaking and cowering.

A single word came from her mouth in the form of a whimper.

"No!"

"What happened to Gella?" Kyong said, her face filled with alarm.

"I don't know—" Axel began when he saw it. There, in the darkness, was that animal that the Mother had at her side, but it had grown enormously, like it had developed years in the span of hours. Then he saw another, and another. But for some reason, they seemed to be running in the area of the caves. What was going on? What were they?

Axel pointed. "They seem to be running away. To the caves." He put his arm around Gella. "Hey. Gella. It's me. Your favorite lawbreaker, Axel."

Gella had managed to put her arms down and blink, reorienting herself. She pointed into the darkness.

"Oh no. I think that's Master Sun!"

In the distance, there was a solitary glowing blue lightsaber. It was deflecting blaster bolts, with a cadence that reminded her so much of Creighton's fighting style. But he seemed to only be defending himself. The lightsaber abruptly dropped closer to the ground; Master Sun was on his knees, about to fall.

"Master Sun!" Gella gasped. She tried to get up and fell over, still weakened by the effects of those creatures.

"Gella, no. Wait," Axel said, holding her back.

The blue lightsaber deflected more blaster bolts before it paused, hovering in the darkness. Abruptly, it spun in the air and fell onto the ground. The low roar of a speeder rose and fell.

"Creighton!" Gella yelled. She pulled free from Axel's grasp and ran far into the field, dodging blaster bolts, with Axel right at her heels.

Master Sun was motionless on the ground. He lay in the mud, darkened from his own blood. A gash ran across his face where a knife had cut him, and a blaster shot had hit his chest and abdomen. Nearby, Aida Forte lay on her side, eyes closed.

"No! Aida!" Gella said, kneeling between the two fallen Jedi. Axel was shooting at attackers behind them. "Creighton. Is she . . . did she . . ."

"She's not dead. But she's lost so much blood, Gella." Creighton closed his eyes, and Gella reached for him, clutching his face.

"No, Creighton. Don't give up. Never give up."

Kyong had run up behind them, also shooting at unseen adversaries in the distance that were assaulting them with blasterfire.

"We have no cover here!" Kyong said, getting down on one knee. "Axel, get low. We're easy targets."

"We have to take them back toward the ship," Axel said. "It's the only thing nearby that will give us any cover."

Gella reached for Creighton's comlink, taking it off his wrist. "This is Gella Nattai. Creighton Sun and Aida Forte are down. We are above the cave system, east of the main Path buildings, near a downed Republic shuttle. We need help!"

"This is Char-Ryl-Roy." His voice sounded tired. So tired. "We're surrounded. I've lost sight of my Padawan, Enya. Our casualties are enormous." There was a pause. "I don't think we'll be able to help you. We—"

Axel knew what Master Roy wasn't saying. They couldn't even help themselves.

"Master Roy. We'll try to come and help as soon as we can," Gella said, but here she was, holding on to a dying Jedi Master. Her hands were literally full. Gella's words were useless, and she and Axel knew it.

"Something's coming," Char-Ryl-Roy said, his voice raspy and out of breath.

"What? Master Roy—"

"It's coming," he repeated. "Tell Enya—"

There was a piercing scream before the comlink cut off.

Gella's eyes widened. "No!"

She was still several meters away from their fallen shuttle, cradling the unconscious Creighton in her arms and holding his comlink. She shut her eyes hard, as if something painful had burst within her, and she was trying hard not to pass out. Axel crouched down closer to her, holding her shoulders.

"No!" she repeated, this time barely a whisper. She looked up at Axel with stricken eyes. "He's gone. I felt it. Master Roy is gone, Axel."

Cannon fire blazed over their head, and they ducked.

"No one is coming to help us. What about going after Binnot?" Axel said.

Gella looked back at him. Master Sun was seriously injured, as was Aida. She had no idea where Enya was. Kyong was shooting into the night. They were being fired upon from all directions, with no help in sight. A blaster bolt singed Kyong's arm, and she dropped a pistol.

"Dammit!" Kyong seethed.

"Mom, are you okay?"

"It's just a glancing blow. Keep shooting, Axel." Her face was grim. She gazed at Creighton and Aida, and then up at the sky. She had a look of fierce steadfastness. Axel's mother would fight to her death, she knew. She would fight for him, after all he'd done.

Axel turned around and began shooting into the distance, seeing enforcer droids and Path members enter their field of vision from the inky darkness beyond. But soon, it wasn't just a handful of droids and Path members. It was two full lines of them. Three. Gella spun around. More were entering their battle zone.

"Gella," Axel said, helplessly.

"Believe in the Force," Gella said as she gently lowered Creighton to the ground. She picked up Aida and Creighton's lightsabers, igniting them in glowing blue and green. She turned to Axel and Kyong, her face lit with purpose and ferocity. "Fight, until you cannot fight anymore. For life. For light. For all of us," she said.

Axel reached for her shoulder, but Gella ran forward, the two lightsabers twirling and striking so fast, they were merely blurs of color. She stayed several meters in front of them, a formidable shield. But they were completely unprotected behind. Even Gella could only do so much.

"Axel!" his mother cried.

He turned. Kyong was lying on the ground, a wound in her stomach. She looked less terrified and more angry, like her wound was a massive irritation in her life. He ran to her side, his hand on her belly, feeling blood beneath his palm.

"Look," she said weakly.

"I'm looking," Axel said. He pulled off his jacket, balling it up and trying to stanch the bleeding.

"No, not at my wound. At that," she said, pointing to the sky.

Axel looked up. In the southern sky, no less than thirty ships, some of them enormous cruisers, descended from the dense cloud cover above.

Gella was also looking up, as were the Path members that had surrounded them. A faint voice crackled from the comlink that Gella had taken from Master Sun.

"This is Captain Xiri A'lbaran, leading Thylefire Squadron from E'ronoh."

"And Phan-tu Zenn, leading ground forces from Eiram."

Master Yoda's voice spoke. "Fight together, we will."

A familiar sleek E'roni starship roared overhead, spinning as it shot down a junker over a fallow field. Axel knew it must be Xiri. The other ships began to land throughout the Path compound, with E'roni troops in copper-hued uniforms and Eirami troops in blue uniforms taking to the fields in droves. Phan-tu, wearing Eirami military gear, was directing troops to the different areas of the compound. Starships lit up the sky, engaging the Path-aligned ships and brightening the sky with their cannon fire. Path members began fleeing from the onslaught.

Gella exhaled with her eyes shut. "It's about time they finally realized that the Jedi are on their side."

Axel began to gently pick up his mother, cradling her in his arms. He winced in pain, probably from that chest wound. "I'm getting you help."

"I always thought Chancellor Mollo would do the literal dirty work, and now look at me," she said, her head leaning against Axel's chest.

"You're a wonder. A wonder that needs a vacation," Axel said, winking.

As he stood, a large group of E'roni troops surrounded them, backs to the wounded, and began to return fire. They rebutted laserfire from the enforcer droids and the Path on the ground, who were now scattering in the face of the overwhelming forces coming in. Eirami and E'roni soldiers were spreading out in clusters, flooding the battlefield in the hundreds. The enforcer droids were no match for the cannon fire coming from the E'roni Thylefire Squadron now whizzing over the battlefield.

Gella spoke into her comlink. "We have a lot of wounded on the ground, including Kyong Greylark."

"Gella! It's Phan-tu. Medics are already on the way," he reported back.

"It's so good to hear your voice, Gella!" Xiri said. "Our view shows that the Path members are scattering. We are sending ships to the edges of the compound and will spread out to keep an eye on the skies. Whoever has wings will flee."

Several Eirami and E'roni voices agreed, and signed off.

"I will be on the ground in a moment. What is your assessment, Jedi Nattai?" Master Yoda said.

"Head to the cave system," Gella said. "They may still have untold hundreds ready to fight down there. But keep your forces aboveground where it's safer."

"Agreed," Yoda said. "Underground activity, we are sensing."

Xiri spoke again. "Gella, the underground activity could be seismic. Could be explosions. We're getting in more readings as we speak. I'll update you shortly."

Axel headed to meet the medics on their way. Perhaps it was his imagination, but the rain seemed to be lessening finally. A Longbeam ship flew over, landing closer to the southern edge where the cave system was. Gella had run back to Creighton, who was breathing shallowly near Axel.

"Master Sun. We did it. We're going to win. Look."

Creighton cracked open his eyes, grimacing at the bright lights flying around above him.

"They came," he said. "They got our message." His eyes began to roll back into his head as delirium hit him. "I am with you," he said faintly.

"You always were, Master Sun. Now rest." She settled him down next to Aida, who was still breathing, but barely. A group of Eirami personnel wearing red armbands arrived with stretchers. Medics.

"We'll take over here," said an Eirami woman, her face spattered with green freckles. She commed her ship. "We have two wounded Jedi here, human male and Kadas'sa'Nikto female. Heavy blood loss by the looks of it. And another human female with a blaster shot to the abdomen. Oh! It's Chancellor Greylark!"

Kyong lifted her hand, still in her son's arms. "Just Kyong. Thanks," she said, before losing consciousness.

"Still giving orders to the last," Axel said, laying her down on a stretcher. She was quickly whisked away by medical personnel.

Axel looked at Gella. "I did this. I'm the reason she's hurt."

"Go with her," Gella said.

"I can't," Axel said. He turned away, swiveling his head. Path forces were being overrun and overwhelmed. All around them were Eirami troops, E'roni troops, Jedi that Gella had never met before, fresh and ready to fight. "I can't. I have to find Binnot. I can't let him get away."

Gella nodded. "Fine. Then I'm coming with you."

Medics gingerly lifted Kyong's stretcher, hooking on medicine patches and inserting an IV. Axel watched as the Eiram medics carried her away.

I'll see her again, Axel said to himself. *I will. I promise, Mother.*

In the air, Thylefire Squadron quickly maneuvered to chase the remaining junkers and prospector ships that had come to the battle. The ones firing back were being shot down, raining down on the rolling hills of Dalna beyond the Path compound. Some appeared to have surrendered in the face of overwhelming superior firepower and were now being escorted to the ground.

A Pathfinder ship circled nearby, and a voice commed in to Gella. "Kenny of the Kenny Night Clan, covering you, Jedi Natty!"

"Kenny? Piti?" Gella said, mouth open.

"We're here to help! You and Jedi DarkEye!"

Gella looked like she wanted to sob, but held it in. "Jedi Darhga is gone, Kenny. He died fighting."

There was a whimpering sound. Piti's voice commed in. "I'm sorry to hear that. What can we do to help, Gella?"

"Cover us. Please."

"Copy that."

The ship began to circle protectively as Axel and Gella ran back toward the wreckage of Kyong's shuttle. Nearby, the octagonal building Gella and Orin had previously snuck into had been destroyed from a fallen pirate ship. Some of the walls had layered upon each other. "I swore I saw Path members hide under here, right before we crash-landed," Axel said.

"That's where they went." Gella put her blasters away. "Stand back, and cover the opening when I expose it."

Axel trained his blaster on the ground, crouching low, while the Pathfinder ship fired on Path members approaching at a distance. Gella reached out with her hands, lifting and flipping one wall of the building at a time. It must have been strenuous for her, as she was concentrating so hard that perspiration dampened her face. She'd flipped three walls before Axel called out.

"Stop. Look, there's a trapdoor in the rubble."

"It probably connects to the cave system to the south, where I was imprisoned."

"Figures they'd have other exits from there." Axel gingerly lifted the door, keeping a blaster trained on the opening as he cracked it wider. He flipped the trapdoor backward.

It was dark in the passageway, the floor of it steeply sloping with carved rock against the bottom, like rough stairs. Rain pattered gently into the darkness below. Axel listened for voices, but only silence answered him.

"It's been a while since they went down here. What if they're gone?" Gella said.

"One way to find out." Axel jumped down the first set of stairs and began quickly taking the rest of them deeper into a corridor lined with stone and clay that had turned slick from the rainwater. Gella followed. Every few minutes, they paused, listening, but there were no voices. No yells, or hollers.

"Are you sure this connects to the cave system?"

"I don't know. But look at this."

The passageway seemed to head downward and deeper, but in the same direction as where the caves would be. Their feet splashed in water with every step. They'd just passed by a narrow crack in the wall when Axel stopped. He paused with his pistols, looking left and right, sniffing the air.

"Smell that?"

Gella inhaled tentatively. All she could sense was the dirt and rocks lining the walls. "Not really. What is it?"

"The faintest odor of perfume. Spiceflower, actually. And brandy. A hundred-year-old vintage, if I'm not mistaken."

Gella raised her eyebrows. "You can smell that?"

"From a kilometer away. It's the smell of money and power. Which means the Mother has been in here at some point." He looked down the leftward corridor, following his nose. At the crack in the corridor wall, he sniffed deeply. "There's a door back here." He put his hands on either side of the narrow opening, and it gave way. It was a sliding door, cleverly concealed in the mudlike wall. He slipped into it, followed by Gella. After a hairpin turn, there was another door. He pushed it open with the tip of his pistol.

Inside, four bodies lay lifeless on a richly embroidered carpet five centimeters deep in water, stained with blood. The fallen all wore Path robes. The room was long, and a table with several chairs around it took up the end of the space. On the table was a decanter of liquor; several cups, some of which had been knocked over, sat next to a bowl of water filled with floating blossoms. Gella poked one of the flowers, and a heady, rich floral scent rose. Beyond it was another door. This time, it was shut. Gella leaned in. They both heard voices behind the door.

"There are no more ships left! I'm telling you, it's swarming with Jedi and Eirami and E'roni troops up there."

"Aren't there other ships? What about the shuttles?"

"The last one went with the Elders, an hour ago."

There was a rustling sound. "Binnot. We have to surrender. We can't hide. Everyone knows you've been orchestrating parts of this battle yourself. You can't hide. This is it. It's surrender, or die."

There was a long pause, and then: "I see you've made your choice."

There was a muffled sound, and knocking, like someone kicking the rungs of a chair. The knocking sound continued erratically, until it stopped. After a rustling sound, the door opened.

Axel backed up, face-to-face with Binnot Ullo. He heard Gella turn on both the lightsabers behind him.

"Axel!" Binnot blinked several times. His mouth twitched, as if unsure what its brain wanted it to do. Surprised, shocked, and confused expressions flitted across his visage, until he settled on relief. One hand was still on the door, and the other gloved hand on the doorjamb. He wore a heavy coat, as if he was ready to leave. Despite the two pistols trained on his chest, he didn't raise his hands in surrender. "You made it! Are you okay?"

Axel frowned. "I'm impressed. Even now, you're almost a better liar than I am. Am I okay? I had shrapnel coming out of my chest. Clearly you didn't care to do anything about it."

"I had no choice, Axel," Binnot said, shaking his head. "I thought you were dead. I was willing to give you another chance. I was."

"Like that fellow?" Gella said, pointing her lightsaber at the figure just behind Binnot, now facedown on a table.

"He didn't know what he wanted. That's what I always liked about you, Axel," Binnot said. "You have ambition." He stepped closer.

"Don't move another step," Gella said, pushing ahead of Axel and letting Creighton's blue lightsaber come close to Binnot's face.

"You got new lightsabers! Good for you, Jedi," Binnot said, his voice dripping with condescension.

"Not for long. I'd like my own back," Gella said.

"Perhaps. Perhaps not." Binnot slowly moved around the table, not letting Gella get close to him.

Gella squeezed her lightsabers so hard Axel could hear her hands squeaking on the metal.

"And here you are, Binnot," Gella said. "Left behind by the two people you thought you trusted. You're fodder, don't you see? They never cared about you. Especially the Mother."

"Throwing you away, the same way you threw me away," Axel said.

"You'd do that to me, brother?" Binnot said. "When you were younger, I was all you had. I was the only person who cared about you. Your mother? After her own glory." He extended his bare hand. "Let's start fresh. New beginnings. We know each other. Friends fight and they make up. You'll never be alone again, with your brother at your side."

Axel hesitated. His pistols were shaking ever so slightly.

"Axel. He's going to say whatever it takes to slither his way out of here," Gella reminded him.

"Remember that day we swam in the ocean at Canto Bight? Stole those pies and ate them under the sun?" Binnot said, his voice softening. "We can do that again. Be the princes of this galaxy. You and I both still have friends who can help us. We'll be stronger than ever. Forget the chancellor. The Mother. The Herald. Just you and me, Axel."

Axel let his pistols fall at his side.

"You and me," Axel said.

"Axel, no!" Gella whispered.

"You and me," Binnot said. He smiled, a brilliant, handsome smile on his Mirialan face. "All the family we'll ever need."

"You and me," Axel said again. "And Quin."

Binnot's eyebrows contracted. "What?"

"That little insignificant droid that you destroyed."

Binnot blinked, his mouth open slightly. He took a slight step backward, before he quickly reached beneath his long coat and pulled out both of Gella's lightsabers, igniting them. The bright purple light made Axel stagger back. Binnot swung the lightsabers forward, but Axel wasn't fast enough. One of them burned hard against his shoulder, and he cried out, falling to his knee with a splash. He lifted a pistol, but Binnot crashed one of the lightsabers down and the blaster fell to the floor, split in half. Axel ignored his pain and picked up a nearby chair, throwing it at Binnot, who batted it away with a lightsaber. It was just enough to allow Axel to scramble backward to put the table between him and Binnot.

"You simpleton," Binnot yelled. "Never mind. We could have escaped this place, but looks like you'll die here along with your mother and that silly droid of yours."

"Nice soliloquy," Gella said, moving forward. She twisted her wrists, making her lightsabers circle the air before her. "You want to fight, Binnot? Then let's fight."

Binnot smiled, and brought the purple lightsabers crashing down and forward. She parried him easily, pushing him to the side. When he tried to hit her again, she twirled her blades against Binnot, whose wrist couldn't handle the torque. One of the purple blades went flying into the air, landing behind Axel. Binnot roared, thrusting his remaining lightsaber toward Gella, who brought hers down on his, forcing his arm down as she jumped in the air and kicked him hard in the chest. Binnot went flying back, dropping the other lightsaber and hitting the floor with a splash.

Gella stood back in her fighting stance. Axel stood up, his hand clutching the burn wound on his shoulder.

"It's over, Binnot," Axel said.

Binnot got up slowly, holding his hands up in surrender, when an explosion sounded from far away. It was almost like a groundquake, but then there came another boom, and another.

Axel looked at Gella. "Are we bombing the caves?" he said.

"I don't know!" She listened to another boom as the very ground beneath them shook. Crumbled bits of the ceiling began to fall, plopping into the flooded water on the floor. Dust and pebbles rained down on all three of them. Gella looked up and around her.

Axel saw it before Gella did. Water, rushing into the door with a wave, and splashing against their legs. The next thing he knew, he had been swept off his feet. He landed hard, his head slamming against the wet ground. Axel blinked, dazed and disoriented. He felt pressure against his windpipe and couldn't breathe. At first he thought a deluge of water had carried him off his feet, but he could feel it, only about a few centimeters deep and splashing against his cheeks. He opened his eyes and found Binnot sitting atop him, hand on his wrist, and his leather glove raised high.

"I don't think I'm coming out of this alive," Binnot said, a hollow look in his eyes. He saw Gella start toward him with her lightsabers, and he held up his glove. Axel could see tiny, shining points emerging from the palm. "Poison. He'll be dead the second I touch him. You know there's no antidote. Even you're not that fast, the great Gella Nattai."

She halted. "Let him go, Binnot. You owe it to him."

"Owe him? The galaxy owes me!" he said, clenching his teeth. "The Closed Fist was supposed to be the future. My future." He looked at Axel, whose hands were trying to pull Binnot's fist off his trachea, but Axel could already feel the darkness enclosing his vision as the blood was being cut off from his brain.

Axel saw the glove with its embedded, shining needles descending toward his face. He thought of his mother, injured on the battlefield. All his failures. And Gella, standing there, unable to save him.

No one could save Axel. It was never up to other people. It was always and only ever Axel himself that could spell out his fate. Even now.

He let go of Binnot's wrist, and Binnot smiled. Axel was giving up, weakening, it seemed. But Axel instead closed his eyes, gathered up every shred of strength he had, every disappointment, every fury he'd experienced since he was a child. He felt how deeply he loved his fallen father, and his mother, despite all the disappointments. Despite the despair. He pulled his hand back as far as he could, feeling water dampen his arm.

And then he punched Binnot square in the face with all his might.

Binnot didn't expect to be hit. His head jerked back from the impact. Axel pulled his other fist back, punching Binnot's face again before Binnot had even a chance to respond to the first strike. Binnot fell backward.

Axel scrambled out from under him. Binnot clutched his bloodied nose, holding his gloved hand out in front of him as he tried to keep his balance. Axel sprang back and hefted all his effort into a kick. The sole of his boot thrust forward, shoving Binnot's gloved hand hard into his chest. Binnot lost his balance and fell backward, splashing in the rising water that was now knee-deep.

Gella ran toward him, her lightsabers ready to strike, when Axel held out a hand.

"No. Don't touch him," Axel said.

Binnot was faceup in the shallow, muddy water, unmoving. His eyes were open, eyelashes wet from the water. And his entire palm of poisoned needle points was embedded into his upper chest and neck. A purplish, sickly color had already spread from his neck to his jawline. His mouth was open, a silent scream of shock as the poison worked quickly. Muddy water entered his gaping mouth and he gurgled helplessly. His eyes moved from Gella to Axel, full of surprise as if, even now, he could not fathom his fate.

His light-blue eyes grew dark, dilating widely. The gurgling ceased.

"He's gone," Axel said, closing his eyes. He suddenly felt exhausted, like he'd just aged twenty years in a minute.

"Come on," Gella said. "With all this rain, this place is flooding unbelievably fast. We've got to get out of here."

The water was rising so fast that it quickly went from splashing against his thighs to his waist. Suddenly, a large wave of water came crashing into the room, knocking the floating chairs against one another. Gella and Axel both lost their footing. They grabbed for the table, but it was starting to float, giving them no stability.

"Watch out!" Gella yelled. "Don't touch Binnot's body. He's still poisonous!"

Binnot's corpse had disappeared under the rising tide. With all the floating furniture and the brown, clay-colored water, he couldn't be seen. Axel tried to keep near the wall, pushing himself closer to the door. When Binnot's body bobbed in the water nearby, Axel kicked it away with his boots. One of his legs got tangled in the rungs of a floating chair, and Axel's head briefly went under the surface.

He came up, disentangling from the chair, spitting water into the air.

"Swim, Axel!" Gella yelled, already buoyant and near the exit. She held open the door, which kept trying to shut, by jamming her legs in the frame. Axel managed to swim over and grab the edge of the doorway. He turned around one last time to see Binnot's body floating facedown beyond the table. The bowl full of spiceflowers had been overturned, and the beautiful blooms bobbed gently against his corpse.

"Let's go!" Gella yelled.

"Wait!"

Axel dived beneath the surface and swam back toward Binnot. When he surfaced, Gella was hollering at him, words like *are you crazy* and *are you trying to get yourself killed.* But Axel wasn't listening. He was near Binnot's body now, and he carefully pushed his body aside, avoiding the poisoned glove. He felt for the ground near the wall where Binnot had dropped Gella's lightsabers, grabbing one and then the other. He broke the surface, gasping for air.

"If you die, Greylark, *I am going to kill you.*"

Axel lifted up the two lightsabers in his hand as he swam forward. He handed them to Gella.

"Okay fine, I forgive you," she said, smiling brightly and slipping them into her tunic.

Axel touched his chest, then raised his wet hand out of the water. It was bright red at his fingertips. The wound in his chest stung terribly, and he realized it had opened back up and was bleeding again.

Gella saw the blood on his hand. "That's from you?"

Axel nodded, his other hand pressing against his chest. The water was now about two-thirds of the way high.

"We've got to get out of here. It's okay. Stay close to me."

They began swimming forward, but Axel lagged behind. The wound in his chest made it difficult to use his arms, and one of them still burned painfully from the lightsaber strike. His boots and clothes were waterlogged, making it almost impossible to swim. He could barely catch his breath between splashes of water cresting by. As Gella progressed forward, she had to pause and occasionally tug Axel behind her by the scruff of his jacket, beneath his neck.

Axel nodded weakly, but a new wave of water filled his mouth, and he coughed and sputtered. Something caught his leg and pulled him under. Axel reached down, his hands frantically scrambling to find what had snagged his boot. It was a hand. He would have yelled if he could, but instead he kicked the hand away, trying to surface for air.

When he came up, there was a Path member flailing in the water two meters away. The woman's forehead was a blur of blue paint, and her eyes were panicked.

"This way!" Gella yelled, motioning toward the passageway back to the surface.

"No!" the woman yelled, hatred in her voice. "Never."

But even as she spoke, she could barely keep her head above water. She flailed again, and her face went under. A single hand surfaced, grasping the air, before it went below again for good.

"Dammit!" Gella said. "Axel. Come on. Keep going."

Axel's legs were starting to cramp painfully from the effort of kicking. One arm was hardly useful, and his chest screamed with pain every time he pushed at the water. Darkness encroached at the edges of his vision before retreating. He was going to pass out soon. He was still bleeding.

"Gella," he said, between gasps. "I can't do this for much longer."

"Flip onto your back. Relax."

He did as he was told, and Gella tugged him by his jacket. She was able to swim and yank him past the hairpin turn, then rightward up the corridor that led to the surface. But the water was pushing and gushing upward, faster than Gella was able to swim.

Axel's vision was blurry from water splashing over and over against his face, but he could see the end of the tunnel—about five meters away. They passed the dead body of another Path member, facedown in the roiling water, which continued to rise at an alarming rate. Very soon, there would be no air to breathe.

The tunnel was made of compacted soil and clay, carved out who knew how many decades or centuries ago, but it was not fortified with much stone or cement. Which meant the water was eating away at the soft, clay walls like ocean waves against a sandcastle. The walls began to crumble as Gella cried out.

"Help!" she yelled, gurgling and coughing, her face halfway under the turbid water.

Gella would only ask for help if she knew things were bad. Very bad.

Axel's mouth was full of water. If he spoke, he'd inhale water. Which he did, trying to tell her with his last breath that he was sorry, so sorry for all the trouble he'd caused. And that he loved her very much, the way that friends did when they realized their existence had shifted in a way that changed them forevermore.

But what came out of his mouth was a gurgling, coughing gulp. The darkness once again began tunneling his vision. His legs were cramped into uselessness. His limbs were numb from the cold water, and the pain in his chest would not abate. He was dying for real now, and Gella, with him. Her hand pushed against the roof of the tunnel, her fingers gripping mud as even the ceiling began to soften and collapse.

And collapse it did.

Chapter Thirty-One

THE PATH COMPOUND, DALNA

Enya Keen had just felled the last standing enforcer droid before her and was wiping the sweat from her eyes. She had lost count of how many droids she'd destroyed since the second wave had been unleashed on the compound. The odor of smoke permeated the air, and the Eirami and E'roni soldiers were now everywhere. The Path was scattering.

She had paused, looking for another droid to attack, when she felt it. An unspoken voice calling out to her. A feeling of light and darkness, tangled together. Within it, a purity of intent, so beautiful, being snuffed out like a candle choking under a glass. Without understanding the sensation, she spoke almost involuntarily.

"Master Roy," she whispered.

Her head twisted to the south, nearer to the caves. She ran through the rain, dodging fleeing Path members. Everywhere around her was fighting. Path members were shooting ground missiles at ships in the air. Farther south, there were Path members once again emerging from the caves, fighting Dalnans and Jedi and the fresh reinforcements.

Somewhere around here was Master Roy.

An irregular, short fence of stones had made for some low cover for several Dalnans. Their bodies now lay inert, scattered along the wall. And then she saw it.

A familiar lightsaber, lying on a wet patch of grass, alone.

Enya knelt upon the ground. She carefully picked up Master Char-Ryl-Roy's lightsaber. Perhaps he had just dropped it. She didn't sense him, no matter how far she reached out with the Force.

It was only when she stood up that she saw the ashy remnants of a Cerean man in Jedi clothing lying on his back a few meters away, with palms facing upward as if surrendering to the sky itself, slowly melting in the rain.

Master Yoda and Master Yaddle spoke under a sky whose darkest edges were weakening. The rain had lessened, and stars could actually be seen near the horizon.

"Too late, we are," Master Yoda said.

"The battle is not yet over," Master Yaddle said, under the now gentle rain. She looked over her shoulder to where Cippa was sleeping, her head propped on Priv Ittik's substantial and uninjured biceps. Priv had been given medication to sleep after her wounds were tended. Despite the calm scene, they could still hear the sound of blasterfire.

"Master Yoda. Master Yaddle." Xiri ran to them, now on the ground with Phan-tu at her side, E'roni and Eirami military flanking them. "Skies are clear and we have control of the Path grounds. But we are now getting readings of massive tremors underground."

"Groundquake?" Yoda asked.

"No. Something artificial. We think explosions, deep underground," Phan-tu said.

"We have not cleared the caves yet," Yaddle said. "Who set them off?"

"Don't know," Phan-tu said. "There was fighting going on in the cave system before we came. Master Sutan and several others have been fighting there from the beginning of the battle. Someone reported animals entering the caves, we're not sure. We need to clear the area. I've already informed the Eirami and E'roni personnel." He and Xiri turned to the soldiers nearby who were helping coordinate the effort.

"Alert everyone to clear out of those caves!" Xiri ordered them.

Yoda glanced at his fellow Jedi.

"We need to gather what help we can," Master Yaddle said. "Things are going to get worse."

The ground shook. It was unlike anything Yaddle had ever felt, as if the stone beneath her had begun undulating, almost more liquid than solid. Both Yoda and Yaddle crouched, keeping a hand on the ground and staring at the simple mounded curves of terrain to the south. There was reportedly a deep and intricate cave system here. Master Char-Ryl-Roy, before his comlink went dark, had been able to keep Path members from pouring out and filling the fields by holding them at bay. Since the arrival of the massive numbers of E'roni and Eirami forces, some of the cave doors had been shut with small internal explosions, to purposefully keep the newcomers out.

It was a death trap.

"We have to go and—" Yaddle began when an enormous boom sounded, followed by another and another. Once again, the ground shook and felt liquid.

Yoda pointed. Ahead on a tiny hill, a dark dot appeared, widened, and grew. Yaddle finally understood what she was seeing. A sinkhole in the hill, drawing the ground and turf into itself like a hungry maw. More holes began appearing, and an entire section of the top of the cave system, the size of two or three Longbeams, simply disappeared into the depths. There was a rumbling, splashing noise as the sinkhole appeared to almost bubble and froth, like a giant pot of boiling water.

"The water is going to overwhelm the entire area," Yaddle said.

"No one is going to survive that," Xiri said. She spoke into her comlink. "Inform the rescue teams. The entire cave system is collapsing in on itself. Ready the ships to lift out any survivors." She ran away toward the medic encampments. "Clear the area! I want a half-kilometer radius around that sinkhole!"

Yoda began to back away, but hesitated. Yaddle did, too.

"Did you sense it?" Yaddle said.

Yoda nodded. He began to walk forward, closer to a pile of wreckage. "It's close. Not near the caves."

"A Jedi. In distress," Yaddle said.

"And another." Yoda and Yaddle began running. They could hear Phan-tu behind them.

"Master Yoda! Master Yaddle! You're . . . you're going the wrong way!"

They ran until they were in the shadow of a downed Republic shuttle and the nearby wreckage of a pirate ship. The latter seemed to have decimated a building, whose walls had folded upon themselves. There was a door in one of the walls that was flat on the ground.

Thick, muddy water was bubbling forth from beneath the door.

"There," Yaddle said, holding out her hands. She reached into the Force, pulling the entire wall and attached door upward. It landed behind them. Where it once lay was now a bubbling geyser of water that spilled out onto the ground, rushing against the Jedi's robes. Chunks of dirt and rocks bubbled up, tossed in the muddy water as if they weighed nothing. The two Jedi Masters leaned into the onslaught of water, digging their clawed feet into the muck.

Water and wind and air cannot move this body. The Force is with me, Yaddle said to herself, calming her hands as she reached forward.

Master Yoda, like Yaddle, had closed his eyes. She felt what he knew was there—two hearts beating, very fast at first, but now slowing from the approach of asphyxiation. Yaddle felt the fight within them. One, attuned to the Force. She knew her lighted life was soon to be extinguished, and with it, sadness and peace stirred inside her.

I want to seek, her heart said. *I want to learn. I am not ready, but I am willing to bear what is to be.*

The other being possessed a tangled soul full of regret, anguish, and love. Much love, and strength beyond his own conscious abilities. Unlike the Jedi, he was not at peace with his possible fate. He had amends to make. He was not ready to die.

Yaddle spoke to Yoda. "The land," she said simply.

"The water," he replied.

Together, they reached forward. Yaddle felt the ground in all its beauty and consequence. The tiniest grain of clay, dissolved in so much liquid, and the great stones beneath the surface of the ground that moved only with centuries of past glaciers, formed in magma, cooled into stones as everlasting as hope.

She gathered them, pulled them from the water, and felt them as if molded clay in a child's hands—pulling. Pushing. Thrusting tons of dirt and stone up and away. Peeling it from the bodies, now nearly lifeless, deep below.

She opened her eyes. Master Yoda was twisting his clawed hands, and the water was emerging from the widening hole in the ground like a piece of carved glass, a bloom opening and spreading outward from what was now a large crevasse.

"Gella!" a voice cried. Jedi Enya Keen had rushed forward from a nearby rescue tent. Despite the cries of warning from others, she ran forward, knee-deep in the muck and glancing only for a second at the walls of water and soil, like enormous giants of glass and flowers of clay, ever growing, and being manipulated by the two Jedi Masters. A thick wavy mass of clay peeled out of the crevasse, and a human hand appeared in the bubbling water, covered in mud.

Enya reached for it, grasping the wrist, pulling with all her might. Gella, covered in mud and with an open mouth full of dirty water, emerged. Gella's hand was fixed tight to something deep in the ground, and Yaddle exhaled, dropping enormous twin clods of soil to the side, and reaching in deeply with the Force.

The body of Axel Greylark, similarly obscured in mud and limp as wet leaves, emerged from the watery hole. Gella's hand held fast to the back of his jacket.

Yoda let the water fall in an enormous wave several meters away. Master Yaddle lowered her arms, the torturous structure of extracted mud falling with a boom at a distance. She exhaled.

Enya pulled both Gella and Axel away from the gushing water and mud. Several medics ran over with stretchers, gathering them up and dashing back to the rescue tent. Enya ran alongside them, out of Yaddle's view. A single voice hollered to them seconds later.

"They're alive!"

"The others? In the caves?" Phan-tu hollered.

Yoda turned toward the watery sinkhole, no longer splashing but settling with a calmness that belied the violence that once was there. There were people at the edge crawling out, and hundreds of bodies floating within its vast cavernous hold. E'roni soldiers, tethered with ropes, were already helping the survivors get to higher ground. Some survivors were immediately being placed in manacles by Eirami soldiers.

The skies were no longer a cacophony of cannon fire. The storm clouds, once a blanket over the sky, now cleared along the eastern edge of the Path compound. A glint of peach warmed the horizon. The unrelenting rain had finally ceased. Morning was coming. The terrain of Dalna no longer shook from explosions. Many tiny voices cracked the stillness of the fading night, crying in grief. Though distant and small, the voices were loud as screams in Master Yaddle's ears.

"It is done?" Yaddle asked, knowing the answer.

Yoda turned to her. "Yes."

Chapter Thirty-Two

ABOARD THE MEDICAL FRIGATE, NEAR CORUSCANT

Gella Nattai tried to open her eyes but failed. Her eyelids felt weighed down by the gravity of ten suns, and her entire body ached as if she'd been swimming through mud.

Wait. She *had* been swimming through mud.

She finally managed to open her eyes and found herself attached to wires and IVs, with a physiology scan board nearby reading out her vital signs. Around her, other people were lying in a medbay, similarly attached to treatments. To her left was the vast darkness of space, but through the viewport she could see a few Republic ships nearby, and a starship or two flying at a leisurely pace.

"It's about time you woke up. I was getting pretty bored."

Gella turned her head. Axel Greylark was sitting in a chair nearby, one hand folded on his lap. He smiled at her. One of the planet-shattering, celebrity smiles she had been so used to seeing. At the door to the medbay, not three meters away, were two very large Coruscant guards staring at Axel as if afraid he might disappear into thin air.

"How long have I been out?" Gella asked, trying to sit up and finding it rather painful. It hurt to breathe. "Where are we? What happened?"

"Whoa, slow down." He stood up and went to her side. "Relax, Gella. You've still got a lot to recover from. You've been in a medically induced sleep for a few days, actually. They released me yesterday." He gestured to the viewport. A planet of silver and gray, strewn with intersecting lines, came into view. "We're aboard a medical frigate orbiting Coruscant. As for what happened, well. We survived."

Gella lay back down, trying to get her mind to remember everything. The fight with Binnot. The explosions and the cave system flooding. Knowing their underground passageway was collapsing in on itself. The feeling at the very center of her being that she was dying quickly, and nothing could be done about it.

"So . . . we won the battle?" Gella said.

Axel sat back down, his eyebrows and mouth turning down in sorrow. "I think as a Jedi, you'd understand better than me that there was no winning that battle. Even if our side did, technically, end the fight."

"That's awfully wise of you, Greylark."

"I'm not that wise. Maybe that's wisdom in and of itself?" He laughed lightly.

"I would agree," a woman's voice put in.

They looked up and saw Kyong Greylark walking into the medbay. The two guards nodded at her, and she passed through. She was wearing a simple robe of white that signified she, too, was a patient. Axel touched the chair he'd just left, and she took it gratefully.

"How are you feeling, Mom?"

"Better and better. A blaster shot to the gut is one helluva wound, but I'm okay. You?" She reached out and squeezed Axel's forearm.

"Okay. My wounds are so much better already," he said, touching his chest. His left arm was in a sling. "I may have to buy a new cape to wear with this sling. I'll look like quite the statesman."

"Just like you, Axel, to twist a hospital stay into a fashion statement," Gella said, laughing. "Oof, that hurts," she added, touching her chest.

"Between the two of you, Gella, you suffered far more when that passageway collapsed," Kyong said. "You got a bad chemical pneumonitis and your whole body took quite a hit. But you really turned it around."

"That's what she tends to do," Axel said. "Take an impossible situation and make it better."

Gella caught Axel's eye, wondering if he meant Dalna, or himself.

Axel lifted his eyebrows knowingly.

"And what will you do, now that you're not chancellor?" Gella asked Kyong.

"Well, first things first. I need to answer this deluge of requests asking me to take back the position."

Axel cocked his head. "Will you?"

Kyong leaned back into her chair. "Never say never, but in this case, I don't think so. I'll fill in here and there, to ease Orlen's transition. But you know what I'd really like to do?"

Axel raised his hand. "Go on a vacation for the first time in ten years?"

They all laughed. "Does recovering from getting a blaster shot to the gut count?" Kyong asked.

"No!" Gella and Axel chimed in simultaneously.

"Okay. Well, maybe a good long recovery period. And then . . . I've been thinking about starting up a school. Intergalactic affairs, for emerging, new Republic civilizations. We have a lot to learn from one another, and navigating those new cultures would be the foundation."

Gella noted that Kyong had a shining look in her eye, one she hadn't ever seen before. It must feel quite different, working to create a new good, instead of patching up other people's problems.

The two burly guards took a few steps forward. One of them spoke loudly.

"It's time."

Gella looked at them, and then at Axel and Kyong. "Time for what?"

"Time for me to leave." Axel turned to the guards. "Give me one more minute?"

"That's it. Your shuttle is already set to leave in five."

"Got it."

"Where are you going?" Gella said.

"To Coruscant. Not to my fancy digs, but to the incarceration units in the Federal District, in the northern hemisphere. Chancellor Mollo was kind enough to let me recover here with you, and my mother. But it's time to go and finish out my sentence. Plus the extra time I earned for breaking out of Pipyyr."

Gella sat up, despite the pain it caused her. "Wait. I only just woke up." She shook her head. There was so much more to say.

"I know there isn't time to talk. My mother and the rest of the Jedi will fill you in on what happened on Dalna." He reached out and held her hand. "But I have to go. If I'm ever going to start over, I'd like to start right away."

Gella's eyes began to smart, and she was almost angry at herself for feeling so emotional toward the one person who had failed her time and time again. This person who had lied, and smiled through those lies, and hurt everyone around him. She had built up so much frustration, but now all she felt was a hollowness. The hollowness hurt just as much. But then she thought of the varying emotions running through her—what they meant. She knew part of her Wayseeking journey would be to examine them, as difficult as that would be.

"I don't know what to say, Axel," she said.

"That would be a first for you!" Axel smiled, then took a deep breath. "I'm the one who should say it all. I am sorry for all the pain I caused you, and everyone else. I'm going to pay my dues now. But I also want to thank you."

"For what?" Gella said, blotting her eyes on the back of her bandaged hands.

"For always giving me a chance to redeem myself. Even when I threw those opportunities away. For years, I was so blinded by my anger with the Jedi that I couldn't step past it. You taught me how to go beyond hurt, and hate. It's a new experience for me." He squeezed her hand. "I can go do my time, knowing that out there in this big old galaxy, I have a real friend. Come visit me sometime? I won't have the best wine and cheese, but I promise to provide some good conversation." He smiled again, the edges of his eyes crinkling. "Goodbye, my Jedi Knight."

Gella said nothing, only squeezed his hand back. Kyong turned to Gella, her face softened with emotion.

"Thank you, Gella. For everything."

Together, Axel and Kyong walked into the corridor, flanked by the two guards. Gella lay back on her medbay bed, blotting the last of the moisture from her eyes. It occurred to her that this wasn't sadness. And it wasn't weakness, either. Her tears were part of her. And they would evaporate and leave their faint watermarks upon her, like so much of the last few months.

She turned her head toward the viewport, seeing Coruscant's metallic sphere. Soon, she would head to the Jedi Temple. She would pay her respects to the Kyber Arch, and then finally travel to Jedha where she could begin her Wayseeker journey.

She watched a shuttle pass by the viewport on its way to Coruscant. In it, she knew, was Axel. She closed her eyes and reached out, sensing the emotions of those it carried in its belly.

Purpose, from those who piloted the shuttle and guarded the prisoner aboard.

Peace, from the prisoner. And one other thing. Something she had never sensed in him throughout all of their time and travels together: hope.

She watched the shuttle descend into Coruscant's atmosphere and disappear. Gella smiled then pursed her lips.

"Well. Maybe there's time to do a quick visit to the Republic Judiciary Central Detention Center before I head to Jedha," Gella said, smiling, before she closed her eyes and took quite possibly the best nap she'd ever had.

Kyong Greylark stood before a viewport, watching the shuttle fly her only son back to finish his incarceration. His honest admission of all that he had done wrong, as well as new internal information about the Path of the Open Hand (and the Closed Fist, as some of its followers had morphed into), was salient in helping to understand the conflict. But none of it negated the wrongs he had done.

As she'd walked him to his shuttle, Axel had draped his arm over his mother's shoulders.

"You'll visit?" he asked.

"Of course," she said, reaching up and holding his hand. "So often, you'll probably get tired of me."

"Never."

The docking bay was now ahead, with several small shuttles coming and going on board the medical frigate. When they drew closer to their shuttle, the guards had stopped.

"Sorry, can't go farther than this, Ms. Greylark."

Kyong smiled. She was still getting used to not being called Chancellor Greylark. She liked it.

"This is goodbye then," Axel said. He held out a hand to shake.

Kyong reached forward and embraced her son. Axel hugged her hard and long, the same way he used to when he was a small child. By the stars, she had missed it, and didn't realize until now that she had.

"You know I'm sorry, right?" he said quietly.

"You know I'm sorry, too?" she said.

They both nodded. They separated, but before Axel turned toward the shuttle, he tipped his head down and kissed his mother on the forehead.

"I'll be all right," he said, smiling.

And she had smiled back, because she knew he was right this time.

When Axel's shuttle was no longer in view, she turned and headed toward one of the meeting rooms deep within the ship. It took her some time, and she got a little winded, but eventually she opened the door to a wide room with a long table within it.

Inside, Master Yoda and Chancellor Orlen Mollo were sharing cups of tea and talking in earnest. At the sight of her, they stood.

"Kyong!" Orlen said. He quickly made his way to her and held out his hands. Instead, she went straight in for a hug. She was getting good at this. She let go and smiled broadly.

"Good to see you, Orlen."

"Are you feeling better?"

"Much. Remind me that next time I pick up blasters and knives, I should train a little beforehand. My muscles took a beating."

"Seems like a lot of your foes took a beating, too," Orlen said.

She bowed to Master Yoda. "It is good to see you. I trust you are well."

"Very well, I am," Yoda said.

"Kyong. Can I not ask you to reinstate your chancellorship?" Orlen said. The Quarren's tentacles waved with some trepidation.

"You may ask, Orlen, but I will likely give you the same answer," Kyong said, sipping a cup of tea poured by a protocol droid at her elbow.

"Two chancellors. Worked well, have they not?" Yoda said.

"Worked well, and in some ways, not so well," Kyong admitted.

"We shall see. In any case, if I'm the chancellor you think I am, you'll be back, Kyong."

"And if you're the chancellor I know you to be, you shan't be needing me." She sighed. "But there is much work to be done. Our efforts to expand communications and alliances in the galaxy and prospect new hyperlanes is far from finished. There are conflicts still brewing that need the Republic's help."

"And yet, the Republic grows more reachable with every hyperlane established," Orlen said. "As it expands, the village becomes smaller in a way. Every home is easier to reach. A positive paradox."

"Nevertheless, I promise to help out until your transition feels more secure, Orlen."

"Speak to the Jedi Council soon, you should," Yoda said. "We must explain the happenings on Dalna. All that went wrong."

Orlen pointed to his fingers, one by one. "The communications errors. The machinations of the Path. All going back to the failed talks at Jedha. And beyond."

"But we must also speak to all the things that went right," Kyong said. "We could not have defeated the Path without the Jedi."

"And the Jedi could not have defeated the Path without the help of our Republic allies," Yoda said.

"Yes. It is a lesson well learned, and a strength that the galaxy can draw upon, for centuries to come," Orlen said.

Kyong stood. "I shall see you on Coruscant soon. I wish it were for a happier occasion," she said.

"Happy or not, there is much to celebrate. Honor. And remember," Yoda said, standing.

"The Dalnans are calling it the Night of Sorrow. It will not long be forgotten," Orlen said.

The three of them—a Jedi Master, a chancellor of the Republic, and a chancellor that once was—stared into the viewport at the stars and planet beyond, each immersed in their own, intertwining visions of the future.

Master Yoda soon left the medical frigate for the Jedi Temple on Coruscant. There was always a comforting, familiar feeling when landing on the planet. His expression remained neutral, but his left ear twitched. Always, he was listening, sensing what was beyond the obvious in his surroundings. Sensing what was in himself that was not always so obvious. The visions of the aftermath of the Battle of Dalna were all too fresh in his mind. He recognized the slight distress, then allowed it to pass. He watched the multiple lanes of air traffic that flew in varying altitudes above the dense city, marveling at how the city hummed like a plucked chord of harmony. The sun shone brightly, reflecting off the panes of glass and durasteel on the buildings, making the entire globe feel like a sparkling, faceted, complex jewel.

His shuttle landed on the roof of the Jedi Temple, and Yoda disembarked, with several Jedi greeting him. They busied him with notes and updates from the Jedi community on Coruscant, but his left ear continued to twitch.

"The queen and consort of Eiram?" Master Yoda asked.

"Arrived and resting in their quarters."

"And E'ronoh's Monarch?"

"Also arrived, along with the others in the party."

Yoda nodded. He retired to a room to meditate, take a repast, and prepare himself for what was to come. There were many things on his mind, beyond the upcoming ceremony. The events of Dalna. The Path. The nameless creatures that preyed upon the Jedi.

It was evening when Yoda climbed one of the spires of the Jedi Temple, following a line of other Jedi before him. The room at the top of the spire was spare and large, with tall beams of light set into the wall, reminiscent of the Jedi lightsabers. In it, Queen Adrialla of Eiram stood next to the queen consort, Odelia. Nearby, Monarch A'lbaran had his hands folded, looking ahead, where there were three stone tables. The shrouded forms of Jedi lay upon two of the tables, with a lone lightsaber laying upon the third.

People gathered around the tables and tiered seating surrounding the room. Muffled sobs could be heard. The ceiling of the room opened to show the clear, dark sky above Coruscant. As requested, all air traffic above the Temple was halted to give a clear view of the night sky, the shining stars, and beyond.

Princess Xiri and Phan-tu Zenn saw Yoda and bowed. They held hands and retreated between the queen, the consort, and the Monarch. There were several Jedi in attendance, many who had been fighting on Dalna. The number of Jedi they had lost was nearly half of those who had come to help. The loss of life had affected all. A heavy sadness hung in the air, and at Yoda's entrance to the remembrance room, a hush fell over the mourners.

Master Yaddle nodded at Yoda. The youngling Cippa was standing next to her, a tall, hulking Iktotchi female at her side. The Iktotchi wore bandages over one arm. In her Coruscant Republic uniform, she kept her hands folded formally, but Cippa pulled a large clawed hand free and draped it over her own shoulder. Yoda noticed the edge of the Iktotchi's mouth curve into a minuscule smile. The child had rested and physically recovered, but Master Yaddle was already ensuring that Cippa would be carefully supported in the aftermath of the battle.

Yoda raised his arm, and the murmurings around the room quieted. He made a simple gesture toward a group of Jedi, and withdrew into the small line of mourners behind him.

A bent-over figure rose from a chair and, using a walking stick, slowly entered the center of the room to stand before the pyres.

Master Creighton Sun stood in the dim light of the room, beneath the starshine. His body was still healing and in pain, and it was with great difficulty that he stood before the gatherers. He looked about the room and saw friendly faces—Xiri and Phan-tu. Masters Yoda and Yaddle. Chancellor Mollo. And Enya Keen.

His new Padawan. Enya smiled uncertainly at her new master while a red-and-brown astromech unit nestled at her side.

Unconsciously, Creighton put his hand to his heart. It had been beating ever so slightly faster ever since he'd woken up aboard the medical frigate, femur broken, two blaster shots to his body. When he had broken through the sedating medication, he had tried to sit up, delirious and in pain. The first thing he had done was yell.

"Aida. Where is Aida? What happened to my friend?"

An FX-2 droid had spun away from him in alarm, bleeping for assistance. A 2-0A medical droid came quickly to his side. Her eye-lights were bright and she tried to gesture reassuringly.

"You must stay calm, Master Sun. You are still quite ill," she had said.

"Aida Forte. Where is she?"

"We have no such person registered aboard the *Renascence,* Master Sun. But we are a single medical frigate. It is possible she is elsewhere. Please, do lie down. You'll hurt yourself more."

Creighton had lain back in the medbay bed, wishing to tear out the IV lines and other monitors attached to his body. But he still felt awful, nauseated, and terribly weak. He'd looked left and right, and saw other Jedi and figures from Dalna receiving treatment.

He knew why Aida wasn't on the ship with him. He knew, and despair threatened to overwhelm him. The droid 2-0A was still at his side.

"Can I help you, Master Sun?" she asked quietly.

For a long time, he had stayed silent, but oddly, the droid did not leave his side. He thought it had perhaps shut down after a while, or quietly left. But when he opened his eyes again, he found that she was still there. Quiet. Waiting for something. Perhaps nothing. He must have passed out. Hours later, he woke again to find her in the same position, at his side.

And Creighton thought, *If this droid can stand here for an eternity trying to heal these impossible wounds, then so can I. Aida would want me to look on the bright side.*

Take her with you, an internal voice said. *She had said to you,* I am with you, Creighton. *Do her the honor of believing her.*

Now, standing before the fallen at the top of the Jedi Temple on Coruscant, Master Sun took his hand away from his heart and swelled his pained chest to begin speaking.

"Our Republic friends," he began. He gestured to Chancellor Orlen Mollo, wearing dark clothing of mourning. "Our new friends and allies, far beyond the Core." Here, he swept his hand to the queen and queen consort of Eiram, Princess Xiri and Prince Phan-tu, and the aged Monarch A'lbaran. "The Night of Sorrow is over, but the brave warriors who fell will not be forgotten. These Jedi came to answer our call of need without hesitation or doubt, because at the heart of the Jedi is a heart that fights for good. These Jedi fought bravely and selflessly, against the darkness that is ever-present in this galaxy. Beautiful, bright lights have gone dark. I am truly saddened to say that there are pyres burning throughout the galaxy tonight." Master Sun looked to the two fallen Jedi to his left, and the lone lightsaber. "And now here, in the Jedi Temple, we gather to honor three exemplary Jedi. Master Orin Darhga, Master Char-Ryl-Roy, and Jedi Knight Aida Forte."

He paused, trying to still his racing heart. He was still too ill to be here, in all honesty, but he had to. He glanced to his left, where the 2-0A droid stood in the shadows waiting to attend to him if he needed. C-2C was her name. He had finally cleared his mind enough to ask a day after he'd woken up.

"Many lives were lost on Dalna," Creighton said. "Not just Jedi lives. Many friends who came to our aid in our time of desperate need have left us. Their sacrifice will not be forgotten, and we mourn them as well."

He turned around to all the people gathered, felt the pulsations of life and the sadness that seeped past and through them. He lifted his hand, palm to the open sky above.

"All lives have a beginning and an end. With every beginning is born hope and goodness. No matter how short or long those lives are, the galaxy expands to meet them at every tide, every sunset, and every breath. Whenever we are weak, or weary, or doubting, it is this hope and goodness that will buoy us all. They offered their lives to keep this light alive. All of us shall carry the gift they so selflessly gave. And now they are at peace, living within the everlasting light of the Force. A light that exists within everyone here. And so, too, do our fallen comrades exist within us."

Creighton nodded, and two younglings came forward, holding their fists aloft. One went directly to Creighton, handing him the green kyber crystal from Aida Forte's lightsaber. The other approached Enya Keen and gently dropped a kyber crystal into her palm—a green one from Orin Darhga's lightsaber.

The two Jedi closed their fists over the crystals. Creighton took a deep breath, but his hand trembled. Enya shut her eyes and tried to suppress a sob but failed.

"These kyber crystals will be added to the Kyber Arch in their memory."

The tables with the fallen Jedi sank slowly into the floor. Doors slid closed above them, and a single bright beam of light from their joined center rose straight into the sky.

"As stars are born and die," Creighton said, "so does time move forward. Relentlessly so. And yet we fight. We will never stop fighting for the light and life in this galaxy."

The beacons of light grew so vivid in the room that soon, they outshone even the brightest star in the night sky.

After the ceremony, Xiri and Phan-tu walked slowly back to their waiting shuttles. They saw Enya Keen sitting on a bench next to 4VO-TG. She was blotting her face with her sleeve.

Xiri came forward, a blaster scar on her cheek from the battle, and gave Enya a hug. "I'm sorry. So sorry about Master Roy. He helped us so much. As did you."

Enya's eyes shone wet and bright, and she smiled. "I learned a lot from him, and had so much more to learn, yet. I'll be all right. Eventually." She saw them in their long royal coats. "Are you not going to stay longer?"

"We can't. There's a ceremony happening on Eiram and E'ronoh soon. We can't miss it."

The astromech sidled up next to Enya, as if asking for hugs as well.

"We're going to miss you, Teegee!" Xiri said, patting the droid's head. "If it weren't for Teegee, we wouldn't have been able to fly that recon fighter. He helped us get the message out to Eiram and E'ronoh. Helped turned the tide, as they say on Eiram."

Phan-tu stooped down to look at 4VO-TG straight in his blue lens. "You take care, Teegee."

The little droid did a short jig and whined.

"What? You're coming with us?" Phan-tu looked at Enya.

"It's true," Enya said, smiling. "All Teegee wants to do now is astromech work. He's hoping to be a Thylefire Squadron droid, if you'll have him. Consider him a belated wedding present."

Xiri and Phan-tu beamed at the droid. Enya joined them as they walked through the halls. "Enya. Can I ask you a question?" Phan-tu asked.

"Of course."

"I noticed in the ceremony that Master Darhga's and Jedi Forte's kyber crystals were to be put into the Kyber Arch. But they didn't give Master Roy's to anyone."

"It's because I have it," Enya said.

She pulled two lightsabers from her belt and held them out. "I used Master Darhga's lightsaber throughout the battle, when I didn't have my own. And I realized that it was somehow encouraging me the whole time. Or rather, the Force did. So when I got my original kyber back from Elder Onning, and Master Roy's lightsaber, I sat with them both for a long time. I couldn't help but feel like Master Darhga's was ready for the arch, but Master Roy's was not. I talked to Master Yoda about it, and he agreed that in this case, I could carry two lightsabers, if they truly harmonized with the Jedi carrying them."

She ignited both lightsabers, a deep blue and bright yellow. She turned off the lightsabers and hooked them to her belt again.

"What will you do now?" Xiri asked her.

"Continue my training with Master Sun. Begin my trials to become a Jedi Knight. Trust in the Force. And perhaps . . . find another droid to fix."

They all laughed softly, and the sound reverberated far down the hallways of the Jedi Temple, warming the hearts of those who heard it. Because it sounded like Aida laughing.

Creighton Sun and Yoda walked together down the central corridor of the Jedi archives within the Temple. Their footfalls were quiet, and the archives were dimly illuminated in cool blue light. Creighton walked with a cane, his leg still far from healed.

"Troubled your mind is, Master Sun."

"Yes. About Dalna." Creighton stopped walking, and leaned upon his cane. He wanted to see Yoda's expression as they spoke. "There are details that have come together that are troubling. Those, creatures. They have an effect upon the Jedi and Force-sensitive persons. Master Roy succumbed to one. The husks of other Jedi, seen on Jedha. Aida Forte and I witnessed it in the killing of a prisoner, and we felt it ourselves."

Reflexively, he grimaced a little. The pain was an uncomfortable mix of physical discomfort, the memory of being mired in terror, and, of course, sadness. He missed his friend.

"Great pain, I sense."

"Yes. With time and understanding, two sources of my pain will fade. But I cannot understand the third." He lowered his voice almost to a whisper. "Which is why I needed to speak to you. Master Yoda, those creatures—I might be the only one who realizes they are related to this disorienting, torturous effect upon the Jedi. What do you know about these nameless creatures?"

Yoda dropped his eyes to the floor. "I, too, know of them." He looked up and locked eyes with Creighton. "Powerful beings, they are. Dangerous, they are. But in pain, they could be. Only a few understand them. You, and I. And still, much to learn is there."

"Where did they come from? Is there a larger danger here?" Creighton asked.

"Many unanswered questions we have. Much we have to discover. But most important—yes. A larger danger, there is." Yoda looked away. *What else did he know?* Creighton wondered.

Yoda did not elaborate, he simply began to walk, and Creighton kept in step with the diminutive Master Jedi, despite his ailing leg. Creighton imagined what might happen if word got out that there was a living weapon against the Jedi. How it could decimate the Order. Against his will, a swirl of terror, like mud grabbing at his legs and trying to pull him down entered his mind. He felt like he was suffocating, and he took a deep breath and shook his head.

No. They needed to keep this quiet until they knew what its true nature was.

"You realize how catastrophic—if word gets out—" Creighton began.

"Quiet, we must be. Reveal these nameless creatures, we cannot."

"Perhaps it was isolated to Jedha and Dalna. Since the Night of Sorrow, we have heard of no further reports," Creighton said.

"Gone, they could be," Yoda added. "Find out more, you and I must."

"It may also be best if we keep it out of the archives entirely."

They had reached the end of the archives. The doorway awaited them. Master Yoda looked into Creighton's eyes and nodded.

"We will not speak of this again," Creighton said. "Not until we know more, and with certainty."

Yoda nodded again.

They exited the archives, each walking away in a separate direction as if they'd never spoken.

Two weeks later, the ceremony was held on, of all places, the Time-keeper moon of Eirie, as it was called by the E'roni. The two planets had hurriedly worked together to build a simple celebratory platform amid the salt flats, decorated with seashells and pearls from Eiram, and burnished red marble and sunstones from E'ronoh. Twinkling lights hovered throughout the platform, making the guests feel as if they were walking among the stars themselves. The finest mountain water that ran into the Erasmus Sea had been shipped over to create a fountain, from which guests drank freely. The pirates in the Eiram-E'ronoh system had been chased away, thanks to the Jedi and Republic support that had been welcomed to the area in the last week. As a result, multiple shipments of food, medicine, and supplies had flooded in, gratefully accepted by both planets.

The people of both planets had collectively sighed in relief.

"There's a lot of work to do yet," Xiri said as she sipped the sweet, clear water in her glass. The view was stunning from here. Half of the swirled, blue planet of Eiram rose above one horizon, and on the opposite side of the moon's sky, the red-gold planet of E'ronoh dipped its half over the horizon.

"A new peace treaty. One that will last," Phan-tu said. He stood by her on the dais, where they were to speak soon.

"Yes, and this time, you and I will work on it directly," Xiri said.

"And not on Dalna, I hope!" said a booming, female voice.

The queen consort, Odelia, stepped upon the dais, her wispy veil fluttering in her wake. Queen Adrialla followed behind her.

"Mothers," Phan-tu said, smiling. He leaned in to kiss each on the cheek. Xiri hung back a little, but they both waved their arms forward.

"And does our daughter not deserve our embraces, too?"

Xiri smiled and gave each a warm hug and kiss. She was still not used to such outward displays of affection, but it was rapidly growing on her.

"And so you survived . . . not just this terrible battle, but a war, and your first foray into ambassadorship," Queen Adrialla said. She gently touched Xiri's face. "With scars to prove it."

"It was worth it," Xiri said. "Phan-tu was right. Eiram is my home, too. We'll do anything to defend both planets."

The queen waved a hand and sat down on one of a group of plush loungers. "After the fiasco on Jedha, we would not entrust the ambassadorship to anyone else."

"I heartily agree!" Monarch A'lbaran said, stepping onto the dais with a group of attendants, one of whom assisted him with walking up the steps. Another attendant began to hand out glasses of frothy, peach-colored wine. "The Path has fled Dalna and Jedha. The remaining members have scattered to the distant barrens of the galaxy and have gone quiet." He received a glass of wine from an attendant, sniffing it. "The scars of the Forever War are deep." He opened his mouth to say more, and saw Xiri shaking her head slightly.

"Indeed, they are. They may never fully disappear," Queen Adrialla said. At this, Phan-tu put a hand gently on his mother's, and she said nothing more.

Jedi Enya Keen and Master Creighton Sun came onto the dais, along with Chancellor Mollo who was dressed in blue-and-red robes that reflected the two planets' colors.

"Are we ready?" Chancellor Mollo asked everyone.

They nodded. The group fanned out, and Chancellor Mollo turned to the small crowd of dignitaries, ambassadors, Jedi, and Republic representatives from several nearby planetary systems.

"We welcome you, all, to the first joint celebratory event hosted by the people of Eiram—" Here, he bowed toward the queen and her consort. "And E'ronoh," he continued, bowing to the Monarch. "The good people of these two planets are now looking forward, not back, to a time that shall be filled with healing and prosperity. In good faith, both will partner with the Republic, and I am thrilled to announce that currently, due to the hard work of our tireless Pathfinder team, Seventy-one-Beenine—" Chancellor Mollo gestured to a group that included Kenny, Piti, two Jedi, and a comm droid. "We can now celebrate the opening of a new hyperlane that will bring Eiram and E'ronoh access to one of the most resource-rich areas in the Outer Rim. The Hetzal system."

He turned his bubbling wineglass toward the horizon, in between the two planets' globes. The entire party also turned in that direction. At a distance, two ships rose above the salt flats of the moon. One, a copper colored E'roni cruiser, and the other, a sleek, large Eirami transport with the bluish-silver coloring of a krel shark. Together, they rose in parallel and turned toward the southern sky of the moon. They grew smaller and smaller, lifting into the darkness.

Seconds apart, the lights on the vessels stretched impossibly and winked out as they entered the hyperlane.

A chorus of cheers, applause, and music rose from the platform of revelers and musicians perched around the dais. Xiri and Phan-tu embraced, taking advantage of the celebratory cacophony to make their kiss last just a touch longer than was publicly appropriate.

Chancellor Mollo turned back to the crowd. "Now begins the time for the future. For healing, and for prosperity."

"Hear, hear!" the Monarch said, holding up his glass.

"To rebuilding," Xiri said, her voice clear as a bell, as she held up a glass.

"To allies," Phan-tu said, holding up his.

"And to peace," Odelia and Adrialla said, their hands entwining.

"To Hetzal!" the crowd roared, glasses clinking like musical chimes in the night.

Acknowledgments

Not a day goes by without my witnessing a reference to *Star Wars* at the office, in a random movie, or on someone's coffee mug. When the Lucasfilm Ltd. logo appears on the screen when I'm watching *Andor,* my heart does a little disco dance.

I'm behind the magic curtain now, too. It is an absolute honor to be included in this grand world of creative people, in this galaxy far, far away. I thank my lucky stars every day.

However, closer to home, there are many to thank as well. To the Lumineers who welcomed me so warmly into the High Republic world—Claudia Gray, Cavan Scott, Daniel José Older, Justina Ireland, and Charles Soule—you guys are brilliant. To the other High Republic freshmen—Tessa Gratton, George Mann, and Zoraida Cordóva, so happy to be here with you. And a special shout-out to Zoraida and Cavan, who conversed with me for endless hours during the writing process. I couldn't have finished this book without you.

To Mike Siglain, thank you for your vision, boundless optimism, energy, and thoughtful support as our leader. To Robert Simpson, Brett Rector, Lindsay Knight, Jennifer Pooley, and Jennifer Heddle, I very much appreciate all the behind-the-scenes heavy lifting you do.

I will always be so grateful to my editor, Tom Hoeler, whose insightful and tireless work helped to make *Cataclysm* the best book it could be. Thank you to the many people behind the magic curtain at Random House Worlds, including Elizabeth Schaefer, Lydia Estrada, and Gabriella Muñoz. Thank you also to Yihyoung Li for this incredible cover featuring Axel Greylark. The artwork brought tears to my eyes.

Thank you to the Lucasfilm Story Group for your bountiful wisdom. You are all superstars, and it's been truly amazing to work with all of you.

To Ben, Maia, and TG, you guys are the light of my life. And a humongous thank-you to Bernie, who told me I should do this even though I was terrified of the responsibility of writing a *Star War*! As always, thank you to Sarah Simpson Weiss for also being the coach in my corner and the voice of positivity. To friends and family who have supported me nonstop—Alice Kang, Richard Kang, Angie Hawkins, Felicity Bronzan, Gale Etherton, Sarah Kosa, Tosca Lee, Ann Kim, Phil Smith, Lindsey Baker, Jasmin Marcelin, and so many more—big hugs. To my patients and my team at Nebraska Medicine, thank you for bringing balance to my world.

And finally, to the fans. You've already heartily welcomed me into the fold. This book was written with love. It's now in your hands. Enjoy, and may the Force be with you.

About the Author

LYDIA KANG is an author of adult and young adult fiction, poetry, and nonfiction. She is also a doctor and practices internal medicine in Omaha, Nebraska. She became a *Star Wars* author with the inclusion of the short story "Right-Hand Man" in the 2020 anthology *From a Certain Point of View: The Empire Strikes Back,* which describes the critical scene when 2-1B attached Luke Skywalker's prosthetic hand. Her historical fiction includes the bestselling titles *Opium and Absinthe, A Beautiful Poison, The Impossible Girl,* and *The Half-Life of Ruby Fielding.* She is the co-author of *Quackery: A Brief History of the Worst Ways to Cure Everything,* an NPR Science Friday Best Science Book of 2017, as well as *Patient Zero: A Curious History of the World's Worst Diseases.* She lives with her three kids, her physician husband, and her two very codependent dogs, one of whom looks uncannily like an Ewok.

lydiakang.com
Facebook.com/AuthorLydiaKang
Twitter: @LydiaYKang
Instagram: @lydiakang

About the Type

This book was set in Hermann, a typeface created in 2019 by Chilean designers Diego Aravena and Salvador Rodriguez for W Type Foundry. Hermann was developed as a modern tribute to classic novels, taking its name from the author Hermann Hesse. It combines key legibility features from the typefaces Sabon and Garamond with more dynamic and bolder visual components.

A long time ago in a galaxy far, far away. . . .

STAR WARS™

Join up! Subscribe to our newsletter
at ReadStarWars.com or find us on social.

 @DelReyStarWars

 @DelReyStarWars

 StarWarsBooks